BROOKE L. FRENCH

THE CAROLINA VARIANT

Black Rose Writing | Texas

The author grants the final approval for this literary material.

First printing

This is a work of fiction. Names, characters, businesses, places, events, and incidents are either the products of the author's imagination or used in a fictitious manner. Any resemblance to actual persons, living or dead, or actual events is purely coincidental.

ISBN: 978-1-68513-218-7
PUBLISHED BY BLACK ROSE WRITING
www.blackrosewriting.com

Printed in the United States of America
Suggested Retail Price (SRP) $22.95

The Carolina Variant is printed in Baskerville

*As a planet-friendly publisher, Black Rose Writing does its best to eliminate unnecessary waste to reduce paper usage and energy costs, while never compromising the reading experience. As a result, the final word count vs. page count may not meet common expectations.

For the smartest man I know.
I love you, Dad.

PRAISE FOR

THE CAROLINA VARIANT

"*The Carolina Variant*, by Brooke L. French, is one of those books that, while fiction, is so close to reality that it becomes more and more terrifying as you read. And read, you will. Once you start, you're completely drawn into this gripping story about a possible bioterrorism event, all the while hoping that such a thing never occurs in our world. Filled with compelling characters fighting not only for their lives, but humanity itself, you won't be able to put it down."

–Jeffrey Jay Levin, author of
Watching, Volume 1, The Garden Museum Heist

"*The Carolina Variant* is a taut thriller that terrifies with a too-damned-frighteningly plausible story about what happens when a deadly virus escapes. It's the kind of book that makes you afraid to turn the page, but you will. You definitely will."

–Christopher Amato, author of
Shadow Investigation* and *A Letter from Sicily

"What a ride! *The Carolina Variant* is Blake Crouch's *Upgrade* with the pacing of Fox's *24*. Brooke L. French's eidetic heroine is the only one standing between a mystery virus and a worldwide pandemic—but the last time she used her skills, she almost died. Good luck putting this adrenaline-laced thriller down!"

–Cam Torrens, author of *Stable*

THE CAROLINA VARIANT

PROLOGUE

September 13, 2018

The girl on the video monitor stared up at the ceiling as blood trickled from her eyes and nose. Her only movement an occasional spasm of coughing.

Nothing unexpected, given the progression of the disease.

Dr. Edmund Haley shut off the overhead fluorescent lights and let himself adjust to the dim glow of the screens lining the back wall of the office. Only the girl's monitor still played a live feed, but it lit the room well enough.

And, either way, darkness suited him fine.

He'd spent so much time stuck in this tiny godforsaken place, he could've found the desk and computer with his eyes closed. Haley dropped into a chair and adjusted his glasses, trying to ignore the sharp tang of antimicrobial soap that clung to his hands. It smelled like life in the hospital. Like the servitude of medical practice.

He hated it as much now as he had before he'd lost his license. But at least this time, he'd be well paid for his efforts. And soon, it would be over. He refocused on the girl's image. The only question was when.

Light sliced into the room behind him as Margaret bumbled inside. He made no move to acknowledge the nurse, even as she pulled up a chair beside his. As idiotic as she otherwise seemed to be, she'd know by now not to bother him. He shifted his attention from the video monitor to the computer, where he pulled up the patient's chart.

Patient: Octavia MILLS, 18 yo, Af-Am, F, #4
Vitals: 5'5", 110 lb. updated (9-10) 108.8 lb. updated (9-11) 106 lb. updated (9-12) 104.1 lb.
Provider Notes: Click to open

He scrolled to the section for his notes and, after a click of the mouse, entered the details of that day's exam. "9-13-18; Liver and kidney function both continue to decline. Discrete purpuric patches expanding from face and trunk now merging. BSA involvement approximately 80%. Note third spacing."

The third spacing, a condition where the skin separated from the tissue beneath and filled with blood, was something new. Margaret's report of it had been the primary reason he'd put himself through the nightmare of protective gear and protocol it'd taken to do a physical exam himself. He wasn't going to let it be said that he hadn't been thorough.

Haley glanced back up at the monitor in time to see a bubble of blood form between Octavia's lips. The thing grew with each shallow breath. When it reached the size of a small orange, it burst, splattering more droplets of blood onto her face and neck.

Octavia made no move to wipe them away. He'd given her enough morphine. She would be long past caring. And, more importantly, the extra dosage meant she'd finally quit staring out at him with that awful, confused look on her face.

He didn't care. Not really. Except that it had been distracting, and he needed to focus. Needed to understand why was she still alive. What had he missed? Perhaps another round of blood work would—

The blare of an alarm sounded over the video feed and, more faintly, from the hall. Three more followed.

Octavia's body spasmed, convulsing again and again as she vomited up a grainy black-red mix of blood and tissue. The progression was as repulsive as it was now familiar. The vomit mixed with the brighter red flowing from her eyes and nose as the virus moved into its final stage. Blood, still unable to clot, flowed until it covered her face and chest. Until the bedsheets were saturated and no longer white.

Octavia's muscles tensed, seizing all at once before releasing. Her body too gruesome to look peaceful, even as she finally came to rest.

Neither he nor Margaret moved from their chairs.

The alarms echoed unanswered down the empty hall. Haley clicked off the monitor and most of the noise with it. "That's better."

God knew it had taken long enough. He turned back to the computer, closed Octavia's chart, and opened another document saved to the desktop as "Subject Outcomes." He scrolled down, missing Octavia's name the first time, then tapped the cursor back up until he found it. She'd been number four of twenty-five subjects, and hers was the last empty field in the column marked TPOI for Total Period of Infection. From the time she had been exposed, it had taken four days for the disease to take its course. At least a full day longer than any other subject.

"About fucking time." He spoke under his breath as he typed the final entry in with one finger. He still didn't know why the girl had survived so long, but it was no matter. By any measure, his work there had been an overwhelming success. Haley pulled off his glasses and tapped them against Margaret's shoulder. "Get me a copy of the subject files, including all of the relevant video footage."

Margaret flinched away from him. "Yes, doctor." She pulled a thumb drive from a desk drawer and plugged it into the video system. The system — which had been his idea — had not only allowed them to observe the patients from a safe distance but also recorded the progress of the disease in each subject.

Having such an accurate, time-stamped record of their experiments would be invaluable to his employer. As he had been. Haley cleaned the lenses of his glasses with the edge of his lab coat. And knowing what was coming, it didn't hurt to have insurance. Which was why he had contingency plans stashed in safe deposit boxes across the city. It was a point he would be sure to make when he and his employer spoke.

No matter what, he wouldn't end up like the others.

He pointed to Margaret as she collected the files. "Once you're done, wipe the system clean."

She looked at him, her eyes a question. What happens now?

He didn't bother responding. Some part of her had to know already.

Stupid.

The kind of people who would hire her to do what she'd done weren't the type to assume money would be enough to keep her quiet. She was a loose end who — unlike him — had no continuing value. Not that what happened to her mattered. And if she hadn't been smart enough to see that going in… Well, she'd as much as made her bed, hadn't she?

He put a layer of steel in his voice. "Do it."

Margaret's gaze flicked away. She pressed a few buttons on the keyboard and waited for the computer to comply, removed the thumb drive, and dropped it into his waiting hand.

He turned the small device over in his palm. Amazing that so many lives could be held in such a small device. But then, these lives weren't the kind anyone cared about. Nobodies and throw-aways. The kind of people who would volunteer for a drug trial for pennies and not be missed when they didn't come back. He'd done the world a service, really.

Haley slipped the thumb drive into a padded envelope, scrawled the address he had memorized at the outset of the project on the front, checked twice to make sure he'd stuck on enough postage, then slid the envelope into his briefcase.

“Take care of that, won’t you?” He tilted his head toward the hallway leading to the patient rooms, where the girl’s body lay waiting.

Margaret didn’t look up from the computer. “Of course, sir. Same as with the others.”

Haley tucked the briefcase under his arm, whistling as he left the facility for the last time. With his part done, the rest could finally begin.

CHAPTER 1

By any objective measure, Tess Oliver's office was a pit. The walls, the spotty carpet, even the desk chair that had come with the rented space bore the sickly yellow-gray shade of corporate beige. One off-center window looked out on Atlanta's constant gridlock. Someone had painted it shut, the office's A/C was permanently set to arctic, and the contraband space heater under her desk did nothing to help win the war on office climate control.

But it's mine.

Or at least it was, for now. Tess twisted her curls onto the top of her head and shoved a pencil in the center to hold it in place. It didn't work. She blew the strand that slipped loose out of her eye and flipped through the pile of bills on her desk, adding them in her head. Most were past due.

What now?

There had to be an answer.

But damned if she could find it. She shoved the invoices into a folder and slid it under a stack of notepads and case files, trying to ignore the knot in her stomach. In the six months she'd practiced law on her own, Tess had lived on her savings. But hardly any of her nest egg remained, and the dribble of money coming in from clients wasn't enough to make ends meet. Not even her malpractice insurance had made the cut this month.

The knot in her gut drew tighter.

"Knock, knock." Gail came in from the hallway, her slow South Carolina drawl making even that sound melodic. "Want a doughnut?" The petite, sixty-something receptionist carried a Krispy Kreme box to where Tess sat behind the desk. As usual, her friend was perfectly put together, today in a plum-colored sheath dress with a matching cardigan draped over her shoulders.

"Always." Tess flipped open the lid, as glad for Gail's company as she was for the sugary distraction.

"Some court reporter left them for the new guys in 302, but I don't think they'll mind." Gail leaned closer. "The one with the man bun's been looking for an excuse to meet you. And he's kind of cute, in a dirty-on-purpose sort of way."

"I'm pretty sure that's not a thing." Even if it was, and assuming Tess was interested — she wasn't — whoever'd had first crack at the doughnuts was of questionable taste. The plain glazed and the chocolate cake ones were all still there.

Tess took a huge bite and chewed with her eyes closed. Any day was better with a mouth full of deep-fried chocolate heaven. At least, it seemed that way until she noticed the paper hanging from Gail's hand under the doughnut box. Tess couldn't see the fine print, but the words "Notice of Delinquency" were clear enough.

"That for me?"

"Sorry, hon." Gail shifted the box so she could hand it over. "George asked me to tack it to your door. But I could forget for a few days, if you want."

Tess shook her head, shoulders drooping. She'd already been avoiding her landlord for two weeks. And even if Gail "forgot" to give her legal notice, "a few days aren't going to make a difference."

"Really? But you've been so busy." Gail wrinkled up her forehead.

"I don't get paid until the client does. And we haven't collected anything yet." Tess shrugged and looked out the window where traffic crept by below. The cars stuck in a relentless crawl toward nowhere, baking in the afternoon sun. "Anyway, mostly I've been chasing that developer that screwed over the Ashbys."

"Whole thing's such a shame." Gail closed the doughnut box and propped it against one hip, holding it in place with her wrist. "If Sam Ashby wasn't happily married and a hundred and twelve…" She raised her eyebrows.

"You're a mess." Tess took another bite of the doughnut, but it didn't taste as good with a delinquency notice in her other hand.

Sam visited their office every few days to check the progress on his case. Always in what her grandmother would have called "church clothes," with a pocket full of butterscotch candies to share. It broke her heart to disappoint him. "I can't face him again without any money. They're living with water seeping into their living room, a construction disaster next door, and a foundation that might buckle at any minute." Tess crumpled the notice. "Everything we did to get a judgment, and the damned developer might as well be a ghost. He's just… gone."

The ringing of a phone echoed down the hall, and Gail made a run for it. Or as close to a run as she could get in kitten heels. "Be right back. Gotta grab that."

Tess smoothed the delinquency notice but didn't bother reading it. She knew well enough what it said. It was the second one she'd gotten, which meant she had thirty days before she was out on her ass.

So much for that unfair advantage.

Tess shook off the thought. Nothing good would come from going down that road. She threw back the last of her coffee and got a mouthful of dregs. "Ick."

Gail's voice came faint from down the hall. "Good morning. This is the office of Tess Oliver, Attorney at Law. May I help you?"

Tess waited for Gail to launch into the standard brush-off she knew to give creditors, but it didn't come. A prickle of hope crawled up the back of Tess's neck. If it wasn't a creditor, it could be a lead. She leaned forward, listening.

The phone on her desk shrieked to life, and Tess jumped, knocking over her empty cup. It rolled off the edge of the desk and disappeared into the footwell, but she didn't bother going after it.

She focused on the phone, letting it ring again, willing her heart rate to come down. Not wanting to seem overeager.

Even if she was.

Please let it be good news.

Tess cleared her throat and picked up the receiver. "This is Tess Oliver."

"Afternoon. Brandt Goodman, branch manager at East Atlanta Savings and Loan. I'm calling in reference to the GA Investments, LLC garnishment."

A grin spread across Tess's face. Of the dozen sets of garnishment paperwork she'd sent out, hoping to find where the Ashbys' developer stashed his money, this was the first possible hit. "Thanks for getting back to me."

"You're very welcome. Most of the garnishment paperwork we receive is in a state you would not believe. I appreciate you providing us with everything we need, especially given the recent changes in the law."

"Of course." Tess dug through the stacks of paper covering her desk, searching for the Ashbys' file.

"I wanted to return the courtesy by letting you know that we filed our answer with the court this morning. I don't usually communicate this directly to counsel, but it may help you to know in advance that the garnishee's checking and savings accounts are both empty."

"Shit." Tess put down a stack of yellow notepads and squeezed her eyes shut. "Sorry, language. Thanks for getting back to me." No money in the accounts meant no money for the Ashbys.

Or her.

"I can understand your frustration." Goodman let a few seconds of silence stretch out before he spoke again. "I don't know if this will help, but the customer also has a safe deposit box. We've placed a hundred and twenty day hold on it, as we're required to do, but, if you were to get a court order," he paused, "we could turn the contents over to you." A desk chair squealed, as if he'd turned around before continuing, more quietly this time. "It's one of our jumbo boxes, and it seems to me you only pay for the big one if you have a good reason."

Tess could think of a few good reasons, all of them lucrative. Banks made a point of not tracking what customers put into a safe deposit box, which would make it an ideal spot for the developer to have hidden his assets. Her mouth went dry with the possibilities.

Tess said her goodbyes, tossed her laptop into a computer bag, and hustled out of her office. "I'm off," she called to Gail. "And don't forget you're on your own for brunch Sunday. I'm headed to Gran's tomorrow."

"Have such a good trip, honey. Shoot me a text when you get there, and make sure to give your grandparents a squeeze for me."

Tess blew her a kiss and hurried toward the stairs. A quick stop home to change into a suit, and she'd be off to court to try and get an audience with the judge. The first step would be to see if she could turn the developer's disappearing act into grounds for an ex parte order. If the other party refused to be found, there was no reason to wait for them to speak up before the judge allowed her access to their assets.

Or, at least, that's what she'd argue. And there was no time to go through normal channels, anyway. By the time the court took up a standard motion, waited for the developer's response not to come, and issued an order, she'd be out of business.

CHAPTER 2

East Atlanta Savings & Loan sat in the middle of a strip mall between an ancient pizza joint and a salon with You've Got Nail emblazoned above a striped awning in matching candy pink. Only a few cars dotted the parking lot, but the lights inside the bank glowed through their front windows. According to the hours posted on the door, she had twenty minutes before they closed.

Nothing like coming in right under the wire.

Tess hurried inside. No other customers waited in line, and every surface in the place had a sheen to it, as if it had just been wiped down for the day. The place reeked of some artificial fruity floral cleanser. She wrinkled her nose. Hard to imagine what could smell bad enough to make that an improvement.

A gangly man in a cheap three-piece suit emerged from a back office. He crossed the lobby and offered a clammy handshake. "Can I help you?"

"Hi…" She glanced down at his name tag. "Mr. Goodman. I think we spoke on the phone earlier about the Georgia Investments accounts?"

"Of course. You must be Ms. Oliver." He followed her gaze through the open vault door to the rows of metal boxes inside. "I can imagine you're anxious to get started." He looked back again but, this time, focused over her shoulder, toward a man who had come in after her and seemed not to understand the basics of personal space.

She pretended not to notice, even though she could feel the pressure of his closeness on the back of her neck.

"Someone will be right with you, sir." Goodman gave the customer behind her a bland smile and led Tess a few steps away. He gestured to the satchel she carried. "You have the legalities handled?"

"I do." She rummaged around in her bag. "I have an order from the court allowing the immediate seizure of any assets in the box up to the amount of the judgment, which was for forty-eight thousand dollars." She found what she was looking for and handed Goodman a stack of paper bound with a binder clip. "And I'll file a sworn inventory of the box's contents once I get back to my office."

"Good, good. Naturally, without the account holder here, we'll have to address a few formalities before you can get started." The bank manager reviewed the documentation she'd provided, took a quick look at her identification, and gave a nod. "That ought to do it."

He led her to the vault, and a round-faced woman came around from behind the bank counter and followed. She carried a set of keys in one hand and a clipboard in the other.

She lifted the latter toward Tess. "If you can sign here."

Tess scratched out a signature, and the two bankers inserted keys into their respective locks, turning them until something clicked.

Here we go.

The box swung open with a faint squeak of the hinge.

"I'll just leave this here for you." Goodman placed the rectangular metal container on a bar height table in the center of the room. It made a promising thud.

Please let it be cash.

How much could fit into a box that size? Enough that Tess's cut would pay her rent? "Thank you." She said to the bank employees' backs as they left her to it, counting the seconds until they had gone.

Tess threw open the lid.

A single, plain manila folder sat in the center. A seed of resignation took root in the center of her chest. Small enough for her to ignore, but too big not to feel.

It could be bearer bonds.

She opened the folder and wilted. An over-sized piece of paper folded several times over waited within.

Shit.

Whatever it was, it wasn't money or anything that could be used as money. She should've known this would go sideways. Most everything did these days. She chewed the edge of her thumbnail. Still, if there was any chance the document was something she could use, she needed to know.

Tess tried to unfold the document without ripping the paper. Failed. Then tried again, twice, before finally smoothing the enormous thing out on the table.

Dense markings covered the page. She blinked, trying to focus.

I'm getting old.

She held the paper a foot in front of her face. It looked like a color-coded March Madness bracket or a family tree, but instead of teams or names, each line bore only a series of letters and numbers. It started with a single entry on the left side of the page and branched out until there were hundreds of entries against the far right. Each notation was either red or blue, but no key indicated what the colors might mean. The only other marking on the page was a series of numbers handwritten on the bottom left corner in black ink.

She re-folded the document, failing — despite her best efforts — to consolidate the beast to its original size.

Like trying to fold a fitted fucking sheet.

And she may as well have found a cache of Egyptian hieroglyphs. She let out a deep breath as she shoved the rumpled document back into the folder.

She was back where she started. With a judgment worth exactly the cost of the paper it was printed on and rent looming due at the end of the month.

. . .

Tess pulled her ancient Volvo into the pay-by-month garage across the street from her office, driving up past the reserved floors to the cheap first-come, first-served spots on the top level of the parking deck. If there was any chance what she'd found could be monetized, she needed to figure out how. She cranked the steering wheel again and again to the right. Something unidentifiable, but no doubt expensive, squealed in protest under the hood.

The markings on the document didn't look like any corporate structure she'd ever seen. It was too linear, each line branching off into others that branched off into more. And it was too big, even the biggest conglomerate wouldn't be made up of that many entities. Maybe some sort of trade secret? Which might explain why the developer had it in a vault.

Whatever it was, if it didn't lead her to money or the identity of whoever was hidden behind all the corporate shells and subterfuge, it wasn't going to do her a damn bit of good. Tess pulled into a spot on the top floor of the garage and climbed out, a gust of balmy late summer wind slamming the door closed behind her.

The sound echoed through the parking deck, which, at this time of night, was mostly empty. And eerie as fuck. What she wouldn't give for some available on street parking right about now.

Tess adjusted the strap of her computer bag and glanced around, her gaze drawn to the shadows beyond the security lights. Had she seen something move? A flicker of something now just out of view? She peered out into the darkness. But, of course, nothing was there. Just her imagination.

Too many damn movies.

She hurried to the stairs but stopped before she went in. Tess took a deep breath and threw open the door. It was a long climb down, and the whole stairwell smelled like pee.

She clambered down the steps. It wouldn't be long now, and she could go home to the sweet comfort of sweatpants and boxed wine. Just a quick call to the Ashbys to give them the bad news and then she'd draft the notice setting out what she'd found — or more accurately, hadn't found — in the developer's safe deposit box. Once she'd electronically filed the notice with the court, she was done for the night.

She'd figure out the rest tomorrow. Somehow.

She had to.

She didn't have any other choice.

. . .

Martin Bannon pulled a burner phone from his pocket as he stepped out of the parking garage. He dialed his boss's number from memory. As often as he'd called it, he never punched in those digits without an uncomfortable flutter in his chest. And today, he had reason to worry.

He counted every ring with a mixture of dread and relief. No part of him wanted to have the conversation that was coming, but it wasn't news he could leave in a voicemail, and the longer he waited to try and explain—

The ringing stopped. "Is it done?" The question was as close as Martin was going to get to a hello.

He swallowed hard. "Someone got it before I could."

"What do you mean, someone got it?" His boss barked out the question. "Who?"

Martin popped the rubber band on his wrist. "I don't know yet, sir. But I'll take care of it. I'm tracking her now."

"It's a woman?"

"A lawyer by the looks of it. She went into a Midtown office twenty minutes ago." Martin eyed the front entrance of one in a row of mid-rise office buildings. "I checked her car. It's empty except for a half dozen coffee cups in the floorboard." He popped the band again. "She must have taken it in with her."

The voice was cold as it came back across the line. "You need to retrieve it. Or at least make sure no one else does."

"Yes, sir." Martin crossed the street to a multi-use development catty-corner from the lawyer's building. "And the woman?"

A pause stretched out.

"Deal with it." His boss didn't wait for a response before disconnecting the call. When he gave an order, the answer was always "yes."

Sliding the phone back into his jacket pocket, Martin's fingers brushed the passport he'd carried into the bank. He'd gone to a lot of trouble to have it made, and it was real top of the line stuff. Now it might as well be kindling.

Not that it mattered. His employer had plenty of resources. And Martin would get the job done, one way or another. He settled into the shadow of a bagel shop's awning and waited.

He was good at waiting. Especially when he wanted something.

A few lights glowed in the apartments on the floors above him, but the bagel shop on the ground floor sat dark, chairs turned upside down and stowed for the night on top of the tables. He flipped up the collar of his jacket and fished out the hood of the sweatshirt he wore underneath. The air still held the warmth of the day's sunshine and hung heavy with humidity. But the hoodie and jacket provided good cover, making his thin frame seem bulkier. Out of habit, more than necessity, he kept his face tilted down in the shadow of his hood, listening for any sign of danger or detection.

The night was quiet for Midtown. Just the whoosh of traffic and the wind whistling through the narrow openings between the office buildings and the newer multi-use developments, which had sprung up all over the city.

He checked his watch, 7:05. A heavy-set blonde in a passing SUV seemed to look his way, but then, the light turned green, and she was gone. Martin shifted further into the shadows, slumping down against the building. Nothing but another invisible homeless man on the streets of Atlanta.

Martin rolled the rubber band back and forth against the tender skin on the inside of his wrist. He had begun wearing it, or one like it, at the suggestion of his first state-mandated therapist. She wasn't a terribly attractive woman. Her eyes were too closely set, her lips too thin. But she had nice legs. Shiny and smooth, like the vain bitch put lotion on them every day. He checked his watch again, 7:32.

The lawyer came back out the same door she'd gone in. Curls bouncing with each step, she jogged across the street, taking advantage of a break in traffic to cross without waiting for the light. He let his gaze drift to her chest, appreciating how her breasts moved underneath her shirt.

Martin waited until she reached the garage, then stepped out of the shadows.

CHAPTER 3

September 14, 2018

Tess's phone rang just as her romp with Jason Momoa started to get interesting. She ignored it, ran her hands one more time down his tan, tattooed chest, and burrowed into the duvet, willing the dream to pick back up where she'd left off.

The damn phone rang again.

Tess cracked open one sticky eye and smacked the cell phone off her bedside table. The alarm clock she hadn't bothered to set went with it, both clattering to the floor. Where, with any luck, they'd break into several, quiet inoperable pieces. She clamped her eyes closed.

Where'd you go, Jason?

The phone rang a third time from under the bed. And, as if insult needed injury, the whine of a neighbor's leaf blower joined the party.

Neither helped the cheap wine hangover taking residence behind her temples.

Tess dangled upside down off the edge of the mattress, blood rushing to her head as she felt around in the dark. She grabbed the receiver and smacked it to her ear. "What?"

"Tess, honey. Something's happened." Gail spoke over the clamor of sirens and raised voices.

Tess snapped upright, the movement too quick. The throb in her head became a pounding, her tongue like sandpaper in her mouth. "Are you okay?"

"Yeah, I'm fine. There was a fire at the office last night."

"What?" Tess rubbed a hand over her face. That didn't make any sense. She'd just been there, and everything had been fine.

"They haven't let us inside yet. But the firefighters listed your office as one of the ones that burned."

"Oh my God." Tess blinked, instantly awake. She was already broke. There was no way she was coming back from this. The pounding in her head picked up tempo.

"All the offices on your side of the floor did. And, from out here, it looks like the fourth floor, too, maybe."

"That's crazy. Do they know how it started? Is everyone okay?" What the hell was she going to do now?

"Yeah, so far as we know. George says they're thinking it was something electrical."

Tess swallowed hard. Had she turned off the space heater when she left? What felt like cymbals joined in the percussion inside her skull. She couldn't remember. But she'd been so anxious to get home, so ready to be done with the day, it was completely possible she hadn't.

Gail lowered her voice. "But I overheard one of the officers who was here say that the fire alarm never went off. They think someone tampered with it."

"No shit? Like someone might've started the fire on purpose?" The realization that the arsonist could've been in the office with her the night before crept in tingles up the back of her neck. Someone could have been hiding in any one of the dozen darkened offices she'd passed on the way in or out.

"No shit. They only got it under control because a neighbor saw the smoke and called it in. If they hadn't, who knows?"

"That's crazy. Why would anyone want to burn down our building?"

"Goodness, girl, who knows? I'm just glad no one… what?" The murmur of a voice in the background cut in. "George says he needs for you to get him an inventory of whatever was in your office so he can submit a claim to the insurance company. Can you come by?"

Tess closed her eyes, then opened them slowly. A Saturday morning visit with the landlord she owed back rent was the last thing she wanted. Especially not without a penny to her name and a hangover on board. "Sure, of course. I'll be right there."

She said a quick goodbye, stumbled out of bed, and scrubbed her face with a wet washcloth. There would be no make-up today. She shoved her legs into the closest pair of jeans she could find.

What all had been in her office?

The short answer was, not much. She'd never bothered to decorate or even hang her diplomas. There was the standard office furniture, the same as had been provided to each of the other 'furnished' spaces on the third floor. Plus her laptop, an old landline phone, and her paper files. Thankfully, she had those backed up in the cloud. The only real loss was her computer. And her work bag, which was nearly worn out anyway and didn't have anything of value in it — notepad, pens, sticky tabs.

Shit.

She'd left the document she retrieved from the bank the day before in the bag. She pressed her palm to her forehead. "Dumbass." She'd had no way to scan in something that size from her office — the document was bigger than a blueprint. So, she'd filed a notice electronically with the court, noting her intention to supplement the filing as soon as she was able to properly attach the document. And then she'd gone home, planning to deal with it later.

Except now the only copy was gone. Literally, up in smoke.

"I am so screwed." Tess put on a pot of coffee and plopped down on the couch, trying to think of any scenario which wouldn't involve her having to tell the Ashbys she'd lost the only lead they had on getting the money they were owed. She put that thought in the "shit I'm going to ignore for now" pile. What she needed to deal with first was how she was going to buy another laptop with money she didn't have.

But she couldn't deal with that either. Not now.

One more thought for the pile.

Tess zigzagged her finger through the thin film of dust that coated the side table as the coffee maker burbled and spit in the kitchen. There wasn't a damn thing she could accomplish without her computer.

"Fuck it." She went to grab a go-mug.

Three cups with extra sugar, and she was finally ready to adult something. She made two calls, first to the court and then the bank to let them know the document had been destroyed. She would need to file something official with the court to make a record of the loss as soon as she had access to a computer. But, for now, that ground was, at least temporarily, covered.

Tess made a quick list of what had been lost in the fire and emailed it to Gail from her phone, along with an apology for not making it to the office in person. She was in no mood to deal with George. Besides, she was supposed to have been on the road by 8:00 a.m. And at a quarter to 10:00, her suitcase still waited unopened in the back of a hall closet.

She had been looking forward to spending a long weekend at her grandparents' house for months. And if ever there was a time to get the hell out of Dodge, this was it.

. . .

The trip from Atlanta to Southern Mississippi meant an eight-and-a-half-hour drive on the world's least interesting stretch of highway. But, after a seemingly endless parade of pine trees, eighteen wheelers, and low-end fast-food joints, Tess finally turned onto her grandparents' long gravel drive. She rolled slowly under overgrown wisteria vines, rocks popping beneath her tires as she pulled into the clearing. The double-wide hadn't changed a bit.

Hanging planters circled the porch, an assortment of stone gnomes lined the steps, and an oversized Ole Miss flag waved proud from the holder Pop had mounted by the kitchen window.

Even before she'd opened her car door, the barking of dogs from the nearest outbuilding was hard to ignore. Gran and Pop usually had twenty or thirty of them boarded on the farm, in addition to the dozen rescues that lived with them full time. It was endlessly loud, almost always chaotic, and one of the things she liked best about coming home. Dogs made for better company than people.

Tess waited for the dust cloud her car kicked up to settle and climbed out. Pop's German Shepherd, Badger, found her before she'd even shut the door. He yipped and jumped in circles.

"Hi, big boy!" Tess grinned at him. "I missed you, too!"

He jammed his nose in her crotch and sat down at her feet, tail thwacking back and forth at top speed.

Gran yelled over from the front porch, "Badger! Let her be. Tess, you come on up here and get a plate! We've been holding dinner for you, and you look like you haven't eaten in a week." Wheel of Fortune blared out through the open screen door behind her. "And leave the suitcase in the trunk. Pop'll come get it."

"Yes, ma'am," Tess called back, giving Badger's ears a quick rub before she jogged to the house. She stopped halfway up the porch steps. "Badger, where'd you go, buddy?" The dog never missed an opportunity to be under foot.

She scanned the clearing, finally spotting him by the back of her car, head shoved under the bumper. Tess tilted her head to the side, expecting to see a barn cat peeking out from underneath.

Something under the car blinked red.

Tess went closer, crouching down beside Badger so she could see. Road grime coated the Volvo's undercarriage, painting everything the same shade of mud brown. What had she seen?

"Tess!" Gran called from inside. "It's gonna get cold."

"Coming." Tess took one last, long look under the car.

Nothing.

The dog looked her way, and she shrugged. "We better go, or there's gonna be trouble." Tess got to her feet, following Badger up the porch steps. God knew it seemed to be following her around.

CHAPTER 4

September 15, 2018

Luke Broussard checked the flight calendar, but there was still nothing on it. No record of any flights for the day.

And this particular unscheduled passenger was not a pleasant surprise.

Mr. Smith hadn't given a first name. And he'd refused to wait in the lobby of the main Cobb County airport terminal building while Luke sorted out the missing reservation. Instead, the man had followed Luke into the hangar, where he now seemed intent on wearing grooves into the concrete floor.

Smith paced in front of the 1978 Cessna Skylane, that was Luke's bread and butter, muttering and typing what was probably a business-ending Yelp review into his iPhone.

Luke swiveled the chair so that his back was to Smith and tried his partner's cell phone again. But, as usual, Nick Parker didn't answer.

Luke rubbed at the ache brewing behind his temples.

Had Luke known they had a client, he would have worn one of the company polos rather than his ratty LSU shirt and maybe brushed his hair. He put a hand up to his face and huffed out a breath. Had he at least remembered to brush his teeth? Even if he had, he was sure he'd made a terrible impression, on top of the reservation being lost and the state of their "office" — which was really just a desk shoved into the back corner of the hangar.

"Listen." The voice came from directly behind him, and Luke jumped in his seat.

Shit.

Smith didn't seem to notice. "We need to go. Now."

He turned and looked up into the man's pinched face. With every ounce of professional gravitas he could muster, Luke smiled. "Let me just try to reach my partner one more time, sir. If I can't, I'll fly you to Mobile myself."

Luke dialed, knowing the chances were less than slim that Parker would answer. "Uh, hi, Nick. It's me again. I don't know what you did with the reservation for Mr…" putting his hand over the receiver, he asked the client, "What was it again?" Luke knew the name, but for some perverse reason, wanted to make the guy repeat it.

"Smith."

"Right." Luke nodded, certain it was anything but. "Mr. Smith understood that he had booked a 9:00 a.m. flight to Mobile. If I don't hear back within the next ten minutes, I'll…"

Call waiting beeped in Luke's ear. He smiled again at his passenger and slowly turned his back once more, trying to give Smith a subtle cue he'd like some privacy.

Luke waited until the client's footsteps cleared the sliding metal doors of the hangar before he spoke. "Parker, you dumb fuck, where the hell are you?"

"Sorry to leave you hanging, man. But I met this girl at Chino's last night, and she was so worth it. I mean, dear God, this thing she does with her mouth—"

Luke cut him off. "Okay, yeah. I don't want any part of the details or the antibiotics you're gonna need after that." He shook his head. It didn't matter how many times Parker made a mistake. Given half a chance, he'd do the same damn thing again. "I thought you were trying to work it out with Cassie?"

"Shit, man, aren't we always trying to work it out?"

Luke let it go. Nothing he said was going to matter while Parker was off on a bender. "What's going on with this morning's charter? Can you get here?"

"Um, no," his answer was interrupted by giggling in the background. Along with what sounded like someone smacking Parker's bare ass. "Sorry, I forgot to log it in. But the Cessna's ready to go. Smith's all paid up. I did pre-check last night. You're fueled and ready. Everything's sorted, all you have to do is climb in and go."

"You owe me, Parker. Big time."

"Thanks, buddy." And then, somewhat muffled, but still unfortunately clear enough for Luke to hear, "No, no don't bite it." The line went dead.

Partnering on the charter business with his best friend had seemed like a good idea at the time. For all his shenanigans, Parker was a good dude at heart, easygoing, and, maybe most importantly, had enough family money to buy a plane. So, when neither wanted to re-enlist with the Navy, it seemed like a perfect option. Except, since Parker's marriage had hit the skids, he only showed up for work when he felt like it and was usually hung over when he got there.

Luke had been giving Parker space to figure it out, but that couldn't go on forever. He gathered up his things and walked out into the sunshine to find Smith. "Let me just run through our pre-flight checks, and we'll get going."

Luke ignored the man's eye roll and went about his routine, going through his checklist, making sure that everything was in good working order, that they had sufficient fuel on board, and that their flight plan had, in fact, been filed. You never knew with Parker.

But, for once, Parker seemed to have checked all the right boxes. Luke turned to Mr. Smith, "Let's get you boarded."

Luke popped open the passenger door and moved out of the way so Smith could climb in. "I'm happy to stow that for you," he indicated the bag, still pressed to Smith's chest.

"No."

Luke blinked. "I'm sorry?"

"The bag stays with me."

"That's not going to work, sir. There isn't room in the cockpit for you to hold it." Luke reached in to demonstrate the path of the yoke, which was otherwise known as the knees and nuts test. Because, if you weren't sitting all the way back in your seat when the yoke landed in your lap, you were going to damage both.

Smith pursed his lips, and Luke tried again. "Sir, it needs to go in the back." There was no way he was taking off with a loose bag in the cockpit. "The last thing you want is to have a bunch of crap flying around hitting you in the head if we run into turbulence."

Smith's expression didn't change.

Luke crossed his arms over his chest. "It'll be hard for me to fly the plane if I'm knocked unconscious."

"Fine." Smith sighed loudly through his nose, as if he was growing tired of humoring a petulant toddler. "But I'm going in the back seat with it." Normally, clients chose to ride in the front seat. The view was better, and the back seats in the older model Cessna didn't have shoulder harnesses. But, given the man's attitude, Luke decided not to argue the point. He just smiled his assent, hoping the "good riddance" he'd muttered on the inside wasn't evident on his face.

Luke waited for Smith to climb in before closing the passenger side door. He gave the plane a final once-over as he rounded the tail and climbed into the cockpit.

"Okay, here we go." Luke yelled over the engine noise, then pulled on his headphones, gesturing for Smith to do the same. To his surprise, Smith complied, and Luke continued, this time at normal volume, "My apologies for the delay. I'll have you to Mobile in no time." Smith said nothing, his attention focused on picking lint from the fine weave of his trousers. Which was just as well. Were it not for his passenger, it might be a day Luke would really enjoy being in the air.

The sky stretched out before him, a bright cornflower blue and cloudless. He checked in with the tower, got his clearances, taxied to the runway, and took off due west on runway twenty-seven. Then, he quickly turned southwest on course and climbed up to cruising altitude. Once there, he let himself relax, to enjoy the feeling of being aloft, the late September morning a little cooler at 6,000 feet but still sunny and beautiful. He watched the western outskirts of the Atlanta suburbs fade into the more rural surroundings. With any luck, he'd be rid of Smith and back in time to get their invoices out before the end of the day.

In what felt like minutes, they'd crossed over the state line and into Alabama. Luke pulled on the yoke, but the nose of the plane didn't lift.

What the hell?

He tried again, but the elevator, a long, horizontal flap running along the stabilizing crossbar on the tail of the plane, wouldn't respond.

"What's going on?" Smith asked from the back seat, leaning forward as Luke fought with the yoke.

"We've got a control issue." Luke pulled harder, but the elevator was jammed in a partially down position, which meant the plane was similarly and intractably stuck pointing down. If he couldn't get the nose to lift, the plane wasn't going to stay airborne. He forced away the bubble of anxiety rising in his chest and pulled, once again, on the yoke.

Still nothing.

"Has this ever happened before?" Smith's voice, already high-pitched and nasal, came across the headset as a falsetto.

"Never." They'd been careful to make sure the plane was well maintained, but she'd been built in 1978 and had more than ten thousand hours of time in the air. Even with the best upkeep, and no turbulence, things would eventually break. At least until now, they'd had the courtesy to bust when he wasn't six thousand feet above the ground.

Luke radioed air traffic control. "Atlanta Center, this is Cessna Skylane N227EchoTango, we need to declare an emergency. We're about six miles northeast of Wedowee, Alabama, and we're having a control issue."

The response came within seconds, "Two-Two-Seven-EchoTango, can you give me the number of souls on board and fuel remaining?"

"Two souls and— " He eyed the gauge. "About 50 gallons of fuel remaining." Luke continued pulling at the yoke, desperately trying to raise the nose of the plane, but it stuck firm. "We have loss of vertical control."

"Roger, 227EchoTango, please switch frequency to 121.5 and squawk 7700."

"Understood, switching now." Luke changed over to the emergency frequency, which would give him a way to communicate, uninterrupted by the normal communications of Atlanta air traffic control. Then, he switched his squawk to 7700, changing ground control's radar image of their plane to one identified as a plane in immediate distress.

If he couldn't control the pitch of the plane with the elevator, he'd have to do what he could to control it with speed. He pushed the throttle forward. That gave them a little lift, the speed of the plane buoying the nose of the plane up. And it slowed their descent, at least a bit. The increasing speed, counter-intuitively making them lose altitude more slowly. He watched the speed gauge rise,

... 160 knots ...

... 165 knots ...

... 170 knots ...

... 175 knots.

He considered pulling back but waited a beat and watched as the gauge pushed up to 185 knots, at least five knots over the airplane's stated speed not to exceed. When the plane started to shimmy, he yanked back the throttle to cut velocity. And, in response, the plane tilted forward. The trick was to add enough speed to slow their fall from the sky, while, at the same time, not going too fast. Exceeding the speed the plane was built to withstand might cause it to break apart mid-air.

There was no victory in having the wings fall off before he could land the damn thing.

"What's happening? Is it supposed to do that?" Smith asked, gripping the back of Luke's seat as the plane's shaking finally subsided. "What kind of bullshit operation are you running?"

The truth was bleak, and he couldn't come up with any way to make it sound better than it was. "We're having a mechanical issue, and we're going to have to find somewhere to put her down."

"Put it down?" Smith whipped his head side to side, as if he might spot their problem from one of the rear windows. "What're you talking about? You need to fix it."

Before Luke could answer, air traffic control came back over the headset, "Two-Two-Seven-EchoTango, wind is 230 at 10. You are cleared to land at the Roanoke Municipal Airport, roughly 15 miles to your southeast. Can you give me some more information?"

"My elevator is jammed. I'm at 4000 feet in an uncontrolled descent. I don't think I can make it to Roanoke. Looking for a place to set down." Luke pulled a laminated cheat sheet from the door pocket where it had been gathering dust for years and double-checked his emergency checklist. He had done everything he was supposed to do. Which, as it turned out, didn't make him feel any better.

He ran through the possibilities in his head, but they kept coming out the same. They'd be lucky to make it another five miles, even under the best of conditions. Which this wasn't. And that wasn't going to be enough. Even before they'd begun to descend, when he'd had a view several miles ahead, there had been nothing but pine trees and the glimmer of Lake Wedowee in the far distance. No possible landing sites opened up on the horizon.

The radio went silent while Luke continued the dance of throttle and descent.

The crackling returned. "Two-Two-Seven-EchoTango. Can you give me more information?"

"We're at 1500 feet. We're not going to make it." The words caught in his mouth, a lump climbing into his throat. As if saying it out loud made it true. Who would tell his mother he was gone? His sisters? He swallowed hard, forcing himself to stay in the present. "Request search and rescue activation."

"Wait, what?" Smith threw himself back against the seat. His voice grew louder, nearly hysterical. "You need to do something. This isn't acceptable. You have to fix it!"

Luke ignored the man, gritting his teeth as he used the rudder to shift the tail of the plane left and then to the right, crabbing the plane across the sky to create more drag. They were coming in way too fast.

Smith again, this time nearing a yell. "Did you hear me? Do something, damnit!"

Air traffic control came back on the radio before Luke could tell the man to shut up. "Say aircraft color."

"She's white, blue tail. We're not going to make it."

"Two-Two-Seven-EchoTango, can you repeat?"

Every muscle in Luke's body held tense. "We're not going to make it."

Smith keened from the back seat, his wailing interrupted only by the calm voice over the radio. "Roger. Just do as you were trained. Set up for emergency landing."

Even as Luke did what they asked, he couldn't reconcile what was happening with reality. And maybe that was for the best. Panic would be the worst possible thing to do. He forced himself to focus only on what he needed to do next.

Air traffic control again. "Radar contact lost."

It seemed to take an eternity and, at once, no time at all as they closed in on the treetops. A mass of continuous green pines, and the ground waiting for them beneath the trees. Luke left it as long as he could, until they were a few dozen feet above the tree line, and then did the only other thing he could think to do that might help. He cut the engine power, dropped the flaps to full, and adjusted the trim. It wasn't perfect, but between the lack of throttle and trim, the nose rose, slowing their fall to earth a bit more.

The belly of the plane connected with the treetops. Each tree they hit snapped off, the sound a sickening screech of metal, punctuated by the popping cracks of the stalks of timber as they broke.

"Brace yourself," he yelled into the headset, but it was too late for either him or Smith to do anything more than hold on in whatever position they found themselves. Luke kept his hands locked tight on the controls, even though he had lost any actual control over the plane. They plunged forward fast, down through the trees, the body of the plane rolling onto its right side as they fell. Smith's bag flew forward into the cockpit, slamming against the side of Luke's head before it crashed into the dash. Luke held his breath, pain searing along the side of his head. The plexiglass windshield cracked in two with a loud pop, a branch jutting into the cockpit. More tree limbs punched in through the passenger side as they neared the ground, and then the plane finally collided with the earth and bounced, hard.

Luke squeezed his eyes shut, afraid of what he might see. He took a shuddering breath. Everything hurt. And he was wet.

Fuel?

No, that didn't make any sense, not really. Not inside the cockpit. But…

The thought slipped away.

In its place, an image of his mother's tear-streaked face the day he left home. Of his family gathered around the table for Sunday supper, everyone there but him. The pain in his head became a throb, his mind too jumbled for him to tell memory from fear. He should've given his sisters one more hug before he left. Should've told Charlotte how much he loved her. He squeezed his eyes tighter. His thoughts barely surfaced past a loud, constant buzzing in his ears. He was going to die if he didn't get out. But even that threat wasn't enough to keep his hold on consciousness.

He'd done everything he could. And knowing that made him feel at least a little better about letting go.

CHAPTER 5

Tess stood in a drafty, prefab stall under a shower head gone brown around the edges. Goosebumps prickled her arms and legs. The water was barely more than tepid and, worse, it smelled of rotten eggs. Her grandfather might call their well "artesian," but sulfur was sulfur no matter what you named it.

She squirted a dollop of a fruity Herbal Essence knock-off into her hand and lathered up. The sooner she got clean, the sooner she could get out and get warm. The shampoo was an improvement over the stink of the water, but only by a little. The scent reminded her of something she'd smelled before. She checked the bottle.

Tropical breeze, my ass.

It smelled like the cleanser they'd used in the bank where she had found the Ashbys' document.

And just as it had happened dozens of times before, she wasn't in the shower stall anymore. Only, she was. She could still feel the pathetic patter of water on the back of her head. But she was also caught inside a memory, looking at the rows of safe deposit boxes lining the inside of the bank vault.

Every detail of the room — the oak table where she'd spread the document out, the flicker of the cheap florescent light above her head, and even the text of the document itself — came into focus, as sharply defined as if she was standing there again. The feeling of intense disappointment she'd had when she realized the document was likely useless, that she'd failed again to find anything that might help the Ashbys, or herself, was back again, too. The image floated out in front of her, and she scanned the document again. It was still gibberish.

Except, was it? She focused the memory on the bottom left-hand corner at the scrawl of black handwriting.

Each of the four rows of numbers had just enough digits to be a phone number. The digits were clumped altogether, not separated by dashes as a phone number would usually be written. Which was why she hadn't recognized the possibility before, although the "251" that started the first number should've been a clue. It was the area code for most of Mobile. Could the number be the developer's? Other homeowners he'd scammed? Maybe it meant something else entirely. She scanned down the list of numbers again, but none of the others started with area codes she recognized. Could be they weren't phone numbers at all.

"You almost done in there?" Pop's voice came through the bathroom door, and she blinked. The document gone. Her grandparents' plastic shower curtain in its place.

"Sorry, Pop. I'll be right out." She kept her voice even, not wanting him to know she'd had another episode. The less her grandparents knew about what her memory spells really were, the better.

"No rush, Tess-bug. Just wanted to make sure you didn't fall in." He laughed at the tired joke, his chuckling fading with his retreating footsteps.

Tess went through the motions of rinsing her hair, even as her mind spun, the aftermath of the memory making her feel out of place and off-balance. And, of course, the usual headache set in.

Crap.

It had been a solid three months since she'd had one of her spells. Long enough she had begun to hope — as she always did — that the previous eidetic memory had been the last. The last time she'd deal with the sickness that followed or the problems she knew would come if she tried to use it for anything. She shut off the tap, trying to shake off the heavy feeling of failure that had come back to her with the episode.

But that wasn't the only thing she remembered. She stepped out of the stall, the goosebumps finding all the spots they missed the first time. If she closed her eyes, she could still see the first row of handwritten digits from the document. It was faint, but it was there.

A lead for the Ashbys? Maybe. But what else would it bring?

Consequences.

There always were, and they were never good. She pulled a brush through the snarls of her hair, wrapped herself up in a threadbare, yellow robe and stuffed her cell phone in the pocket.

Tess marched into the kitchen, damp but clean. She found Gran transferring buttermilk pancakes from the griddle to a turquoise Fiestaware platter, already heaped high. She planted a kiss on her grandmother's cheek, helped herself to coffee, and then shook two pills from the bottle of ibuprofen Pop kept above the refrigerator.

The medicine was probably a waste of time. She'd tried everything — over-the-counter, prescription, old wives' tales. Nothing put a dent in the brutal headaches that followed her spells. But she settled in at the table and swallowed the tablets dry anyway. Couldn't hurt.

And if I'm going to have a headache anyway...

Tess pulled her phone from the pocket of the robe and focused on the screen, her stomach going sour as she tried to invoke the images from the bank vault again. Nothing. She took a sip of coffee, which only served to add more acidity to her growing nausea.

My body knows I shouldn't be doing this.

But what choice did she have? Declare bankruptcy? Start scouring want ads? If ever there was a time for desperate measures…

Tess tried to reach the memory again, training her mind on the image of the document.

She did her best to tune out the smoky sweet smell of crisp bacon, the clink of Gran's spoon against the bowl as she coaxed pancake batter onto the griddle, the old oak chair hard under her backside. Tess pulled a lock of her hair to her nose and breathed in. With the whiff of fruity floral scent, the first set of numbers came into focus again, along with a burning in the back of her throat.

As quickly as they'd appeared, they were gone again. She chanted the numbers to herself, trying to make sure she got them right as she pressed them into the phone's keypad, then waited while it rang.

Pick up, pick up.

A voice croaked through the line. "Hello."

Gotcha.

"Hi, this is Teresa Oliver, I represent Sam and Eleanor Ashby. I'm trying to reach someone with GA Investments, LLC. Would that be you?" She paused, but there was no response. "This is in reference to the judgment entered in Fulton Superior Court."

Tess cringed. If anything was going to scare him off, leading with a reference to the lawsuit would. The flame of hope that had lit when the man had answered sputtered as quickly as it'd caught fire. Why hadn't she planned what to say before she called?

A sharp inhale of breath came over the line.

Which was something. At least they hadn't hung up. Maybe she could start over, try a softer tactic or—

"We need help." The man's voice cracked. "I, I don't know where we are exactly. But I think he's dead."

Tess sat up straight in the chair, dread fizzling under her skin. "Who's dead?" She clutched the edge of the table, her breath coming fast and shallow. "Where are you? Who is this?"

Gran pivoted in place at the stove to stare at Tess.

Tess held up a hand, a silent plea for her grandmother to wait until Tess knew what the hell was going on. Gran nodded, her eyes wide.

The man's voice sounded more distant this time. "I think we were still near Wedowee when we went down… couldn't get it to respond… near the dam, I think." His voice faded in and out, and she struggled to make sense of what he was saying. But the last sentence couldn't have been clearer. "There's blood everywhere."

Tess's lungs seized and her breath caught in her throat. "God, where are you? Who's dead?" She waited for a response, but none came. She tried again. "Have you called 911?"

Only a dial tone answered.

. . .

Tess hit redial again and again, but her calls still went straight to an automated voicemail. She didn't bother leaving a message. Whoever had answered hadn't sounded like he'd be in any condition to check them.

What now? She shifted forward in her chair, a chill finding the still damp skin on the back of her neck. She had to do something. Had to help somehow, but—

"Who's dead? What happened?" Gran came closer.

Tess shook her head but didn't look up from the phone. "I don't know yet, Gran."

She dialed 911 and stumbled through the details of what little she knew "…and someone's hurt. The man I spoke to said there was blood. That they went down near the dam in Wedowee. I think he meant they were in a plane crash."

As Tess answered the dispatcher's questions a second time, she glanced up at Gran, who was frozen in place beside the table, the spatula still in her hand. Tess wrinkled her nose and tilted her head toward the stove, where smoke rose from the griddle.

Gran spun back toward the pancakes as the tap tap tap of the dispatcher typing in notes filled the phone line. The tapping stopped. "You said this all happened maybe five minutes ago?"

"Yes, that's right."

"Okay, we have what we need. Thanks." The dispatcher disconnected the call.

Tess pulled the phone away from her ear and looked at the now-dead receiver. What the hell was that? The acrid stink of ruined pancakes grabbed hold of her nausea and gave it a squeeze. Did she not believe what Tess had told her?

"What's going on?" Gran came back to the table, wiping her hands on her apron.

"I'm not even really sure." Tess put the phone down on the table and rubbed her temples. "It was the weirdest thing. You know how I've been trying to collect on that judgment I told you about?"

Gran nodded.

"I had one of my episodes, just now, in the shower." She swallowed, trying to get rid of the bitter taste in her mouth. As much as she hated talking about her memory, she couldn't think of any other way to explain what had happened. "I was back at the bank, looking at a document. And I realized some of the numbers on it could be phone numbers. Maybe a way to track down the defendant in the Ashbys' case. You know, if I got lucky. But when I called..."

"What?" Pop spoke up from the doorway, and Tess jumped, adrenaline still winding her nerves tight.

Pop gave her a small apologetic smile. "What happened?"

"The man who answered said someone was dead, and there was blood everywhere. He said they went down near the dam in Wedowee." She leaned back in her seat, rubbing her arms against the chill that'd now gone bone deep. "It has to be a plane crash, right?"

"Sure sounds that way." Gran dumped burned pancakes into the trash bin, the lid thwacking shut as she stepped off the foot lever. "Goodness. Those poor people."

Pop shook his head, worry crinkling his already lined brow. "Whether it was meant as a phone number or not, I'd say that fella was mighty lucky you called." He took the platter of surviving pancakes and a paper towel lined plate of bacon from Gran and put them on the table.

Maybe.

If what little she'd been able to tell the dispatcher wound up helping.

And that was a big if.

She wrapped her hands around her coffee cup for warmth. There was nothing she could do now but hope what she'd done had been enough. Tess took a deep breath and let it out slow.

But even as her heart rate finally came down, a residue of worry remained. What if the rescuers didn't make it in time? What if she was the last person that man ever spoke to? Could she have said something to give him comfort? Or asked for some detail that might've helped the paramedics find him faster?

Tess got up and pulled plates from a cupboard wedged into a corner of the tiny kitchen, hoping the movement would shake the ice from under her skin. "It didn't sound like the 911 dispatcher took what I said very seriously." She set a place at the table for each of them and settled in between her grandparents.

Pop squinted at her over his glasses. "Even if they weren't convinced, there are protocols for that kind of thing. They'll send someone to check it out."

Gran crunched into a piece of bacon. "I know that part of Wedowee. Near the dam, it's all trees, except for a fancy lake house here or there. But most of those are second homes. If something happened out there, might be no one would know. You could go for miles in those parts and not see a soul."

Pop nodded. "You may have saved that man's life."

"Maybe." God, she hoped so. She could still hear the desperation in his voice. "It was just so surreal, especially right after. You know." She shoved a bite of pancake into her mouth, wishing she hadn't brought the memory up again. She'd only avoided a lecture the first time because the circumstances of how it came up had been so crazy. Dodging that bullet twice?

Not likely.

And even as a distraction from what had just happened, it wasn't a conversation she'd choose.

"God gave you that gift, my girl." Gran put down her fork and reached to take Tess's hand. "See what good things can happen when you let yourself use it?"

Good things.

What a joke. Good things like an aneurysm that almost killed her. Good things like her mother running off because her daughter's "gift" was too much to handle. Tess forced a smile and squeezed her grandmother's hand, even as the food on her plate lost its appeal. The bacon too greasy, one of the pancakes spotted black.

It wasn't Gran's fault she didn't understand. Tess had made sure Gran and Pop didn't know the truth about her eidetic memory. Didn't know how sick it made her. That the aneurysm had been her fault. That she'd brought it on by forcing a memory, even when she knew the consequences.

Her selfishness had ruined their lives.

And there was no way she could ever let them know it.

Gran returned the squeeze and let go. "All those fancy doctors your daddy took you to, way over in Mobile. They all said the memories would go away by the time you were twelve, thirteen at the latest. Remember? 'Eidetic memory doesn't last through to adulthood.' That's what they said. But God had other plans. He knew that one day you'd use that gift to do his work." She dabbed her mouth with a napkin. "You probably don't remember what happened to your Great Aunt Berta, on your mama's side. Now, she had a voice like an angel. Ever since she was an itty-bitty girl singing in the choir. It was something, I tell you." Gran took a sip of coffee and shook her head. "But then, one day, she just up and quit. Didn't use her gift. And Berta didn't ever do nothin' after that but work herself into old age out at that truck stop on I-10."

Tess waited until Gran looked away and made a help-me face at Pop.

He put a forkful of pancake in his mouth and shrugged. Once Gran got started in on Tess's episodes, there was nothing to do but nod and wait it out.

CHAPTER 6

Martin's cell phone rang as he pulled into a spot in a half-empty Wal-Mart parking lot. He didn't need to check caller ID. Only one person had the number. And he'd been waiting for the call since the doctor's tracker beacon had stopped moving in middle-of-nowhere Alabama. Martin could only see the hand of God in the fact that he'd been so close when it did, already on his way to their facility in Birmingham.

Martin connected the call. "Sir?"

"Are we contained?" The voice came out flat, business-like.

"I believe so, yes." Although, for the second time in as many days, that was only half the story. He snapped the rubber band on his wrist.

"You believe so?"

"I've retrieved the hatbox and the tracker. Still no sign of any rescue efforts when I left." Martin swallowed. There was nothing he could do except spit it out. "But the package was damaged in the crash."

"Did you recover the contents?" This time, his boss spoke with urgency. "Are they intact?"

"One of the samples got smashed." Martin closed his eyes. The gore he'd found when he'd climbed into the broken shell of the cockpit flashed in his mind. He shook it off. "The remaining four are intact. I have them with me now. I'll need to repackage them, but there shouldn't be a problem with delivery."

A heavy silence followed, and his boss gave a deep sigh before he continued. "Did the doctor survive?"

"No, sir. Dead when I arrived. Tree limb got him clean through."

"I see. That's… unfortunate. And the broken specimen?"

Martin's mouth twisted. "Given the doctor's condition, no one's likely to notice anything out of the ordinary." He paused again, waiting for a response.

None came.

Martin pushed on. "I also retrieved the doctor's phone and ID. The scene is clear."

"And the pilot?"

When Martin had left, the pilot had barely been breathing. The man wouldn't know anything that could hurt them, even if he survived. Which seemed unlikely. He'd been collapsed forward in his seat with an ugly gash on his forehead. "If he isn't yet, he will be soon."

"Some things can't be avoided. And can I assume you're on your way to the auxiliary lab now?"

Martin fidgeted with the package, shifting it carefully to the floor on the passenger side of the car. "I had to make a brief detour to get a few things to make sure the remaining samples are secure. But delivery should still be before nightfall."

"Good man."

A blush of pleasure rose to Martin's face. He almost hated to continue. "I should mention, though, we may have another problem." He popped the rubber band on his wrist. "I checked the call logs on the doctor's phone. There was activity shortly before I arrived."

"A call for help?"

"No, it was incoming." Martin closed his eyes again before he continued, and then forced himself to get it out. "I ran the number. It comes up for the lady lawyer in Atlanta." He didn't breathe in the few heartbeats it took for his boss to respond. Martin had been so careful, so sure he'd made sure nothing like this could've happened and—

"You assured me she was no longer in possession of the document. Which is the only place she could've gotten that number."

Martin's grip on the phone tightened. "She was empty-handed when she left the office. The original was destroyed, and I searched the office for duplicates." He knew he was talking too fast and, worse, making excuses. That wouldn't go over well. Martin stopped. He snapped the rubber band again. And, again, harder. On the third pop, it broke, the remnants falling off of his wrist and into his lap.

"It seems unlikely she called the number at random." The sound of ice cubes clinking into a glass came over the phone line.

Martin swallowed hard. He couldn't think of any other explanation except that the scheming bitch lawyer had played him somehow. Heat rose under his collar.

"You'll need to get the document from Ms. Oliver once you finish up at the lab. Things have changed now that the doctor's dead. Retrieving the document is our priority, and it's essential there are no more surprises. No more mistakes."

"Yes, sir."

"And Martin?" Another clink of ice cubes shifting in a glass. "No loose ends."

CHAPTER 7

Tess eased herself into a ladder-back chair at the kitchen table. Her muscles protested the movement, sore from a full day helping Pop around the homestead — exercising the dogs, repairing fence line, spreading mulch. It felt good to be outside, away from her desk, doing something physical. Even better, that morning's headache had finally abated.

But despite her best efforts to get lost in the routine of the day, Tess couldn't get her mind off what had happened when she'd dialed that number. And she couldn't decide what to do about it. She pulled a giant, yellow bowl full of pole beans across the table and snapped off a few of their ends.

"You better quit it." Gran worked at the stove, her back to Tess.

Tess looked up. She wasn't sure if Gran was fussing at her or an uncooperative Ball jar. A few pieces of Gran's hair had come loose from the bun she wore high on the back of her head, and a mix of brown and gray strands stuck to her neck.

Gran rearranged the pots she had going, each one screeching as she slid it over the grate of the gas cooktop. "You're going to give yourself wrinkles if you keep on making that face."

Tess willed the muscles in her forehead to relax and smirked at her grandmother's back. "Yes, ma'am." How she knew Tess was making a face was a mystery.

"I hear that sass." Gran said with a smile in her voice as she used a chipped coffee mug to fill each of the waiting jars with the stewed okra and tomatoes she had simmering in a soup pot.

"I still feel like there's something more I should be doing." Tess returned to her job of snapping beans.

"You're doing plenty. These old hands start to ache once I get half-way through a bowl of those things." She poked a wooden rod down into each of the filled jars, popping any bubbles that might be hiding in the okra before she wiped the rim of each clean and settled their lids gently into place.

"I'm glad to do this for you, Gran," Tess paused, adding a handful of scraggly bean ends to her growing compost pile, "but, I meant for the man I called this morning."

Gran lowered the last of the second layer of jars down into her pressure cooker. "If God wants more of you, more of your gift, he'll find a way to let you know." She placed the metal lid of the cooker on top and twisted it down into place.

That was Tess's cue to leave. Not only did she not want to talk about her "gift" — now, or ever again — there was the issue of the pressure cooker. She eyed the small metal rocker on top of the pot. Any minute now, it would begin to clatter, a ribbon of highly pressurized, barely contained stream escaping around it.

It didn't matter that Tess had spent her entire life watching the women in her family preserve anything that would sit still. Or that she knew it was objectively silly. The damn canner made her nervous. All it needed was a little shrapnel, and there wasn't much difference between that and a bomb.

Tess forced her shoulders down from her ears. "I'm going to go check on Pop." The blare of the evening news gave her a pretty good idea where she'd find him.

Gran gave her a knowing smile over one shoulder. "Okay, Tess-bug."

Tess carried the bowl into the living room, where Pop was just as she expected. Fast asleep in his recliner, despite two pundits yelling at each other on TV. The fat one had a blob of spit in the corner of his mouth.

Gross.

She balanced the bowl against her hip and found the remote control on the side table, nestled between stacks of Reader's Digest and daily devotionals. She was all for the news showing both sides of the issues, but the way the guest host oozed self-importance as he talked over the usual newscaster made her skin crawl. She hit the mute button as the program switched over to its local news segment, and a stylized image of a plane appeared in the upper left-hand corner of the screen.

Oh my God.

Tess scrambled to turn the sound back on.

The anchor leaned toward the camera. "Authorities report that a small plane went down this morning in a heavily forested area just east of Wedowee, Alabama. At this time, we can confirm that the plane was en route from Cobb County International Airport in Kennesaw, Georgia to Mobile, Alabama at the time of the crash. There was one fatality and another man, believed to have been the pilot, was seriously injured. Rescuers life-flighted the survivor to Grady Hospital in Atlanta. The identities of the pilot and passenger have not yet been released, nor has there been any statement from authorities regarding the cause of the crash. We will keep you updated as we learn more."

The man she'd spoken to had been on that plane. She knew it. Her heart beat faster.

But was he the passenger or the pilot?

Was he still alive?

She couldn't know for sure. She sank into Gran's chair, resting the bowl of beans in her lap. She should feel better, more settled, given the news report. But she didn't.

Tess muted the TV and went back to working on the beans. She could go try to talk her way into the hospital. But that seemed like something that would only work in movies. She could call and pretend to be a family member or friend, but that didn't really seem plausible either. Or sane. And what was she hoping to get out of it, anyway? Closure? She didn't even know the guy.

She reached for another bean and pulled out a pair of limp ends instead. Her piles were now a single, mixed mound.

"Well, shit." She was so addled, she couldn't even snap beans properly.

CHAPTER 8

September 16, 2018

Tess stumbled her way to the coffee pot. The thought that had kept her awake the night before still circled her mind. Had the man she'd spoken to survived? The percolator burbled, but the indicator light still showed red.

Brew faster.

She'd thrown a Hail Mary last night and called an investigator who'd done work for her old firm in Chicago, hoping he could find some answers. But Boris didn't promise anything. He hadn't said what the work would cost or when she'd hear back. And the need to know what had happened was driving her insane. Even though she had no real connection to whoever had been on the other end of the phone, except maybe as a lead in her case. The man could've been the developer, another homeowner he'd scammed… or just some poor random person who'd been in a horrible accident.

Tess pulled one of Pop's dented metal coffee cups down from the cupboard. No matter who the man was, something in her gut wouldn't let Tess move on until she knew if he was okay. She tucked her cell phone in her back pocket, filled the cup, and took the steaming brew down the hallway to the laundry room. She needed to keep herself busy, and there always seemed to be a load of something that needed folding in the dryer.

The phone rang as she popped open the dryer door.

Boris.

A rush of possibility trilled through her as she answered, suddenly and completely alert despite not yet having touched the coffee. "Thanks for jumping on this for me." She scrunched up her face. "I should have asked before I told you to get started. What's the going rate these days?" Tess cringed while she waited, visions of overdraft fees dancing in her head.

"How 'bout a beer?"

She relaxed, pressing the phone to her ear with one shoulder as she reached into the back of the dryer. "Well, that depends." She swept the pile of clothes into a waiting basket. "Does beer mean a nice IPA or… something else?"

"Just a beer." Boris choked out a laugh. "I always knew I liked you." His laughter tapered off into a smoker's cough. Tess had known the grizzled old investigator for a half-dozen years. He'd worked with her on at least twice that many cases. And she'd never seen him without an unfiltered Camel in his hand.

She waited for the coughing to subside. "So, did you find anything out for me?"

"Please. Next time, call me with a challenge." He exhaled deeply, and Tess could as much as smell the smoke. "The pilot's name is Luke Broussard. He's still an in-patient at Grady Hospital in Atlanta, room E304. They have him listed in stable condition."

Tess wasn't sure she wanted to know how he'd gotten the room number. No way that was meant to be public information.

"The number you dialed is a burner." Boris coughed again. "The rest you probably know from the news. The passenger hasn't been identified, no ID on him. He died at the scene from multiple penetrating and blunt force trauma."

Tess grimaced at the image that conjured up. "Yikes."

"Yeah. Given where the crash happened, it's amazing the pilot made it out. Pretty minor injuries, too, from what I could gather." An ambulance siren wailed in the background. "Hang on."

Tess waited until the noise faded. "That's odd, isn't it? For the passenger to be traveling with no ID?" She didn't run in private plane circles, but the fact that he'd been found without a wallet seemed off.

"Not so odd on a charter flight specifically, but unusual in general. Nobody goes anywhere these days without a stack of credit cards and a smartphone."

"Hmmm." She chewed that over, fishing a sock from the back of the dryer. "True. Are you sure I can't pay you for your time?"

"Once you get on your feet there, maybe you can send me some business. In the meantime, a six-pack'll do it."

"Done. And thank—"

Boris cut in. "But none of that millennial IPA bullshit."

"You got it." Tess grinned as she hung up the phone. It might be crazy, but there wasn't a doubt in her mind what she needed to do.

She dumped her clean laundry into her suitcase, not bothering to fold it, and told Gran and Pop she'd been called back to Atlanta early for work. In the grand scheme of things, it was a white lie and far more efficient than trying to explain to them what she was actually doing. She wasn't sure she could even explain it to herself.

Except that going to talk to Luke Broussard felt like a step she needed to take. The first down a path she couldn't quite see and yet felt compelled to follow. It could lead her to the developer. Tess rooted around the house until she found her keys. Besides, even if Broussard knew nothing about her case, she'd find out what had happened to the man she spoke to. And that was enough.

. . .

Tess swung open the front door, and a wall of heat and noise hit her in the face. Only the periodic barking of dogs interrupted the cicadas buzzing in the trees. She thunked the suitcase down the porch stairs and wheeled the overstuffed bag toward her car. It wasn't even lunchtime yet, and it already felt like soup outside.

She had another headache brewing, and neither the heat nor the noise helped.

The screen door smacked closed behind her. "You need help with that?" Gran followed her down the porch steps.

"No, ma'am." Tess dropped the suitcase into the trunk and closed the lid, the license plate cover rattling as it clunked into place.

"You should've let me or Pop know you were loading up. He could've carried it out for you." Gran made a face Tess knew well, but the lines around her mouth softened as she came closer. "It's always so good to have you home. I hate that you're leaving so soon. You just got here."

Gran handed Tess a go-mug of coffee and tucked half a lemon pound cake wrapped in wax paper into Tess's shoulder bag. "For the road." She patted Tess's cheek with a smile.

Tess looked into her grandmother's clear brown eyes, and her lie stopped feeling so small. But there was nothing to be done about it now, she was already in too deep. And the need to go was a steady pull that wouldn't let her be. Broussard could lead her to the developer, to answers for the Ashbys, to the payday she couldn't go much longer without.

"That cake smells good." Tess returned Gran's smile before she put the bag on the passenger seat and the Ole Miss cup in the center console. It didn't quite fit, and the cup leaned precariously forward toward the gear shifter.

"Thanks, Gran." She dropped into the seat and slid the key into the ignition. "Where's Pop? I wanted to say goodbye before I..."

In the rear-view mirror, Pop rounded the back corner of the trailer with a dirt brown Pit Bull pulling against a leash. The dog rooted in place every few feet as Pop coaxed him toward the car.

Tess stuck her head out the door. "You brought a friend?"

"You know Tater." Ten pounds overweight, missing one eye, Tater looked like a potato. Pop gave the leash another soft tug, murmuring something to the dog she couldn't hear. "You shouldn't be living by yourself in the city, like you do. The thought of you there alone…" He shook his head. "I'll sleep better knowing you've got some company, and he sure could use a person of his own."

Tess eyed Tater. "I can't take a dog home with me. What's he gonna do when I'm at work?"

"What they all do, until you finish training them properly. Sleep, poop, and chew on your things." Pop winked and opened the back car door to let Tater in. "You've been training dogs with me long enough to know what you need to do." He closed the door as soon as Tater's tail was out of the way, held up a hand for her to wait, and then jogged back behind the house.

She raised her eyebrows at Gran. "Really?"

Her grandmother raised an eyebrow back. Tess knew that look, too.

"Right." Tess pulled her door shut and rolled down the window. Apparently, she was getting a dog.

"Humor the old man, Tess. He worries about you. We both do. And don't wait so long before you come back next time."

Tess nodded. She knew they worried. She was the only family they had left, and they were hers. "I love you guys." Her eyes got wet. Stupid, silly things. What did she have to cry about?

Gran pulled a tissue from an apron pocket and handed it to Tess. It was folded into a perfect square and smelled of peppermints. The same kind Gran had given her as a bribe to "sit still and hush" when she'd been a kid in church.

"Sorry, Gran. Don't know what's wrong with me." Tess used the tissue to blot at the corners of her eyes. "You must think I'm looney. Especially after," Tess waved her hand back and forth, "you know, everything that happened in Chicago." Shame tingled up the back of her neck and spread hot across her face. The cicadas started up again, the pulsating buzz seeming somehow one with the heat. Tess started the car to get the A/C blowing and adjusted the vents so the air could reach Tater's perch in the backseat.

"Whatever you think 'everything' is, it's nothing to me or your grandpa. And you don't have anything to be sorry for." Gran blinked a few times, but her eyes stayed dry, and her voice was firm when she continued. "You are the best thing that's ever happened to us."

That couldn't be true. She knew her grandparents loved her, that they would do anything for her. But, if it weren't for getting stuck raising her, they'd have been off enjoying their retirement years ago. Not still stuck in small town Mississippi.

Pop reappeared behind the car with a huge sack tossed over one shoulder. He made a thumbs-up gesture, bouncing it up and down. Her cue to open the trunk. She pulled the lever, and he dropped the bag inside with a heavy thunk.

"What the heck was that?" She twisted around in her seat.

"Just a little kibble to get you started." Pop eased the trunk closed and tapped the top with his palm before walking over to drape an arm over Gran's shoulder. He wore a collared shirt and Levi's despite the heat, and the faded plaid of the shirt's fabric had darkened with sweat under his arms. "Drive safe now." The skin around his eyes crinkled with his smile, weathered from too many years working in the sun.

Tess nodded and waved goodbye, trying to ignore the dull ache in her heart as Gran and Pop stepped back inside. Leaving home was always hard, and somehow, this time felt worse. Because of the financial mess waiting for her in Atlanta? Or maybe because she'd lied?

A sharp pang of guilt told her which.

Tess snapped a quick picture of Tater in the back seat and texted it to Gail. "Check out my new roomie." Gail was going to think she was crazy. Tess smiled at the thought, righted the coffee cup in its holder, and put the car in reverse. With the windows rolled up, the inside of the car smelled of dog.

The culprit gave a low chuff from the back seat as they zipped backward down the drive.

"Don't be so judgey. You don't even know what I'm up to." She shot Tater a look in the rearview mirror. "Besides, they'd think I was nuts if I'd told them where we were really headed."

She took the dog's silence as agreement and pulled out of the driveway in a cloud of dust.

CHAPTER 9

Warren Sullivan sat in the sunroom of his D.C. brownstone, scrolling through a draft presentation to the Maeler Pharmaceuticals board of directors. Each tap of his finger on the laptop's down arrow landed harder than the last. He scrubbed a hand through his hair, still thick but, in recent years, gone silver-white.

The draft was far from the finished product he expected from Quinones. He had hand selected the man as VP of Maeler's vaccine R&D department after Quinones showed remarkable success in their efforts to develop vaccines for the Third World markets, making strides toward the Marburg vaccine that were all but unheard of before he became involved.

That early success made it all the more disappointing for Quinones to be floundering with their current project. It was one thing to simplify the complicated science behind what they did to make it comprehensible to those members of the board who, unlike Sullivan, hadn't gone to medical school. It was quite another to fill a dozen pages with unsupported conclusions about how many lives would be saved or profits made. They needed to show clear, undeniable results. Or, at the very least, progress.

He looked out a big bay window at the birch trees his wife had planted in the courtyard, back when she'd been able to get around unassisted. The sun's rays were just beginning to shine between the branches, a light wind tossing the leaves. Usually, this view gave him a sense of calm, but not today. It had been a struggle to get board approval for the project when it began, harder still to get the last extension. It was going to take a Herculean effort to get it funded this time.

Never mind that vaccines were second only to clean water in saving lives. The only thing that mattered to the Board was that they weren't money-makers. Too little profit and too much potential for liability.

The whoosh of his wife's wheelchair rolling over the thick carpets that lined their front hall pulled him back from his thoughts. "There you are." He pushed his heavy, upholstered chair away from the table and rose to greet her. "How about some bagels?" He brushed a lock of auburn hair from Lynn's forehead and planted a kiss in its place.

"You do know the way to a girl's heart." She wheeled her chair up to the sunroom table and set the lock.

He pulled their breakfast together and carried it back to the table, the coffees sloshing onto the tray with each step.

Lynn put down the Wall Street Journal and took her cup, carefully sipping enough so she could sit it down again without spilling. "This is perfect. Thank you, Sully." Unlike her black brew, his was half milk, half sugar, with a splash of coffee. Lynn eyed his cup but said nothing.

He spread a healthy slab of cream cheese on his bagel. "I'll try to make it home early. And Joseph will be here today to keep you company until I'm back." They'd started in-home care after the accident, when it became clear Sully wouldn't always be able to be there for her. Not with work and the travel it required. "Soon, I won't have to go in at all."

"I'll believe it when I see it." Lynn raised her brown eyes to his above her coffee cup. "You've been saying that for years." The buzz of an incoming email came from his shirt pocket, as if to make her point.

Lynn went back to slicing up the strawberries on her plate as he pulled the device free. "And anyway, I'm fine here. Joseph's been teaching me to play poker."

Sully mmm-hmmm-ed, his thumbs flying over the tiny keypad. Quinones's secretary seemed not to understand that his request for a meeting with her boss wasn't an invitation. It was a summons.

"We started strip poker yesterday." Lynn's words were muffled by a bite of her bagel. "Joseph says he likes my black lace bra best."

Sully nodded as he punched out another email, this time to Quinones's lab manager. He'd have his VP in the hot seat before lunch, one way or another.

"Earth to Sully. You're not listening."

"I'm always listening, just not always hearing." He chuckled, still looking down. He hit send on the email. "And the lace bra is my favorite, too, by the way." He finally glanced up at her, letting mischief dance in his eyes.

She smacked at his arm, and he snorted a laugh as his phone rang. Sully glanced at the display. It lit up, R. Quinones.

Finally.

Sully got up from the table. "I've gotta take this. I love you."

He connected the call but waited to speak until he'd crossed into his home office and pulled the pocket door closed. "Richard?" He hoped his voice conveyed every bit of his irritation.

"I just finished reviewing the notes we received from the team in the secondary lab." Quinones's voice shook, but it wasn't with the fear Sully was used to from the man. Quinones sounded giddy. "Sir, I think we've done it. We only have preliminary results at this point, but from what I can tell, the process works just as we hoped. And it seems to indicate a common antigen amongst every type of cancer we tested."

Sully blinked, allowing himself a minute to digest what Quinones had said before he responded. "How sure are you?"

"We'll need to do our own separate analysis, but what we received this morning looks pretty conclusive. And, before you ask, I checked their work twice. I'm waiting for the supporting data to arrive now. I'll go through it and report back as soon as I'm able to confirm it checks out. But, sir, this is incredible. It's the first indication we've ever seen that a real cure for cancer might be possible."

A warm glow of affirmation built deep in Sully's chest. It had taken significant capital to make it happen, but he had believed it was the right thing to do. Few people would ever have the chance to do something so important. And it changed everything. "I'll be in the office by 10:30 this morning. I'd like to have you walk me through all the data we have so far. We'll need to start distilling it so we can update our presentation to the Board. And, of course, I'll want copies of everything, including the underlying data, sent to my email so I can do a deeper dive tonight to prepare for the meeting…" Sully trailed off, twisting his wedding ring on his finger as he pondered his next steps. There was so much to do. So many possibilities opening up.

"Sir?"

"That's all for now." Sully hung up, his mind spinning with the implications of their discovery and what it might allow them to do.

Sully's gaze drifted to the framed photo of his daughter, which sat in a place of honor on the corner of his desk. He picked it up and leaned back in his chair. He was finally going to be able to do something worthy of her memory. Something that would keep other families from losing their children. Carly had been seven when the photo was taken. They'd been on a family trip to the Cape, and her golden hair was windblown. She had a bucket of sand in her lap and a look of pure joy on her face. A small silver cross hung from her neck, a gift from Lynn to commemorate her first Communion. Even now, so many years later, it didn't seem possible that she was really gone.

A series of dings from his desktop signaled the usual morning flurry of emails, and he forced his mind back to the present, gently putting Carly's photo back where it belonged. There was work to do. It was going to take everything he had, but, in the end, they were going to change lives.

No, they were going to change the world.

CHAPTER 10

Thunder rumbled outside, a deep guttural shaking that seemed to insist Luke had slept long enough. But even the dim light of the room hurt his eyes, pain flared in his chest with each breath, and his head throbbed in time with something beeping nearby. What the hell had happened? He pressed a palm to what felt like a gash on his head and flinched at the bite of something sharp in the back of his hand. An IV needle and line.

That can't mean anything good.

A woman in light blue scrubs bustled into the room. "Good afternoon. How are you, Mr. Broussard?" She spoke with the lilt of an accent he couldn't place, wrote her name on a small whiteboard to the right of the door, and turned back to face him. "My name is Sarah. I'll be your nurse this evening. I just need to get your vitals, while we're waiting on final authorization from your doctor to administer pain medication." She moved the wheeled table beside his bed out of the way. "Can you tell me what your pain level is on a scale of zero to ten?"

He blinked at her, still trying to make sense of his situation. He was in the hospital. He'd been asleep, or maybe unconscious, and it was gray outside the window. Because it was almost night? Or just bad weather?

He couldn't tell.

Was it even still the same day as… as what?

Luke forced himself to push through the fog. He remembered the unexpected charter, trying to reach Parker, the client pacing the hangar with that bag clutched to his chest. And then…

He clutched at the bedsheet, memories flooding back.

He'd crashed. The plane had gone down, and there'd been nothing he could do. His head filled with the sound of his last radio calls with Air Traffic Control. The crackle of the radio. *"Do as you were trained. Set up for emergency landing."* His body tensed already constricted muscles, and pain shot through him. He grew hot and cold all at once, a sheen of sweat breaking out on his forehead and along the top of his upper lip.

Luke blinked up at the nurse, his eyes wide. He shook his head, but no words would come out.

The nurse patted his arm with a purple latex-covered hand before she spoke. This time, her voice was soft. "I'm not sure how much you remember. You were life-flighted here to Grady Hospital after the crash. I was working an extra shift down in trauma when you arrived." She held his gaze for a moment. "I'm glad to see they've moved you here, instead of the ICU. That's a very good sign."

He forced himself to breathe deeper, to relax his shoulders. Once he had regained control, he nodded, and the nurse — Sarah, she'd said — gave him a small smile. She pulled a blood pressure cuff from a pocket on the wall. He tried to pay attention to what she was saying, but his mind was busy re-playing what he remembered of the flight. Trying to make sense of what happened.

Where was Smith? Had Luke seen him after they went down?

It was all a blur.

The blood pressure cuff tightened around his arm, then stopped. Sarah dropped her end and coughed several times, hard, into the crook of her elbow. "Sorry." She threw her latex gloves in the waste bin, sanitized her hands, and pulled on a new pair of gloves. "Now, let's try that again, shall we? What is your pain level on a scale of zero to ten?" She squeezed again, the cuff tightening around his arm in quick increments.

This time, he answered. "A seven, I think. My chest hurts when I breathe, and my head is killing me."

"Breathing is going to hurt for a while. You've bruised one of your ribs." She watched as he struggled to breathe without pain. "Not like that. You need to take deep, full breaths so you don't develop a chest infection." She inhaled an exaggerated breath, stifling another cough with a shake of her head, before exhaling.

He forced himself to take a full breath and grimaced. It hurt like a bitch.

"Good," she said, "like that." She moved to the laptop mounted on a standing workstation near the door. "Now let me just check a few things here."

Luke shifted in the bed. "I don't know if you can answer this, but I had a passenger with me, Mr. Smith." No matter what position he was in, he couldn't get comfortable. "Was he admitted with me?"

Sarah finished typing and shifted the workstation toward the wall. "The doctor will come by in a bit."

There was only one logical reason she wouldn't answer his question.

He swallowed, trying not to jump to conclusions, but his guilt didn't wait for confirmation. It settled over him, a sickening, heavy weight. Luke dropped his head back onto the pillow.

What if he was responsible for someone's death?

The weight grew heavier, making his already labored breath burn in his chest.

Sarah moved back to the bed and scanned a bar code printed on a plastic wristband he didn't remember putting on. She handed him two fat, white pills and a small plastic cup of water, watching while he swallowed the medicine. It left a hard, bitter trail down his throat.

He couldn't just lie there, not knowing what'd happened. "My passenger. He isn't okay, is he?" Luke clenched his teeth, holding his breath as he waited for an answer.

Something flickered over her face — indecision, maybe. She leaned her head to one side. "No."

Luke closed his eyes. He had wanted to know, needed to know. But now he had his answer, and it only made things worse. The fire in his chest spread to his heart.

It wasn't as if he'd never considered the idea that he might be responsible for the loss of a life one day. He'd joined the military knowing he might have to use lethal force in combat. Maybe have to kill someone else to protect himself, his unit, or his country. This was different. Smith hadn't been an enemy combatant. He'd been Luke's passenger. His responsibility. Luke had failed to return someone in his care safely back to earth.

Sarah's voice pulled him back from his thoughts. "When you came into the ER, you were non-responsive and covered in blood. The first responder who brought you in said it was a miracle you survived. Much less walked away with only contusions, a concussion, and a few bruised ribs." She squeezed his hand. "Try to focus on that."

Luke didn't open his eyes again. He wasn't sure he could meet her gaze. As he listened to the nurse move quietly around the room, it became more and more difficult to hold on to his thoughts, the medicine softening the edges of the pain and everything else with it.

. . .

A knock at the door pulled Luke from near sleep. It was probably Sarah. She'd checked on him half a dozen times already, usually just after he'd finally drifted off. He rubbed his palms against his eyes, but it didn't make them any less sticky or him any less exhausted. "Come in."

A tall woman walked in. She had angular features, a spray of freckles across her nose, and strawberry blonde curls swept up in a tangle on top of her head. He didn't recognize her, but with the head injury and the pain meds, that didn't mean they hadn't met.

Although it would be hard to forget someone who looked like she did.

"Hi." The woman leaned a still dripping umbrella beside the door. "I'm Tess Oliver."

Luke nodded a hello, waiting for her to hand him a stack of registration forms or maybe something to do with insurance. But that didn't make sense. She'd obviously come from outside, and she wasn't dressed like someone with hospital administration. In sneakers, an oversized hoodie, and a pair of running shorts, she looked more like a co-ed than a paper pusher.

But something about her did seem familiar.

She came closer, her shoes squeaking on the faux-wood vinyl floor, then paused, as if she wasn't sure what to say next. "It's nice to meet you."

So, we haven't met before then.

In the faded light filtering in through the window, her eyes were an unusual shade of gray. Or green. Maybe both.

"Nice to meet you, too." He shoved his hand through his hair, which had to be standing up in all directions. "Luke Broussard."

She shifted on her feet. "I just wanted to come by, and…" Thunder boomed loud enough to rattle the window in its frame. She hunched forward. "Goodness." Tess laughed as she straightened back up, a small dimple appearing on her cheek.

"Sounds bad out there." Luke searched for the bed's remote so he could sit up. Something about laying down while she stood next to him seemed decidedly unmanly.

"I'm glad you're alright." She tucked a loose strand of hair behind her ear, and glanced around, still looking like she was somehow at loose ends.

"I suppose, under the circumstances, this counts as alright." Giving up his search for the remote, he pushed himself up on an elbow, and pain lanced through his chest. He grimaced, gesturing toward an extra pillow waiting in a chair near the window. "Would you mind?"

"No, of course not." She retrieved it and came around the side of the bed. Then stopped, a few inches away. "Okay if I reach across you?"

"Yeah." His voice came out deeper than he intended. He cleared his throat but found himself looking into her eyes again. Up close, they were green after all. A pale shade, more blue than yellow and flecked with gray. Like sea glass. She sat something on his bed, reached for the pillow, and slid it behind him. He breathed in. She smelled like fresh rain and coffee.

"See if that helps." Her cheeks were pink when she straightened, and he had the uncomfortable feeling his might be, too.

It had to be the pain meds. He'd never been shy around women, and there was no reason this one should get under his skin. He needed to snap out of it. Luke smiled at her. "Thanks."

He glanced down at what she'd left on his bed. A short stack of business cards.

The top one read, Teresa M. Oliver and, under that, Attorney at Law.

Heat flushed through his body. Blood pounded in his ears.

How dare she?

He dropped her hand, the pain in his chest an afterthought as he forced himself to lift his torso higher. "You're barking up the wrong tree, lady."

"I'm sorry?" She blinked at him and took a step away.

Luke held back as long as he could, but he was too tired to be polite. Some bottom-feeding ambulance chaser didn't deserve his courtesy or his respect. "How did you even get in here? You people have no shame."

"What?" Her eyes narrowed, the muscles in her face tightening as she drew up to her full height and squared off to face him. "What people? What the hell are you talking about?"

Now, he could see it. She looked like a lawyer.

"It's Smith you're looking for, right? That's why you're here." He stared at her.

She shook her head, but before she could come up with any lame excuse for trying to profit off what he'd been through — what Smith had been through before he died — he answered for her. "Sorry to ruin your plans, but Smith's dead. Maybe if you scurry off now, you can find one of his heirs in the hallway. I bet that'd be even better, as far as you're concerned."

"You have no idea what you're talking about." Thunder boomed again outside. Only, this time, she didn't flinch. "I think I should go."

"Yeah, I think so."

The beeping of the monitors grew loud in the silence as they stared at each other.

Tess threw up her hands and turned toward the door. She paused half-way, her back still turned. "I'm glad you're okay."

Luke blinked. Whatever he'd thought she might say, that wasn't it.

In two long strides, she crossed the rest of the distance to the door — and walked right into Parker.

"Oh, sorry. My bad." He gave her shoulder an apologetic squeeze as they danced around one another in the doorway. Left, right. Right, left.

Tess stilled, but instead of taking the opportunity to pass, Parker turned to Luke. "You're up. Finally. I never thought I'd be so glad to see…" He stopped, his gaze darting from Luke's face to Tess's. "Everything okay?" Parker moved into the room and out of the lawyer's path.

"It was nice to meet you, Nick." Tess walked out of the room without another glance at Luke.

"It's Parker, remember?" He called down the hallway after her. "Only my mama calls me Nick."

Luke couldn't hear if she answered. Either way, good riddance.

"I see you haven't lost your way with the ladies." Parker grinned at him and sat at the foot of the bed, barely missing Luke's legs. "You doing okay?"

Luke grimaced. "More or less. Everything hurts." He shifted to make room. "You heard about Smith?"

"I heard." Parker shook his head, and they both sat silent for a moment.

Parker continued, his voice soft. "You did everything you could."

Luke looked toward the window, where rain pelted the glass. "Did I?"

When Luke finally looked back, Parker nodded slowly. "I heard the recording."

"I can barely remember anything, just pieces. The damn yoke wouldn't budge." Flashes of memory came back. Him pulling at the controls, long after he knew the plane wouldn't respond. Smith yelling from the back seat. The crack of trees breaking off against the underbelly of the plane. The blood.

"From what we can tell, you had a mechanical failure. They're still figuring out the details. But you did everything possible to put her down safely. It's amazing you managed to land."

Luke hissed out a breath. There'd been nothing amazing about it. "I didn't land. I crashed."

"You gave yourself a fighting chance. How you managed it in that terrain… I wouldn't have." Parker held Luke's gaze, his eyes, for once, serious. "If the plane had rolled left, instead of right through the trees, we wouldn't be having this conversation."

Guilt squeezed Luke's chest. "No, you'd be talking to Smith."

"Nah, man. You'd both be dead."

The thought of those final minutes made Luke's stomach turn. He forced himself to stay in the present. "How long have I been here?"

"They brought you in yesterday morning. Your mom's been calling me every half hour for updates. They should be getting here soon."

Luke nodded and looked out the window again, where the rain had calmed to a patter. His mother must be hysterical, but damn he'd be glad to see his family. No doubt they'd all be caravanning north, husbands and children in tow. Whatever the Broussards did, they did as a tribe. "How'd you get your hands on the recording anyway?"

"How do you think?" Parker coughed out a dry laugh.

"Right." Luke didn't need to ask more to know what that meant. Parker's father was connected — politically, financially, and otherwise.

Luke nodded his head toward the door. "I haven't been here twenty-four hours and the jackals are already circling the carcass. Can you believe that shit? The security in this hospital must be a joke."

Parker raised an eyebrow at him. "What the hell are you talking about?"

Luke sighed. "That was a lawyer looking for survivors. Trying to figure out a way to make money from the crash."

Parker's other eyebrow rose to meet the first.

Damn, sometimes Parker was thick. Luke tried again, this time slower. "She's looking to sue me. Us. The business. For the crash. Who knows how she talked her way in here."

Parker broke into a grin. "Dude. You're an idiot."

Luke narrowed his eyes, trying to determine how he could kick Parker off the bed without doing further damage to himself.

Parker leaned forward. "I let her in."

Of all the idiotic… "You what?"

"You've been asleep forever, and I was starving. They have really good tater tots in the cafeteria. They'll do them extra crispy, if you ask." Parker pulled a box of Tic Tacs from his pocket and shook a few into his palm.

Luke stared at his friend, waiting for any part of his story to make sense.

Parker popped the mints in his mouth. "When I got down to the first floor, she was at the front desk. I overhead her asking about you. So, I introduced myself and offered to walk her upstairs." He held the box out to Luke, shaking it so the candies rattled around inside.

Luke waved him off.

"I mean, damn, did you get a good look at her?" Parker sat the candy box beside him on the bed. "You know, before you started acting like a dick."

Luke spoke slowly. "You walked the lawyer that wants to sue us upstairs to meet me?"

"She's not trying to sue us." Parker rolled his eyes. "She's the one who called Smith's phone. You don't remember? You talked to her after the accident. When you got disconnected, she called 911. She saved your life, man. With where you went down, who knows how long it would have been before someone found you otherwise."

Luke shook his head. That didn't make any sense.

He focused hard on the last things he could remember, pushing deep into the memories he'd been trying unsuccessfully to avoid. The mangled fuselage creaking around him as it finished settling to earth. The wet that seemed to coat his skin. The pain that was at once everything and somehow separate from him, as if it were happening to someone else. And then there'd been a ringing in front of him. A phone on the dash.

Smith's phone.

He'd spoken to someone. He remembered gripping the phone in his hand, but he couldn't remember what he'd said. Just that he'd been alone in the wreckage, maybe knowing even then Smith wasn't really there anymore, and then there'd been a voice on the phone, someone bringing him back, anchoring him to reality. The voice — her voice — was the last thing he remembered before waking to find himself in the hospital.

Parker crunched a Tic Tac. "She came to see how you were doing. I told her she could stick her head in and check. But that I thought you'd still be asleep. Anyway, I said I'd pass on her number. You know, if you were." Parker held up one of the cards the woman had been holding. His had something scrawled across the bottom, a phone number. Probably her cell. She'd still had the cards in her hand when she'd come in to see him.

Luke cringed. "I'm such an asshole." If he hadn't already been so on edge, he might not have jumped to the worst possible conclusion. He might have considered things like the fact she hadn't been dressed like a lawyer or acted like one. At least not until he'd yelled at her. An embarrassed heat crept up the back of his neck.

Parker cocked his head to one side. "I'd go with douchebag, but okay."

"Thanks, buddy. Love you, too."

Parker made a smoochy face at him as the first bars of "Pour Some Sugar On Me" rang out from the pocket of Parker's cargo shorts. "Here we go again." He fished out the phone. "Dad? Yeah, hi. He's up and grouchy as hell." Parker covered the receiver and mouthed "Be right back." His flip-flops smacked against the soles of his feet as went back out to the hallway. The door closed behind him, but it barely muted Parker's voice. "What does the NTSB guy say?"

Oh shit.

Luke dropped back onto the bed, causing another shock of pain across his chest. Of course the National Transportation Safety Board was involved. There'd be an investigation into what happened. Into him. And as if that wasn't all bad enough already, now, he wasn't just a murderer.

He was also a douchebag.

CHAPTER 11

Sarah pushed open the door to her flat and dropped her umbrella into the porcelain holder her mother kept by the entry table. She sagged against the wall, letting her purse clunk to the floor. Even her bones hurt. The four block walk home from the MARTA bus stop had taken half an hour today.

Ahmed rounded the corner from the hallway, and a smile crept onto Sarah's face. "Speak of the devil. I was just thinking of you."

Ahmed wore his coveralls, heading out to start his workday just as hers ended. "And I you." He pulled an old raincoat from the wooden pegged rack above her umbrella and stooped to kiss her cheek. "You look exhausted. Long shift?"

"I think I'm—" A coughing fit cut her off. She kept her eyes closed and her face pressed into the crook of her elbow until the stars cleared from her vision. "I think I'm coming down with something."

"Ah, that's too bad. I was hoping you could come by when you got up." He grinned at her, revealing the gap between his front teeth. "You know, for lunch." He pulled her into a hug. Trying to get pregnant had proven difficult with their opposing work schedules. And the fact that they shared their small flat with her mother hadn't helped. They'd been forced to be creative in where and when they could try, including nearly getting caught in the hospital break room the day before.

Sarah laughed, leaning her head on her husband's chest.

"Why don't you go lie down, sweetheart. I'll see you before you leave for work tonight." Ahmed tilted her face to his and gave her a soft kiss.

His closeness was a comfort, but she broke the embrace. "I don't want to get you sick."

"Nonsense. I'm healthy as a horse." He flashed her one more gap-toothed smile and left.

Sarah closed and locked the door behind him. If she'd made it home faster, they could've at least had a few more minutes together. She frowned and leaned against the worn wood of the door again. They were both making good money, but what use was that if they couldn't—

Women's voices spilled from the kitchen, and Sarah's frown turned to a grimace.

To get to her bedroom, she'd have to walk right past them.

No helping it now.

"I'm home," she called and gave in to another coughing fit. With each cough, more pain bloomed behind her eyes.

Her mother popped around the corner. "Ah, Sarah, you sound terrible." Fatima bustled into the foyer with the five elderly women that made up her weekly Bible circle in tow. Dressed in various shades of pastel polyester, they descended in a cluster, clucking, double-checking Sarah's forehead for temperature, and arguing about what soup or tea might be best.

"Thank you, Aunties. I think I just need to lay down for now." Sarah hugged each of the women, promising to rest, drink fluids, and eat citrus, then started toward the bedroom. Halfway there, she changed course, with her mother on her heels. "I think I'm going to be sick," Sarah whispered, tilting her head toward the audience still gathered by the front door.

Her mom gave her a quick pat on the back and turned to shoo the other ladies back to the kitchen.

Sarah barely made it to the toilet in time.

She flushed her sick away, sunk to the floor, and pressed her cheek against the wall's pale green tile. It offered a cold relief against the heat of her body, but she still felt terrible. Her hair stuck to her neck, damp and sweaty.

Sarah fought the nausea and lost, her bouts of vomiting punctuated by short reprieves where she lay spent on the floor. Too tired to do anything but listen to the chatter of women's voices in the kitchen. Then, the clank of pots and pans being washed.

Fatima's voice came through the bathroom door. "I left a fresh cup of tea for you on the bedside table, love. And don't forget to take some ibuprofen." The bang of a cabinet door sounded through the small apartment. "There's a new bottle in the cabinet over the stove. I'm going to pick up a roast for dinner. Call if you need me." Then, a moment later, her mother's voice came from farther away. "You know, Sarah, all that nausea could be a good thing!"

The front door clunked closed.

Sarah had never been pregnant before, but there was no way morning sickness felt like this. This was something else entirely.

▪ ▪ ▪

Sarah woke to the soft murmur of a man's voice, his words in a language she didn't know. "'As'alu Allah al 'azim rabbil 'arshil azim an yashifika. As'alu Allah al 'azim rabbil 'arshil azim an yashifika." Their neighbor Mohammed sat on the floor next to her bed.

He finished the prayer, and Sarah retched again. Bile and mucus splashed over the side of the bed and into her mother's largest cooking pot.

Mohammed held the pot to her mouth, while her mother hovered behind him, wringing her hands. She didn't just look worried. She looked terrified.

What's wrong with me?

And what must Mohammed think with her in this state? Sarah tried to thank him — to ask how she'd gotten from the bathroom to her bed — but she couldn't. Her throat was too raw from hours of coughing and vomiting, every breath leaving a trail of fire in its wake.

"It's okay, Sarah." He put the pot on the floor and pressed a washcloth to her forehead, damp and cool. Then dabbed her face with it. "Here, Fatima." Mohammed handed her mother the washcloth. "Would you rinse it out again, please?"

Fatima took the cloth, her eyes going wide as she looked down at the blood splotched material. "Yes, of course." She said but didn't move. "We need a doctor. She's getting worse. I haven't been able to reach Ahmed. I had hoped to wait until he was home." She swallowed and shook her head. "But I don't think we should delay any longer."

"We could call an ambulance." He raised a shoulder. In their neighborhood, who knew how long that would take to arrive. "Or I can drive you to the hospital."

Fatima nodded, twisting the cloth in her hands. "What would I have done if you weren't next door?"

"It's nothing. I would have been upset to know you'd needed help and hadn't come to find me." Mohammed shifted to his knees. "Time to go." He slid an arm underneath Sarah's back and eased her weight toward him.

The movement sent a shockwave of pain through her body. "No, no." Her words came out with a gurgle, the swelling in her throat making them thick and harsh. Sarah waved him away, her movements jerky and uncoordinated.

Mohammed slowly pulled his arm from under Sarah's shoulders, looking from her to Fatima, his eyes a question. What should they do? He shifted Sarah's weight back to the pillow, the movement sending another avalanche of unbearable cramping through her abdomen. She curled into herself, willing it away.

Mohammed got to his feet. "I'll call for the ambulance."

"No." Sarah forced out the words, the tremors making her teeth clack together. "I want Ahmed." Her vision blurred with tears.

One fell to the bedsheet, a jagged circle of blood red.

CHAPTER 12

September 17, 2018

Tess sat cross-legged on the couch, computer in her lap, with a throw blanket over her head. It had taken a solid hour, but she finally had the new laptop set up, which meant she had access to her client files.

And a maxed-out VISA to go with it.

Nothing to be done about that. Tess typed in a search for available office space, increasing her target area in wider rings out from the city center. She scrolled through the results — over-budget, over-budget, way over-budget. Even outside I-285, the highway that circled the city and served for most Atlantans as the demarcation between in-town and suburban living, there was nothing.

Tess clasped her hands together, reaching both arms overhead, the tension in her shoulders finally releasing. She'd never been afraid of hard work. She wasn't going to let fear become paralysis. It was time to get her head back in the game, push her cases forward, drum up business, and pinch every thread until she collected the Ashbys' money. Even if she had to do it working from home. She was going to figure it out.

Tater edged his snout underneath the blanket and poked his cold, wet nose into the arch of her bare foot.

Tess yelped, tucking the blanket back in. "Don't you have anything better to do?" She glared at the dog. But the desperation in his good eye was hard to miss. "Oh. Sorry, dog."

She kept the blanket pulled tight around her shoulders as she lumbered over to check the window. The morning drooped outside, gray and waterlogged. But this time of year, when the South seemed stuck between summer and fall, that could go one of two ways — sticky-hot or freezing. She unlocked the window and pulled it open. Swollen from rain and lack of upkeep, the sashes stuck in the casements, glass rattling as she finally shoved the window skyward. A cold breeze carried in the slow patter of rain on the overgrown hydrangea lining the front of her rented bungalow. The perfect soundtrack for staying in her pajamas tucked up at home.

Tater nosed her leg.

Or it would've been, if not for her new houseguest.

She scoured the house for an umbrella or a raincoat, with the dog pacing and pushing between her legs, but couldn't find either.

Screw it.

She pulled a sweatshirt from the laundry pile, took a quick whiff, and jerked it on over her head. "Let's go." Tess connected the leash to his collar. The sooner they went, the sooner she could get back home and focus on figuring things out.

They stepped outside, and Tater put his entire body weight into trying to propel them off the porch. "Keep your pants on." Tess shot the dog a look as a droplet of water from the awning above her door found its way inside the collar of her shirt and down her back. Tater gave another tug.

"You're the damn gift that keeps on giving." She stepped on the leash so she could use both hands to turn the misaligned lock into place. It finally engaged, as the leash slid from beneath her foot. "Shit!"

Tess chased Tater down the steps, stomping on the leash before he could run for the street. She looped one end around her wrist and gave him the stink eye. Her life was already crazy. What on Earth made Pop think a dog would help?

Tater paced the small patch of dirt that was her front yard, found one of the few remaining green spots, and peed on it.

Typical.

Tess stared down the street, waiting for him to finish. Most of the houses looked like hers, ramshackle bungalows built in the early 1900s, long on potential and short on repairs. Weathered plastic toys and dollar store lawn chairs lay abandoned in a few of the yards. It looked like a ghost town, which was usual for this time of day. Her neighbors tended to leave for work at dawn. The only other sign of life was a shiny black sedan parallel-parked half a block down.

Definitely not a local.

Leaving a luxury car in her neighborhood was like sticking an engraved invitation to the windshield — Free money. First-come, first-served.

Something moved inside the car, and Tess stilled. A shifting of the shadows, a subtle darkening behind the back window glass. Had it been a trick of the light? Or was someone in there looking back at her? She shivered. The window tint made it impossible to tell, and Tess didn't want to get caught staring. She looked away.

She had probably imagined it anyway. She'd been on edge since the fire.

Even so, when Tater finally finished, she led him in the opposite direction. No reason to go looking for trouble when she already had plenty.

And somewhere between the half-way house at the end of the street and the Bojangles Chicken and Biscuits two blocks over, she stopped minding the walk or the wet. It was good to be outside and moving. The rain made the cracked pavement smell earthy and fresh. They wandered her neighborhood until the drizzle turned to downpour, her side-stepping the puddles, Tater plowing through potholes with water up to his midsection.

When they got back to the house, the sedan still waited at the curb. But she did her best to ignore it. Whoever it was had probably braved the trip into her neighborhood looking for a place to score a fix. She led the dog back inside, kicked off her soggy sneakers, and filled her Notorious RBG mug with the last of the coffee.

Instead of settling back in with her laptop, Tess found herself at the window. She stood to one side, careful to stay behind the curtain where she could see out but, hopefully, not be seen.

A drug deal did seem to be going down under the eaves of the duplex across the street. A thin man waited as another approached. They huddled together, both turned in toward the building. The shorter of the two shoved something into his jeans pocket, flipped up his hoodie, and turned back toward the street — toward the sedan — this time moving with purpose.

He strode past, his gaze never lifting from the sidewalk. And a prickle of something not quite right crept over Tess's skin.

She still couldn't see into the black void behind the glass, but an instinct she couldn't name kept her from looking away. As if she were playing a childhood game of Statues and could only be tagged when her back was turned. She edged further behind the curtain as a cold wind cut in through the window, binding the drapery around her legs.

The window.

Shit.

She'd left it open while they went on their walk. Tess slammed it shut. What a stupid thing to do. Anyone could've come in and—

The sedan eased away from the curb, gliding unhurried into the distance. As if the driver knew he'd been noticed and wanted to make it clear he didn't care.

She smacked the window lock into place. The sedan's driver might be gone, but that didn't mean she was alone. Tess held her breath, listening for any noises in the house that didn't belong.

A sloshing whir came from her dishwasher in the kitchen. Tater shifted on the floor. But it was otherwise quiet. She stared down the hall toward her bedroom. Even in her tiny house, there were places someone could hide. Tater hadn't acted like anything was off, but he wasn't exactly a trained guard dog, and—

Her cell phone dinged.

Tess yelped, and Tater scrambled to his feet, his nails scratching against the floor. He looked around, then at her. His expression a clear "are you crazy, lady?"

All signs lately certainly seemed to point to yes. She swiped her sock over a splatter of coffee she'd spilled when she slammed the window and checked her phone. The message read only "hi." Tess watched for something more, but it didn't come. The sender had a 404 area code, which meant it was someone local. But the number wasn't in her phone, and she didn't recognize it.

She carried the phone with her as she moved through the house, opening closet doors and checking behind the shower curtain. Nothing waited but the usual assortment of dust and clutter. She checked under the bed for good measure, then made her way back to the couch. "Definitely losing my mind."

Maybe she should've filled the mug with wine instead of coffee.

Another ding came from her phone. "Sorry for being an asshole."

That didn't narrow the list of possible senders down by much.

Ellipses, then, "I have your umbrella."

My umbrella.

"Holy shit!" She must've left it at the hospital.

Tater raised onto his front paws again and cocked his head to one side.

She mirrored the movement. "I gave Parker my number." She'd purposefully avoided thinking about the nonsense at the hospital. She had enough stress without looking for more. But, with this text, it all tumbled back. Luke Broussard. Dark eyes, wavy black hair, and a nasty attitude.

Tater gave a low chuff from the floor, as if to confirm his earlier assessment of her sanity.

"Mind your own business, nosey-bones." She flexed her fingers over the phone's keypad. Then, typed and re-typed possible responses, a process made harder by auto-correct's refusal to accept that fuck-face was a word. She briefly considered telling him where to stick the umbrella instead, but finally settled on "Keep it."

She hit send and immediately regretted it.

The high road was so unsatisfying.

She stared at the phone, waiting for a response. But none came.

And maybe that was for the best. The likelihood he'd know anything that would help the Ashbys was slim at best. He'd been a pilot doing his job when something terrible happened. That was all. If there was a connection between his passenger and her case, she might never know what it'd been. And she wasn't doing anyone any favors obsessing over leads that hadn't panned out or keeping tabs on the local drug trade from her window.

A muffled ding and another text bubble appeared. "I owe you an apology."

Tess raised her eyebrows.

The ellipses danced, stopped, then started again. "Give me a chance to explain?"

Tess stared at the text, then at Tater as he sniffed around, probably looking for crumbs. "Do we answer or make him suffer?"

Tater didn't look up, his concentration fully engaged in licking a spot of God knows what he'd found on the floor.

"You're no help." Tess turned back to the phone. She wanted to see Broussard again but had no idea why. So what if he was hot? That made it even more likely he'd be trouble.

A new message appeared on the screen. "The hospital released me this morning. Could we meet somewhere and talk?"

As much as she knew she shouldn't go, she wanted to. The same feeling that had compelled her to drive eight hours to find him in the hospital was back. A little itch in the back of her brain, begging to be scratched.

She typed. "Know where Righteous Coffee is on Moreland?"

And before she could come to her senses, Tess hit send.

CHAPTER 13

The body lay naked on the morgue slab, a Y incision crossing the width of the chest and extending down to the base of the abdomen. Mara circled the stainless steel table, one of a pair sharing space in the autopsy suite of the Midtown Atlanta Medical Examiner's office. She moved with care. The bulk of her biohazard suit could be cumbersome, and this kind of work required absolute precision.

She paused periodically as she went about her external examination, making notes on a white board that took up most of the room's back wall. The deceased was male, looked in his early to mid-thirties, five-foot-ten or eleven, dark haired, of Asian or possibly Middle Eastern descent. He was the first dead body Mara Eugenia Nuñez had seen in more than a year.

She spoke without looking up. "He's a floater?"

"Yes." Emmy's voice was hoarse, terse even.

Mara glanced at her friend. Emine Polat was the Deputy Chief ME and never prone to use one word when twenty would do. Maybe Mara's request that Emmy let her take a look at the body cold, without the influence of first knowing any conclusions Emmy had drawn, rubbed her the wrong way? Or the fact Mara made her suit up in full protective gear when she arrived?

Not that it could be helped.

Emmy had been wearing a simple surgical mask and latex gloves when Mara got there. And that wouldn't provide half the protection she'd need if they were dealing with a filovirus. As unlikely as that seemed, until they knew what had killed the man on the table, they needed to take every precaution.

Mara made an effort to soften her usual resting bitch face. "Do we have any identification?"

"No." Definitely terse.

Mara moved around the windowless room, cautious not to snag her suit on any of the sinks, scales, pans or other instruments that cluttered the dingy space. Pale pink tile covered the floor and walls but did nothing to make it less depressing.

She adjusted the directional light that hung above the body and leaned down so she could get a better look at the skin on the man's fingers and the backs of his hands. "He must not have been under long. There's no maceration present." Mara moved to the bottom of the table. "Usually, with a floater, I'd expect to see wrinkling of the dermis. Some sort of swelling as it absorbed the water." None of that would be news to Emmy, but the silence in the room was stifling. Mara felt compelled to fill it. She used a gloved hand to grip the man's heel, noting the amount of pressure it took to twist the foot toward the light. "Still in rigor mortis." She replaced the foot on the perforated metal table and looked up. "His skin is bruised but still smooth."

Emmy nodded but didn't speak. Something was definitely wrong.

"What gives, Emmy?" Mara crossed her arms over her chest. "I haven't seen you this quiet since your mom caught us sneaking back into your house summer after freshman year."

Emmy didn't even crack a smile. When she finally spoke, her voice came out tight. "From what I can tell, he wasn't in the water long at all. Less than an hour, I'd say."

"Timing explains the lack of bloating." Mara adjusted the motor on her belt. It was necessary to push clean air up and into her respirator, but it was also damned uncomfortable.

"Right." Emmy shifted backward, bumping into a metal shelf lined with gallon jugs of Formalin.

Mara waited for Emmy to continue, but she didn't. And the strain on Emmy's face unnerved Mara even more than the silence.

Mara snapped. "You know I'm not even supposed to be in the field anymore. This is gonna get me in deep shit, and I'm not exactly person of the year at the CDC as it is. You barely told me anything when you called me, at 6 a.m., to ask for an unofficial consult. And you've told me even less since I got here." She threw up her hands. "What gives?"

Emmy flushed behind her respirator. "There's some… unusual symptomatology."

Mara took another look at the body. She had noted redness around the eyes, but nothing out of the ordinary, even for a drowning. She looked back at Emmy, eyebrows raised. "Unusual enough for me to be here?" The chances of Ebola or Marburg showing up domestically were miniscule. She forced a smile into her voice, trying to cut the tension between them. "Seriously, Emmy. Did you kill this guy? Am I here to help with the cover-up?"

"This is what I wanted you to see." Emmy took a deep breath and pulled open the left flap of skin at the top of the Y incision, then the other.

Dios mio.

Now Mara understood why Emmy had called. She took an involuntary step back.

"I noticed the widespread bruising in my external examination and the redness around the eyes, but I didn't become concerned until I opened him up." Emmy shifted aside to give Mara room. "So far as I can see, the hemorrhaging is present in every major organ. I haven't opened up the skull. Once I saw this," Emmy waved her hand over the exposed cavity. "I hesitated to use the saw. But I expect we'll find bleeds there, too."

"Good call." Mara nodded. "Nothing good is going to come from making an aerosol of potentially infected tissue and bone." She kept the rest of the thought to herself. Unless whatever they were dealing with was airborne already, then a light misting of gore would be the least of their worries.

Mara took her time, examining the organs one by one. Hemorrhaging was an understatement. The internal bleeding was extensive. The man's liver and kidney had lost their structural integrity, disintegrating in place. She looked up at Emmy, her voice strained. "You were right to reach out."

"Shit." Emmy shook her head. "I was hoping you'd tell me I was crazy."

Mara retrieved a scalpel from a tray on the counter beneath the white board and made a quick incision through the man's small intestine. Like his other organs, it was filled with blood. "With this level of internal damage, there must have been an extensive amount of external bleeding."

"Yes." Emmy cleared her throat, but the words still came out strangled. Something new in her voice Mara couldn't identify. "Given the scale of the internal damage, I agree."

Mara glanced up.

Emmy's face was pale behind her face mask. "They found him floating in one of the holding ponds at the Hemphill water station."

Mara shook her head, the lack of comprehension apparently evident on her face.

Emmy swallowed hard. "They pulled him from the city water supply."

CHAPTER 14

"Hey, Kelly." Tess waved to the barista, who was wiping down an espresso machine with a white cloth. The machine gleamed, a perfect match to the stainless steel of his nose rings.

"Welcome back, stranger." Kelly leaned over a shelf of pastries, one hand on his hip. "Where have you been hiding?"

"Work." She scrunched up her face. "I'll come say hi in just a minute. I'm looking for someone."

"Aren't we all, sweetheart?" Kelly tucked the towel into his apron and worked the dials on the machine. It whirred to life, the air filling with the rich scent of freshly ground coffee.

Customers packed the small shop. But then, it was always busy. She scanned the people who waited in line — blondes, brunettes, hipsters, bankers, and construction workers. Everyone hugged the counter, waiting to order or scanning for cups bearing their names on the opposite end.

It took her two passes over the tables and sofas crowding the room to spot Luke.

He sat at a small round table, facing the street, his back to her. An "S" shaped tattoo peeked out from the bottom of his shirt sleeve on one arm. Tess pushed her still shower-damp curls into place, checked to make sure her bra straps weren't hanging out of her tank top, and walked over. "Hi."

Luke stood slowly, wincing as he straightened his body. He was bigger than she remembered, his muscles clearly defined under the thin fabric of his t-shirt. He'd looked a lot less imposing lying in a hospital bed. "Thanks for coming."

Something fluttered in her chest as they came eye to eye, and she wasn't sure she liked it. He made her feel off-balance somehow. "Sure, of course." She cleared her throat and looked away. The table sat empty except for a pair of folded sunglasses. "Did you want a coffee?"

"Yeah, I was just waiting until you got here to order." Luke shifted around the table toward the line, his body slow. "What would you like?"

Watching him move made her hurt. "I've got it. You sit, rest. What can I get you?"

"Are you sure?" He pulled a wallet from his back pocket. "Can I at least give you some cash for it?"

"No, I'll get it." Because why wouldn't she buy the guy who yelled at her a four dollar coffee?

He hesitated, then seemed to think better of arguing the point. "Thank you." He eased himself back down into the chair. "I'd love an Americano."

She eyed him from the line, waiting for her turn to give Kelly the order. Luke was even better looking than she remembered. Taller, yes. But also, the color had returned to his skin, a healthy olive-toned glow. And an intelligent sparkle lit his eyes where it had probably been dulled by painkillers before.

Tess could tell by the look on Kelly's face as she approached the counter he didn't mind the view either. She pretended not to notice. "Two of the usual."

"He's letting you buy?" Kelly asked in a stage whisper.

She shrugged as the barista frothed a small carafe of milk and poured it into a porcelain mug. He handed it to a man who was busy yammering into his Bluetooth and turned back to Tess. "I guess I'd buy that a coffee, too. Are these for here or to go?"

She glanced at Luke. "Better put them in to-go cups. Just in case."

"Keeping your options open." He pulled two cups from a stack. "I like it."

She paid for the coffees and left Kelly to ogle Luke from a distance.

Hopefully, she wouldn't need to make an early exit again. But after what had happened at the hospital, she wasn't taking any chances. She handed Luke one of the too hot cups and settled into the chair opposite his.

"Thanks." He turned the cup in his hands. "So, let me start with an apology. You didn't deserve how I acted. Especially not after what you did for me." Luke swallowed before he continued, his gaze intent on hers. "I found out my passenger didn't survive right before you came in." Luke stopped, swallowed again.

He looked so sad, so earnest, she couldn't give him the coal-raking she'd planned. How could she, after what he'd been through? "I can't even imagine how awful that must've been."

He nodded. "I didn't know him, I mean, not before that day. But he was in my care when he died. And I can't help but think whether there was something more I could've done. Something that would've made a difference." Pain creased his face.

She had no way to know what'd caused his plane to crash, but she could see in his face he'd have done anything to keep it from happening. "I'm just glad you're okay."

"Thanks." Luke put the cup down. "When I saw your card, I jumped to conclusions. I was so angry with myself, with the situation… I took it out on you." He leaned forward, resting his elbows on the table. "I want you to know how much I regret that." Luke studied her face, his eyes a question.

"Apology accepted." After what he'd been through, letting him off the hook was the least she could do. It wasn't hard to see how, if he was already blaming himself, he might have misunderstood her intentions. Might have seen her appearance there as confirmation he was to blame for Smith's death.

The tension lines around Luke's eyes relaxed, and he settled back into the chair. He picked up his coffee, taking a careful sip. "How did you know him?"

She blinked, trying and failing to make sense of the question. "Who?"

"Smith. My passenger who…" He cleared his throat, his voice coming out hoarse. "The man who died."

Tess shook her head. "I didn't. I misdialed, I guess, or I had the number wrong." Or she hadn't, and her only lead was dead. "I don't know. I was trying to reach a defendant in one of my cases. And, instead, I got you." She shrugged. "The whole thing was surreal."

He looked out the window at the traffic creeping down Moreland Avenue. "I only remember parts of it. I didn't even know I had talked to you on the phone until after you came to see me. Parker told me." He looked back at her. "You saved my life, you know."

Her face warmed. She definitely couldn't take credit for that. "I didn't do anything but call 911 and tell them what you told me. That's all."

"If you hadn't, I wouldn't be here." Luke reached up to touch the side of his chest, his mouth tightening as he did. "Where we went down, it was trees as far as you can see. It could have taken days for search and rescue to find us if you hadn't told them where to look."

She didn't even want to think about that, and she couldn't think of a damn thing to say. Whatever she'd expected from Luke, the earnest, unabashedly vulnerable man in front of her wasn't it.

He held her gaze. "You're like a guardian angel."

"Angel, I'm not."

He gave a low chuckle. "Good to know."

If she'd blushed before, now she must be beet red. The heat spread across her face and down her neck. She looked away and shifted in her chair, her knee knocking into his. "Sorry." The contact made it impossible to ignore how close he was. The size of the body he'd somehow managed to stuff into that chair.

"It's okay." He didn't move. Their legs still touched under the table. And that tiny point of contact was all she could feel.

His gaze drifted to something above her head, and his smile faded. "Crap."

She twisted to look through the window behind her. A white Jeep Grand Cherokee idled at the curb. Luke's friend Parker sat in the driver's seat.

"He was supposed to wait until I texted him I was ready. That's my ride." Luke braced himself on the table as he rose from his chair, and his eyes seemed to grow darker. "Can I see you again?"

"I'd like that." The words left her mouth before she realized she'd opened it.

"Me, too." His voice was lower, softer when he spoke again. "I'll call you?"

Two short beeps sounded from the Jeep.

Luke ignored his friend, still focused on her. He waited until Tess nodded before he started toward the door.

She wouldn't have known he was in pain if it weren't for the set of his jaw as he passed in front of the shop's plate glass window. He looked back, flashing her one more smile before he climbed into Parker's Jeep, and it pulled out of the lot.

Tess stared down at her still mostly full cup of coffee. Under no circumstances was it a good idea for her to get involved with anyone—she needed to stay focused on getting her career back on track. Wasting time with some hot, complicated, possibly volatile guy wasn't going to pay her rent or keep her firm's doors open.

Once she had doors again.

A ding sounded from her purse, and she pulled the phone free.

A text from Luke. "Sorry we got interrupted. Dinner tomorrow? Maybe 7 at Taqueria del Sol?"

She couldn't contain her grin.

Fuck caution.

Tess texted a quick yes, finished her coffee, and dropped the cup in a trash can. Kelly waved back and forth in her direction, then made a thumbs up followed by a thumbs down. His eyebrows formed a question mark.

Tess mimed a zipper closing her lips and winked.

As she reached the door, a young man in a maroon hoodie approached, coming the opposite way. The brim of a Braves cap peeked out from the hood, his eyes red and swollen underneath. He got to the door first and held it open for her. "Thank you." She quickened her pace, trying not to make him wait. As she reached the exit, he doubled over in a fit of coughing.

Tess held the door until he'd recovered. Her hand where his had been only a moment before.

CHAPTER 15

Mara fumbled with a roll of tape, her thick rubber gloves making it hard to coax an edge free. Nothing about this situation seemed real. She finally peeled up a corner, tore off two long pieces, and handed them to Emmy. Surely there was some other explanation for the dead man's symptomatology, something she'd missed. But if there was, she couldn't think of it.

Anxiety prickled under Mara's skin, even though she knew there wasn't time for it. She tore off another piece of tape. She needed to keep a clear head. She knew the protocol. All they had to do was execute it. Which, at this point, meant securing the site.

They moved as quickly as they could, using the tape to seal the space between the doors, the surrounding walls, and the floor. Emmy worked in absolute silence, no doubt as freaked out as Mara but still holding it together. Which was what Mara needed to do. When every inch of the opening was sealed tight, she tossed the remainder of the roll onto one of the empty gurneys lining the hall. "Better turn off the HVAC, too. Until we know whether it's airborne, we need to assume it is."

Even though the prospect of that was too horrific to seem really possible.

"Right." Emmy eyed the dusty vent on the wall above their heads.

Mara did the same, forcing a calm into her voice she didn't feel. "Do you know where the thermostat is?"

Mara followed Emmy into the morgue's administrative office, talking to her friend's back. "In theory, the virus could float through the air duct, even with it off, but at least it's a start." She would've thought the idea of that happening was ludicrous.

Except it had happened before.

Years ago, in an animal research facility outside D.C. In a place designed to stop the spread of pathogens. Where the first line of defense wasn't just her and a roll of duct tape.

"How comforting," Emmy finally responded, her voice flat.

Whatever Emmy was thinking, she obviously didn't want to talk about it. Mara clammed up, watching as Emmy adjusted the thermostat and moved to a tall metal cabinet. Emmy tugged on the door twice before it squeaked open. A ball of rubber bands fell out, bounced off one of her boots, and rolled under a battered oak desk against the far wall. Normally, Mara would have gone after it. But missing office supplies seemed like the least of their worries.

Emmy emerged from the cabinet waving a biohazard sign.

"Good call." Mara led Emmy back to the hallway, retrieved the tape, and tore off two much smaller pieces. The sealed doors already bore multiple notices warning visitors about radiation, the dangers of formaldehyde, and cautioning "All Bodies & Body Parts, Including Fetuses, Must be Signed Out."

Mara cringed and taped the biohazard notice over the top of that one. Nothing would be coming in or out of that room anytime soon. Not without multiple levels of oversight and red tape. "Lets get out of here."

They took turns spraying the outside of each other's protective suits with virucidal detergent, removed the safety apparatus, and left it in a pile outside the autopsy suite doors. Even knowing they were doing everything by the book, her skin itched with the irrational fear that she'd been contaminated. That every minute she spent inside the morgue increased the chances she'd end up like the man now entombed in the autopsy suite.

"This way." Emmy pointed back the way Mara had come in, and Mara followed her friend toward the main door, the reality of their situation a burn rising up from her stomach to clog her throat.

She'd trained for this, dealt with filoviruses in the field and in the lab, but this was different. This was on American soil. Her friend could be infected. And she wasn't flying in like she usually did, fully briefed and prepared to manage the CDC's well-thought-out, coordinated response.

She was on the ground level of whatever this turned out to be, and there were no safety precautions that felt like enough.

Near the end of the hall, they veered off into a small locker room with a long metal bench running down the center. Mara stepped inside and stopped. A shower stall and water closet sat to her left, two sinks and a series of wooden lockers on her right. The one nearest the door stood open with scrubs in varying shades of blue piled inside. It all looked so normal.

But nothing was.

Even knowing how ridiculous it was, Mara wanted to strip out of all of her clothes and burn them, shower until she'd scrubbed herself head-to-toe clean, and then maybe shower again.

Emmy brushed past her on the way to the sinks, and Mara followed, forcing her body into motion. Seizing up from fear would be the worst thing she could do.

The two stood side-by-side, scrubbing up to their elbows with antibacterial soap. Steam billowed from Emmy's sink, the skin of her hands turning pink as she held them, longer than what must be comfortable, under the burning water. Mara eyed her friend but said nothing.

She wasn't the only one struggling. Emmy was the one who had already been exposed. She'd need Mara to be there for her when she was ready to talk about it. Which meant it was time for Mara to get her shit together.

They stepped outside, into the bright sunlight of a beautiful day. Mara gulped in clean air. Birds chirped from the phone lines overhead. A jogger in neon yellow shorts cut across the parking lot and down the sidewalk. Traffic flowed beside him as people went about their day, completely unaware of how close they were to what might be one of the most feared diseases known to man.

"I'm going to go make sure all the exterior doors are locked." Emmy disappeared around the side of the building. It was a good idea. But there was a solid chance Emmy was just looking for a moment alone. And Mara could see why. Emmy'd done most of the autopsy in nothing but a paper mask, smock, and a pair of latex gloves — normal for that procedure — but, if they were dealing with what she feared, terrifying.

Mara dug out her cell phone and dialed her boss. It was going to cause an absolute shit storm, but it had to be done. "Jerry, it's Mara. We may have a domestic outbreak of something that looks like Ebola or maybe Marburg. The Midtown ME called me for an unofficial consult this morning, and my initial examination is consistent with a filovirus."

A long pause fell over the line. Jerry Pulaski might be as mild-mannered and Midwestern as they came, but Mara had just delivered a bombshell. On top of the fact she wasn't supposed to be there to begin with.

He had to be angry, but his tone stayed even. "Tell me what you know so far."

Mara gave him the details as efficiently as she could. She finished with a description of the steps they'd taken to secure the site, just as Emmy reappeared with a cell phone pressed to her ear. She looked to be deep in a conversation of her own.

"I see," Jerry said, still the professional. "Wait there until Thomas's team arrives."

Mierda.

Jerry continued. "He can take over on securing the site and begin interviewing any of the ME's personnel who had contact with the body. I'll make the necessary arrangements for the body to be transferred back to the CDC."

Mara closed her eyes.

Of all the people he could send, why'd it have to be him?

Thomas Dietrich had spent the better part of a year trying to pretend Mara hadn't been promoted to be his manager. Mara swallowed the protest. She'd disobeyed a direct order in being there. Now wasn't the time to air her grievances. "Thank you, sir."

"Mara?"

"Yes, sir?"

"I'll expect you to be with the body when it arrives. We need to talk."

Mara tried not to think too much about what that might mean.

As soon as she hung up, she made the other calls required by protocol, first to the Department of Health and then to the Georgia Emergency Management and Homeland Security Agency.

With that done, she put her cell away and listened while Emmy tried to convince the local police department they needed to bring in the FBI. "Yes, I understand the body was found in your jurisdiction. What I need for you to understand is that a body infected with a highly infectious disease that, until now, didn't exist on U.S. soil outside of a laboratory, was just found floating in one of the City of Atlanta's primary water sources. It's entirely possible he was dropped into the water supply on purpose, as an overt act of bioterrorism. It's time to stop tripping over your dick and get someone from law enforcement here who is properly prepared to handle it." Emmy's face had turned a bright red. "Right, yes... Right." She hung up.

"Damn, girl." Mara gave her a nod of appreciation.

Emmy pulled a limp cigarette from the front pocket of her shirt. She let it hang unlit from her mouth as she paced the concrete walkway running between the morgue entrance and the roll-up metal doors used to load bodies in and out of the building.

Knowing her friend probably needed a moment to regroup, Mara launched into what she'd learned on her calls, leaving out the part about the reprimand she expected once she got back to the CDC. "There will be an all-hands meeting at one today, which is as soon as the State Epidemiologist said he could pull someone from each of the necessary agencies into a conference room together. In the meantime, they've stopped operation of the Hemphill station, rerouting supply as much as they can from the other two water treatment facilities. That won't work for very long before we start having shortages, but it'll at least buy us some time to see when Hemphill can be reopened."

Emmy dropped onto a dingy wooden bench to the right of the door. "That makes sense."

Mara joined her. "They're also working to identify the deceased, so they can determine who he had contact with before his death. They, and everyone who was exposed to the body post-mortem, will need to be brought in and checked out. What else?" Mara extended her legs, crossing them at the ankle. "They're shutting down access to Hemphill and to this building. I'm assuming there's another facility where your normal traffic can go?"

"That was my first call. It won't be a problem." Emmy pulled the crumpled cigarette from her mouth. "And what happens to the people who had contact with the body? The city employees who found our guy in the water, the medics who pulled him out, our intake team. That's got to be, what? Eight, nine people who went home after their shifts to kiss their kids goodnight."

Emmy had to be wondering what was going to happen to her, too, even if she didn't ask. She wouldn't have known to put on a face shield, much less a respirator, until after she'd opened the body. All they could do was pray the paper mask and gloves had been enough.

"They'll be in quarantine for some period of time, depending on what it is. The incubation period for both Ebola and Marburg is between three to eighteen days, so I'd expect isolation and observation, probably at the CDC, for about twenty."

Emmy nodded, and Mara continued. "Their first priority is always to identify the bug, which is really just a matter of getting a blood sample into one of the Level 4 labs so they can look at it under an electron microscope. They compare it to the other virus samples we have on file. And, with any luck, that will tell us which of the nasties we've got and how to deal with it. Then, we've got to try to figure out if John Doe's our index patient and how he was exposed, so we can eliminate whatever pocket or reservoir of infection is out there."

"Right." Emmy stood back up and paced the loading bay again. "Damn, I wish I hadn't quit smoking." She hung the broken cigarette from the corner of her mouth. "But I'd settle for a lighter." Emmy crossed her arms over her chest and stared into the distance. When she finally spoke again, her voice came out hoarse. "How bad is it?"

Mara shifted in her seat, trying to decide how to answer. "Well, you know there are three ways to stop the spread of a virus. Drugs, vaccines, or containment. There's no real treatment for filoviruses, so drugs are out. All we can do is try to mitigate the symptoms. But there's been a lot of progress in the past few years with a new Ebola vaccine, assuming that's what this is. They had tremendous success with it in the last outbreak in the Democratic Republic of Congo."

Emmy shoved the cigarette back in her pocket. "And Marburg?"

"No vaccine yet. And I suppose we shouldn't assume it's one or the other. Could be something entirely new we haven't seen before."

"Okay," Emmy nodded, "so we're hoping for Ebola."

"Said no one ever." Mara tilted her head. A faint sound of sirens cut through the background noise of Atlanta traffic, but she couldn't tell if they were headed her way.

"If the Ebola vaccine isn't effective against whatever this is, then what?"

"Containment." Which given the number of people who'd had contact with the body, was going to be a mess.

Emmy stopped her pacing. "Okay, and if we can't contain it?"

"Scientifically speaking, we're fucked."

CHAPTER 16

September 18, 2018

"Not bad, not bad at all." Tess turned, checking the fit of the dress across her backside in the mirror. "And it only took fifteen tries." In the end, she'd settled on a simple navy number that hit her mid-calf, gold hoops, and sandals. It was casual enough for tacos but still managed to show off her figure. She'd tried to play it cool, pretending she wasn't nervous. But now that it was almost time to go, her stomach stirred with something between anxiety — what did people even say on first dates? — and excitement.

She hadn't been out to dinner with a man since she'd left Chicago.

Since Jay had broken their engagement.

Tess sagged, the flutter in her belly stilling to a leaden weight. Was that the last time she'd worn this dress? Out to dinner with him and their law firm friends. The ones who didn't speak to her anymore. She toyed with one of her earrings. Maybe she shouldn't go. What was the point in putting herself out there when she knew how it would probably end?

Badly.

Tater ambled up beside her and gave her a look in the mirror.

Pure canine skepticism.

"Okay, you're right." Gran and Pop hadn't raised her to be chicken shit.

Tess gave Tater's ears a good rub. No matter what happened, she had him to come home to. And, as pathetic as it might be, that helped. "Wish me luck." She dropped a rawhide treat onto the folded blanket she'd made into his bed. "Chew on that and not the shoes, big boy." Tess got to the front door, purse in hand, before doubling back to make sure her closet was closed — just in case.

Then she headed out into a dark, starless night. None of the usual neighborhood noises filled the air. No swoosh of traffic from the busy street near the end of her block or thump of music from the apartment complex across the street. Nothing moved except the flicker of a dying streetlight. Like something out of a low budget horror movie.

Stop being ridiculous.

She hurried into the car and plugged her phone into the USB cord trailing from the lighter. Her nerves might be getting the better of her, but it was nothing a good soundtrack wouldn't cure. She flicked through playlists until she found the song she wanted.

Nina Simone crooned through the car's speakers. Tess finally relaxed as she pulled onto Ponce de Leon. The dividing line between the gentrified Virginia Highlands neighborhood and the part of the city where she could afford to live, Ponce also served as the main, and usually clogged, thoroughfare between Atlanta and the city of Decatur.

She started west and ran directly into a wall of brake lights.

Of course.

She glanced at the clock on her dash. At quarter after seven, she should've expected gridlock. And it explained why she hadn't heard any traffic noise. Nothing was moving. The line of cars in front of her inched forward then stopped again.

Crap.

The light at the next intersection cycled green to red without a single car making it through. If she didn't figure out a way around this mess, she was going to be late. She pulled Waze up on her phone and let it reroute her. Assuming she found a better way there and didn't hit any more traffic, she could make it in time. Just. She merged over and turned onto one of the less traveled, and seedier, side roads.

Several cars followed her lead as she zig-zagged around a blocky set of condos and behind the aptly named "Murder Kroger," where you could pick up a bullet wound along with your milk and bread. Then she worked her way toward Midtown. Tess sang along with the stereo, loud and off-key. She made a right onto another cut through, dodging cars and delivery vans blocking the shoulder on both sides before picking up speed.

She sounded awful. Tess turned up the volume.

Better.

A sharp bang came from the back of the car.

She jerked her gaze away from the radio and back to the road.

What the hell?

Tess gripped the wheel, as the back tires fish-tailed. The pit of her stomach left behind.

No, no, no.

She fought to bring the car under control, even as the tires lost traction, and the old Volvo slid sideways. Moving as if of its own volition.

Whirling like a carnival ride gone mad.

A shriek tore out of her throat as the car continued its spin to the right, then lurched up over the curb. She bounced hard against the seatbelt, and her purse went flying to the floor.

Tess cranked the wheel again, trying to correct course while slamming down on the brake with every ounce of strength she had. But she couldn't stop. The car slid toward a traffic signal on a path she couldn't change. Tess closed her eyes and waited for impact.

▪ ▪ ▪

Something exploded, like a kick to Tess's face and chest.

She slammed back into the bucket seat, her safety belt cinching tight as the air whooshed from her lungs.

The airbag deflated in her lap with a low hiss.

Holy shit.

She took a deep breath in. The car smelled like fireworks at a backyard Fourth of July. She let the breath out. It was just a car accident. Another deep breath in. Her face and arms stung, but she was okay. Tears pricked behind her eyes anyway.

Oh my God. I could have died.

She pushed the withering bag away as movement flashed in the rearview mirror. A tall man with blonde hair held something in his hand. It gleamed in her taillights as he came closer. A badge? In the lights' red glow she recognized some kind of uniform. A policeman. He would probably give her a ticket, but who cared? Help was there, and that's what mattered.

He leaned down near the back of her car.

Probably looking at the tire.

Tess tilted her head back against the headrest, closed her eyes, and listened to the ticking coming from what was left of her engine. She had no idea what had happened or if it had been her fault. But she was alive.

Thank God.

She let go of the tension she'd been holding in her muscles, the knots in her shoulders melting away from her ears. Whatever happened next, she could deal with it.

Something bright glowed from behind her closed lids, and Tess raised a hand to shield her eyes from the light.

A voice. "Hey, lady. You okay?"

The beam shifted to her lap, and she blinked spots from her vision. An old man in a dirty Falcons jersey and a Sun Oil cap stood outside her window. She unlocked the door and tried to undo her seatbelt, but her hands were numb and clumsy.

Where had the officer gone?

The old man opened her door. "Can I?" He gestured toward the lap belt, a tiny flashlight dangling from what looked like a set of house keys in his hand.

She nodded, grateful for the help. Nothing about the accident made sense. She hadn't hit anything. The sound had come from the back of the car, not the front. A blow out?

"What happened?" He stooped down, pulling the lap belt free. He smelled of beer and clove cigarettes.

"My tire, maybe? I don't know. I was just driving, and then… I don't know."

He glanced toward the back of the car, his brow furrowed. Then, with a shrug, he clipped the keys to his belt, and helped her hobble to the curb. He kept a hand under her elbow to steady her as she sat down. The pavement felt damp and gritty against her palms, but it helped to anchor her to reality. To make this strange version of the world seem real. People emerged onto the sagging porches of the few lit houses across the street, whispering and pointing in her direction. But, otherwise, she and the old man were alone.

She leaned to look around the far side of her car. "Do you know where the policeman went?" He had to be there somewhere. "He was just here."

"I didn't see nobody else." The old man pulled a flip phone from his jeans. "Don't you worry yourself. I'll call for help." He sat down next to her, pulled a pair of bent reading glasses from his pocket, and squinted at the buttons on his phone as he dialed 9-1-1.

She'd been so sure she'd seen a policeman. But then, her head ached, and her memories jumbled, and everything that'd happened seemed so much less concrete.

She didn't think she hit her head, but maybe she had and didn't realize? Or maybe that wasn't what was going on at all. A chill crept over her skin. The other possibility was almost too horrifying to consider. She'd known forcing the memory at Gran's house would have consequences. It always did.

What if this time, it was worse? What if she lost her memory altogether? Or her grip on reality?

Tess dropped her forehead to her knees and waited. Forcing memories had only ever caused harm.

The old man sat quietly beside her until the ambulance arrived, then shuffled off with a "you take care of yourself now" as the first responders took over. She tried to think of a way to thank him, something that might measure up to the comfort he'd given her just by being there. But as the EMTs descended, she got caught up in the whirlwind of trying to explain what had happened, and he disappeared into one of the houses lining the street.

This time, as Tess repeated what had happened to the EMTs, even she didn't think it made sense. She gave up, going quiet as they loaded her into the back of the ambulance. There was no point in explaining again, no one was going to believe her. The shorter of the two EMTs climbed in with her, closing the doors behind them.

"Can I have my phone? From the purse, there." She pointed to her bag, where he'd loaded it onto the stretcher by her feet. He handed her the cell without a word and settled back into a jump seat, his gaze fixed on the screen monitoring her vital signs.

Even though it all looked normal, so far as she could tell.

They'd probably have let her Uber home if it weren't for her reporting the phantom policeman. What a waste of time. And money. Tess drew in a deep breath as the ambulance picked up speed, swaying back and forth as it sped through the narrow city streets. She made a quick call to Gail to make sure Tater would be covered if the hospital kept her overnight, then found Luke's number and connected the call.

"Hi, are you here?" Dishes clattered, and a dozen voices blended together on his end of the line. An animated, persistent roar. "I can't find you in this mad house. Sorry I'm so late. Traffic was a nightmare." A short pause. "Is that an ambulance siren?"

"Yeah." Nothing like making a memorable first date impression. "I'm not gonna make it to dinner."

"What? Hang on." The restaurant clamor dimmed, and he came back on the line. "That's better. I stepped back outside. Everything okay?"

"I was in a car accident. They're taking me to the hospital now."

“The hospital?” The subtle Cajun in his voice now unmistakable. “Jesus. Are you alright?” He didn’t say it like a platitude. It sounded like he cared.

Tess smiled, and she caught the EMT looking at her like she was crazy.

She shifted to the other direction, not that the back of the ambulance provided any actual privacy. The guy could probably hear both ends of her conversation. “I think so. Just a little shaken up.” She looked herself over. “Maybe some bruises and a burn on my arm from the airbag.”

“Which one?”

She lifted her arm, turning it to inspect the red splotches. “The left.”

“What hospital?”

“Oh.” That made more sense. Heat crept up her face. “Grady.”

“What happened?” His question held none of the accusation that’d seemed implicit when the EMTs had asked the same thing.

And this time, she didn’t force herself to relate what she remembered in objective, logical detail. She let the words tumble out, and all the fear and apprehension over what might have happened — what had almost happened — came with them. “I don’t know. One minute I was driving, I looked down at the radio, and wham! I’m spinning out of control and I’m headed for a light pole and I can’t stop…” She paused, unable to get the rest past a lump that had formed in her throat.

“It was the same for me.” He said with a quiet kindness. “With the plane crash. I did everything I could, everything I’d been trained to do. But nothing worked. Nothing helped. It seemed like it went on forever and was over in an instant.”

She leaned her head back against the stretcher. What a pair they made, him needing her comfort as much as she needed his. “But it did work, you know. You survived. Parker said what you did, landing the plane like that, was a miracle.”

He puffed out a breath. “It sure didn’t feel like one.”

"I mean, you didn't crash trying to crank up the radio, like I did. But it's something."

He laughed, a deep resonant sound she liked almost as much as the thought that she might've made him feel better.

The paramedic tapped her shoulder. "You'll need to hang up now. We're pulling in."

"I've got to go."

"Do you need a ride home? It sounds like your car probably got towed."

Oh shit.

He was right. Tess pressed a hand to her forehead. Could she even afford to get it out of impound? As much as she wanted to see Luke — and she did, maybe too much — she needed time to catch her breath, to find her equilibrium.

To figure out what the hell she was going to do about her car.

Her life.

"I've got a friend coming to get me." Tess only had one friend in Atlanta, and Gail was already on her way to get Tater. But that sounded less pathetic than saying she'd be calling a taxi to pick her up from the ER. "Thank you again, Luke. I'm sorry our plans for tonight got ruined."

"Can I come check on you tomorrow? See how you're doing?"

A slow smile spread across her face. No matter what else she had going on, it didn't change how she felt. "I'd like that."

CHAPTER 17

Mara spun her office chair toward the window, rubbing at what felt like a permanent phone-shaped imprint on her ear. It had grown dark outside while she'd exchanged updates with the half-dozen agencies working together on the Midtown outbreak. She'd been managing a thousand moving parts. There was still more than she could ever hope to do. And all she could think of was Emmy.

They'd have finished her interview hours ago. It wouldn't take long to trace her post-exposure contacts, not when she'd been in the morgue the whole time. Which meant she was most likely in quarantine. Either somewhere in the CDC complex, if she'd yet to show symptoms, or — Mara swallowed a lump in her throat — in the neighboring hospital on Emory University's campus.

She stared off in the direction of the hospital. It was too far away for her to see, buried somewhere behind a dozen of the university's identical beige stucco buildings, their terra-cotta roofs turning a murky blood red in the starless night. The trees around them scratched at the night sky, jagged and black. She couldn't just sit there and wait. Mara snatched back up the phone and tried Emmy's cell again.

It still went straight to voicemail.

Mierda.

She let the receiver clatter back into its cradle. The walls of her office, always close — near enough she could almost reach both opposing walls if she stood in the center and stretched both arms out wide — now seemed to be closing in. No matter how much the urge to race out and do something itched beneath her skin, she was desk-bound until Jerry finally appeared.

Mara glanced at the wall clock, 8:44 p.m.

She'd expected him hours ago. But that hadn't been realistic. With everything going on, her ass-chewing could wait.

And, as much as she hated it, she'd have to, too.

She shifted her head side to side, stretching out the kinks in her neck, then pulled up her call list. She had more messages to return. Mara leaned over, caught the edge of the office door, and pushed it closed.

It bounced off Thomas Deitrich, who stood on the threshold wearing his usual plaid shirt, black socks with sandals, and scowl.

Of all the complications she didn't need right now…

She did her best to paste on a smile. "Sorry about that. Didn't see you."

"Jerry wanted me to get your thoughts on the press release." A crease ran between his brows, like he suspected she'd closed the door in his face on purpose.

If only.

"No problem." Mara took the loose pages, making a conscious effort not to let irritation creep into her tone. He was no doubt pissed he needed her approval. She held the papers under her desk lamp so she could see, pretending not to notice he was still hovering in the doorway. If she ignored him long enough, chances were, he'd get the hint and go away.

"Right." He cleared his throat. "I'll need your comments within the hour."

Mara whipped up her head, dropping the press release to the desk. "You're a valuable part of our team. And I appreciate your work on this." She forced her voice to remain level. "But it is not appropriate for you to give me deadlines."

Thomas threw up his hands. "You really need to get your ego in check."

She gripped the edge of her desk, trying to get herself under control. Despite every cell in her body screaming to give him an anatomically correct suggestion for what he could do with his opinion.

Fuck it.

"I don't know who you think—"

Jerry appeared in the hallway. "Thomas." Jerry nodded a hello, then shifted his gaze to Mara and back to Thomas. "Everything okay here?"

"Yes, sir." Thomas shifted to let Jerry pass. "Just dropping off the press release. I'll get out of your way." Thomas smirked at her as he passed behind Jerry's back, disappearing down the hall to whatever hole he'd crawled out of.

Probably wishes he could stay and watch Jerry tell me off.

"Sorry it took so long for me to get over to see you. It's been a long day." Jerry leaned one shoulder against her doorframe, his blazer rumpled, something that looked like soy sauce spotting his tie.

"Not a problem." Mara offered the other seat in the room, a one-armed desk chair she'd scavenged from storage. "I've been on the phone or in meetings since we got back with the body."

"Press?" He pulled the chair from where it sat wedged between the desk and the wall.

"Not yet, thank God. Although, I expect we'll spring a leak any minute." She pointed to the press release. "Should have this ready soon. Maybe we can still get out in front of it." With people from dozens of government departments involved, it would inevitably get out to the press, probably before the sun came up tomorrow.

"Let's hope so." Jerry shook his head and looked out the window, silent. He took off his glasses, resting them on one knee. "I take it you understand the scope of your duties as director of the CDC's filovirus team."

Here we go.

"Yes, sir. I do."

"Then, you know field visits, particularly unsanctioned interactions without support and without proper safety protocols in place, are not within your scope."

"I do." An image of Emmy's face, ashen behind her respirator, sprang to Mara's mind.

"You have a cell phone?" He asked in a tone that made clear he didn't expect an answer.

Mara stared ahead.

Jerry leaned back in his chair, tapping the glasses against his khakis. He pursed his lips, dark brown eyes considering. "I know you think your promotion to this post was only one in name. I'm aware it would have been your preference, your strong preference, to remain in the field. But my job is to put the most qualified people in the positions where they can do the most good. And you, Mara, are the person most qualified for this job. You are excellent in the field. But you are better here."

She had expected a variety of things from Jerry — a reprimand, a demotion to a basement office doing ringworm research into eternity, maybe removal from the team assigned to work the outbreak — but, not a compliment. Her face warmed.

Jerry watched her with eyebrows raised, as she shifted in her chair.

"Thank you, sir." She finally managed.

Jerry relaxed his arms, leaning forward as he slid his eyeglasses back on. "Good. Now we've got that dealt with, we can get to business. What do we know from the lab?"

"Nothing since they confirmed the virus as Marburg this morning. It looks like we're dealing with a new strain." Mara ran through the details of what little she'd learned so far and listened while Jerry did the same. So far as she could tell, Jerry's morning had primarily been spent negotiating the division of labor between government agencies.

"There'll be more bureaucrats jousting for control tomorrow, but we don't have the bandwidth to deal with it anymore. We have to get in front of this thing, and we have to do it now." Jerry rose from his chair. "Get that done." He tilted his head at the press release. "Then go home and get some rest. You'll need to be fresh tomorrow. I want you to take point on this for the CDC."

She sat up straighter, realizing the trust he'd placed in her.

The responsibility he'd put on her. It was the best and worst thing she could imagine.

No one joined the CDC for money. They were there because they wanted to make a difference. And this was her chance to do something truly important. Something that would save lives. "Thank you."

Jerry pushed his chair back against the wall. "I know it's a big ask, so I've cleared Thomas's plate. He'll be your right hand on this one."

She forced herself to nod. Knowing Thomas, he'd have interpreted the assignment to mean he'd be running the CDC's response with her. Or he'd be busy plotting how he could use the opportunity to show her up.

Which explained his smirk.

CHAPTER 18

September 19, 2018

Tater's barking turned into one long "Arrroooooo." Tess grabbed his collar and blocked him with a hip, his nails scratching into the foyer's ancient hardwood floors as he fought her hold. Her landlord would not be stoked.

"Sorry about the dog." She looked up to Luke.

He stood frozen, one foot on the porch, the other hovering above the cracked concrete of her front steps.

Tess turned back to the dog. "Tater, sit."

The dog took his time complying.

Luke gave her a small smile, then eased down into a crouch. "Hi, Tater." He offered the dog the back of his hand. Tater edged closer for a sniff, backed up, and tried again. After a few rounds, he gave Luke's hand a lick that almost looked like approval.

She pushed the door the rest of the way open, ignoring Pop's voice in her head, *"Christ on a cracker, girl. You thought you'd just invite a very large man you don't know over for tea?"*

No reason to start making smart choices now. She waved Luke inside. "Come on in." Tess made the short trip around the corner and into her kitchen to pull a clean mug from the cabinet. "Want something to drink? I've got water, Diet Coke, wine."

No answer.

She waited another second. "Luke?"

"What? Sorry?"

Tess leaned around the kitchen wall.

Luke sat stiff on one end of the couch. Tater had claimed the remainder. He lie sprawled across both cushions, his head resting on Luke's thigh. A self-satisfied grin stretched wide across the dog's face.

Tess hid a smile. "Water, soda, wine? I have a red open."

Luke glanced up, before refocusing on the seventy-pound dog in his lap. "Yeah. Sure. Wine would be great."

She left him as Tater's captive, humming to herself as she slid honey wheat rolls into the oven and set a timer. Bob Marley's *Three Little Birds* played in her mind. She'd always associated the song with lazy, sunny days, bare feet in the grass, and time to spare. She filled two coffee mugs with wine. So why was it in her head now? She re-corked the bottle, still humming the refrain.

It was her soundtrack for happiness. Always had been.

Which didn't make any sense with her life in chaos. She carried their drinks to the living room, where Luke still sat pinned under Tater. But now, the two looked like old friends. Luke rubbing the dog's ears, Tater's eyes closed in doggy bliss.

Bob Marley started another verse.

You're losing it, Oliver.

Luke looked up at her, a slow smile spreading across his face. "One of those for me?" His bayou accent gave his words a gentle lilt, like suede on her skin.

She nodded but, "I didn't think to ask before I poured this. Is it okay—" she paused, shifting her weight. Was it weird for her to ask? Or careless not to? "Is it alright for you to have alcohol with your pain meds?"

"I weaned off this morning." Luke's smile crinkled around his eyes. "Got tired of my chauffeur."

She returned the smile. Parker seemed like a good guy, but maybe one better taken in small doses. Tess handed him his cup and took a seat on the tiny slice of couch Tater hadn't claimed. "And you're still feeling okay? Without the pain meds, I mean?"

"Still a little sore but not nearly as bad as I expected." Luke rested his cup on the couch arm. "What's that smell?"

She glanced at the dog.

Luke took a deep breath in. "It's amazing."

Not Tater then. She hadn't registered the scent of the stew she had simmering on the stove until he'd mentioned it. "Dinner. It's not much. Just some soup and bread." She'd pulled a few tried and true recipes from Gran's repertoire, enjoying the excuse to cook for someone again. Since she'd been living alone, she mostly ate cereal for dinner.

"Well, it smells great." He wrapped both hands around his mug, and the room fell quiet. Too quiet.

Why couldn't she think of anything to say?

She took a deep drink from her cup, while the silence expanded. Until it felt like a balloon about to pop. "So, did you always want to be a pilot?" She blurted out the first thought that floated into her head.

"I sort of fell into it. Joined the military to get out of Louisiana." He shrugged. "But they taught me to how to fly, and it's all I've wanted to do since."

"And now? I mean, do you still—" Tess froze. The question was half out before she'd thought about what she was really asking. Would he ever be able to go back to his normal life? What would he do now? Not exactly first date material. Assuming that's what this was. Her face got even hotter.

If he minded the question, he didn't show it. "I can't imagine doing anything else. Although I didn't think my mother was ever going to forgive me for moving to Atlanta to fly with Parker after I got out of the Navy. Her people have lived in Iberia Parish since the British kicked them out of Acadia in the 18th century. And all my sisters still live on family land."

"All your sisters?" She took another sip of wine. "How many are there?"

"My parents had four girls and then me."

She laughed. “I bet they spoiled you rotten.”

He cocked his head, a mischievous smile on his face. “My father would probably agree with you.” His voice had love in it when he talked about his family. And it made him even sexier than he already was. Which was saying something. His dark hair tousled, his t-shirt just snug enough to show off the muscles underneath. He looked like a snack.

The kitchen timer rang out in a series of beeps.

Tess blinked, the spell broken. Had she been staring at him?

Something like amusement danced in his eyes.

She cleared her throat, setting her wine on the coffee table. She definitely had. “I’ll be right back.” She didn’t look to see if he still watched her as she moved into the kitchen. She could feel his eyes on her.

And she liked it.

Tess didn’t stop herself from humming this time as she piled a tray edge-to-edge with bowls of soup, a basket of bread wrapped in a linen towel, a dish with salted butter, napkins, and spoons. She moved slowly back to the living room, watching to make sure she didn’t slosh either bowl over the edge. Luke dislodged Tater, who jumped down from the couch, sneezed twice, and went directly back to sleep.

She took his spot beside Luke, each of them blowing steam from their bowls.

“Did you always want to be a lawyer?” Luke picked up a spoon from the tray.

“Hardly. I think I only went to law school to feel close to my Dad again. He was a small-town prosecutor for thirty years. That man loved the law.” She pulled a roll from the basket and focused on making sure she covered the entire thing in butter, rather than making eye contact. “He died when I was twelve. Cancer.”

“I’m sorry.”

She could feel that he was watching her again, but she couldn’t meet his gaze.

Why did I tell him that?

She pushed chunks of carrot and celery around her bowl.

"And do you? Love the law, I mean."

Tess tore a piece from her roll. "I don't know. It isn't what I thought it'd be." She put the bread into her mouth, washing it down with a swig of wine. "I left my firm in Chicago because I thought practicing would be better with a fresh start. My own shop. But..." She drank again. "It hasn't really turned out that way." She left out the rest of what she'd left behind — an offer of partnership in the firm she'd worked toward for seven years, a piece-of-shit ex-fiancé, and the upside-down house they'd bought together.

She gave him the abbreviated version of her time in solo law practice, ending with the office fire and her current financial predicament.

"It sounds like you need a stroke of luck." Luke helped himself to a roll.

"You mean like totaling my car?"

"Not exactly what I was thinking." He grimaced. "Did you figure out what happened? Was it a blow out?"

"I don't know anything yet. It was just crazy. Which is probably what the paramedics would say about me." She shrugged.

Luke raised an eyebrow. "What, why?"

She told him everything she could remember about the accident and the phantom policeman. It sounded even less believable every time she said it out loud. She glanced up at him, waiting for him to tell her she must've hit her head or gotten confused in all the chaos of the crash.

"That's bizarre." Luke said, but nothing in his face looked like disbelief.

Tess relaxed. "Damn right it is. One second he was behind my car, looking at the damage. The next, he was just... gone."

She picked up her mug. Empty. His was as well. "I'm out of wine."

"That's okay." He spooned the last of the soup into his mouth and helped her stack their empty dishes on the tray.

She dropped her napkin on top. "But I have bourbon."

"That's even better."

Most of a bottle of Woodford Reserve later, she and Luke sat side by side on the couch. Each cup of the warm, amber liquid had drawn them closer together, until she'd found herself settled in snug against him. Her body a perfect fit to his.

"Is this okay?" He rested his arm on her leg, the bourbon still in his hand.

"Very." She smiled, breathing him in. He smelled of sandalwood and clean laundry.

He shifted, his eyes locked on hers as he closed the last few inches between them. He brushed his lips against hers, his thumb on her chin. His breath mixing with hers. She wound her hand into his hair, pulled him closer, and caught his mouth in a kiss. Gentle, then hungry, a flame lit and growing. She broke away, took the mug from his hand, and put it on the table in an invitation she hoped like hell wasn't subtle.

Luke pulled her to her feet, her body coming flush with his, their mouths joining again in a kiss that she could feel all the way to her toes. They stepped over the dog, still sleeping on the carpet, and stumbled through the house, tugging at each other's clothes, tripping over half-off pant legs. Only to wind up standing beside her bed in their underwear. He was good-looking with clothes on. The man was beautiful with them off, even with the bruises.

She traced the damage from the plane crash with her fingertips. The bruising to his midsection looked painful, a mottled reddish-pink stain that started under his left pectoral and wrapped around the side of his body. "Are you sure this is okay? I don't want to hurt you."

He stepped closer, and she lost her breath. The air between them crackled with possibility, a gap begging to be closed. He lifted her arm and kissed the marks left by her airbag. His mouth moving soft as a whisper against her skin. “I’ll say when if you will.”

Yes.

She meant to answer, but her words disappeared. Lost to sensation, to the trail of pleasure his lips left every place they touched. The inside of her wrist, the crook of her elbow, the sensitive spot at the base of her neck where it met her shoulder.

Heat stirred in her core and spread outward until every inch of her flushed with need. His hands, warm and strong, slid down her bare back to her bottom. He pulled her toward him, her breasts pressed against his chest. Solid, steady. He walked her backward until she leaned against the wall, his weight pressing into her, his hands still exploring her body.

His leg slid between her thighs and she rocked against him, kissing him harder. He tasted of bourbon. His lips firm and hot on hers.

They moved in cadence, their kisses becoming hungrier. But no matter how much of him she had, she wanted more.

CHAPTER 19

September 20, 2018

Moonlight sifted in through Tess's window, just enough for her to make out the ceiling fan's lazy rotations. The longer she watched the blades move, the more it felt like she was the one spinning.

She wiggled her wrist, waiting for her watch to glow to life. All she got was a faint green apple on the screen. Dead. She looked over to the side table, but her alarm clock was missing. Still somewhere under the bed where she'd knocked it the day of the fire. Not that the time mattered all that much. Morning or not, she had to pee.

Tess eased back the covers, careful not to wake Luke. Even though he seemed to be out cold, asleep on his stomach with one hand under his head. In the quiet, she stilled to watch his back, a muscular triangle that tapered from shoulder to waist, moving rhythmically up and down.

He looked younger this way. The hard angles of his face softened by sleep. His dark hair tousled and falling in messy waves over his forehead. She lowered her head back down to the pillow, her face inches from his. Tess slipped her legs back under the blankets and willed herself to go back to sleep. It had been ages since she'd had someone in her bed.

Never mind someone who looked like he did.

But damned if she didn't have to pee.

She slid out of bed and immediately regretted standing up. Not only did it make the spinning worse, her whole body ached. Most of it from the accident. But the other sore parts had been more fun to earn. A smile spread across her face.

Some bad decisions were worth it.

Tess plucked Luke's T-shirt from the floor and pulled it on with some soft terry cloth shorts from the pile of clean laundry on her dresser. The fact that he'd seen her without clothes the night before did not mean she was ready for the walking-around-naked stage. She stumbled to the bathroom and back, head fuzzy, her body half awake. Nothing had ever sounded better than climbing back into her warm bed to sleep for a dozen hours. She glanced at Luke.

Or maybe not sleep.

Something hard connected with her big toe. "Shit." A cell phone skittered from under her discarded bra to the edge of the bedroom rug.

She picked it up and, on her way to put it on the bedside table, tapped the button to check the time. The screen lit up, 4:45 a.m.

Under the glowing numbers, a picture of Luke smiled out at her. He had his arm draped around a beautiful Black woman. A little girl grinned beneath the pair. The girl looked up at them with joy in her eyes, her arms not quite reaching all the way around a giant pumpkin in her lap. The woman had her hand resting on the girl's shoulder, and on her ring finger, an emerald cut diamond glinted in the sun.

She stared at Luke's phone. The image didn't make any sense. Until it did.

He was married.

With a family.

What had his friend Parker said at the hospital when they'd met in the lobby? That he was holding down the fort until Luke's family could get there. She hadn't put two and two together. Hadn't been thinking Parker might mean a wife. A kid.

But now it all made sense. She couldn't breathe. Couldn't think. Except for knowing — beyond any shadow of a doubt — she couldn't be there anymore. Tess sprinted into the living room, and Tater scrambled to his feet.

He trotted after her as she grabbed her phone from the kitchen charger, stuffed her feet into the battered Chucks she'd kicked off by the door, and snapped a leash onto his collar. It didn't matter where they were going as long as it was away. They ran out into darkness broken only by the few working street lamps lining the road. One block, two, four.

How could she have been so stupid? Did she even ask if he was married?

No. She hadn't. She closed her eyes, and her foot missed the edge of a curb. Tess went down hard, the pain as her knee connected with the edge of the sidewalk a resonant shock that radiated up her back. Her phone clattered to the ground a few feet away.

She twisted to sit, pulling her knee into her chest and rocking back and forth on the rough pavement, the lightning bolt of pain in her leg becoming a deep, continuing throb. Tater nosed his way into her lap, and they both eyed the scrape. Should she turn back for home? Wash out the dirt, maybe get some Neosporin?

No.

She'd left Luke in her house. Which was crazy.

What was wrong with her?

She'd run away from him like she did everything thing else when things got hard.

Like Mom did me.

Fresh tears pricked behind her eyes as she blew on the abrasion, waiting for the stinging to calm. No matter how insane leaving Luke in her house had been, there was no way she could face him. Not yet. Not until she knew she could yell at him without tears. He didn't deserve to know she cared that much.

Tess pushed herself back up to her feet and went for the phone. Cracks spider-webbed the surface.

Fuck.

She hit the home button, and the face of the phone lit, but nothing else happened. The keypad didn't respond to her passcode. She held her thumb to the home button.

Come on, come on.

Nothing.

Double-fuck.

She shoved her phone into the pocket of her shorts, looped Tater's leash around one wrist, and limped to a run. It was five in the morning. She had no car, no keys, no wallet, and no plan. In a way, she welcomed the pain pulsing from her knee. It gave her an anchor to something that wasn't the thoughts in her head.

Failure.

She'd done it again. Let someone in who didn't deserve it, opened up to the wrong man.

Her mind flashed to the memory of Jay packing his things. The indignation in his voice as he'd shoved polo shirts into a duffle bag, not even looking at her. "I can't believe you used your fucking magic memory to take my spot. You aren't even supposed to be up for partnership until next year." He yanked the bag's zipper closed. "You knew what this meant to me." The fact that he thought she could do something like that, would do it to him… after everything she'd done for him, the affairs she'd forgiven. One after the next. The summer associate he'd screwed at the firm's annual retreat. The years of her life she'd poured into making their relationship work.

She jogged past darkened houses, then auto repair shops.

Fuck up.

Past fast-food restaurants opening for the day.

Idiot.

She focused on a Waffle House shining bright in the distance, its windows full of truck drivers and drunk people.

Tess counted footfalls as they thumped down Tenth Street to Park Tavern, the bar abandoned and dark. Her lungs burned, and her knee ached. She pushed harder, cutting left through Piedmont

Park. The dew-covered grass soaked her feet through the thin canvas of her sneakers as she punished herself, one step after another. When she neared 14th Street, she knew where to go. Tess changed course again, giving wide berth to the dark figures sleeping on the park's benches. By the time she spotted Gail's duplex, her feet were soaked and her body heavy. Her breath came out in shallow, irregular bursts. Tater didn't seem to be faring much better.

The dog plopped down at the foot of the building's front steps. And Tess did the same, collapsing onto the cold stone. It was too early to wake Gail. The sun had barely risen, a dull gray glow behind the jagged Atlanta skyline.

The building across the street blocked the light and any warmth it might have brought with it. Tess pulled her knees inside the t-shirt and dropped her head. It smelled like him.

She turned her head, burying her face in her arms instead. Why did everything always have to turn out like shit? She sat until her body was stiff, her skin as cold as the step beneath her. She should've known better than to think it could have been different this time.

The rumbling of a passing FedEx van broke the morning silence.

Tater scrambled to his feet. He gave a long series of loud barks, staring down the delivery truck until it turned a corner. The dog looked back to her with a softer woof that sounded like a "you're welcome" and settled back into place. She dropped a hand to his head.

A window rattled open above her. "Tess? Honey, is that you?" Gail called down from the second-floor unit. "What're you doing out there?" She didn't wait for a response. "Hang on, I'm coming down."

Her friend appeared seconds later, barefoot but dressed for work and in full make-up. She lowered herself to sit on the steps. "Are you okay?"

Tess shrugged. "Sort of."

She gave Tess a once-over. "What happened? When I looked out to see what the ruckus was all about, you were the last thing I expected to see."

"I... It's a long story."

"Most of them are." Gail raised an eyebrow. "Why didn't you call me? I would've come let you in."

Tess pulled the broken phone from her pocket, holding it out to show Gail the screen. "It lights up, but that's it. Might as well pitch it." Except, if there was any chance she could have it repaired and save herself the money, she needed to try. She leaned back on the steps and slid it back into her pocket. Then took in her friend's outfit. Pale peach pencil skirt, ivory silk blouse, a chunky gold necklace. Flawless, as always. "Why are you all dressed up so early?"

"I've got an interview. Woke up early with nerves and thought I may as well go ahead and get dressed." Gail shrugged.

"You look great. But you're going to get yourself dirty." Tess stood, pulling Gail to her feet and brushing bits of loose gravel from Gail's behind. One left a faint smudge on the fine weave of the skirt. "Your beautiful outfit. I got it dirty." Tears burned behind Tess's eyes and choked her words. It was a dumb thing to cry over, but it wasn't just the skirt. Not really. She ruined everything.

Gail pulled her into a hug. "Hush now. Silly girl. You two come inside." She urged Tater toward the stairs as she spoke. "You're covered in goosebumps and bruises."

Tess looked down. Where her skin wasn't marked up from the car accident, or scraped from her fall, it was an unhealthy gray blue in the cold morning light. She was a mess. Tess followed Gail back into the building, with Tater crashing up the stairs ahead of them. He sat waiting by the door once they'd caught up.

"You knew right where to go, didn't you, buddy?" Gail scratched the dog's head before digging out her keys to let them in.

The apartment looked exactly the same as it always did, cluttered but clean. A vase of cut hydrangeas sat surrounded by half-burnt candles on the dining table. Silver-framed family photos covered every other surface. Gail settled Tess into a plump leather couch and wrapped a throw blanket around her shoulders that smelled like Opium perfume. The old-fashioned musky scent reminded Tess of playing hide and seek in her mother's closet as a child.

She pushed the memory away before it could take hold.

That had been before.

When her mother still wanted to find her.

Another pang of regret — this one more familiar — sliced her chest. And the tears threatened to come again. She shook it off. Why couldn't she get herself under control? With everything that'd been going on, the fire, her law practice circling the toilet, why was it Luke that seemed to have pushed her over the edge? There was no good reason for her to care as much as she did. Tess blinked hard and glanced at Gail, hoping she hadn't noticed.

But Gail had already turned away. "Let me get you something warm to drink." Her voice trailed off as she disappeared down the hall. Then running water and the clang of a bowl on the floor sent Tater loping off toward the kitchen.

Leave it to Gail to take care of them both.

She carried a coffee mug back to Tess. "My oldest son bought me a fancy new coffeemaker for my birthday."

Tess took the coffee. It helped to have something warm in her hand. "Thank you."

"Want to tell me about it?"

"No." Tess sat for a moment, rolling the hem of her shorts between two fingers. But maybe she needed to. "I went out with Luke. He's the one I told you about, the pilot. It didn't quite go as I'd hoped."

"He can't have been that bad in bed."

Tess choked out a laugh and a splatter of coffee with it. "That is definitely not the problem." She wiped droplets from the sofa and dried her hand on her shorts. "Turns out he's married. With a kid.

And as if that wasn't bad enough, my hangover may actually kill me."

"Men are pigs. Nothing to be done about that. But I can at least help with that hangover." She turned back to the kitchen. "You smell like a distillery," she said as the refrigerator door opened and slammed shut. "I'm out of Bloody Mary mix."

Tess put down her coffee, raised one arm to her nose, and inhaled.

Yikes.

She needed a shower. Bad. And to brush her teeth. Her mouth tasted like bourbon and bad choices.

Gail came back with a frosty blue Powerade in one hand and a laptop in the other. "I've got to run. The interview's at a doctor's office in Alpharetta at 8:00, and I want to make sure I get there a little early." She put the bottle and laptop on the coffee table. "Drink this. Then, get online and order delivery. Something carby."

Tess scrunched up her nose. "Food sounds appalling."

"You'll feel better once you feed the hangover. Do it, and then make yourself at home." Gail tossed the TV remote onto the sofa next to Tess. "Wish me luck!"

Tess stood, pulling her friend into a hug. "All the luck in the world." She tightened her arms. "Thank you for everything."

Gail squeezed back. "It's nothing. I'll be back by in a few hours, and I can drive you home then. Order two of whatever you want for breakfast. I'll eat when I get back." She whistled for Tater as she made for the door. "Come on, Tater. I'll let you out to chase some squirrels on my way. Best thing about this place is the backyard."

Tess ordered a pile of food, snuggled into the blanket, and flipped on a re-run of Forensic Files, trying to pretend she wasn't still thinking about Luke while she nursed the Powerade.

She didn't actually believe all men were pigs. But she seemed to have an uncanny ability to find the ones that were. She'd just finished an episode and the last swig of Powerade when a knock came from the door.

That was fast.

Delivery from Flying Biscuit usually took at least an hour.

She padded to the front door, her bare feet sinking into the carpet.

Thank God.

Gail had been right. Her mind might not feel like food, but the acid in her stomach had other ideas. Tess could almost taste the towering biscuits with apple butter, the grits, topped with fried green tomatoes, bacon, and eggs.

The door had a transom at the top, but it was too high for her to see the delivery person on the other side. "One second." Tess flipped back the deadbolt and swung open the door. "That has to be a land speed record for grits delivery."

A tall man in an orange hazmat suit loomed over her, his face distorted by a plastic shield. He said something she couldn't make out, his words lost to the vacillating whir coming from his suit. He looked like something from a movie. The kind she didn't watch because they gave her nightmares. The world telescoped away from her, nothing certain except that she wanted no part of whatever this was. She gripped the door to swing it closed.

The man stepped over the threshold. "Are you Gail Brubaker?"

Tess's breath stopped in her chest. "Why?"

CHAPTER 20

Mara stepped into a conference room several sizes too small for the meeting it was meant to hold. An oak table sat in the middle, surrounded by leather chairs. Behind them, plastic folding chairs lined the walls in double rows. All were filled.

The CDC team clustered around the head of the table, where a single chair sat open. Jerry had taken the seat to its left and was mid-conversation with Jim Lester, who she recognized from the State Epidemiologist's office. Thomas hovered behind them, a pen tucked behind one ear, head tilted as if to absorb every word Jerry said.

Suck up.

As she nodded hello to the few other faces she recognized, Jerry caught her eye and pointed to the empty chair.

Oh shit.

He'd put her at the head of the table.

Mara swallowed the acid rising in the back of her throat. She took in the crowd as she worked her way to the front of the room. The scientists and military had gravitated to opposite ends of the room, middle school dance style. And none of the faces at the other end of the table looked familiar, or friendly.

Mara moved through the cramped, stuffy room. Then slipped into the empty seat, her throat going tight. She'd prepared for today, had her remarks ready to go, but now that she was here… now that so many faces stared back at—

Jerry rapped his knuckles against the table, and Mara jumped.

"Good morning, everyone. Thank you for coming in so early." Jerry raised his voice, bringing the room to attention. "Let's get started with an update from Dr. Nunez on our progress with contact tracing and what we've learned of the virus so far." He turned to her. "Mara?"

Mara stood, gripping the table to quiet the adrenaline tremors from her hands. "Good morning, everyone. We've identified the virus as a new strain of Marburg hemorrhagic fever. We usually think of Marburg as the gentle sister amongst the other filoviruses, Ebola Sudan and Ebola Zaire. In this case, I'm afraid she is no such thing." Mara found her stride, comfort with the science giving power to her voice. "The new strain, which we've named Marburg Hemphill, based on its first known place of appearance, has an extremely truncated incubation period of 12-24 hours."

A few muted exclamations came from around the room. Jerry spun a hand beneath the table. A gesture she understood to mean she should continue.

Mara pushed forward. "And, unlike other filoviruses, we believe it may be transmitted without physical contact. Like the Ebola Reston strain, we have seen patients contract the illness despite having had no apparent physical contact with an infected patient or material. We believe it is likely airborne and, unlike Reston, fatal to human primates."

The military end of the table erupted in noisy disbelief.

Mara looked at her watch, then at Jerry. "We don't have time for this."

Jerry had one hand pressed to his temple. He shook his head but didn't respond.

A uniformed man with heavy eyebrows and unnaturally black hair raised a hand.

Silence fell.

Instead of addressing her directly, the man turned his attention to her boss. "Jerry, when we agreed the CDC could take lead on this, given Ms. Nunez's discovery of the presumed index patient, I assumed you would be personally involved in the CDC's assessment of the virus. No disrespect to you, Ms. Nunez," he tilted his head in her direction, still not making eye contact, "but the CDC's assessment doesn't seem credible. What is the likelihood Marburg would mutate in so many ways at once and show up in the middle of a major American city?" He paused to look at the officers seated around him, all nodding their agreement. "Why don't you let USAMRIID take an independent look at what we're dealing with?"

Son of a bitch.

That explained the attitude. The United States Army Medical Research Institute of Infectious Diseases was the government's main institution responsible for combatting biological warfare, and he was protecting his turf. Although the implication that she might not recognize the distinctive shape of a filovirus under a microscope was infuriating. Mara forced herself to take a breath before responding.

Jerry got there first. His voice even but his face bright red. "Colonel Fitzgerald, I assure you this assessment is the result of not just Dr. Nunez's work — which I can promise you has been exemplary — but of independent and redundant testing done by other senior members of the CDC staff, including myself." He leaned forward, looking over his glasses at the colonel. "I'm sure I don't need to remind you this is not the first time we've seen a filovirus show up on American soil. We've known for more than twenty years, since Ebola Reston appeared outside D.C., that this was a possibility."

Fitzgerald's already thin lips nearly disappeared in a grimace. "Nonetheless, we would ask you to reconsider the Army's role in managing this outbreak." He softened his tone. "It is, after all, in everyone's interest to have as many qualified minds on this as possible."

Mara chose to ignore what she was pretty sure was another dig at her qualifications and, this time, responded before Jerry could.

"Colonel, we would welcome the Army's input and aid." She didn't look to see what her boss thought of that olive branch. "When we finish our meeting today, I would be happy to personally escort any members of your team with the appropriate clearances to our labs to observe the results of our research in person."

She still couldn't see Fitzgerald's lips, but he stayed silent and nodded for her to continue.

"As I was saying, we have identified an Iranian-American man, Ahmed Baqri, as our likely index case. His wife, Sarah Baqri, was admitted to Grady showing late-stage symptoms of the disease shortly after Mr. Baqri's body was discovered floating in the Hemphill water treatment facility. Mrs. Baqri died of a massive hemorrhage half an hour after being admitted. Several family members and friends of the Baqris, two of Mr. Baqri's co-workers, and six of the patients seen by Mrs. Baqri on her last shift at the hospital, were subsequently admitted with symptoms of the Marburg Hemphill virus. None survived their first night in care. In the last twelve hours, we've seen a secondary wave of infection, including several members of the hospital staff who cared for Mrs. Baqri before her condition was identified and one of the paramedics who responded to the 911 call from her apartment. All are currently under quarantine and receiving treatment, to the extent we can provide it, at Grady Hospital."

She paused to dig yesterday's water bottle out of her bag, and the room devolved into argument and discussion.

The reedy voice of Jim Lester rose above the others. "What we need to decide first is how to handle the water supply issue. I assume the water station was shut down when the body was discovered?" Mara nodded, and he continued. "Will the normal treatment protocols eliminate any threat from the virus? Can the water currently stored in the system be released?"

Mara tried not to let her annoyance at the interruption show on her face. "Unfortunately, we don't know. The Marburg virus can survive at least five days in water. But, as far as I know, it's never been tested to see how much longer it might survive beyond that. And, given this is a new strain, we can't assume it would behave similarly. For the same reason, we can't know for certain the normal treatment protocol would eliminate any trace of the virus. Most likely it would, but, at minimum, a boil water advisory would seem prudent."

This time, the room stayed silent. Jerry swiveled his chair to face Jim's. "For now, it may be best to source the city's water needs from one of the other two treatment facilities. At least until we've been able to do sufficient testing of the water, post-treatment, to know whether there is any risk of infection. And, even then, Mara's suggestion of a boil water advisory would seem wise."

"And what do we tell the public? This is going to cause shortages, city-wide." Jim again.

"Doesn't matter as long as it's not the truth." Fitzgerald said, his voice soft. "If you tell them what's actually going on, you're going to create panic in the streets."

He wasn't wrong, but Mara's chest tightened. What he'd suggested would mean hiding risk from the public, and she particularly hated that they might release the water without warning people of what could be in it. She opened her mouth to say so but caught Jerry's cautionary look just in time. His meaning was clear — this wasn't an issue she was going to win. Especially not here, where Fitzgerald had such a large and influential audience.

This is the same crowd who couldn't even come to consensus on a damn press release.

She snapped her mouth closed, picked up her notes, and continued with her remarks. "Our efforts at contact tracing continue. Having identified the man we believe to be our index patient, we are tracing and isolating all contacts to the furthest extent possible. Unfortunately, because the disease progresses so quickly, we were unable to question most of the earliest victims before they became incapacitated. On the upside—" She swallowed. Was she really about to say that there was a benefit to how fast people were dying?

Like it or not, it was true. "The speed of this strain may help to limit its spread. Unlike previous Marburg strains, and Ebola, which can lie dormant for as many as eighteen days, leading to the connection between that person and the index patient becoming more attenuated, here, infection becomes evident quickly. In most cases, Marburg Hemphill virtually takes over the host's body in as little as twenty-four hours." Mara looked up from her notes, and locked eyes with Fitzgerald.

He cleared his throat. "I understand the 911 call from Ms. Baqri's apartment was made by a recent immigrant to the U.S., an Indian man by the name of Mohammed Patel?"

Mara blinked at the sudden change in topic. "Yes, that's right. But Mr. Patel was not among the infected, which is most interesting because of his report that, in nursing Ms. Baqri prior to her death, he came into physical contact with both her blood and vomit."

"I would agree it is most interesting indeed." Fitzgerald raised his eyebrows. "To recap what we've learned today, our index patient was found, infected with a Level 4 hot agent, floating in one of the city's primary water sources. Our first two patients are Iranian. The man responsible for bringing first responders to Mrs. Baqri's home — subsequently infecting at least one of those medics and multiple caregivers at the hospital, in addition to however many others we've yet to identify — was a recent Muslim immigrant to the U.S. from a small village near the India/Pakistan border. We've identified no travel to countries where Marburg is known to exist by either of our possible index cases. Nor have we identified any contact with monkeys or other wild animals that might explain the source of the infection. And, if your assessment of the virus is correct, this new Marburg strain seems to be a perfect killing machine." He scanned the faces around the table. "Almost like somebody planned it that way."

Her face went hot. "I do not recall saying Mr. Patel was Muslim."

"But he is, is he not?"

"As far as I know, yes. Although, I fail to see how that has any relevance."

The smile on Fitzgerald's face told her she'd walked right into whatever outcome he'd planned for the conversation. "You may be too young to remember the mass salmonella outbreak perpetrated by the Rajneeshee cult in rural Oregon in the mid-eighties. You were likely still in diapers then. But nearly eight hundred people became ill."

"I am aware of the Rajneeshee incident," she answered, her voice tight. The suggestion she might not be was ridiculous. It had been one of the largest biological attacks ever perpetrated on U.S. soil, and she had to assume the statement was calculated to get under her skin. Which made her all the more careful not to react.

"Good. Then you are likely also aware, during its investigation of that attack, the CDC refused to seriously consider the Rajneeshees as the source of the contamination because of their fear it would seem bigoted to do so. The truth wasn't uncovered until a year later, and only then because one of the cult members revealed it. We aren't dealing with salmonella here, Dr. Nunez. The CDC doesn't have a year to figure it out." He looked down his nose at her before he continued. "We need to recognize the facts as they are without concern for how it might look."

The heat in Mara's face spread to her ears. His description of the Rajneeshee incident, while not entirely inaccurate, was completely unfair to the all the dedicated doctors and scientists who had worked the outbreak. "I can assure you the facts are our absolute top priority, and no one at the CDC will allow the race, religion, or nationality of any of the Marburg Hemphill victims, or anyone else connected to the outbreak, to influence our medical or scientific judgment."

"Yes, of course." Fitzgerald dropped his clasped hands into his lap. "My point, Ms. Nunez, is that there appears to be a distinct possibility we are dealing with an act of bioterrorism and, if so, whoever is behind it may not yet be finished."

CHAPTER 21

Sully wiped sweat from his forehead, careful to tuck the handkerchief away before the elevator doors dinged open. Now was not the time to show weakness. He strode into the sky lobby with his shoulders back and his head held high. Unlike the executive floor, which housed Sully's office and the rest of the C-level team, Maeler's public areas were about form, not function. Wide swaths of exorbitant square footage stood open, allowing unobstructed 180-degree views across spotless ivory marble floors to plate glass windows overlooking the city.

A heavy-set woman he recognized as a secretary on one of the lower floors waved to him from the opposite end of the lobby. She wore a loud floral blouse and too much make-up. "This way, Mr. Sullivan. Mr. Bellows and Ms. Clark just arrived. I think everyone's ready to get started."

He followed the woman around a corner toward Maeler's conference rooms and forced himself to relax.

You have a lead on the cure for cancer in your pocket.

Act like it.

He arranged his face to convey the right mixture of confidence and superiority before pushing open the heavy wooden doors of Maeler's main board room.

The company's directors sat around a massive stone conference table. Most had half full coffee cups or water bottles on coasters in front of them. But not Rolland Bell. The board chairman sat at the head of the table with a bottle of Diet Coke gripped in his fist, an empty one on the table in front of him.

Rolland looked up, his beady black eyes holding Sully's gaze a half-second too long before he nodded a hello. Sully tipped his head toward the man as he made his way to the open seat at the opposite end of the table. He shook hands with each of the directors he passed along the way.

Rolland called the meeting to order. The low hum of chatter quieted, and he ran through the opening formalities. The chairman finished by pointing to Sully. "Warren, you're first up on the agenda. I understand you'll be presenting a proposal to again extend funding for the common antigen project?"

"That's right. Good morning, everybody." Sully pulled copies of the rewritten presentation from his bag. He split the stack in two, and handed one half left, the other right. He waited until each person at the table had a packet in hand before he began. "If you'll take a look at the lab results summarized on page two, you'll see that our team has done what we previously only dreamed possible. We've found solid evidence of what may be a common antigen amongst the various diseases known as cancer."

A murmur circled the table, every eye on him. He had them now.

Sully took his time, going through the process followed by Quinones's team and finishing with a summary of what would need to be done next. Just as he'd practiced, he presented the evidence in a dispassionate, concrete way he was sure left no aspect of what they'd discovered in dispute — a cure for cancer might actually be possible.

He finished and sat down, flushed with confidence.

Until he made eye contact with Rolland.

Rolland steepled his fingers, leaning back in his Aeron chair. "We are so grateful to you and your team for your years of dedication to this cause. It is truly in the same spirit of healing that guides all actions of this board and this company as a whole. And I am sure I speak for everyone when I say I am genuinely excited to see what can be done with Dr. Quinones's research. Once we have it patented, I am certain there will be numerous medical organizations dedicated to pursuing this possibility through to its logical end."

Sully sat bolt upright. "We can't put this project on hold while we pursue a patent. That process can take years. We need to keep this in-house so we can move forward with the research while we do what needs to be done to get patent protection." This couldn't be happening. He looked around the room at the other board members. "Denise?" Sully appealed to a woman in a tailored black suit two chairs over. "You know this is game-changing. Maeler. Could. Cure. Cancer."

Denise Petit, one of the few other board members who had, like Sully, spent time in medical practice before joining the board, turned to Rolland. "He's not wrong. This is the first time anyone's found a lead on a common antigen. I know it's not an expense we budgeted for, but if there was ever reason to rethink where we put our resources..."

Heads around the table began to bob, a few here and there.

Sully rested his elbows on the table. "That's exactly right." He looked across the table to a stocky man with watery gray eyes and a drooping face. "David, I know you lost Ellen to breast cancer last year. The value of this research can't be underestimated for other women like Ellen and their families."

Sounds of agreement circled the table.

So close now.

Rolland patted the air in front of him in a calm down gesture. He turned to Sully. "I am correct in reading this report to say that you have not, in fact, identified a common antigen?"

Shit. "That's correct, but— "

Rolland raised a hand again, cutting him off. "Your team has uncovered promising signs, yes. But that's all. You have the promise of a discovery. Not a discovery." Rolland lifted his head and gave a deep sniff, his expression like a pig scenting a truffle. "In my view, the Board cannot approve continued funding for what, even with this auspicious step forward, remains a project with only the slimmest possibility of success. Perhaps if this was the first budget extension. Or if your team had managed to stay within any of the prior budgets given for the project…"

Sully choked back a protest. For once, Rolland wasn't wrong. The project's costs had far outpaced what they'd projected, and Sully had no way to explain why. There were things he couldn't explain. Not now, not to them.

Rolland rubbed the short, round fingers of his right hand across the swell of his belly. "It is, after all, our responsibility to ensure this company remains profitable and delivers the returns our shareholders expect. And, while I'm sure we would benefit from the positive press this promising advancement would yield, the Board simply cannot authorize the additional spending it would take to see if this dream might materialize." He paused, as if considering. "Unless there are other departments willing to offset the expenditure with cuts to their own budgets?" He made a show of looking at each person around the table, giving them an opportunity to volunteer.

As if any of them would.

And, of course, Rolland knew that already.

Son of a bitch.

No one spoke up or looked in his direction. And only David had the decency to look ashamed; he stared out the conference room windows, mouth pressed in a hard line.

"I see." Rolland slid his copy of the presentation to one side. "In that case, I move to eliminate further funding for the common antigen research program. Is there a second?"

"Second." A voice came from Sully's left, but he couldn't focus well enough to tell whose. He knew Rolland's when it followed. "All in favor?"

The ayes took it seven to five.

What a bunch of traitorous, self-serving, backstabbing—

Rolland turned to the next item on the agenda, the slightest hint of a smile on his lips.

Sully couldn't meet the man's eyes. He looked down at the agenda but saw nothing. Every ounce of his energy focused on making sure he didn't give Rolland the satisfaction of even a flicker of emotion while the meeting droned on around him. Only snippets — audits to be completed, best practices, good corporate citizenship — reached him through the static of regret in his head. Taking his company public had been the worst choice of his life. He had thought it would give him more time with Lynn. More time to focus on what mattered.

Knowing what he did now, he'd give every penny back if he could.

Even as the meeting finally wound to a close, Sully forced himself not to bolt from the room. He kept busy gathering his things while the pleasantries and prolonged farewells around him turned to conversations of golf and upcoming tropical vacations. At least he was too far away to hear whatever pompous nonsense Rolland spewed now. The man hadn't moved from the far opposite end of the table, where he was deep in conversation with the secretary in neon floral.

When at least half of the others had gone, Sully let himself get up. He strode toward the exit, careful not to look too hurried.

The secretary caught up as he reached the door. "Mr. Bell asked me to make sure there was nothing you needed."

Sully stepped into the hallway and lengthened his stride. He had no doubt Rolland's request was meant to reinforce what his board room antics had already made clear — this wasn't Sully's company anymore. Not since he'd sold it to the wolves. As if he'd need an escort to find his office, in his building, by a secretary paid out of his company's damn operating budget.

She followed him through the lobby, moving at a half-jog to stay beside him. "Are you sure there's nothing I can get you? A coffee, maybe?"

Sully punched the elevator's call button. "You can have my car brought around." There was no way he could go sit behind his desk and pretend things were okay. He stepped on to the elevator and threw up a hand in dismissal. "That'll be all."

Thank God, Rolland's lackey didn't follow. He left her standing open-mouthed on the other side of the doors as they closed, a smear of fuchsia lipstick on her front teeth.

Who the fuck did Rolland think he was?

Sully was the one who'd built Maeler from a specialty market player, into what was now the single largest pharmaceutical company in America. Rolland Bell didn't have a damn thing to do with any of that. Sully clenched his teeth as he watched the digital display count down the floors. It'd been his hard work. His sacrifices.

Sully barreled through the lobby and out onto the sidewalk, which was thankfully empty. The last thing he wanted right that minute was to be forced to make polite conversation with any of those fuckers who had voted against him. Frustration bubbled inside him, like he was a shaken soda, his composure under pressure and ready to burst.

A shiny black town car pulled to the curb, and Sully collapsed into the back seat, pulling his tie loose at his neck. "Take me home, please, Matthew." He tossed his briefcase onto the other side of the bench seat. It fell over, spilling a jumble of paper, breath mints, and both his cell phones onto the seat and floor. He made no move to retrieve it.

The car slid into traffic. And Sully stared out the window, where the frenzied streets of D.C.'s central business district faded into the wealthy restraint of Georgetown. His mind calmed along with the scenery. Hadn't Quinones's group already done what he needed them to do? It might be slightly more complicated to finish things now. He might have to be a little more creative with how he sourced the funding. But that was hardly a first for him. Sully loosened his tie more and relaxed back into the seat. Let Rolland think he'd won. Sully hadn't gotten where he was by giving up, and he wasn't going to start now.

He gathered his things from the floor of the town car's backseat. As he cleaned carpet lint from the face of his smartphone, a CNN alert popped up on the screen, "10th Patient Dies in Atlanta Viral Outbreak." Sully's mouth went dry.

He clicked through to the article. "Oh no. No, no, no." Forty people sick. Ten confirmed dead from an outbreak of the Marburg virus in a major American city. Sweat broke out on his forehead. Sully scrolled down through the rest, skimming details of the disease, a brief history of previous international outbreaks, along with instructions to the public on what to do if they suspected they, or someone they knew, might be infected.

So much information and none of it what he needed to know. How far had the disease spread? He scrolled until he found an answer.

"An anonymous source close to the CDC investigation tells CNN the CDC's request for infected persons to quarantine at home has not been successful in stopping the spread of the virus. While most of the known infected reside in the Edgewood neighborhood of Atlanta, our source indicates the virus is likely to spread to adjacent neighborhoods before it can be contained. Additional unconfirmed cases have already been reported in other in-town areas, including Midtown, the Virginia Highlands, and as far north as Smyrna."

Sully dropped the phone to his lap.

God help them all.

CHAPTER 22

Tess clambered into the back of the ambulance and stopped, not sure what to do next. A metal gurney crisscrossed with black straps sat in the middle. She'd ridden to the hospital on one just like it the day before yesterday, but that was after a car accident. Not… whatever this was. She didn't need an ambulance. Or a gurney.

She needed to understand what the hell was going on.

Tess turned back to where Gail and the orange-suited man waited on the sidewalk. "Could you at least tell us—"

"Sit there, please." The man indicated a jump seat under a small window looking into the ambulance's driver's cabin.

Gail gave her a short nod.

Tess swallowed the rest of her question as she edged past the gurney and buckled in. Everything about the doctor's collection of her and Gail from the apartment had been done with rapid efficiency. His words clipped, his face tight behind his respirator, his movements so precise they could have been choreographed. Maybe now wasn't the time for questions.

Tess adjusted the face mask he had given her. But, no matter how she shifted it on her face, she still couldn't draw a full breath through the thick material covering her nose and mouth.

The doctor settled Gail into the furthest of two other seats along the outside wall, facing in toward the gurney. "Remember to keep at least six feet of distance between you." He looked to Tess, then Gail, waiting until they both nodded before he thunked the back door closed. Almost immediately, the whoop, whoop-whoop of a police car sounded from in front of the ambulance.

"What now?" Tess depressed the latch of her safety belt and stood to peer through the small window above her head. A police car pulled in front of them. "We have an escort." A softer thunk came from the front of the ambulance, and it jerked forward. Tess stumbled, catching herself on the gurney. She dropped back into her seat, fumbling for the loose ends of the seatbelt. "They're not wasting any time, are they?"

She wrapped her arms around her chest, rubbing the cold from her arms. At least they weren't running the siren.

"There's one back here, too." Gail stared through the back glass, where another cruiser pulled away from the curb and into place behind the ambulance. Its lights and sirens started up, and a heartbeat later, the ambulance followed suit.

Crap.

"Do you have any idea what's going on? Or why the CDC would be looking for you?" Tess raised her voice to be heard over the noise but kept her tone as even as she could. She didn't want it to sound like an accusation.

"You know what I know." Gail tossed up her hands. "I was on my way to the interview, and some doctor called just as I turned onto Peachtree. Said something about an infectious agent. That I should go straight home. I ran through a red light and nearly off the damn road. You know there are traffic cameras all through there. I'm getting a ticket for sure."

"That's what you're worried about?" Not why the doctor would be looking for her or why the hell they would need to put on a spacesuit first. Tess smiled at her friend. But, of course, it was hidden by her mask, and Gail didn't look amused. Tess couldn't blame her. "What the hell is an infectious agent?"

Gail lifted one shoulder, and the lines around her eyes tightened. "I don't know. But I don't think it's the flu." She looked away.

Tess rubbed at her arms again, but the cold had settled in to stay. She sucked in another suffocated breath, and they rode the rest of the way in silence, both staring through the rear glass at the cars lining the side of the road. Mini-vans, commuters, and delivery trucks all pulled off to the right to make room for their motorcade. Tess watched until the world outside the window became a blur.

The flu might not be that far-fetched. Not the normal kind, but maybe some new bird flu? The doctor's hazmat suit had made her think chemical spill or even terrorist attack at first.

God knew what people were capable of these days.

But that didn't make sense — not with the CDC there. They only handled diseases. Really, really bad ones. Despite the chill under her skin, a sheen of nervous sweat coated her forehead and the back of her neck.

The ambulance arrived at Grady Hospital to a flurry of activity. More orange-suited doctors waited with wheelchairs, while other figures in different protective gear, white with yellow plastic aprons and smaller respirators, worked setting up what looked like a perimeter. They adjusted barricades that had been erected across the sidewalks to either side of the entrance.

This doesn't look like the flu.

Tess gripped the edges of her jump seat, her nails biting down into the vinyl.

This looks like fucking Ebola.

. . .

The same doctor who'd loaded them into the ambulance rolled Tess's wheelchair down a long hallway lined with patients. Each one faced in toward the hall and wore a thick paper mask identical to her own. Some stared straight ahead, others had their eyes closed in what looked like prayer. She scanned their faces but recognized no one.

Where the hell had they taken Gail?

Somewhere between realizing she had none of the forms of identification the hospital needed and pondering whether they could just take a kidney out while she was there — which was the only way she was going to be able to cover the costs of her second ER visit in as many days — Tess had lost sight of her friend.

And the longer she was surrounded by strangers, the harder it got to keep her shit together. The place reeked with the sour bleached smell of sickness. Fluorescent lights flickered overhead. And her anxiety simmered, threatening to boil over. She shifted in the chair, unable to sit still even though she had nowhere to go and nothing to do but wait.

Worse, she still had no idea what the fuck was going on.

The doctor parked her wheelchair against the wall, six feet from the next patient. "Give me one second. I'll be right back." He hustled to a nursing station, where a group of what she guessed was medical staff gathered around a waist-high counter. Doctors, maybe nurses, or orderlies? Except by height or weight, the orange-suited figures were impossible to distinguish one from another.

This is insane.

She needed to borrow someone's phone so she could call Gran. And what about Tater? He was still out in Gail's backyard. How long would he be okay out there? She hadn't even had a chance to feed him that morning.

One of the orange suited figures approached a young Black man whose wheelchair was parked down from hers on the opposite wall. The figure crouched beside the patient, and the two spoke briefly. The patient nodded along, then stilled in his chair. They rolled past Tess in silence. The man's eyes bounced from one side of the hall to the other, but landed on nothing, his body locked in place. They travelled the full length of the hall, past the nursing station, and out of view.

Tess leaned forward, straining to see where they went. But he was gone.

The fear welling inside her went to a full roiling boil, and her skin went clammy again. If she didn't already have whatever disease this was, this is where she'd catch it. Didn't that happen all the time? People came in with a sprained ankle and got hepatitis from a doorknob on the way out. And what if it didn't matter what she touched? What if she could get it just by breathing? She adjusted her mask, feeling for gaps around the edges as her breath came fast and shallow.

A squeak of tires on linoleum, and she turned.

Gail.

One of the medical staff wheeled her chair to the wall a few feet from Tess's, and some of the tension leaked from her shoulders.

Thank God.

"Hey, girlfriend." Gail's voice was even, but she had a white-knuckle grip on the purse in her lap.

"There you are." Tess dropped her hand from her mask, finally taking in a full breath. "Have they told you what the hell is going on yet?"

Gail shook her head.

"I think I can help with that." The doctor who'd gathered them from Gail's house stepped back from the nursing station, now with a tablet in hand. "Sorry not to have given you more details when we picked you up. Our priority this morning was to get you and the others to a secure area with as little delay as possible. You're here because there is a chance you may have been exposed to the Marburg virus, which is a highly contagious hemorrhagic fever." He looked from her to Gail and back. "We're bringing in anyone with possible exposure for testing."

Tess blanched. She didn't know what Marburg was, but she knew from watching TV "hemorrhagic" meant something was going to bleed.

Fuck.

The doctor focused on Tess. "We believe you may have come into contact with an infected person during a recent visit you made here to the hospital. A nurse, named Sarah Baqri." He tucked the tablet against his chest. "Do you recall speaking with her?"

"I, maybe. I don't know. I've been in twice this week, first to visit a… friend. And then after a car accident." She tipped her head toward the bruising on her arms.

The doctor followed her gaze and nodded. "This would have been on your first visit, when you came to see a patient named Lucas Broussard?"

"Okay." Damn if Luke wasn't the gift that kept on giving. Tess leaned back in the wheelchair, trying to remember who she'd talked to besides Luke and his friend. "I spoke to someone at the front desk. And I didn't catch her name, but there was a nurse in the hall outside Luke's room. I asked her for directions."

"Did you have any physical contact with the nurse?"

Why would they have had physical contact? She shook her head. It wasn't like she went around hugging random strangers. The nurse had come up as Tess was looking for Luke's room, and she'd seemed sweet, approachable. They'd talked and, "I gave her a lozenge. From my bag. She was coughing."

Holy shit.

Tess wrapped her arms around her middle.

It'd never occurred to her that the nurse's cough could've been more than a cold or allergies. Not even in a hospital, where she knew people could be really, truly sick. She hadn't worried about catching anything herself. Especially not from a nurse.

But now, in the matter of only a few days…

Every sniffle or stifled cough seemed like a threat.

"I understand." The doctor's face tightened behind his mask. "And you also spent time with Mr. Broussard after his release?"

Spent time with.

Tess cringed. "Yes, that's right."

Did she need to tell him they'd slept together? It might matter. You could obviously catch things that way. This conversation was making her want to vomit. "Is he here somewhere?"

"All I can tell you is that we're bringing in everyone with whom Ms. Baqri had contact. And anyone who had immediate contact with them. You're here because you had contact with Ms. Baqri and Mr. Broussard."

She winced.

She'd been exposed twice. She'd be twice as likely to be infected.

Gail crossed her arms over her chest. "But that doesn't make any sense. You didn't come for Tess. You came to my house, looking for me."

The doctor nodded. "You were listed as Ms. Oliver's emergency contact in the discharge paperwork from her accident. That she was at your house when we arrived was a stroke of luck."

Tess raised her eyebrows.

That's one weird-ass interpretation of luck.

He turned to Tess. "The team that went to your house..." He paused and cleared his throat. "Didn't find you. Nor were they able to reach you on the phone number the hospital had on file."

Heat rushed to her face. Her mind conjured an image of Luke awaking in her house to a team of doctors in hazmat suits with her gone, along with his shirt. If the whole situation weren't so terrifying — so completely screwed up — it would be funny.

"Oh my God." The rest of what the doctor said hit her, and her chest constricted. Gail was only there because of her.

She cringed at her friend, but Gail had her attention focused entirely on the doctor. "So, what happens now?"

"One of us will do a detailed interview with you to establish who you've had contact with, where you've gone in the last few days, and then we'll get you checked out."

"What does that mean? Checked out?" Gail fiddled with the clasp on her handbag. The metal made a faint click, click-click as she opened and closed the fastener without seeming to notice.

"Just a simple test. We're fortunate this strain of Marburg is detectable using the antibody tests the CDC already developed for prior strains. And that we're seeing reliable results much earlier than we'd see with those other strains. Which means we can do it today. We'll draw some blood, test it for the relevant antibodies, and, if you're cleared, you'll be free to go home." He delivered the speech as if he'd said the same thing a dozen times before, finishing with the crinkle of a smile around his eyes.

"If we're cleared?" Tess glanced at Gail, then back to the doctor. "And if we're not?"

Another click, click-click of Gail's purse clasp.

The doctor shifted on his feet. "You'll be given the very best treatment we have available."

Tess pressed her eyes closed.

Something about that didn't sound reassuring.

▪ ▪ ▪

Tess shifted in the wheelchair. In the time they'd been waiting to have blood drawn, the crowd around them had grown. She'd counted seven people who'd been wheeled away, but each spot was then almost immediately taken by a new face. Some waited in desk chairs, a few sat cross-legged in the floor. Like the hospital was already running out of supplies. And every minute they waited took her deeper down the rabbit hole of what she should've done differently. She pulled a loose thread on the blanket one of the nurses had given her. If she hadn't forced the memory of the Ashbys' document… If she hadn't gone off on some half-baked plan to find a man she didn't know…

They wouldn't be here.

Gail wouldn't be here.

Nothing good ever comes from using the memories.

"I'm so sorry I got us into this." Tess stared down at her lap, opening and closing her ice cold fingers. "This is all my fault."

Gail said nothing.

Tess steeled herself and finally looked at her friend, but Gail's attention was fixed on something behind her. Tess twisted around in her chair. One of the staff wheeled a gurney down the hall. It had a bulky, rectangular bag on top.

A body bag.

Tess's breath caught in her throat.

The bag was white at the front, back, and along the top but a clear, rigid plastic on the sides. In the few seconds it took to pass in front of her, Tess had an unobstructed view of the man inside. Or what was left of him. Blood smeared his swollen, bruised face, and something black had soaked his hospital gown. A dribble of the same black liquid ran from his mouth, which hung slack and open in death. Activity on the hall stopped, everyone frozen in place as they watched the gurney roll past. A terrible rotten smell of still wet blood and human waste followed.

Tess clasped her hands over her nose and mouth, smashing the paper mask to her face. They were all going to die. She'd wind up encased in one of those bags, airless and alone. Covered in her own blood and filth.

Another orange-suited figure, a tall thin man, hurried from an office, stopping the guy pushing the gurney near the elevator. He leaned over the smaller figure and punctuated whatever he was saying by repeatedly jabbing the air with one finger. Even under the suit, his body language said "you fucked up, bad, buddy." He swiped a pass card at the elevator and stood cross-armed until both the gurney and offender were on board with the doors closed. Then looked up and around the room, where every set of eyes still fixed on him.

They all waited for something. Reassurance? An explanation?

The tall man turned without a word and walked into the room nearest the elevators. Tess stared at the door as it closed behind him.

A young man midway down the hall started to cry.

"It'll be okay." Gail wheeled herself closer, reaching for Tess's hand.

Tess shifted away, a hard lump in her throat as she tried to speak. "No touching, remember?"

Gail made a face.

"She's right." A dark-haired woman in the wheelchair to the other side of Tess's spoke up. "You need to keep as much space between yourself and other people as possible." The woman wore scrubs, which meant she probably knew more than Tess did.

Even if she was a little too free with her unsolicited advice.

Tess smoothed the irritation from her face. The woman was only trying to help. "Thanks." Tess nodded, not trusting herself to put together a response any more coherent than that.

Gail mumbled under her breath, so low Tess almost couldn't hear it through the mask. "If you've got it, I've got it."

"Seriously?" She blinked at her friend.

Gail shrugged. "At least we'll be lepers together."

Tess barked out a laugh. Several heads turned in her direction, but she ignored them, loving that — even now — Gail was as unflappable as ever.

Another member of the medical staff, this one wearing a respirator and rubber apron, approached. "Ms. Brubaker?"

"That's me." Gail raised a hand.

"Let's go get you taken care of."

Tess watched her friend disappear down the hall again and blinked back the tears she'd fought all morning. She was surrounded by people and activity. Alarms sounding from somewhere nearby. The medical staff buzzing from one end of the hall to the other, wheeling patients in to see the phlebotomist and back out again. But, without Gail, she was completely alone. Tess tucked her hands under her arms, holding them tight to her body as she rocked back and forth in the chair.

The woman beside her spoke up again, her voice breaking through a high-pitched buzz of adrenaline in Tess's ears. "Try not to worry too much. The doctors handling this outbreak are the best in the world."

Outbreak.

Is that what this was? Even as she had the thought, the answer was obvious, whether she wanted to accept it or not.

"I'm sure you're right," Tess finally answered, but she couldn't stop thinking about what came next. What the blood test might show. What it might mean for her. For Gail. For Luke. He had to be here somewhere, too.

Maybe in a room already?

She pulled her knees up into the chair, wrapping her arms around them.

He could already be in a white bag.

A new figure in orange appeared at the end of the hall. Shorter than any of the others, with dark hair peeking from beneath her hood and an unmistakable air of authority. The woman scanned the crowd, her gaze stopping on Tess.

The woman strode directly for her.

Holy crap.

That can't be good.

She breezed past, stopping at the dark-haired woman next to her. "Emmy, thank God. How did you wind up here?" The doctor disengaged the woman's wheelchair lock.

"Where have you been? And why did they move us here? What did Jerry say? They didn't put Thomas in charge, did they?" The woman she'd called Emmy gestured with every thought, asking questions she didn't wait long enough to be answered.

"It's good to see you, too." The doctor said as they moved toward the elevators, her voice holding a smile. "Let's get you into a room, and then we'll chat."

Emmy doubled over, coughing. A wet, phlegmy wheeze that sounded like it came from her toes. The chair jerked to a halt, Emmy still coughing, while the doctor wilted into herself.

The gesture said everything.

Emmy had it.

CHAPTER 23

Martin pulled his hoodie tighter against the cold. As the sun dropped lower in the sky, the temperature went with it. Most of the people gathered outside Grady Hospital clutched sweatshirts or jackets around their shoulders, their eyes trained on a preacher wearing a tie the color of orange sherbet. The elderly black man took his time climbing onto a makeshift platform, a bullhorn in one hand and a Bible in the other.

He lifted the bullhorn to his mouth. "Children," he waited for the noise of the crowd to dim. "We are here to support our brothers and sisters who are afflicted with this wretched illness." He paused again, closing his eyes and lifting his Bible toward the sky. "And to thank God for the brave doctors and nurses working tirelessly to see us through this dark time."

Martin half-listened as he made his way through the crowd, being careful to keep his face turned away from the row of television cameras set up on the crowd's perimeter. It didn't take long for the sermon to turn toward the dangers of living outside God's will and the apocalypse to come.

He's not wrong.

Martin glanced back up at the man, noting the dark stains where his dress shirt met his skin. Sweating despite the growing chill in the air. Already infected. A martyr without even knowing it.

Martin kept moving. The narrow, paved area outside the hospital's front entrance barely held the growing crowd. They stood hemmed in between barricades, the busy street running alongside the main hospital building, and the parking deck. Some were silent in vigil or held phones raised, filming the crowd. Others pushed forward, trying to catch the attention of the police officers who were stationed every few yards on the other side of the perimeter. A man with pock-marked skin yelled over the top of the barricade nearest Martin. "Where can I ask about my sister? Officer?"

A policeman on the other side pointed overhead to a digital sign that reminded Martin of the ones used to announce road closures or festival parking. It read, "Stay Back a Minimum of 25 Feet from Hospital Entrance" and, at the bottom, instructed people to call the Marburg Outbreak Hotline for information or to report suspected infection. The man shook his head and started yelling again, but Martin tuned him out.

He popped the rubber band on his wrist as he slid between spectators, careful not to touch anyone. There was no room for error, not after what happened last time. He edged through the crowd until it thinned enough to cut a more direct path to the side entrance of the hospital. The doors were still well out of reach — barricades extended all the way across the hospital's front elevation to the ambulance check point to his right. But it did give him a direct view of the area where discharged patients were leaving the hospital. Some obviously suffered from unrelated ailments or injuries. One wore a cast on his lower leg. A woman in a wheelchair clutched a swaddled baby to her chest. He suspected others were people who had tested negative for the Marburg Hemphill virus. He couldn't be sure. But they looked uninjured and very, very relieved.

The only person he'd seen come out of the front entrance was a short, dark-haired woman in full protective gear. She had emerged twice and, with the help of the pastor's bullhorn, made impassioned pleas for the crowd to disperse.

Instead more gathered.

Won't be long until the police break up the crowd by force.

And that couldn't happen.

Not until he did what he needed to do.

CHAPTER 24

Mara stepped out of Tess Oliver's room. And, for once, no staff waited for her on the other side of the patient's door.

Thank God.

All their people were stretched thin. Many had never worked an outbreak before, much less one involving a Level 4 hot agent, and she'd spent much of her day answering their questions. When she wasn't trying to pull the hospital administration's head out of its ass.

She needed a chance to sit and think. Could the virus have mutated? Or were they just seeing some sort of immunity emerging?

Her first admission to quarantine that morning — a fifteen-year-old boy — seemed to have contracted Marburg by sharing an elevator with someone who shouldn't have been contagious. There'd never been a filovirus transmittable during the incubation stage before. And then, there were other patients, like Ms. Oliver. If what she'd told Mara was true, she had direct, physical contact with Sarah Baqri when the nurse was already exhibiting clear symptoms of the disease. And yet, Tess Oliver hadn't contracted it. The same was true for several patients Ms. Baqri saw on her final shift.

Why did Emmy get it and not them?

Mara shook her head, trying to dislodge the thought she knew she shouldn't be having. Her responsibility wasn't just to Emmy. She looked at the wall clock anyway, doing the calculation before she could stop herself. Given when Emmy had first shown signs of infection, she had less than thirty-six hours before the disease went into its final stages. Nausea swirled up through her gut, and she pushed it away. The team working with Emmy was exceptional. They would do everything they could for her. Hovering behind them, double-checking all the charts, wasn't going to help anyone.

Not that she hadn't tried.

Mierda.

Mara navigated a maze of hospital corridors back to the CDC's make-shift workroom. She shoved open the office door, and it bounced off the wall with a bang. She flinched, looking around to make sure no one had noticed. The medical staff and patients looked to her for answers. To set the tone for their entire operation. She couldn't seem like she was anything other than perfectly capable and in control.

She eased the door shut behind her, blocking out the hospital's constant noise of beeps, alarms, and television sets leaking from patient rooms along the hall. What she needed was a comprehensive analysis of everyone who'd been exposed without contracting the illness — sex, age, diet, exercise, lifestyle, profession, hobbies. She logged onto the computer.

There had to be a pattern in there somewhere. Mara scrolled through contact tracing interview notes and lab data files. What she wouldn't give for the time to do a proper epidemiological investigation. The luxury of a team, of time, seemed unimaginable at this point. She stopped, the cursor hovering above a link to the compiled video recording of Ms. Baqri's last shift at the hospital. It was the closest thing they had to an interview. The nurse, and her entire immediate family, had died before any of them could be questioned. It was a long shot, but it might show why certain other people — like Tess Oliver — hadn't gotten sick.

Perhaps they'd come close but had no actual physical contact?

Mara opened the file and fast forwarded through a mishmash of footage, different clips taken from various cameras as Ms. Baqri moved through the hospital, going about her day. In the ER, on her break, at a nursing station. Mara sat, staring at the screen, until her neck was stiff.

Come on. It has to be here.

A clock showing the time covered by each clip spooled along at the bottom right of the screen. A racing countdown to the end of the nurse's shift, and still she'd found nothing.

Mara closed her eyes, rolling them back and forth to alleviate the sticky dryness that came with too little sleep. It didn't help. She pried them open.

Something flashed on screen.

Was that—

She smacked the rewind button and replayed the footage at normal speed. Sarah Baqri walked down a hospital corridor, greeting Ms. Oliver as she came from the opposite direction. The video had no sound, but Mara read an "Excuse me" on Ms. Oliver's lips. Ms. Baqri had her back to the camera, so Mara couldn't see the reply. She watched the woman's head move in a gentle bob. Ms. Baqri talking. Then, the nurse jerked, her body hunching forward in a series of coughs. Ms. Oliver dug through her bag and pulled out what looked like a peppermint — the lozenge she mentioned — handing it to the nurse while absently wiping at her arm with the other hand.

Mara paused the video, rewound, then watched the gesture again. Tess Oliver wiping saliva hot with the virus from her skin. Ms. Baqri had coughed directly on her. With the increased virulency of the Marburg Hemphill strain, that amount of spittle likely contained as many as a million particles of virus. And yet, here Ms. Oliver was. Her blood free of any of the antibodies that would be present with infection.

How?

If this had been the only instance Mara had seen of seemingly disparate virulency, she might have attributed it to happenstance. Sometimes people got lucky. When it came to filoviruses, more often, they didn't. But it could happen. Only this wasn't isolated. They'd identified seven others so far who hadn't contracted Marburg despite reporting contact, sometimes sustained contact, with an infected person. None of them had Marburg antibodies. She could see there was a transmission pattern. She just couldn't see what it was, beyond the fact that those patients who hadn't contracted the disease all appeared to be Caucasian. And there was no reason that should matter. Diseases didn't work that way.

Mara jotted a list of tests on a pad left abandoned by one of her coworkers at the shared desk. The lab had taken enough blood from Ms. Oliver to do all of them. There was no reason to keep her in the hospital. But her gut said otherwise.

What if I'm missing something?

She leaned back in the chair and tossed the ink pen on the desk. She was being ridiculous. She couldn't let her fear for Emmy — the crushing desire to do something, anything, helpful — color her judgment. It would be safer for Tess Oliver if she went home.

A buzzing came from the desk drawer to her right. Mara fished out the phone she'd stowed there earlier that day. Or was it the day before?

Who could tell anymore?

She connected the call.

"Mara, it's Harriet Chou at Cedars-Sinai. I think we've got your bug here, too."

Mara gripped the phone so hard it hurt.

If the virus was already on the west coast, there'd be no stopping it.

. . .

Mara hung up with Harriet and immediately dialed Jerry.

He answered on the first ring. "You've got perfect timing."

He might not think so once he heard what she had to say. Mara cleared her throat. "Hi, listen I just got a call—"

"Colonel Fitzgerald is here with me. I'm putting you on speaker phone."

"Before you do—" Mara said, but not quickly enough.

"Ms. Nunez, I assume you're calling with an update of things there on the ground?" Fitzgerald's voice was nasal and flat.

Mara pushed out a breath.

Dios dame paciencia. Don't be petty, let it go.

"It's Dr. Nunez." So much for letting it go. Mara pushed forward before the man could respond. "I just received a call from Cedars-Sinai. They think they may have a Marburg Hemphill patient in their ER."

A heavy silence filled the line.

Mara went on. "I've confirmed they've implemented proper containment measures, both as to the patient and each of the hospital doctors and staff with whom she had contact before the nature of her condition was suspected. Harriet Chou runs the show there — Jerry, I think you know Harriet from her work with the AMA — she'll do whatever needs to be done until we can get there."

The line went silent again.

They muted it.

The sons of bitches were discussing what to do without her. Like she was a child put to bed early so the grown-ups could talk. Mara clenched her jaw and pulled the list of tests to run back in front of her. Jerry and Fitzgerald could only waste her time if she let them. She made it through the list twice before Jerry's voice came back. "We'll get Thomas's team out to LA. You just focus on what we're dealing with here. I assume you've uploaded all your data to the system? I'll want to make sure I have a full picture going forward."

Her throat constricted. "Yes, sir." She'd been waiting for the other shoe to drop since news of the outbreak leaked, and here it was. Jerry had assumed control of the national response, and she was back to being just another pair of boots on the ground.

She'd wanted to be back in the field. Hated her promotion to management. But now that it had been effectively taken away…

It felt like crap.

"What update do you have for us on Atlanta, Doctor Nunez?" Fitzgerald put an emphasis on the word "doctor" that set her teeth on edge.

Asshole.

There was no way he was going to take her theories on disparate transmission seriously. Especially not when she wasn't ready to articulate them clearly yet.

Even if she could, he wasn't going to give it real consideration coming from her.

She'd wait to talk to Jerry alone, and, assuming he agreed with her that something meaningful could be learned from further studying the transmission patterns, let him raise the issue. Mara forced a respect she didn't feel into her tone. "We have seventy-one dead and, as of an hour ago, nineteen in quarantine. Those numbers are constantly in flux, as new admissions and fatalities occur." She waited for questions before she continued, but none came. "The mobile lab is set up and functioning well. We've taken over the old J wing of the hospital. Initially, we believed it might be necessary to retrofit additional space so that we could keep up with the flow of patients. But given the…" She stopped, choosing her words carefully before she continued. "The speed with which the disease progresses means no additional space will be required." An image of Emmy, her face swollen and purple with bruising, intruded into Mara's thoughts.

"Mara? Did we lose you?"

"Sorry about that. Still here." She forced herself to think only about what needed to be done. Just the facts. Just the job. "The re-routing of non-viral incoming patients to other area hospitals has been as seamless as we could have hoped. That along with our ability to test so early for this strain — which means a much shorter quarantine period — and we've effectively alleviated any overcrowding issues we might otherwise have had. I know we had a lot of resistance to closing the city's only Level 1 trauma center, but it was the right move. No good was going to come from bringing more patients into a hot zone."

She braced herself for a fight before continuing. "I was also hoping to revisit the issue of whether the entire hospital should be quarantined. Grady has nearly a thousand beds. And while we've taken every step to prevent it, any one of those patients could carry the virus out of the hospital with them."

"Given recent events, USAMRIID agrees," Fitzgerald responded.

Mara blinked at his acquiescence. She'd tried before to get the military side of the team to agree to a hospital-wide quarantine and been shot down. Fitzgerald's voice had been the loudest amongst the group, arguing that forcing non-Marburg patients to stay in the hospital would cause too much panic and backlash in the community.

"Thank you, Colonel. This decision will save lives."

Jerry cleared his throat. "What else do you need, Mara?"

No question about that. "What we need most now is medical staff reinforcements. We haven't had anyone walk off the job yet, but this is extremely stressful work, and many of the staff have been pulling double or even triple shifts to keep up. If we don't get support soon, we will start to lose people. Or, worse, they'll get careless."

"Understood. Ideally we could source both professional and support staff from some of the neighboring— " A murmur of indistinct voices in the background cut Jerry short. The sounds of chairs scraping back and a door closing followed. "Mara, hang on one second." The line went silent.

She wiggled the computer mouse, waiting for the screen to come alive so she could check the time. She'd wasted another half hour while the clock kept running for Emmy.

And I'm on fucking hold.

She scrubbed her hands through her hair, the chair swiveling away from the desk. Her gaze settled on a battered calendar hanging askew on the wall. Above a scribbled mess of last month's dates, a calico kitten dangled from a clothesline above the words "Hang in there" in cheery neon-yellow cursive.

Suck it, cat.

She spun her chair back to the desk, as Jerry's voice came back over the phone. "I'm back. Just me now. Sorry about that. I wouldn't have taken the call with Fitzgerald here if I'd known why you were calling." He sighed. "Now we'll have to get military buy-in every step of the way."

"He left?" She tried to keep the incredulity from her voice but failed.

"Summoned to the White House. A command performance, it sounds like."

"They'd be better off with you there." Fitzgerald had been nothing but a thorn in the CDC's side since the outbreak began days before. Fighting them at every turn, even to the point of insisting that the outbreak response be handled from this hospital, across town from all their resources at the CDC.

God knows what he'll convince the President to do next.

"Ah, maybe." After a pause, Jerry continued, "Mara, this is highly confidential, but you should know that you may be stuck there a while."

"I assumed as much, given the quarantine. Everyone at the hospital will be."

"No, that's not what I mean. The White House is calling the outbreak an act of bio-terrorism." He stopped and took a deep breath before he continued, his voice lower. “There’s talk of cordoning off the entire city.”

“But they’d only do that if they thought…” Things began to fall into place, one after the other, like bodies into a mass grave. The sudden flood of antibody tests. Nurses whispering in the hallways. Lighter than what should-be hospital security. And now Fitzgerald’s sudden acceptance of a hospital quarantine. “Shit, Jerry.”

“I know.”

The virus was already loose in the city.

CHAPTER 25

The room hadn't been made for two beds. They sat against opposite walls, the foot of one extending past the other, like snaggleteeth in a clenched jaw. Tess sat on the one she'd been assigned, cheap hospital sheets crinkling beneath her as she pressed the phone to her ear. "I'm fine. I promise."

"I must have tried to call you a dozen times." Gran's tone struck an even balance between anxiety and annoyance.

"I'm sorry I made you worry. My cell's broken, and I didn't have a way to reach you until now." She glanced up at her hospital roommate. Rachel sat on the other bed leafing through a battered copy of Us Weekly. Tess adjusted the phone. "They say I'm in the clear. They're gonna release me any minute."

Rachel gave an exaggerated eye roll and tucked a strand of dark, pink-tipped hair behind an ear. She'd been cleared that morning. But when they wheeled Tess into the room at quarter past seven, Rachel was still waiting to be discharged.

She didn't feel great about lying to her grandmother again, but if the alternative was making her worry, it seemed like the lesser evil.

"Are you sure you don't need us to come there?" The sound of dogs barking muffled Gran's voice, followed by the clunk of the kennel door closing. "Pop just put new tires on the truck. We could be in Atlanta before breakfast."

"No, Gran. Please don't come here. I know you don't like to drive at night, especially not in Atlanta traffic. And I couldn't bear it if you guys got sick."

Gran went quiet.

Oh no.

"Gran?"

"I'm here." She sniffled into the phone.

"Don't cry." Tess scrunched her face up in a grimace. Gran wasn't usually one for tears.

More sniffling and the metallic twang Tess recognized as the hinges of the trailer door.

Tess softened her tone. "I'm fine, I promise."

"Teresa Marie, this is your second time in the hospital in a week. That is not my idea of fine." Gran's voice broke on the word "fine."

"I love you guys. Everything is going to be okay. Really. I'm going to head straight home as soon as they bring by the discharge paperwork."

After I figure out how to get there with no car.

And no money.

And somehow pick Tater up on the way.

"I love you, too, sweetheart. Please be careful out there."

She disconnected the call and glanced up, meeting Rachel's gaze across the room. Tess tilted the phone in her roommate's direction. "Thanks for letting me borrow this."

"No problem. But I don't think we're getting out of here anytime soon." Rachel fiddled with one of a series of hoops running from the cartilage of her ear down to the lobe. "I overheard a nurse saying they're about to shut the hospital down. No one leaves, not even the doctors."

That didn't make any sense. "But we were cleared." Tess crossed her arms over her chest. She'd known it would take longer than she'd told Gran, but they couldn't force anyone who was healthy to stay who didn't want to. "Why wouldn't they release us? Don't they need the beds?"

"Something about extending the quarantine." Rachel looked out the window, and Tess followed her gaze. A MARTA bus rumbled by on the interstate two stories below.

All Tess could think of was Tater. Stuck outside, alone and hungry. "Fuck that." She threw back the covers, knocking a plastic bag full of her clothes and shoes off the bed. It clunked to the floor, one sneaker bouncing loose along with a single sheet of paper that floated free and under the bed. The Marburg Hotline print-out had been the nurse's only answer to Tess's questions about Gail and Luke. She stooped to gather everything up, a draft of cold air coming in through the back of her gown at the same moment the tangy stink of ammonia hit her nose. "Gross."

"What?"

"I think they treated our clothes with something." Tess pulled the t-shirt and shorts from the bag. Bringing them closer to her face, then jerking back. "Yeah, they definitely did." The clothes were an odd mix of damp and crunchy, where the disinfectant had dried.

Rachel laughed. "Why do you think I'm still in this?" She lifted the edge of the hospital smock. "Definitely not a fashion choice."

Tess pulled the shorts on under her gown. "I guess it's still better than climbing into a taxi with my butt hanging out."

"Good luck getting a taxi." Rachel went back to her magazine. "You'd have to be pretty hard up to pick up a fare from the hospital during the plague."

"Crap." Tess turned her back, pulled off the gown, and yanked the t-shirt over her head. Rachel was right; no way was she getting picked up from virus ground zero. Honking came from the freeway below their window. Traffic leaving the city would be a nightmare, but… "MARTA buses are still running. If I can get out of here, I'll walk to the nearest stop." Once she got back to Gail's, she'd pick up Tater, and they could walk home. It wasn't ideal, but they had run to Gail's that morning. She could do the same in reverse, just slower this time.

"Here." Rachel waved something at her from across the room. "You don't have your wallet, right? You'll need this."

Tess padded over in her hospital issue grippy socks and took the Breeze card, trading it for Rachel's cell phone. "Don't you need it? How will you get home?"

"Nowhere to go. Whole family's here with me. Somewhere." Rachel looked away, but not before Tess saw the fear in her eyes.

Rachel cleared her throat. "Anyway, there should be at least twenty bucks on it." She rooted around in her bag while Tess tucked the MARTA fare card into her shorts' pocket and pulled her watch from Rachel's charger.

"Thanks. You're a lifesaver. I'd hug you but, you know."

Rachel kissed the air, left then right.

Tess threw an air kiss back and pulled a mask into place. "I put my number in your phone. Call me when you get out of here. Let me know you're okay."

Rachel nodded. "Good luck, girl."

Tess swapped the socks for her sneakers and peeked out into the hallway. "All clear." Tess grinned at her new friend and eased the door shut.

Halfway to the elevators, a murmur of voices stopped her in her tracks. She edged closer to the wall and leaned around the corner. Two nurses stood in the center of the next hall. Their expressions grim, they stood with their heads close together, deep in conversation over paper cups of coffee.

Crap.

Tess jerked her head back then edged away from the corner, cursing the noise of her shoes on the floor. Her sneakers were still damp with disinfectant, and each step made a sticky, sucking sound as she lifted her foot.

There had to be stairs somewhere. She just needed to find them.

She edged around corners until a flash of motion outside caught her eye. Muffled shouts coming from that direction. A glance over her shoulder to make sure she was still alone, and she moved closer to the window. Police in riot gear and respirators pushed against a crowd, moving them away from the hospital. Some wandered off willingly. Others — those who probably had loved ones inside — surged forward instead, yelling and desperate.

Tess stopped at a familiar face, squinting to be sure. Parker stood in the crowd, holding hands with the woman from the picture on Luke's phone. A police officer stepped toward them, pointing past the television trucks ringing the area. Parker said something to the officer then lifted the woman's hand to his mouth and kissed it, before pulling her away.

Tess rubbed the back of her neck. What did that mean? The fact that Parker and the woman were there together might not mean anything. But the kiss…

What if the woman was Parker's wife? The girl Parker's child? The two disappeared behind a blue and white van with a ragged array of satellite equipment scattered along its roof. Maybe she'd jumped to the worst possible conclusion. And maybe she'd been wrong.

Shiiiit.

If that was true, she was going to owe Luke one seriously awkward apology.

A woman's voice echoed down the hall, snapping Tess back to reality. The nurses, apparently having followed her same path, weren't far behind. Tess tore herself away from the spectacle below and hurried down the hall, away from a one-way ticket back to purgatory with Rachel. A glowing red exit sign hung from the ceiling with an arrow pointing to a door marked "Stairs."

Bingo.

She slipped onto the landing, eased the door closed behind her, and listened for anyone going up or down. Nothing but an eerie muffled silence. No sign of anyone else there. The walls had been painted a bright, stark white, but that made it no less creepy.

An almost inhuman keening came through the walls from the floor above.

She froze, her foot suspended over the first step down.

What the fuck is that?

Whatever it was, she wanted no part of it. She flew down the stairs, away from the noise, barreling toward the ground floor, with no plan for what she would do or say if she ran into one of the nursing staff — or security.

What if the door's locked?

What if I'm stuck in here with whatever that is?

She glanced back toward the wailing as she powered down the stairs. Tess had the momentum of two flights behind her and hit the door at full speed. She smacked the handle down and flew out of the stairwell, a burst of relief filling her chest as the door gave way.

She collided straight into a man coming the other direction. The impact a sudden whomping stop that knocked the air from her lungs. "Oh." She stumbled back a step before looking up at him. "I'm so sorry."

He was tall, more than six feet, but he stood hunched forward. Like someone who'd never grown comfortable with their height. Sandy blonde hair stuck out from under a hood pulled low over his eyes. She'd seen him before. Somewhere.

"My fault." He smiled at her.

She caught her breath. "Not at all."

The man stepped forward, and Tess instinctively shifted back out of his way, her steps taking her into the stairwell again. He followed, letting the door fall shut behind them. She stepped to the left, and he did the same. She tried again. A flicker of a smile crossed his lips as he moved with her.

It wasn't a good smile.

"I should go." She tried to keep her voice casual, stepping backwards again. Once, twice. With the next step, her heel met the stair behind her, knocking her off balance. Tess fell back, and the cold, concrete step connected painfully with her tailbone. A sharp yelp of pain up her spine.

"No need for that, Ms. Oliver."

He knows my name.

Something inside yelled for her to get up and run. But another voice, a deeper animal instinct, knew if she did, he'd chase her.

The man moved closer, one hand extended. She hesitated. Maybe she'd read the situation wrong?

He was probably one of the medical staff she'd met on the intake floor, heading home after his shift. She wouldn't recognize him outside of his protective gear, and that would explain why he knew her name. Why she felt she knew him somehow. Tess gave him her hand. He pulled her to her feet, but his grip was strange, too smooth. She looked down to where their hands met. The man wore a flesh-colored latex glove with a rubber band cinched at the wrist.

If he'd already changed to go home, why would he still be wearing gloves? And what was the rubber band about?

He pulled her closer, the smile still on his face.

A flash of something by her ear.

A syringe?

A hot burst of panic.

She jerked back, as the needled plunged into the side of her neck.

▪ ▪ ▪

Cameras peered down from the corners of the stairwell. Martin took care to keep his head turned away from them as he hoisted the woman's weight over his shoulder. He set off at a jog down the stairs, keeping a steady pace until he reached the subterranean parking level. The cameras might be monitored in real time. Or it could be they were only reviewed after an incident was reported. He would bet on the latter but wasn't willing to take the chance. The last thing he needed was more complication.

He bounced down the last few steps, his nose filling with a putrid chemical tang. He sniffed the air.

It's coming from her.

She was covered in some sort of ammonia-based disinfectant and smelled awful. Turning his head away, he kept moving, trying not to breathe in any more of the sickly-sweet smell than was absolutely necessary. Every minute there increased the chance he'd be spotted, that they'd be intercepted before his mission was complete.

He couldn't let that happen.

Martin sped up. He swiped the ID badge he'd stolen off an orderly earlier in the day and entered the staff parking area. Then dug the orderly's keys from his pocket and hit the unlock button. Nothing.

He adjusted the woman's weight on his shoulder and walked to the next row before hitting the button again. It took him three more rows to find flashing taillights. But the parking deck remained quiet, empty. As if his path had been cleared by God.

He dropped his cargo into the front passenger seat of a gray Nissan Sentra, scooting her back into the seat. He leaned over her to click the seatbelt into place and watched as her breast moved under the strap pressed across her chest. An ache squeezed his groin. She wasn't wearing a bra. He paused, breathing in, and licked his lip. Martin raised one hand to cup the swell under her shirt, to squeeze it, thinking of how satisfying it would be to smash her breast in his grip until she begged him to stop.

He snapped his hand back down to his side, forcing his mind back to the task at hand. He wasn't like that now. He didn't do those things anymore. He said a quiet prayer to himself, popping the rubber band on his wrist before he closed her door and went around to the driver's side.

He had a job to do, and he was going to do it. Martin settled into the seat and looked at his passenger. She sat slumped forward, her head cocked at an awkward angle. It made her look half-dead.

That won't do.

There was bound to be security at the exits. He leaned over, trying to arrange her more naturally in the passenger seat. He put her right elbow on the door, perched beneath the passenger window, then tilted her head to rest in the crook of her arm. Better.

But still not good enough.

He went back around to her side of the car and carried her to the trunk, careful to hold her away from his body. The thoughts would come with more contact. And he couldn't afford that. Not now. He popped the rubber band.

Not yet.

CHAPTER 26

Breaking news, my ass.

Sully pointed the remote at a television hanging above the study's carved stone fireplace. He clicked through half a dozen news channels. None of them had anything new to report. He finally settled on the station with the fiery blonde anchor he liked. She sat opposite her guest for the day, a prematurely gray young man with piercing blue eyes. The man leaned forward, elbows on the table. "I think we can all agree that the Republicans' failure to recognize the importance of properly funding the National Institutes of Health is at least partially to blame for what we're seeing in Atlanta today."

Sully rolled his eyes.

"Can we?" The blonde matched her guest's posture, leaning forward, at least three inches of cleavage on display. "Isn't it more likely a result of the Democrats' insistence on open borders? How else could the virus have gotten in?"

Sully pressed mute and tried Quinones again. Still no answer.

We have a domestic outbreak, and he still can't be bothered to come in?

Sully chewed the last bite of a turkey sandwich he didn't taste and reached for the phone again. Quinones would have to pick up eventually.

Except that wasn't really true, was it?

And what would he do then? What if—

The phone rang in Sully's hand. His heart gave a series of irregular beats as he recognized the extension. The White House.

Dear God.

Sully hadn't expected anyone on the President's staff to reach out quite so quickly, but here it was. He straightened in his seat and connected the call.

A woman spoke, smooth and professional. "Mr. Sullivan, hold one moment for the President."

Sully scrubbed a hand through his hair. Not just one of Nathan Coates's flunkies calling.

The man himself.

Sully had wanted this, dreamed of the day Coates would come crawling to him for help. When he'd be forced to acknowledge what Sully had known all along. The world wasn't the safe place Coates liked to pretend it was. And if the President had listened to him years ago, had done what they'd both known was right — no matter how politically painful it might have been — an outbreak like what was happening in Atlanta now would never have happened.

"Sully?" The President's voice rumbled over the line. The same deep baritone Coates had used to charm freshmen girls in their days at UVA, long before he'd ascended through Congress to become the nation's commander in chief.

Sully cleared his throat. "Yes, Mr. President. I'm here."

"You know you can call me Nate."

"Sorry, sir." Given how their last conversation had gone, Sully wouldn't have assumed that was true.

"I trust you've seen the news coming out of Atlanta."

"I have." Given the extent of the media coverage, it would've been almost impossible to miss. "It's terrible."

"It is." He said, and Sully could almost see the look on his face. Blue eyes serious but kind, a line running between steel gray brows, his face a perfect construct of paternal care and concern. Coates had worn the same expression after God knew how many natural disasters and school shootings. At this point, it might as well be patented.

Coates continued. "It's my understanding that Maeler has a vaccine for the Marburg virus under development."

"We do, sir." A smile tugged at the edges of Sully's mouth. But it was too soon to celebrate. Not when he was already driving on the edge of a cliff he couldn't see. "Mainly thanks to the research underlying the Ebola vaccine deployed in the DRC not long ago."

"The DR… right, right. Africa."

"But, Mr. President, er, Nate…" He hesitated. How much should he say? If he made the situation sound too dire, Maeler might be cut out of the government's response altogether. But if he undersold the challenges they faced, Coates would expect results faster than he could deliver. The President's henchmen would be nipping at Sully's heels, drawing his attention away from the work he needed to be doing.

Everything was happening too damned fast.

"Yes?" Coates prompted.

Sully didn't have a choice but to tell the truth. "We don't have a viable Marburg vaccine ready for production. No one does, as far as I know. And even if we did, we couldn't complete drug trials, get FDA approval, and then produce it in sufficient numbers to help anyone currently at risk from the disease. Which all assumes it would be effective against the current strain and we can't— "

"Don't worry about any of that right now. I want you focused on developing that vaccine."

"Okay." Sully picked at a rough edge on his thumbnail. What would that even look like now with the outbreak in Atlanta? He needed more time. "Sir, what we have has only been through the most preliminary stages of testing."

"Mmmm-hm." The sound of a desk chair creaking was followed by the double-thud of what sounded like Coates's boots landing on the Resolute desk. "And what exactly do you need to take it the rest of the way?"

Sully rattled off a wish list that was all but impossible. An unlimited budget, an absolute waiver of any liability arising from the expedited development schedule, and, probably the hardest ask, access to the research of several private institutions likely to view their work as a trade secret. He left out the other thing he needed — to find the head of Maeler's vaccine R&D group.

Nothing good's going to come of telling him Quinones is AWOL.

Sully paused, waiting for Coates to thank him for his time and disconnect the call. Half of him hoped he would.

"And if I can make that happen? How soon could you have the vaccine ready?"

Sully sat straight up in his chair. Ready or not, this was happening. "Assuming we can confirm efficacy. A month, maybe three weeks, if we work around the clock, throw every dollar we have at it, and do only minimal redundant testing before we submit it to the FDA. It'll take us that much time just to set up the production facility."

"The CDC will have a sample of the virus to the labs at your D.C. office by the end of the day. I'll work on the FDA, the research, and the funding. You go make me that vaccine."

"Yes, Sir." Sully wiped the damp from his palms on the legs of his slacks. "We won't let you down."

"I know you won't," Coates said, in what sounded more like a command than an affirmation and disconnected the call.

Sully clicked off the TV as the weight of what he'd been tasked with settled around him. No matter what good he was able to accomplish, there would be death.

And there would be blame.

But even that didn't change what he needed to do. It never had. And there was no time for it now. He needed to find Quinones. Needed to set everything in motion. They had a mountain of things to do, and the clock ticked faster with each moment that passed. He re-dialed Quinones's cell.

Straight to voicemail.

Son of a bitch.

Sully found his assistant's number and dialed. "Brenda, pull Richard Quinones's file from HR and send me all the contact information we have." Desperate times called for desperate measures.

The information dinged its arrival in his inbox minutes later. Home number and address.

Perfect.

If he couldn't reach Quinones by phone, Sully would drive to his house and pull him in to the office by the scruff of his neck. He punched in Quinones's home number and prayed.

"Hello." An old woman answered, her voice thickly accented and thin as paper.

Of course he lives with his mother.

"Is this Mrs. Quinones?"

"It is. And may I ask who's calling?"

"Warren Sullivan. Richard may have mentioned me, we work togeth— "

"He has." Her tone hardened. "Uno momento." The phone clattered, as if it'd been dropped onto a table. Apparently, Quinones hadn't gone home singing Sully's praises.

Feeling's mutual.

Not that he'd have to deal with it much longer. As soon as this project was over, so was Quinones's career. Muffled voices raised on the other end of the line, but Sully didn't know enough Spanish to make out what they said. The sharp slam of a door, and Quinones came on, his voice tight. "This is Richard."

Sully tamped down the urge to bring up Quinones's failure to respond to his calls or messages, never mind show up at work. There would be time for that conversation later. Right now, he needed the man on board. "President Coates has asked Maeler to spearhead production of a Marburg Hemphill vaccine. Coates is going to handle the FDA. The budget is virtually unlimited, and we'll have access to any research we might need, no matter who holds it. I know we're only in the preliminary testing stage on our existing Marburg vaccine, and it's going to be a lot of work to get this over the finish line. But I promise you'll have the company's full support. Whatever you need, as soon as you need it." He leveled out his tone, like one equal speaking to another. "We can do this, Richard. We have to."

A long pause stretched out before Quinones answered. "I'm afraid that's not going to be possible."

CHAPTER 27

Luke pulled on the top from a borrowed set of scrubs, folded his discharge paperwork in half, and tucked the paper into the still-damp back pocket of his jeans. Whatever they'd sprayed his clothes with smelled awful. He looked both ways down the hospital corridor, but the nurse who'd told him he could go had disappeared.

Voices echoed down the hall from the left. Maybe someone who could point him toward an exit? He followed the sound. Most of the doors he passed were shut, but he got the impression the rooms were all occupied. Monitors beeped, televisions played, and muted conversations floated into the hall. A voice rose from around a corner. "I understand there are rules. But do you really mean to tell me they apply under these circumstances?" The woman spoke in a deep southern accent. "She may not be a blood relation, but Teresa Oliver is as much my family as any of the children I gave birth to. And I'm not leaving this hospital until I know she's alright."

Luke stopped in his tracks. He'd been pretending he wasn't looking for Tess. But he hadn't been stopping outside each room to listen for anyone else's voice, and there was no denying it now. He couldn't have stopped eavesdropping if his life depended on it.

Another woman's voice, muffled and heavy with exhaustion. "Ms. Brubaker, you have been discharged, and I strongly recommend you leave. I am sorry I can't provide you with information on your friend, but, as I've told you several times now, no matter how close you may be, we are unable to give out patients' medical information except to immediate family members."

Luke leaned around the corner. An elegant woman in her sixties stood at the nurses' counter, her platinum hair in a twist, hands on her hips, a scarf cinched around the middle of the hospital-issue gown. Even in profile, she had an intimidating look of purpose on her face. "I am not asking for medical information." She smacked a hand on the counter, gold bangles clattering together. The nurse jumped.

When the older woman spoke again, honey coated her tone. "There's a time for bureaucracy. And this isn't it. What would you want someone to do if it was your daughter?" She tilted her head down toward what Luke assumed was a photograph of the nurse's family.

The nurse blew out a deep breath, yanked the rubber band from her hair and then twisted it back in place. When she spoke again, her voice was so low Luke could barely make out the words from behind her mask. "Ms. Oliver is no longer a patient here."

"Bless your heart, woman. Speak English. Are you saying she was discharged or that she's dead?"

A trickle of fear slipped down Luke's spine.

The nurse looked left, then right. "I'm going to answer your question, and then you are going to go away. Ms. Oliver is not listed among the infected, and she is no longer a patient of the hospital." She raised her eyebrows at the older woman, making a point Luke wasn't quite sure he understood. Her voice dropped even lower. "You need to get out of here, too. You are one of the last patients lucky enough to get a discharge. I understand you want to find your friend, but if you stay any longer, you're not going to be able to leave. The rest of us can't go home to our families. You should." The nurse looked pointedly away, her fingers clacking on a keyboard. "Now, either go get changed and get out of here, or settle in with the rest of us."

Luke jerked his head back around the corner as the older woman turned his way. Should he keep going? Head back toward his room? His moment of indecision cost him the choice.

The platinum-haired woman rounded the corner and pulled up short. "Pardon me." She gripped the loose ends of the hospital gown behind her, turning the open back away from him as she passed with a tight smile.

He was going to sound crazy, but… "Ma'am?"

She turned back, head tilted, hand on hip. "Ma'am is for church ladies." She raised one thin eyebrow. "You can call me Gail."

"Nice to meet you. I didn't mean to overhear, but I was coming this way when you asked the nurse about Tess. I—"

"You must be Luke." She looked down her nose at him, something appraising in her gaze.

He wasn't sure he liked it. "She mentioned me?"

"You could say that." She frowned at him. "Tess and I came to the hospital together, but we got separated after the blood tests."

A thread of worry pulled taut in his gut. Knowing she'd been there was a start. But he'd been trying to figure out where she'd gone since he'd woken alone that morning. And none of what he knew about what had happened since made sense. "I've been trying to call her cell, but she doesn't pick up."

"Her phone's busted. And she doesn't have her wallet, or her keys. The only thing she had with her when she got to my house this morning was the dog."

He blinked.

It was weird enough she'd been gone. But why would she have taken off without her stuff, leaving him in her house alone? She didn't strike him as the type to run from intimacy. If anything, their connection had been immediate. More real than anything he'd had in years. Luke rubbed the back of his neck.

He'd had a few drinks the night before, but not enough that he didn't remember what'd happened. There'd been no question of their chemistry, no hint that anything had been wrong, so far as he could tell.

And why would she disappear alone from the hospital in the middle of an outbreak? “That doesn’t make sense. She wouldn’t just charge out of here with nothing, would she? How would she get home?”

Gail shrugged. “I wouldn’t say her judgment is perfect.” She eyed him. “But something about the whole thing feels wrong.”

He couldn’t explain it. But he knew, in his gut, she was right.

CHAPTER 28

The gate to the industrial park stood open. A silent invitation to a very private party. Martin drove to the third warehouse in a row of identical buildings, parked, and found the building key hanging from a small nail tacked to the left of the door. Right where he'd been told it would be.

He swung open the door to a pitch-black interior. Towering misshapen things loomed in the shadows. Part of him didn't want to go in. Which was silly. A lot of his work required the cover of darkness. This was no different. So what if this place smelled like his childhood basement? Damp concrete, the musty forgotten rot of things no longer wanted. And no way out. He stepped in just far enough to flip the light switch.

Nothing happened.

Super.

Martin straightened his spine. The electricity must be off. That was all there was to it. He turned back and stopped. A plastic grocery bag lay on the opposite side of the entryway. He scooped it up and carried it outside into the beams of the Nissan's headlights, sorting through the contents — a black Maglite, two rolls of duct tape, a Glock G43X 9mm handgun, a box of ammunition, and a new burner phone.

Ask, and it shall be given you. Seek and ye shall find.

He took in a deep, restorative breath. He had nothing to fear. Not since he'd been chosen. He'd been washed in the blood, forgiven for his past transgressions. Deemed worthy.

Martin used the headlights to load the gun, then depressed the button on the flashlight's base, smiling as it flickered to life. Pointing both the flashlight and Glock into the darkness, he stepped back inside the building.

He worked for a higher purpose now, and his path would be cleared by God's hand.

Boxes filled the main center room, stacked high and deep enough to block his view across the cavernous space. He moved methodically around their perimeter to where the warehouse had been sub-divided into smaller rooms along the right outer wall. He shined the flashlight into the corners of each room before moving on to the next. Reams of paper and bankers' boxes filled each of the spaces. But the back room held only a desk with a broken leg, a rolling chair lying on its side, and crumpled packing paper strewn across the floor.

Perfect.

Satisfied he was alone and the building secure, Martin returned to the car, where he shut off the headlights and retrieved the woman. This time, he made sure only to touch her as much as was absolutely necessary. He wouldn't succumb to her temptations. He was better than that now.

Martin dropped her near the back wall, where she flopped over, her head landing hard on the concrete. He nudged her with his foot. No response. But that made sense, the sedative would take time to wear off.

He used the tape from the bag to bind her hands, wrapping them again and again until he was sure she couldn't pull free. He did the same for her feet and, to be safe, taped her hands and feet together. He finished with a small strip over her mouth and stood, looking down at his handiwork. She lay bent in half, her face a few inches from her knees.

That should do it.

He righted the desk chair and settled in to wait. Except for the distant horn of a train floating in on the night air, an empty silence filled the warehouse. But it didn't feel ominous anymore, and he didn't turn on the flashlight. The dark no longer bothered him. Not with the holy light burning so bright within him. He sat until his back grew stiff, his eyes adjusting enough so he could see the woman's silhouette on the floor.

Martin checked his watch. Several hours had passed, and she still hadn't stirred.

He focused on her chest.

Was it moving?

What if she wasn't breathing?

Maybe he had given her too much of the barbiturate. He hadn't known her exact weight when he'd calculated the dosage.

What if she doesn't wake up?

He couldn't come back empty-handed. Martin moved to her, his knees protesting after sitting so long in one spot. He put two fingers to her neck.

The woman's pulse beat strong and steady.

He pressed his hand to the center of her breastbone and shoved. Her body swayed, but her eyes stayed closed. Still out cold.

He let his hand linger, let his gaze find all the places on her body he hadn't allowed himself to spend time appreciating before.

Stop it.

He pulled his hand away, flexing his fingers as he moved backward, his gaze still glued to where she lay slumped against the wall. A rusty spigot jutted out from it a few yards behind her head.

That could be handy.

A way to get her to talk without the temptation of having to touch her again. All he'd need was a hose. And he could get one from the hardware store they'd passed on the way in. A picture formed in his mind of her dripping wet, clothes sticking to her skin, the t-shirt translucent. He popped the rubber band against his wrist, again and again.

But the idea wouldn't leave him be.

. . .

Tess snapped awake. She couldn't see, couldn't breathe.

Water sluiced, frigid against her back. Around her body.

She tried to cry out. But she was underwater, drowning in the dark.

Her screams lost to the water.

No.

Not water. Her mouth had been taped shut.

She sucked air in through her nose, arching away from the icy blast.

Her muscles screamed in protest, pain ripping through her shoulders and down her sides as she fought to straighten but couldn't. Her body was locked in a forward position, her face pressed to her knees. Why couldn't she move?

She tried harder, jerking, panicking.

The water stopped.

"Nap time's over." A voice in the dark.

Tess craned around. She wasn't alone. Her throat contracted, her heartbeat thrashing in her ears. Someone else was there. Behind the water.

Her mind struggled to process what little she could see in the inky blackness around her. Everything seemed to swim in a blurry fog, her tongue thick in her mouth. Even the act of lifting her head a few inches took every bit of energy she had. She held the position as long as she could.

Long enough to see a tall figure looming over her in the darkness.

She shrank away, curling into the floor, her chest going tight. She couldn't move.

Why? What—

She stopped pulling against her restraints, the realization hitting her like a blow. Whoever it was that waited in the darkness had done this to her.

Oh my God.

She wanted to ask what the hell was happening, what did he want? To beg for help, for mercy. But couldn't. Not with the tape welding her mouth shut.

Stomach acid rose in her throat.

Don't throw up.

Don't throw up or you'll choke to death on your own vomit.

She forced her body to still, made herself breathe slowly through her nose. She couldn't panic. She needed to be calm so she could think. Tess let her head drop to the pavement.

Water slammed into the top of her skull. The pounding unbearably loud, drowning out every other sound or thought except the screams echoing inside her head. She twisted, trying to get away, but there was nowhere to go. Water flooded her face, surging up her nose. She fought the urge to breathe in. Willing herself not to inhale until her lungs burned, and the need for oxygen built to an impossible, undeniable demand.

I'm going to die.

Her chest constricted. Her body betrayed her mind. And she sucked in.

Sweet, cold air flooded her lungs.

The spray of water migrated down her torso to her legs, then stopped again. Tess held her body rigid, waiting for another blast.

Instead, footsteps approached.

She squeezed her eyes shut and waited for whatever was coming, wishing she could push her mind outside her body. But she couldn't. If anything, she was hyper-aware. Every molecule of her body on edge. Her pulse counting the seconds in her ears.

She felt his closeness, a sudden change in the air, an absence of space. He hovered over her, the warmth of his breath brushing her cheek.

He smelled like cinnamon gum.

Go away.

She lay frozen in place, every muscle tensed as she waited for him to touch her.

For him to hurt her.

Go away, go away.

She counted another dozen heartbeats. Waiting.

His footsteps receded into the distance. And a door clunked closed somewhere outside the room where she was being held.

She listened hard, straining for any sound. Any sign he could still be nearby.

He could be playing with her.

Or there could be more than one of them.

Her body trembled so hard her teeth clacked together. She clenched her jaw, forcing herself still so she could hear. But the room stayed silent.

And the space felt empty.

Thank God.

Tess curled into herself, rocking back and forth as tears streamed down her face and mixed with the dirty water pooling around her body. As her shaking subsided, the adrenaline finally chased away the last of the fog from whatever drug he'd given her.

She remembered now. The hospital, the pinch and burn of the syringe as he'd jabbed it into her neck, and, most of all, the look on his face as she lost her grip on consciousness.

He'd been enjoying himself.

She pulled against the restraints, but they had no give. She tried again and again, and, still, they held tight.

By the feel of it, he'd used duct tape. No way she was ripping that free. But maybe, if she could position herself just right…

She forced her arms and legs up toward her face, straining until she could pinch the edge of the tape at her mouth with her fingers. It took several tries, but she finally pulled it free, the strip sticking and pulling painfully at her lips and skin as she did.

She sucked in giant gulps of air. One after the next, each a burning, greedy rasp down her throat. Tess froze. Could he hear her? She went rigid, now holding her breath as she listened for any sign of his return.

But there was nothing.

She pulled her arms and legs into her chest and scooted along the floor. The progress came slow, painstaking. Each thrust barely moved her body, and the muscles of her arms and legs shook with exhaustion from the effort. She needed to save her energy for when he came back.

The thought made her heart race again and her skin go clammy. Trussed up or not, she wasn't going down without a fight. She gripped her ankles and rolled to her back, then rocked until she had enough momentum to push herself forward into a sitting position.

Better.

She looked around the space, her eyes finally adjusted to the darkness. She was in a small room with no windows. Concrete floor and metal walls meant something industrial. A garage or a storage locker, maybe? She made out an uneven rectangular shape across the room. A desk. A chair lay to the other side of the door, and a garden hose snaked from just inside the door to a pipe sticking out from the wall not far from where she sat. There had to be something there she could use to defend herself.

The desk held the most promise of holding something useful, but could she get there before he came back?

She glanced toward the door. That wasn't a risk she could take. She needed to focus on getting free.

Tess scooted along the hose toward the pipe instead, her backside landing painfully against the gritty, wet floor with each bounce. She made herself keep going, inspecting the pipe as she grew closer. The metal jutting from the wall had corroded with age, ragged and sharp.

Sharp enough to cut duct tape?

She rolled to her back again, stretching her hands and feet up toward the spigot. She slid them around the pipe, trying to create friction with the bindings. The pipe found skin instead. A jagged edge sliced the inside of her wrist. The pain sharp and immediate.

Tess choked back sobs but kept scraping back and forth against the pipe, now wet with water and blood.

CHAPTER 29

"What do you mean there's nothing you can do?" A scratched plexiglass wall separated Luke from the intake officer for the East Atlanta police station. Luke hunched forward, directing his voice into the perforated metal disc at its center. "She's missing. Her phone is broken, and she doesn't have her keys, her wallet, or a car. She wouldn't just disappear by herself into nowhere."

The officer chewed hard on a piece of gum as phones rang unanswered behind her. "Maybe Ms. Oliver isn't by herself." She eyed him over the top of her glasses, her gaze a mix of assessment and pity.

Luke straightened, his arm brushing a tethered pen off of the counter as the realization hit him — the policewoman thought he was a jealous boyfriend. The pen swung back and forth, stuck in place even as it whipped side to side. That wasn't at all what was going on. But the more he tried to convince her it wasn't, the more pathetic he'd look. The more sure she'd be she was right. Heat rose to his face. He glanced at the line of people growing behind him. No doubt listening and drawing their own conclusions.

The officer went on, her voice flat. "We are aware of your concerns. But Ms. Oliver is an adult entitled to move about as she sees fit, and until we have some reason to believe that she isn't doing so of her own volition, our resources must be spent elsewhere. As I'm sure you're aware, we are already spread thin." She lowered her voice, glancing at the line of people behind him. "And even if we weren't in the middle of some kind of crazy monkey-flu outbreak, the facts you've explained to me wouldn't merit anything more." She snapped the gum. "You became intimate with Ms. Oliver a short time after meeting her. And now she isn't returning your calls." She paused. "Do I have that right?"

Shit.

She wasn't exactly wrong. He forced a nod, his throat too tight to voice a response. Why hadn't he just said he was Tess's friend? There was no reason for the police to know more than that. He should've been more prepared, planned what he was going to say instead of just walking in and spilling his guts.

Idiot.

Another snap of the gum. "Sir, has it occurred to you she may not want to be found?"

It had. But he was hardly ready to admit that to himself, much less her. And it was becoming clear he'd been given as much assistance as the APD was willing to offer. "Thank you for your help," he said, gritting his teeth. "You have my contact information. Please let me know if you learn anything."

She shifted her gaze to the person next in line. "Next."

He'd been dismissed.

Luke schooled his face into a mask of calm, avoided the eyes of all the others waiting in line, and stepped outside. "Fuck." He leaned on the cold stone of the building, watching moths throw themselves against the lights dotting the precinct's ugly gray exterior. He had to call Gail and tell her they'd hit a dead end. Even though it was the last thing he wanted to do. If it weren't for Tess's dog waiting in Gail's backyard — and his virtual blood oath to call her as soon as he had news — Gail no doubt would have insisted on going to the police herself.

She wasn't going to be happy when he came back empty-handed.

Not that there was a damn thing he could do about it. He pulled out his phone. Seven missed calls, two from his mom, one from each of his sisters, and one from his dad. The last was no doubt the follow-up "call your mother" that always came after Luke failed to promptly respond to a voicemail.

Crap.

One worried woman at a time. He pulled up Gail's number and stopped, his finger hovering over the call button. What the officer said made sense. Tess left after they'd been together. He knew from Gail she'd been upset. Maybe she really was off on her own somewhere?

Or not on her own.

The thought festered in his gut. He didn't have any claim to Tess, no right to object if she was with someone else. But he hated the idea anyway. What if she really was just avoiding him? What if he'd come on too strong? Or if she'd woken up that morning regretting what they'd done?

And now he was at the police station acting unhinged.

He looked down the street, where navy blue police cruisers pulled in and out of the station's secured parking area. It had been years since he'd felt this way about someone.

She was under his skin. He could still taste her. Feel the brush of her hair against his chest as she leaned over him, making love to him. It was more than just wanting her. He liked her. Damn it. He drew in a deep breath and let it leak out. He really liked her. And he owed her. She'd saved his life.

The least he could do was make sure she was okay.

Luke pressed "call." The officer's theory made sense… but that didn't make it true. There had to be more to it. He didn't believe Tess was avoiding him. She wouldn't leave behind her keys, her wallet, her dog — that, most of all, told him he was right. No way she'd leave the dog.

Everything inside him cried foul play.

CHAPTER 30

Martin stood in the darkness listening to the muffled sobs coming through the door. He'd paced the same strip of concrete since he left her, trying to calm the urges lurking in his mind. His wrist was numb from snapping the rubber band. And still, all he could think of were the curves of her body under her clothes.

Maybe just scratch the itch.

If he did, he could concentrate. Get his job done.

Her sobs grew louder, and it made the longing unbearable. He could stop her crying. She'd like it. He'd make her like it. He ground his teeth together and forced himself to walk out of the warehouse and into the cool, evening air. The clouds had cleared. The night now bright with moonlight and tinged with the smell of burnt tires. He was past this. He could be better. Martin pulled the phone from his pocket and dialed.

"Sorry to call at this hour." Martin looked at his watch, 11:14 p.m. He hadn't thought to check the time before he'd dialed, his mind consumed with thoughts of her. "I thought you'd want an update."

"Hang on." A rustling, the soft thunk of a door closing, then a long pause before his employer spoke again. "Go ahead."

Martin cleared his throat. "The extraction went as planned. She's awake, and we're about to begin."

"Good, that's good. It's time we put our concerns to rest."

"Understood." Martin looked in through the open warehouse door. From out here, he could hardly hear the woman's sobs. "I'll take care of it."

"I know you will, son."

Martin closed his eyes. His employer's trust settled around him, a comforting weight that smoothed the edges of his darker urges and reminded him of all the reasons he was there to begin with. "Thank you, sir. I'll update you when it's done."

He slipped the phone back into his pocket and strode toward the opposite end of the industrial park, where he'd moved the car. It would've been more convenient to have his tools nearby. But, in the otherwise abandoned area, the car stood out. And it made sense not to draw attention.

Especially when what he needed to do might get noisy.

▪ ▪ ▪

Tess lay in the dark, the cut on her wrist throbbing a steady one-two beat. She pulled against the tape until stars bloomed behind her eyelids, every muscle in her body straining with the effort.

Break, break, break, damn you.

It held fast.

She adjusted the loop of her hands and feet over the pipe and sawed back and forth again, and again, and again.

Fuck you, you fucking piece of shit tape.

Tears streamed down her face as she threw her body back and forth.

A sudden rip, and she flopped to the floor.

She lay sprawled. Her body filled with relief and the aches that came from being held too long in an unnatural position.

But she couldn't give herself time to savor the victory. With her wrists free from her ankles, she could reach the ends of the tape holding her feet together. She scrambled to rip it loose, unwinding layer after layer of the binding until her feet were free. She couldn't do anything about the bindings on her hands. The tape was slick with blood and wound too tight around her wrists, the ends beyond her reach. Tess got to her feet and stumbled toward the door. She wobbled, her feet numb, her body spent from exhaustion and the after-effects of the sedative, but adrenaline propelled her forward.

She put an ear to the door and held her breath. It was impossible to hear anything over the pounding of her heart.

She swung the door open, bracing herself, waiting for the man to leap out of the dark.

But nothing happened.

She seemed to be in some kind of warehouse. A tiny sliver of faint light slipped in near the joinder of the walls with the roof. It lit the space enough for her to see a few yards ahead and the looming black shapes of something in the distance. What, she couldn't tell.

Was he there, in the dark, watching her? Waiting for her?

Or maybe the bodies of his other victims lingered just out of sight, leering at her with dead eyes. Waiting for her to join them in their forgotten, aluminum-paneled grave. The nausea swirled in her gut again, and an acid burn crept up the back of her throat. She forced it down, making herself move faster.

You can do this.

As she came closer, the giant black masses became bankers' boxes, stacked row upon row with narrow aisles running in between. She shuffled forward, her bound hands outstretched and dripping blood.

Maybe she could find something sharp. Scissors or a box cutter. Something to get her hands free. Something she could use as a weapon. She scanned the boxes around her but found nothing that would help. And she didn't have time to stop and search, she needed to move.

Keep going, keep going.

She walked until the row dead-ended into a wall. No doors or windows, just reams of paper arranged in neat piles along the floor.

She listened again but heard only a train whistle somewhere in the distance.

Wherever he'd gone, he'd no doubt be back. She needed to move faster. Tess ran her hands along the metal wall as she went. Every few feet, she hit a joint, most with cobwebs in their corners. She wiped her bound hands down her shirt and kept moving, one step after another. And then it was there. Just beyond another pile of paper rolls.

A door.

She rushed to it, but the handle didn't turn.

Fuck, fuck, fuck.

The urge to sink to the floor and cry, to give in to what was beginning to seem inevitable, was overwhelming. She shook her head hard.

Snap out of it.

There had to be more than one door. Damned if she was going to quit before she found it. Tess continued through the blackness, following the wall. She counted the joints in the metal for no reason except to calm her mind. Her hand hit a ridge. Something inset in the surface, like a window, but with ribbed metal where it should have been glass. She took in a deep breath, her lungs filling fully for the first time since she'd woken in the warehouse.

This could be her way out.

She ran her hands over a rolling metal door covering some kind of pass-thru or window. Another deep breath. She gripped the pull handle she found at the bottom center of the door.

Please God, let it open.

She gave the handle a hard yank. With a loud rattle, the door shot up to the ceiling where it stopped with a bang.

She cringed and hunched forward, then forced herself into action.

No reason to be quiet now.

Tess hauled herself up over the edge and out the other side, where her feet hit the ground with a wet thwack. She crouched down, the muscles in her legs protesting. After the darkness of the warehouse, the moonlight seemed bright as day. She was in some sort of industrial park — a series of metal buildings, as far as she could see. None of them had any signs or markings that might tell her where she was.

She edged along the building until she could see around the corner. Lights shined in the far distance, but she couldn't tell what they were. Not bright enough for a gas station. Maybe a backyard security light? She couldn't be sure, but it was enough to give her a plan. She set off as quickly as she could, running hunched over in the hopes it would make her harder to see. If she could just get to the light, she could—

The man stepped out from between warehouses. A gun in his hand.

Tess stopped breathing. She stumbled as she tried to change course.

Never mind that there was nowhere to go. It didn't matter as long as she could outrun him. Because, if she let him tie her up again, let him put her back in that warehouse, she would never come out again. She knew it in her bones.

Tess sprinted back the way she'd come.

Footsteps slapped the pavement behind her and a heavy weight crashed into her back, knocking her breath from her body.

She tumbled to the ground, the gravel digging bloody tracks into her knees as she scrambled to right herself. She rolled to her back, and he came down hard on top of her, his knee on her chest. The impact a crushing blow that whooshed the last of the air out of her lungs. She didn't need to breathe. She needed to throw him off. To get free. She raked her nails down his arms, leaving raw, red tracks behind.

He pushed himself off her, but his mouth lifted in a small, satisfied smile.

He liked it.

Sick fuck.

She aimed a knee for his balls but hit him in the stomach instead. He grunted, the smile gone from his face, and slapped her cheek with the gun.

The blow whipped her head back against the pavement. Stars fizzled behind her eyes, a throb setting up along her cheek. But even so, she could tell he'd held back — he was playing with her. Like this was a game.

No matter what happened, she wouldn't give him what he wanted. She'd rather die fighting. Tess arched up with everything she had, grabbing the front of his shirt, and yanking him down on top of her.

His eyes went wide, his brow furrowed with confusion. In the moment she'd gained from surprise, she brought her knee up again. This time, it found its mark. He choked out a moan, his face contorted in pain as he rolled off of her.

"You stupid bitch." He grasped at her with the hand not holding the gun.

The gun.

A sudden, telescoping clarity. She had to get the gun.

She twisted toward him, reaching. Scrambling.

He swung the weapon up. The movement too fast for her to register. She couldn't get there, couldn't—

The gun bashed into the side of her head. Another sharp bloom of pain.

And the world went black.

CHAPTER 31

September 21, 2018

Mara bit into a stale Danish she'd fished from the back of the hospital's vending machine. The pastry left her fingers sticky and a too-sweet residue on her tongue, but she kept eating anyway. Her body needed fuel, almost as much as it needed sleep. She should be resting.

Jerry had mandated breaks every twelve hours and, she agreed… in theory. But she was too wired, too amped up on worry and caffeine to close her eyes.

Every time she did, she saw Emmy.

She pushed that thought away, refocusing on her laptop. A live feed of a White House press conference played on the screen as she chewed another bite.

A reporter with dull gray eyes stood from the second row of chairs in the briefing room. "What else can you tell us about the planned containment measures in Atlanta?"

Gordon Schultz gripped the sides of the podium. "As the President has already made abundantly clear, all options are on the table." The press secretary flipped his notebook closed and swept his pointer finger back and forth across the room. "Last question."

Mara half-listened to a question from the CBS correspondent and Schultz's answer. It was the same one he'd given to nearly everything since taking the podium after the President's "thoughts and prayers" address. Schultz was a master at re-framing. Jerry sat on the dais behind him in a short sleeve dress shirt and tie. He shuffled and re-shuffled the papers in his hands. Probably the notes for his presentation. She couldn't decide if she envied him the position or not.

Jerry came to the podium as a Skype window popped up on her screen. Harriet Chou. Mara brushed crumbs from her shirt and connected the video-call.

Harriet's face appeared on the screen, dark crescents under her eyes. "Sorry to intrude on you again, Mara."

"Not at all. What do you need?"

"Something about this virus bothers me. I tried to raise it with your guy, Thomas, but he's kind of an ass."

Mara snorted. "That's accurate."

"First off, there's no logical explanation for a nurse in urban Atlanta to contract a disease we've never seen domestically. At least not outside of a high security lab she wouldn't have been authorized to set foot in."

"True. No contact with any possible animal carriers we're aware of either. We're looking into it." Mara ignored the clang of alarms going off down the hall.

"Okay." The crease between Harriet's eyebrows deepened.

"What are you trying to say?"

Harriet blew out a breath. "I don't think Sarah Baqri got it by accident."

Mara lowered her voice, even though her door was closed. "Between us, we don't either."

Harriet leaned back, folding her arms across her chest. "That's not good."

"I think it gets worse." Mara hesitated.

Harriet gave a short nod. "Tell me."

Harriet was going to think she was crazy, but it didn't mean Mara was wrong. And if she could confirm whether they were seeing the same thing in LA, she'd be able to tell whether the odd transmission patterns were due to the disease itself or just a product of how, and in which communities, it'd spread in Atlanta.

"Have you noticed a pattern in the patients who test negative despite prolonged exposure?"

"What kind of pattern?"

Mara took a deep breath. "They're almost always white."

Harriet stared at her, and Mara continued before she could lose her nerve. "People of color make up sixty-five percent of the patients brought in for testing, which isn't statistically noteworthy. But they make up one-hundred percent of those who've tested positive."

The tension broke in Harriet's face. "Well, yes. That's true so far. But you know as well as I do that germs don't discriminate. This isn't a genetic disorder, like sickle cell or cystic fibrosis. This is a virus. Besides, Atlanta and LA are both diverse cities. It makes sense we might have a greater than average incidence of infection in people of color."

"Of course, you're right. It's just the folks we've seen who test negative despite an exposure you would expect to result in transmission all appear to be of European descent. It seems more than coincidental at this point." She swallowed, her throat dry. She'd gone this far. No reason to stop now. "Is what you've seen in LA consistent with that?"

Harriet cringed. "I suppose it is. We don't have any patients identified as Caucasian on their intake paperwork who've tested positive for Marburg." She leaned forward. "And I don't disagree with you exactly, but I just don't see how that would work."

"I'm not sure I do either, but I can't shake the feeling that there's something to it. And selective susceptibility isn't a new idea. The U.S. government, the Russian government, and I'm sure others, have been trying to use biological weapons to target what they view as 'undesirable' populations for ages."

"Trying, maybe." Harriet shrugged. "But the science isn't there."

"As far as we know." Mara let a moment's silence hang before she continued. "What if someone's figured out how to make that leap? Like a Myxomatosis virus for people, instead of rabbits."

The crease came back between Harriet's brows. "You lost me."

"It was sometime in the 50s, I think? This guy in Versailles released a rabbit infected with Myxomatosis onto his property to try to stop an infestation. Within a year, the disease wiped out nearly half of the rabbit population of France, the Netherlands, Belgium, Italy, Spain, and Britain."

Harriet rubbed a hand over her face. "Mara, I've been awake for more than thirty-six hours. Can we talk about rabbits later?"

"Bear with me. My point is that virus nearly wiped out all European rabbits, and it did the same in Australia when they tried it for population control there, but it isn't lethal to American rabbits. If that's possible in rabbits, who's to say there isn't a way it could also be true for humans, with the right scientific steps forward?"

"You're talking about different breeds. The fact that my paternal grandparents are Chinese doesn't make me a different breed of human than you. It's not apples to apples."

Mara's face flushed with heat. "You're right. Of course, you're right." She was tired and not making sense. "So that's not my best example, but you get what I'm saying. It is possible, at least theoretically."

A long stretch of silence spread out between them.

"Let me think about it," Harriet finally answered.

"Okay." Mara pushed her hair out of her face. It was as much as she could ask for under the circumstances. "Thanks for letting me air it. At this point, I feel like I need to consider every possibility. I know I sound crazy. It's just that I also know the patterns of infection mean something." She held Harriet's gaze. "I can't stop asking myself how many more people are going to have to die before we figure out what it is."

CHAPTER 32

Luke stood on a two-inch piece of painters' tape. The trail of blue marks had begun four blocks over and continued, one every six feet, all the way down the center aisle of St. Agnes's sanctuary. At the front, two men in Hazmat suits sat with laptops behind a folding table. National Guard soldiers policed the line, announcing at regular intervals: "Stay on the tape. Keep six feet of distance from others. If you fail to comply, you will lose your place and not be allowed to rejoin the line." With every pass, the soldiers seemed to assess him.

Probably looking for signs of infection.

Luke leaned over, trying to get a feel for how many people were still ahead of him. At least a dozen, and God knew how many were waiting behind him. Each hoping what was now the Midtown Marburg Information Center might have information on someone gone missing in the outbreak. People like Tess. People like the ones on the makeshift memorial outside.

Photos of those lost to the disease had been tacked up along a wooden fence circling an empty lot next to the church. They fluttered in a breeze heavy with coming rain. He'd counted nineteen before he recognized his nurse and stopped. Bundles of cheap grocery store flowers and a few candles blown out by the wind, sat along the ground beneath.

A child's stuffed dog drooped beside them.

That put a lump in his throat that still wasn't gone.

Thank God he'd convinced his family to leave for home before things had gotten this far out of hand. If anything could give him comfort, it was knowing they'd made it back to Louisiana safe and sound. That they were far far away from the insanity around him. The line moved forward in a coordinated shift six feet closer to the front. He adjusted the paper mask on his face. A smart man would have gone with them. Would be as far away from this place as possible.

But leaving before he'd found Tess hadn't felt smart. It'd felt like cowardice.

He made himself focus on the intricate stained-glass windows lining the walls of the church. The late afternoon sunshine had broken through the clouds as he reached the church's vestibule, and, coming through the windows, it cast a pattern on the floor. Slashes of red and bile yellow under his feet.

Gail appeared beside him with a pale floral scarf tied over her nose and mouth. "Come with me."

"What?" He shook his head. He couldn't leave now, not when he was so close. "I'm almost there. I'll call you when I'm done, like I said earlier."

A soldier's voice boomed from the front of the church. "Ma'am, you need to go to the end of the line."

She raised a manicured hand but didn't break away. Her eyes sparked with excitement. "I know how to find her."

He shifted slightly out of line. That seemed too good to be true. "Really?"

"Ma'am. I'm not going to tell you again." The soldier came closer, a furrow between his brows, his eyes locked on Gail.

Luke turned to the approaching soldier. "It's okay, sir. We're leaving."

He followed Gail out onto the church's tiered front steps, keeping to the side opposite the winding line of grim masked faces. "What's the plan?"

Gail stopped a few steps down, turning back to face him. "Her watch. They would have given it back when she was released. I got my wedding ring and my old Seiko back." She lifted her arm to show the gold band of a delicate bracelet-style watch. "So, she would have gotten hers back as well."

This was why he'd gotten out of line? It had taken him two hours just to make it inside. Luke closed his eyes tight, then opened them again. "And?"

"We can ping it."

"I have no idea what you just said."

"If we go get her laptop from her house, we can ping the watch. It's one of those fancy Apple ones. And maybe ping her phone as well. It was busted, but when she showed it to me, it still looked like it was on. We can track her."

"Really?" A burst of energy straightened his spine. "Is that possible?"

"Yeah, it's so you can find it if you lose it. I don't know what its range is. But it's worth a shot, right?"

Damn right it was.

They piled into Luke's truck, and he wove through town toward Tess's house. The trip from Midtown to East Atlanta should have been short, but as soon as they crossed Ponce de Leon, they hit a roadblock. Then another. And the rain came.

Sheets and sheets of rain.

Luke turned onto a side street and stopped short at a third barricade.

Son of a bitch.

A police officer came to the driver's side window. Under the hood of his rain slicker, his gaze flicked from them back to the streets around them, as if he was anticipating a threat.

Luke rolled down the window, a wet gust blowing in. "Evenin'."

Up close, the officer looked barely out of high school. He nodded to Luke, then Gail, and reached a gloved hand out from under his coat. "Driver's license?"

Luke handed over his ID, used to the drill by now. He and Gail waited in silence, the wipers making a squeaking pass back and forth across the windshield, as he prayed, that this time — unlike all the others — they'd finally get through.

The officer pulled a flashlight from his belt, shining it down on Luke's license. "Only local traffic permitted past this point."

Same thing they'd heard at the last two stops.

Luke tried anyway. "We're going to a local home."

The officer shook his head, his gaze back on the darkened neighborhood around them.

Luke leaned out of the car, ignoring the wet. If he had any chance of getting through, he needed to get the man's attention. "Sir, we're looking for a friend whose gone missing. If you could let us through, we'll only be a few minutes."

The policeman's expression didn't change. "Only local residents are allowed beyond this point. All areas within the outbreak zone are limited to current residents of homes within that area. No exceptions."

Luke knew better than to argue further and, unlike the other two stops, even Gail seemed to realize the same. They weren't getting through here either.

Time for Plan B.

Luke retrieved his ID, rolled up the window, and made a U-turn. He drove a block, turned on the first residential street he saw, and pulled into an on-street parking space. "Trade seats with me."

Gail fumbled with her seatbelt. "You want me to drive?"

"I want you to be able to drive, if you need to. But no. You wait here."

She raised an eyebrow.

"I'm just going to walk in, get what we need, and walk right back out." He put the car in park. "Easy."

Gail pursed her lips. "Don't you watch movies? You say things like that, you're asking for it."

He grinned at her as he hopped out of the driver's seat and into the rain. Several unladylike curse words muffled through the door after it closed behind him. Which made his grin widen.

She slid over into the driver's seat, a scowl still on her face.

Luke waited until he heard the soft clunk of the door locks, then disappeared into the rainy gray without looking back.

CHAPTER 33

Tess's head wobbled side-to-side, the world around her coming back in shards. A flickering light in the darkness. A whiff of cinnamon. A draft of tepid air walking across her skin like fingertips wandering where they didn't belong.

She jerked awake.

Where were her clothes? She'd been stripped down to only her underwear, her entire body on display. She jerked, trying to cover herself, her muscles seizing all at once. But she couldn't move.

Something sharp dug into the skin at her wrists. Zip-ties. Her hands had been cinched down to the armrests of an old desk chair. She pulled against the restraints, hard plastic cutting in to the base of her palms. A sharp sting at each wrist as it broke the skin.

She pulled harder. Fresh slices of pain and a deeper throb as the earlier gash on her arm broke open again. The bindings held.

She tried her legs. But they wouldn't move either — her ankles had been tied to something beneath the seat.

An icy tightness squeezed her chest, making her breath come fast and shallow.

Fuck.

She searched the room for any sign of her abductor, for anything that might give her a way out or explain what the hell was going on.

Looming mounds of bankers' boxes.

A familiar pattern of faint light sifting in near the roof.

She was back in the main room of the warehouse.

But this time, she could see. Kerosene lanterns glowed around her. At least four of them, maybe more behind her. And there was something else, shining in the dark where the flickering light of the lanterns didn't reach. A small orange-red thing. She stared at it.

What the hell is that?

"Aren't burns the worst?" His voice came from beyond the circle of light, and she jerked, her chair rolling to one side.

The man stepped into the light. He had a small metal tool in his hand. Like a soldering iron with a slightly elongated, glowing tip.

She stared at it, at him, then back at the glowing edge, trying to quiet the quaking terror rising within her. She couldn't lose it. Not now. She needed to stay calm. She had to look for an opportunity to get free, to gain some advantage. "What do you want?"

"Just to ask a few questions. That's all. This— " he waved the tool in the air, the glowing end making a figure-8 trail in the air that reminded her of New Year's sparklers. "This is only here in case you need help answering. It's all up to you."

She scowled at him but nodded, slowly.

"What did you do with the contents of Dr. Haley's safe deposit box?"

Her eyebrows shot up, dried blood crackling along her forehead. What the hell was he talking about? She wracked her brain for any connection that made sense. "The only safe deposit box I can think of was one I got access to for work, and there was nothing in it. Just a document that burned up in a fire."

"You know what they say about honesty." He stepped forward. "It really is the best policy." He pressed the iron to her chest. And every molecule of her body zeroed in on that single spot of excruciating pain, lancing into the skin above her right nipple. A scream ripped out of her that ended in an almost animal wail. "Stop!"

"Of course." He pulled the iron away. He ran his tongue over his bottom lip, the flush of arousal in his cheeks. "Like I said. You're in control." He reached toward her, tucking a strand of hair behind her ear. She shrank from his touch. His hand gentle, almost tender. "All you need to do is tell me what I want to know."

She opened her mouth to answer but gagged as the acrid smell of her own cooked flesh filled her nose. Her teeth chattered together. "I am… I am telling the truth." She stopped, trying to get the shaking under control. "The document was lost in a fire."

He stepped forward and put the iron to her chest again, this time on the inside swell of her other breast. She screamed again, and again, until he finally stopped. "I promise— " Her words fell into sobs. "I'm telling the truth."

He circled her chair with the iron in hand. Then sat it down on the ground, removed his jacket, folded it neatly, and placed it by the nearest row of boxes. "This is getting tiresome. I want to believe you. Really, I do." He retrieved the iron and eyed the glowing edge. "But we know you called Dr. Haley after the fire. And the only place you could have gotten that number is from the document you retrieved from his safe deposit box." He looked at her over the glowing tip. "The document you claim not to have."

He stepped closer.

Tess pulled as far away as her restraints would allow, the hard plastic of the zip ties cutting deeper into her skin. That pain all but lost to the searing agony on her chest. She blew out a breath so she could form the words. "I remembered it."

His expression didn't change as he brought the iron an inch from her skin. "There must be a hundred numbers on that paper. And you remembered it?" He moved the iron closer. It hovered just above her chest, close enough she could feel the heat radiating from its tip.

Tess's body finally went still. "I have an Eidetic memory."

His face stayed blank.

She tried again. "It's like a photographic memory."

He folded his arms, holding the business end of the iron away from his body. "Do you now?" Calculation crossed his face, as if he was trying to decide whether to believe her. Or maybe just how to break her.

She had to make him understand, make him believe. Anything to keep that iron away. "It's as if there's a video image of the document trapped in my mind."

"That's quite a story." He clicked his tongue. "Let's assume I decide you're telling the truth. Did you disclose the contents of the document to anyone? Or make a copy?"

Should she lie? Claim there was a copy somewhere else? Somewhere only she could get it? He stepped toward her, the glowing tip of the iron held in front of him like the point of a spear.

Think.

If she said Gail had it, it would put her friend in danger. And if she said a copy was hidden somewhere, and he discovered it wasn't. What then? What would he do to her?

She couldn't risk it. Wouldn't prolong whatever he had in mind for her. Tess closed her eyes tight and hung her head while the burns on her chest throbbed. "No."

"Did you send it to anyone?"

"No." She glanced at him.

"Interesting." He moved closer. "Are you quite sure?" Tess flattened herself against the chair, putting as much room between them as she could. "There are other ways I could encourage you to talk." He let the hand not holding the tool rest against the inside of her thigh, her skin crawling underneath. "If I feel you're being less than completely honest with me."

Her mouth went dry. Every part of her shrinking into nothing at the realization of what he meant. Of what he might do. "I'm sure," she finally answered him. Although it was so strangled, she wasn't sure he understood.

He circled his fingers over her skin in a lover's caress, then stepped back into the darkness. She looked down at the place on her leg where his hand had been. Where she could still feel the nauseating pressure against her skin. Then stared into the darkness, waiting.

Don't come back.

Don't come back.

He reappeared with a laptop. Her laptop. The one she'd lost to the fire... Recognition must have shown on her face, because he laughed. "I thought for sure you'd have put the pieces together after our little car accident. And certainly after our conversation today."

A flush of pure hatred, something worse than hatred came over her. He'd set her office on fire, probably destroying her career with it. She'd had to call all of her clients, tell them their files were destroyed. He'd run her off the road, abducted her, tortured her. Burned her. Threatened to rape her. And now he was mocking her?

A raw loathing she'd never known before coursed through her. Hostility in its purest form, undiluted by guilt or condition.

He sat down on the floor, the computer in his lap. "Password?"

She rattled it off without a blink. If it kept him away from her, she'd tell him anything. The room went silent, except for the clicking of keys on the laptop. He gave a quick nod. "Good, that's good."

She let out a breath. Maybe he'd found what he needed or confirmed what she'd said. Maybe—

He smacked the laptop shut and got to his feet, disappearing again into the dark. Then came muffled words and the shuffling of things being moved around, but she couldn't tell what he was doing. She peered into the darkness beyond the lanterns, searching for any sign of what might be coming. The not-knowing spooling out into a thin cord of panic pulled tight through her body.

He stepped back into the light, the iron in his hand. "Let's go through it all again, just to be sure."

CHAPTER 34

Luke stopped at a rusted chain-link gate, listening for any sign of dogs or trigger-happy homeowners. But the night air carried only the patter of fading rain and the rustle of wind through the trees overhead. He undid the gate's latch and stepped into the backyard of a bungalow with peeling sky-blue vinyl siding. This house sat dark and silent, like most of the others on the block. The few lit from the inside had their curtains drawn, as if blocking the view of what was happening outside would make it go away.

He traveled yard to yard, over hedges and a six-foot security fence, until he was sure he'd gone far enough that the officer at the roadblock wouldn't be able to see him. Then he slipped back out to the street. He'd make better time this way. He trudged block after empty block toward Tess's house, aiming for the light of the few streetlights whose bulbs weren't busted or burnt out.

Until the vague sense of being watched crept up the back of his neck.

Luke moved away from the spotlights of the streetlamps, seeking as much cover and concealment as possible given the terrain. His military training snapping back into place, as if his service had been yesterday and not years before. He plotted a course forward, shadow to shadow, gaining whatever tactical advantage he could in the limited visibility. He could be imagining it. It could be nothing. But experience told him to trust his gut.

People did crazy things in times of crisis. Looting, vandalism, and worse. Much worse. Like the interruption of normal life somehow meant none of the rules applied, until it was all just lawless chaos.

Now wasn't the time to be careless.

He kept to the grass to soften his footfalls and listened for anything to indicate he wasn't alone. He heard nothing. But he still couldn't escape the feeling of being under surveillance.

He slipped from a cluster of pine trees to the shadow of a tarp-covered trailer, and an irregular shape barely outside the glow of a streetlight came into view. Something in the road. He crossed the street, drawing silently closer. What was he looking at?

A trap? Maybe something meant to lure in the unsuspecting, a way to steal whatever money or weapons he had on him.

Or just someone who needed help?

A man lay splayed out on his back, his legs on the cracked pavement of a driveway, his head and torso in the path of any traffic that might come through.

"Hello?" Luke moved closer, wishing he had a weapon.

The man didn't move.

Luke closed the distance between them. "Are you…" His voice trailed off. The man looked as if he'd stumbled out of his house, still in his pajamas. Maybe looking for help. He had blood trickling from his nose, ears, and mouth. And he stared up at the starless night sky with bright red eyes.

Even knowing the man was beyond help, Luke pulled his cell phone from his pocket and dialed 911. He kept his gaze up, sweeping the area around him for danger, while it rang.

No one answered.

He pulled the phone away from his ear and checked to make sure he hadn't misdialed. He tried again. And again, got no answer. Luke flipped through his phone until he found the number for the Marburg information line. It rang once, twice, and on the third ring, someone picked up.

Thank God.

"Hello, we need help. There's a man, I think he's dead— "

A woman's voice. Polite, sedate. "Hello, you have reached the City of Atlanta's Marburg information hotline. All of our operators are currently helping other callers. Your call is important to us. Please leave a detailed message at the tone including your name, physical address, and the number of infected or dead about which you are calling. Help will be dispatched to you as soon as it becomes available. Thank you for your patience during this difficult time."

As soon as it becomes available.

No telling when that might be. Maybe never. And certainly not soon enough to help the man at his feet.

A tone sounded in his ear. He quickly rattled off their location as best he could tell from the few street signs he'd seen on the trek in and hung up. Luke turned to leave but stopped. He couldn't just leave the man lying in the road, exposed and alone.

He had to find some way to move the body out of the street. What if a car came through? The dead man had probably been someone's husband, brother, father. Luke took a faltering step forward, then stopped.

He's probably still infectious.

"Fuck." Luke's words echoed down the empty street.

A curtain twitched in the window of a house two doors down, but otherwise everything stayed perfectly, eerily still.

Luke kept his head on swivel, looking for any sign of danger as he trotted back to the trailer where he'd taken cover moments before. He pulled the tarp free, the crinkling of the heavy plastic impossibly loud.

Anyone nearby would almost certainly have tagged his location already. But still, he ducked his head against the noise.

Luke picked through a pile of scrap wood, found a broken two-by-four, and carried it and the tarp back to the body. He used the lumber to roll the man onto the rectangle of blue plastic, grabbed the sheet by the edge and, in three long tugs, pulled his gruesome cargo away from the road and over the curb. The last tug brought the body onto a short stretch of dirt above a cluster of mailboxes.

As the body came to rest, a thick rivulet of blood snaked across the plastic toward Luke's hand. The virus seeking its next host.

Luke dropped the tarp, heart frozen in his chest. Then made himself pull it up and around the body, careful not to touch any of the areas wet with blood as he made the man a shroud. There was nothing else he could think to do.

Our Father, who art in heaven, hallowed be Thy name.

He hadn't gone to church in years, but the prayer had always comforted him when he was a kid. He had no idea whether the man had been Christian. Maybe not. But even if the words themselves would've meant nothing to him, they were still a recitation of respect. A marking of the man's passing Luke felt, in some fundamental way, everyone deserved.

He made himself get moving again. One block — and three more rounds of the Lord's Prayer later — he saw it. Tess's house glowed in the distance. Her curtains were wide open, the front hall lamp lighting up the street in front.

Please let her door be locked.

If it was, there was a chance she was inside. A chance she was safe.

He jogged the distance, ignoring the tactical advantage of shadows, and twisted the knob.

The door swung open. And he knew, before he called her name, the house was empty. It was too still, too preserved. Everything as he'd left it that morning. Her keys still on the counter, their cups still on the coffee table.

He lowered his head, his lips pressed tight in a grimace.

Remember why you're here.

Luke scanned the room for her computer. It had to be somewhere. He went room to room, which only took a matter of seconds. The tiny house had a combined living, dining, kitchen area and, off a small hallway, her bedroom and bath. Which didn't make for many places to look. But still, he didn't see it.

He went through the house again, this time, pulling the curtains closed as he went. He stopped at an overstuffed chair in her bedroom. Clothes she'd probably either intended to wash or wear again covered the seat and draped over the chair's back. A cord snaked out from underneath. He shifted the laundry to the bed and pulled the phone charger from the wall, his nose catching the light, citrusy perfume he remembered from their night together. It made something in him ache.

Luke went back to the kitchen and pulled open the drawer closest to the fridge. Under a random assortment of batteries and a half-sleeve of thin mints, he found a notepad, right where Gail said it would be. It had Tess's login, Apple ID, and password scrawled across the top.

Now all he needed was the computer.

Except it was nowhere to be found.

He braced his hands on the kitchen counter and jumped up to sit next to the sink, leaning his head back against the wall so he could think. But no bright ideas came to mind. He thunked his head against the wall.

Where hadn't he looked?

He scanned the room again, and his gaze stopped on an unopened bag of kibble leaned against the back wall. Tater must be starved. Could he get the food back to his truck? He thunked his head against the wall again. He couldn't let Tater go hungry. So, yes, one way or another, he would.

It might be the only thing he could do for Tess.

He smacked his head against the wall again, hating that thought. And, from under half-closed lids, caught a glint of silver between the couch cushions. The laptop? With a jolt of adrenaline, he jumped down from the counter, half-jogged to the living room, and pulled it from between the cushions.

Fuck, yeah.

Luke opened the lid. The background for Tess's desktop showed an image of her standing arm-in-arm with a much older version of herself behind a raised planter bed with a single scraggly tomato plant. Both of the women were covered in dirt to their elbows, their faces sunburned, with matching grins ear to ear.

The ache grew stronger.

Luke logged in, went into iCloud, and activated the Find My iPhone feature. Then he scrolled through until he found icons for her phone and watch. "Bingo." He clicked, and a gray compass spun on the page.

Come on, come on.

Let it work. It had to work. The compass stopped, and Luke leaned in toward the screen.

A map appeared of an area not far from the farmers' market in Decatur. Two green dots sat a few blocks off of DeKalb Industrial Boulevard. What the hell was there? Nothing, so far as he remembered. Still, he leaned in, studying the map, committing it to memory. Then pulled his phone from his pocket and snapped a photo.

Just in case.

Now that he had a lead, he wasn't taking any chances.

. . .

The door locks disengaged with a soft clunk as Luke finally made it back to the truck. In the rearview mirror, Gail gave him a thumbs up and a grin. He dropped the dog food in the truck bed and pulled his shoulders back in a stretch. The thirty-pound bag had started to feel more like sixty halfway there.

He climbed into the passenger seat and unzipped the backpack he'd found in Tess's front hall closet, tilting it so Gail could see the laptop inside. "I got it."

"You did?" She leaned forward, her face lighting with a smile. "Did it work?"

"It says her phone and her watch are somewhere close to the farmers market. The big one in Decatur."

She collapsed back in her seat. "That can't be right. There's nothing over there."

He shrugged. "I know. But it's somewhere to start."

She opened her mouth as if to protest again, then gave a quick nod and clicked her seat belt in place. "Alright then." She slid the key into the ignition.

A sudden smack from the driver's side window.

Both of them jumped as a hand slid down the glass, leaving a bloody smear behind. On the other side of the gore, a middle-aged woman with tight black curls looked in at them. The flesh of her face drooped like a mask loosening from the tissue underneath. Blood ran freely from her nose, and her mouth hung slack, revealing teeth smeared black. She looked at Luke with bright red, unblinking eyes. Then her gaze flicked away, bouncing left to right, and back again.

Gail put her hand on the door.

"Stop." He took a deep breath. Then another. The woman was too far gone to help.

Gail looked over at him, a question in her eyes.

"She's infected." He worked to keep his voice even. "If you open the door, we will be, too."

Gail nodded, slowly, then shrugged. "If I don't, we'll be something worse."

Luke looked from Gail to the woman outside. She was right. "Stay here," he commanded, swinging open the passenger door.

Gail grabbed his arm, yanking him back. "Wait."

He pulled the door closed and turned to her, eyebrows raised.

Gail's face lost all its color. "It's too late."

The woman fell to her knees, then backward with her legs tucked beneath her. The flow of blood from her eyes and nose quickened, pouring out of her.

How could she have that much blood inside her body?

She convulsed on the ground, vomiting up more of the dark, viscous liquid until she and the ground beneath her were saturated.

He couldn't look away. And it was like the world had gone still. No wind moving in the trees, no sound but his own pulse loud in his ears. She wasn't the first person he'd seen die. But the others had all been soldiers. People who'd signed on for war, who made choices that brought them to the other end of a gun. This was different.

He forced himself to act, found his phone, and pulled back up the Marburg hotline. The least he could do for the woman was tell someone where they could find her body.

Gail stared out through the glass while he left the message.

"I'm sorry." She said under her breath, speaking to the woman as she started the engine. When she looked over to him, silent tears lined her bottom lids. They stared at each other a long moment until Gail finally wiped the wet from her face. "Let's go get our girl."

CHAPTER 35

September 22, 2018

Tess strained against her bindings but didn't bother screaming. Her throat burned with each breath, raw from the hours she'd already spent calling for help.

None had come.

The man walked back into the area lit by the lanterns' glow, and every muscle in her body went rigid.

"There, there, now. All done with the hard part." He spoke in a placating sing-song voice. Like she was a child who'd cried her way through getting a shot.

The simmer of anger inside her spiked to a boil. She gripped the edges of the chair's armrests, blood pounding in her ears. All the pain and frustration, the crushing helplessness, solidified into something else — resolve.

She wasn't afraid anymore. The pain no longer registered.

He crouched in front of her, and the zip ties around her ankles shifted back and forth against her skin, as if he was cutting her free. But no part of her flickered with hope. She'd seen his face. And, worse, the flush of pleasure in his cheeks. The hiss of satisfaction, each time he'd made her scream. He wasn't planning to let her leave alive.

Her legs came free, and she gave each a short stretch. They tingled and ached with pins and needles, her muscles protesting the movement. She did it anyway. She needed to be ready to run if she had the chance. She visualized herself breaking free, trying to run, but stuck in place. How often had she had that dream? Running away from some dark unknowable nightmare thing, legs pumping, willing herself forward, even as her body barely moved. Everything in slow motion except what was coming for her.

This nightmare couldn't end that way.

When she got her chance, she would be ready.

Another train whistle sounded in the distance as he moved up to her arms, cutting one zip tie and then the next. She rubbed at the raw spots on her wrists and put pressure on the re-opened gash, never taking her eyes off him. All she needed was an opening.

He pointed the knife at her. It was long, curved at the tip and serrated on one side. The flicker of the lanterns reflecting on the metal as he wagged it back and forth in her direction. "Don't get any ideas."

She nodded, body tense. He had to believe she was beaten, no longer a threat.

The man lifted the edge of his shirt to wipe a trickle of blood from Tess's cheek. It smelled of sweat. Everything in her wanted to jerk away, but she forced herself to stay still. Waiting, watching.

"That's better." He leaned in and kissed her. Soft, tentative, like a first kiss. As if they'd been on a date. Her stomach churned. As much as she'd wanted to wait for just the right moment, to buy time until she could distract him and run again. His kiss grew hungrier, his tongue thrusting into her mouth.

No.

She shoved him away, the chair flying out from under her as she wiped his filthy saliva from her mouth and spat in the floor. Glass broke behind her, but she didn't turn to see what it was. She focused everything on trying to get steady on her feet while the room spun around her.

"Not to worry, sweetheart." His tongue, a small gray-pink thing, darted out to swipe his upper lip. "I like it rough." He turned the knife over slowly in his hand and came toward her again. She took a step back and then another, her heel knocking into one of lanterns.

She widened her stance.

Not long now.

He closed the distance, pressing himself against her and bringing the knife to her throat. She didn't move. His other hand fumbled to undo his pants, sweat glistening on his face, anticipation in his eyes. His erection pressed into her leg through the fabric of his trousers.

She waited, hoping her disgust was plain on her face.

He struggled to get himself free. "Shit."

Still, she waited, her breath caught in her throat.

With a frustrated grunt, the man lowered his knife-hand between them. And as he worked to get his pants down, she grabbed the knife hilt with both of her hands and jerked upward. She knew there was a chance she'd stab herself. She couldn't see what she was doing between their bodies, tightly pressed together. But she was beyond caring.

This was going to end, one way or another.

The knife went into his stomach with a fleshy thud. Shock, then realization, flickered across his face as wet seeped out over the hilt and onto her hands, sticky and hot.

She jerked the knife up again.

His body convulsed forward. "Bitch."

She leaned in. "You're never going to hurt anyone ever again." She shoved the knife deeper, twisting the blade even as the handle grew slick in her hands, and she lost her grip.

He fell to his knees, pulling at the knife jutting from under his rib cage as he collapsed. His breath came in shallow bursts, the blood black where it seeped out of him and onto the floor. His hands fumbled, flopping useless around the hilt of the knife before falling limp.

She watched to make sure he didn't get up.

A low buzz hummed in her ears.

She waited for guilt. For relief.

Neither came. She felt nothing.

The dark pool grew around his body, light dancing across its surface.

The light.

She blinked, looking up at the flames spreading around the room. The fire stared back, crackling and hungry. The lantern she'd broken must have splashed its fuel on the boxes behind her. The reams of paper going up like tinder. Her old laptop and two more lanterns were already inside the blaze.

How long until the fuel inside the other lanterns caught, too? Would they explode?

She tried to make herself care but couldn't. None of it seemed real.

The fire jumped from box to box and down to the rolls of paper that lined the walls. Smoke mixed with the sickly sweet, metallic scent of blood in her nose.

She looked back to the man. His eyes stayed fixed forward, reflecting the fiery glow inching across the ceiling above him. His hands lay loose at his sides. She picked his jacket up from the floor and wrapped it around herself — her desire to be covered only a thin breath stronger than her repulsion as she pulled it on.

Tess hobbled toward what she hoped was the door, leaving him to burn.

CHAPTER 36

"Want me to drive?" Luke watched Gail from the corner of his eye. She shook her head but didn't answer. Her knuckles clenched white on the steering wheel. It was one thing to know people were dying from the outbreak. It was another to watch it happen. To see it, face to face, and know there was nothing they could do to help.

They rode down Ponce de Leon, the rough commercial area turning green and lush as they wound toward downtown Decatur. He clicked on the radio to fill the growing silence, flipping through stations until he found the news. "—after a record market decline, the SEC announced its plan to continue yesterday's trading halt indefinitely and extended it from the New York Stock Exchange to all major U.S. exchanges. In local news, the mayor has again asked citizens to use the Marburg information hotline to report any known or suspected infection. Local health authorities have issued a statement requesting that patients suffering from non-life-threatening conditions avoid area hospitals as all are at or above capacity. Help should be sought from your primary care physician, if possible. If you are suffering from a non-Marburg related emergency, you are asked to please dial 911."

Luke snorted, and Gail gave him a questioning look. "What?"

"They don't answer."

She glanced at him again. "Who doesn't?"

He turned the radio back off. "Take your pick: 911, the Marburg hotline, no one answers the phone." Like it or not, they were on their own. "Stay to the right." He pointed in that direction when the road split, then dug out Tess's laptop.

Luke logged in, connected to the wifi on his phone, and looked out the window while he waited for the map to load. Tree-lined streets. Lovely old houses with well-tended yards. Porch lights glowed, and autumn wreaths or wooden signs hung on each door, "Happy Fall, Ya'll" or "Go Dawgs". But the sidewalks and yards stood empty. No sign of any human life but them.

The loading wheel on the computer screen kept spinning.

And spinning.

Come on, come on.

Still, nothing happened. Luke smacked the laptop closed, and Gail jumped.

"Sorry." He grimaced. "I can't get the map to come up." He pulled up the photos on his phone. "But I took a picture of it when I was at Tess's. Let's just hope she's still there."

Assuming she had been to begin with. They crossed DeKalb Industrial Boulevard, entering a desolate area of undeveloped lots and warehouses. Tess would have no good reason to be there. Even so, he looked down at the photo and said, "should be close now."

Gail slowed, pausing at each side street or driveway as he inspected the map, murmuring for her to "keep going." Most of the roads were unmarked, some concrete but many dirt. Several had chain link fences, none had bothered with landscaping. Each time they stopped, the dot showing Tess's location seemed to be close, but not quite, where they were.

They rolled into the farmers' market parking lot at the end of the street, and Luke dropped the phone in his lap. "Fuck." He stared at the ceiling, then looked over to Gail. "Sorry."

"Nothing wrong with an f-bomb when it's warranted, sugar." Gail pulled into a parking spot facing the market, where a hand-painted sign had been tacked up "Closed Until Further Notice." Abandoned cars dotted the lot. The driver's side door of the one closest to them, an old Buick parked catty-corner across two spots, stood open. Like the driver had just climbed out and walked away.

Or worse.

A smear of something oily and dark lay just beyond the open door.

He made himself look away.

“We’ll go back and try each of the side roads until we find the right one.” Gail put the truck in reverse and rolled down the window, sticking her head out to check behind them before she backed up. “You smell that?”

He shook his head, then stopped. Smoke. Luke ducked his head so he could see past the truck’s roof to the horizon. “There.” His heart rate sped up as he pointed beyond the warehouses they’d passed before turning in to the lot. “Something’s on fire.” A dull orange glow stood out against the early morning sky.

“Is that a good thing?” Gail looked at him like he’d lost his mind.

Probably not, but… “Let’s go find out.” It was a long shot, but a fire could mean someone was nearby. And he was out of other ideas.

They followed the smoke to the second side road before the farmers’ market and turned in, driving through an open chain link fence and into an industrial park. Luke peered up at the sky but couldn’t see the fire’s glow anymore. Not with the warehouses so tightly packed around them.

Gail wove around one identical metal building after another. “We’ll take it like a grid.” She started down an aisle of buildings, taking a left when she reached the end.

Their headlights flashed on a figure wrapped in a dark coat.

Gail slammed on the brakes, the tires kicking up loose gravel from the pavement as the truck jerked to a stop.

The person limped toward them. A woman, her bare legs striped with rivulets of blood.

Not again. Not another one.

He couldn't bear to watch anyone else die. The woman reached out a hand, blocking the glare of the headlights as she moved closer. She stumbled, and the light shone on her face.

Tess.

Luke flew out the door.

Gail yelled from behind him. "She's infected. Luke, wait."

But they'd found her, and he couldn't stop. As he got closer, the smell of smoke and blood hit his nose, and the risk of what he was doing finally registered. He froze a few feet away, and a stone of dread settled in his stomach. To come so close and not be able to help. To know that they'd tried so hard and gotten there too late. It gutted him.

Tess stared at him, a puzzled look on her face. "Luke?" She swayed, unsteady on her feet. Then dropped to her knees and slouched sideways to sit on the ground. "What are you doing here?" Her voice came out a whisper.

He went to her and crouched down, his worry greater than any rational thought. "We came to see if you were okay."

"I've been better." Her mouth turned up at the corners — half grimace, half smile.

He searched her face. None of the blood came from her eyes or nose. And the whites of her eyes were clear, not the red of the infected. "You're not sick?"

She shook her head. Another whisper. "No."

Thank God.

His shoulders sagged with relief. "Can you stand?"

She nodded. But when he reached for her, she flinched, her eyes squeezing closed. "Sorry." Bruises covered her face, and she had a cut over her eyebrow that would probably need stitches.

He stopped, an icy realization forming crystals under his skin. She might not be sick, but something else terrible had happened. He kept his voice soft. "It's okay. When you're ready."

She swallowed and nodded again.

Luke helped her up, her oversized jacket swinging open. She wore nothing but underwear underneath. And small burns, each a perfect line about a half-inch long, scattered her chest, her stomach, and… Jesus, the inside of her thighs. His throat tightened until it hurt, but he forced himself to be calm. It wouldn't do her any good for him to lose it.

He took stock of the rest of her injuries. Raw, bloody marks circled her ankles. He pushed up one jacket sleeve, then the other. Matching marks circled her wrists. Blood dripped from one of her pinky fingers to the ground below, leaving a small crescent of red dots on the pavement. Someone hadn't just hurt her, they'd tortured her. Maybe worse. He tried to swallow and couldn't.

He'd fucking kill whoever'd done this. When she was safe, when he'd gotten her the help she needed, he would destroy them.

"She's not infected," he called to Gail. "Just hurt."

He turned back to Tess, almost afraid to ask, but, "What happened?"

She shook her head, unable or unwilling to voice it. He didn't blame her, and he didn't want to push her to talk about it before she was ready. But he needed to make sure whatever had happened was over. Whoever had hurt her might still be nearby. Part of him — the animal part that wanted to tear them limb from limb — hoped so. He tried again. "Who did this?"

Tess looked behind her, down one of the aisles that ran between warehouses. "He's dead." When she turned to Luke again, her eyes stood empty. The fire he'd seen in them when they'd met in the hospital had gone out. Not even an ember left burning. "I killed him." There was no remorse in her tone, no feeling at all.

"Good," he answered, and he meant it. He only regretted not being able to do it himself.

She pulled the jacket closed again, and he tucked a bloodied lock of hair behind her ear. His words failing. If he'd been faster, he could have spared her some suffering, maybe spared her from having to take a life. How was she going to deal with what had happened? With what she'd been forced to do? He knew trained soldiers brought to their knees by less.

Gail appeared by his side. "Hello, love." She moved slowly toward Tess, seeming to take in her friend's condition before wrapping her in a gentle hug. Gail shifted so that she looked at Luke over Tess's shoulder. He gave a small nod, confirmation of the suspicion he saw in Gail's face. Someone had done this to Tess on purpose. Gail squeezed her eyes shut.

When she finally let go, Gail's tone was light, the look gone as she turned to Tess. "Let's get you out of here."

Tess nodded and leaned into Luke, one arm around his back, the other over Gail's shoulders as they limped toward the truck. "How did you find me?"

"We tracked your watch and your phone." Luke pulled open the door and helped her climb in.

Her face tightened in pain as she settled onto the bench seat. "You what?" She reached down, feeling her naked wrist. "I think maybe he took them." Tess shivered, her teeth chattering as Gail climbed in beside her. "When he took my…" Tess pulled the jacket even tighter around her as the rest of her sentence tapered off to nothing.

He had no trouble filling in the rest.

When he took her clothes.

Motherfucker.

Blood pounded in Luke's ears, but he tried to keep the rage off his face as he circled the truck and climbed in next to Tess.

She stared out the windshield, still shaking. He followed her gaze, but there was nothing there. Just the warehouse lot, bare and empty in the gray light of dawn. He clenched his jaw until it ached, turning the heat on high and the vents toward her.

She leaned her head against Gail's shoulder, her eyes drooping before he'd put the truck in drive.

She needed a doctor. But the hospitals were closed or over-run, and any urgent care clinic was likely to be just as bad. He ran through all the options he could think of.

None of them were good.

. . .

Tess awoke to the jostling of the truck as it crossed over a set of railroad tracks.

Luke spoke from beside her. "I'm sorry I didn't call sooner. I—" He moved the phone away from his ear.

A woman's angry voice, brushed with a Caribbean lilt, spilled out into the cab. "I nearly had to hog-tie Parker to keep him from going out looking for you."

Luke's mouth turned up on one side. "That I'd pay to see."

The voice got louder, several of the words in a language Tess didn't recognize. French? Or maybe Creole.

"I really am sorry." Luke pulled to a stop at a red light.

A man with a bandana over the bottom of his face crossed the road in front of them. He peered into the truck, his eyes a pink-red above the cloth.

Tess tensed, waiting until the sick man crossed to the other side of the road and disappeared behind a row of dumpsters before she let herself breathe again. She might've walked out of that warehouse alive, but it didn't mean she felt safe.

Nothing in the world did anymore.

"Listen, I have a friend with me who's hurt. She's not infected, just injured. But the radio says the hospitals are overrun. I'm not sure where to take her. Hang on, I'm going to put you on speaker." Luke tapped a button on the phone, then dropped it in his lap as the light changed. He pulled through the intersection. "Do you know if it's better outside the city? If the interstate isn't clogged with other people who had the same idea, maybe we could find help near my place? Or maybe your boss could help?"

"Our office is closed. Dr. Abboud came down with it yesterday—" She stopped, interrupted by a cascade of little girl giggles. "Sorry, hang on." When she spoke again, her voice was muffled. "Nick? Could you take Charlotte to play in her room?"

The image from Luke's phone came to Tess's mind. The little girl and the gorgeous woman he'd had his arm around. Long black waves, shining brown eyes. The same woman she'd seen with Nick outside the hospital, maybe his wife or girlfriend. After a long pause, the woman continued. "Sorry about that. I know this is going to sound crazy, but you can't get out of the city anymore."

Luke tapped his thumb against the wheel. "What do you mean?"

"The government put a barrier up around 285. We're all stuck here until they get the outbreak under control."

The tapping stopped. "They did what?"

Tess glanced at Gail, who gave a short shake of her head. That didn't make any sense. They couldn't just hold the entire population of in-town Atlanta against their will. Who would even have the authority to—

The woman's voice lowered, probably to make sure the little girl couldn't overhear her from the other room. "There's a freaking fence, running right down the center of the interstate. The news says they've got drone surveillance and soldiers patrolling it. No one's allowed out of the city."

Soldiers.

Of course the military would be involved. No one else would be able to just shut an entire city the size of Atlanta off from the rest of the world. Tess pulled the blanket in her lap up to her chin, then seeing the stricken look on Gail's face, shifted so that it covered them both.

A crease formed between Luke's brows. "I can't believe people let that happen."

"What choice do they have?" The woman's accent got stronger. "They're keeping anyone who resists at the Georgia Dome. Infected, uninfected, all in there together. It's a mess. And now they're saying maybe you can get it just by being near someone. Like it can float through the air to get to you."

Tess heard what she'd said but couldn't absorb it, her mind refusing to accept any more trauma. It was someone else's problem, in a reality that wasn't hers anymore.

She'd killed someone.

The world was falling apart around her.

And nothing would ever be the way it had been before.

The woman spoke again. "Do you have masks? You could come here. I don't have much to work with, just whatever's in the medicine cabinet. But Nick could keep Charlotte in her room, and I'll do my best to help."

"Thank you, Cassie. Really. We're in Midtown now, so at least twenty or thirty minutes from you guys, but we may take you up on that. I'm going to try urgent care first. She's going to need stitches for sure. And—" He looked over at Tess then back at the road, "burn treatment."

A sharp intake of breath came over the line. "Jesus. What happened?"

"Nothing good." Luke's voice came out rough.

Tess stared out the window while Luke finished his call, not seeing anything. The question was enough to put her right back in that warehouse, the man's breath on her face. The iron searing her skin. The acrid smell of her own burning flesh filling her nose. The wet knife slipping from her grip. Her stomach went sour, a fist of nausea tightening around the back of her throat.

"Hey," Gail rested her hand on Tess's knee, "you okay?"

"No." Tess stared out at the city as they wove around abandoned cars and groups of people in paper masks going God knows where.

There was no where for any of them to go.

CHAPTER 37

Miguel Romero clasped Mara's hand over the rail of his hospital bed. The calluses on his palm scraping rough against the top of her hand, even through a double layer of surgical gloves.

"Thank you." He held her gaze, his deep brown eyes clear and unwavering. The monitors behind him made a steady, syncopated beep. "A thousand times, thank you. You cannot imagine what it means to me to know my family is okay."

"You are more than welcome." Mara collected his chart from the foot of the bed. "We'll see what we can do about getting your wife and son moved upstairs so you can wait out quarantine together." While she tried to figure out what she'd missed.

She flipped through the chart, skimming each page of providers' notes and test results. Looking for what, she couldn't say. An explanation? She wasn't likely to find anything that hadn't been there the last five times she'd looked. Mr. Romero wasn't Caucasian, and yet everything seemed to indicate he was immune.

Was it possible all the time she'd spent studying patterns of infection had been wasted?

Had she made any progress, any difference at all?

The words on Mr. Romero's chart blurred on the page, and she fought the urge to rub the exhaustion from her eyes. Maybe she'd missed something because she was just so damned worn out.

"It would be wonderful if my family could be together." Mr. Romero said, his voice thick with emotion.

She looked up from the chart.

He had tears in his eyes. "My son is only twelve. And knowing I'd been exposed, that I might've brought it home with me." He swallowed and shook his head. "I don't like the idea of him alone in the hospital. With all that's going on. He must be nervous."

"Your son is with your wife now." She put the chart back where she'd found it, making herself refocus on what should be a bright spot in an otherwise soul-crushing day. She finally had the chance to reunite a family, rather than watch it be torn apart. "I'll go see about the details of having them transferred."

"Good, good." He settled back, a look of relief on his face.

Mara excused herself to the hall, wishing she could let herself share in his relief. But the facts of his case wouldn't let her. As a funeral home technician, Mr. Romero had been directly and repeatedly exposed to Marburg Hemphill early in the outbreak. In the brief time before the CDC's alert against such contact was issued, he'd not only transported bodies hot with the virus, but, when one of his co-workers failed to show up for work, he had assisted the funeral director in the embalming process. Which meant he'd had direct contact with blood, tissue, and human waste — all of which would have been teeming with the virus. The funeral director had died from the disease that morning, but Mr. Romero remained uninfected.

Why?

Mara headed back toward the nursing station. The fact she now had people of color who also appeared to possess some sort of immunity, or at least resistance, to the disease didn't prove anything. The statistical anomaly was still there — patients who identified themselves as Caucasian on their intake paperwork were dramatically underrepresented in the group who tested positive for Marburg Hemphill. The same pattern was true in Los Angeles and in the small cluster of cases that had broken out in Minneapolis overnight. She had no doubt it meant something.

She just didn't know what.

Mara flagged down a nurse. "Could you see about moving Mr. Romero's wife and son up here?" She tilted her head toward his room.

"I'd be glad to." The nurse hurried off, no doubt happy to deliver good news for a change. Mara watched her go. It might be the last bit of anything good they'd see for a while. They were no closer to finding an effective treatment plan than they had been when she'd started.

She stopped mid-hallway and leaned against the wall, letting her sandpaper eyes drift closed. God, she was tired.

Alarm bells rang out in the distance, a sound now so ubiquitous it was only background noise. Mara turned in the opposite direction, taking the long way back to her office. She needed to stretch her legs, to think. Outside the bank of windows lining the hallway, the gray-blue light of dawn revealed the freeway below. Cars clogged the road, none of them moving. Drivers' doors stood open, cars left at odd angles between the lanes. Probably abandoned by owners who'd given up hope of escape.

She didn't blame them.

A young doctor from the isolation ward hurried past her, already in full protective gear. He was handsome, with dark eyes and deep smile lines. Behind the face shield, he grimaced in Mara's direction. But he didn't slow.

Emmy.

The alarms.

Mara spun around and broke into a run behind him, matching his pace even though it took her two strides to his one. Her panic rose with the volume of the warning bells, every step closer to Emmy's room confirming what she already knew.

They rounded the corner to isolation. Through the glass wall partition, a frenzy of activity filled Emmy's room. A team of doctors, all in full protective gear, moved with fluid efficiency around her hospital bed. There was no effective treatment. Mara knew that as well as the doctors working to save Emmy's life. But it didn't stop any of them from trying.

The dark-eyed doctor smacked open the door to Emmy's room, the alarms growing still louder as it opened. He turned back, tilting his head toward a bin holding stacks of protective equipment. "Suit up."

Under other circumstances, she'd have been annoyed he thought she needed reminding, but people did crazy things when the ones they loved were dying. And right now, she wasn't a doctor. She was Emmy's friend.

"Thank you," Mara choked out, but the door that had already closed behind him. She ripped off the smaller mask she wore outside the isolation ward, sanitized her hands, pulled on two sets of gloves, and yanked a protective suit from the pile. She needed to hurry the hell up. Needed to be there. Needed to give Emmy whatever comfort might come from knowing she was. She shoved herself into the suit but struggled to get the protective booties on. Mara hopped on one foot, sliding on the worn, linoleum floor. She leaned against the glass wall to get her balance and stopped.

Inside, the room had gone still. The team of doctors stood around Emmy. No one moved.

She was too late.

Mara's hands shook as she rubbed at the pain in her chest, a heavy empty space where something lovely used to live.

CHAPTER 38

The windows of the Piedmont Road urgent care clinic gaped dark and empty. The front door had been pulled loose from the hinges. It dangled, still half-attached, and someone had spray-painted "No Help Here" in electric blue across the building's brick facade.

Tess stared out through the rain-spattered windshield of Luke's truck, too tired to care that they hadn't found help. And maybe even a little bit glad. A doctor would want to know how she'd gotten hurt. Would make her say out loud what had happened. Her throat threatened to close at the idea, the nausea back for an encore. Tess closed her eyes, willing it away.

Gail squeezed her hand. "We'll figure something out."

"I know." Tess nodded, even though she didn't. But, no matter what happened, she was beyond grateful to have Gail and Luke there with her while they tried. She whispered her fingertips around the gash on her forehead. "I think the bleeding stopped."

Gail eyed the cut but said nothing. She turned toward Luke, who had pulled out of the urgent care parking lot while they'd been talking. "Take a right up here."

"Do you know somewhere else we could try?" He flipped on the blinker.

"No, but I know where we can go for now." Gail pointed the way, and soon the streets became familiar.

Luke pulled into one of the parallel spots in front of Gail's building, her neighborhood quiet except for the steady barking of a dog.

Tater.

Tess's heart expanded in her chest. It made no sense for her to take such comfort in knowing her dog was there. That he was safe. That she'd be able to bury her face in his fur and cry. But it did. She looked at Gail, the tears already building behind her eyes. "Thank you."

Gail waved her off, then dug a set of keys from her purse and dropped them into Tess's hand. "You go let yourself in. I'll get Tater from the backyard, and we'll meet you upstairs."

They climbed out of the truck into the early morning light. Another dawn on Gail's front stoop. God, how much things had changed since yesterday. Or had it been the day before? She'd lost track of everything, the world slipping off its axis. None of what had happened since seemed possible or real. What she wouldn't give for that to be true.

But it wasn't.

And there was no changing it. No changing what'd happened. What she'd done. She took a deep breath and followed Luke around the back of the truck, where he hefted a bag of dog food onto one shoulder.

Tess stopped. "Where'd you get that?"

"He carried it back from your house, when he went to get your laptop." Gail reached into the truck and pulled a backpack from the floorboard.

"But that thing's got to weigh like forty pounds." Tess shook her head at him.

Luke shrugged, adjusting the bag.

"You're amazing." One corner of Tess's mouth lifted, her heart so full it felt like it might burst. "Both of you."

"Hush." Gail said with a smile. She shut the truck's door and walked toward the building's side yard. "Head on inside."

It took time for Tess to make it up the stairs to Gail's apartment. Exhaustion had settled heavy in her bones, and everything hurt. But once she got there, the familiar warmth of Gail's place — with all its floral patterns and family photos — felt like a sanctuary. A safe, normal place, untouched by the chaos outside.

She lowered herself to the couch, the leather cool against her skin. She'd never been so tired in her life. A thud came from the kitchen, the dog food dropping to the floor, and Luke came to join her. She tensed as he sat down, and he must have noticed because he stiffened, shifting to give her space.

Tess made herself relax. "Sorry. It's not you."

"I know." His voice was rough, but there was understanding in his eyes when she looked up. He pulled a throw blanket from the back of the sofa, holding it out to her. "You're going to be okay. And I'll be here. As long as you need me to be."

She took the blanket, searching his eyes. Nothing in them scared her. She reached out, taking his hand in hers. She needed there not to be anything but truth between them. "Can I ask you something?"

"Of course. Anything."

"The picture on the home screen of your phone, who is it?"

He blinked, confusion passing over his face. "My Goddaughter and her mom. We talked to Cassie on the phone earlier. She's Nick's wife, er, was." He shook his head. "It's hard to tell with them."

Tess closed her eyes. She'd made such a mess of things. "Okay." Later, she'd owe him an apology for jumping to conclusions, for running out on him. But for now, what she needed was peace.

And him.

They sat together hand-in-hand on the couch until a series of rollicking thuds came from the stairwell, followed by a frenzy of scratches at the door. Tater burst into the room, with Gail in tow. She dropped the leash, a smile in her voice as she turned for the kitchen. "Your dog is a menace."

Tater run-waddled his way to Tess and stopped, a few feet from the couch. He cocked his head to one side, a low whine in his throat, and inched closer, dropping to his belly.

"Hi, dog. It's still me."

Tater put his chin on Tess's foot.

"I'm fine, big boy. I promise. I just need a shower and a band-aid."

Tater didn't move. He looked up at her without moving his head. He had the same look of skepticism in his good eye as Luke did when she met his gaze.

"Maybe two band-aids." Tess smiled at them both.

Gail put a pair of metal bowls on the floor outside the kitchen door. "Come eat, Tater." The dog didn't move.

Tess moved to get up. "Can I use your shower?" She'd never wanted anything more.

"We have to deal with that cut on your forehead first and any others that are open like that." Gail grimaced as she inspected it. "Then, the shower's all yours." She disappeared down the hall and came back with a wicker basket under one arm. "Let's see what we have to work with." She settled beside Tater on the floor and dug through what turned out to be a medicine bin, pulling out cotton balls, rubbing alcohol, a tube of Polysporin, burn cream, gauze, and an old bottle of painkillers. She shook the bottle, and a few pills rattled around inside. "Let's start with this." She turned to Luke. "Could you grab some water?"

Luke jumped up, like he was glad to have something to do to help. He banged through kitchen cabinets while Gail soaked a cotton ball in alcohol and dabbed it around the wound on Tess's wrist. The antiseptic stung like a bitch. Tess hissed out a breath between her teeth.

"Sorry." Gail gave her wrist one last dab, soaked another cotton ball, and moved on to the cut on Tess's forehead. Tess squeezed her eyes shut, trying to focus on the sound of water running in the kitchen instead of the searing pain on her forehead. When the dabbing finally stopped, Tess opened her eyes, but Gail was still hovering.

"I'm afraid stitches are outside my skill set. Never did learn to sew, despite my mama's best efforts." Gail leaned in for a better look, then sat back on her heels. "How do you feel about super glue?"

Tess blew on the cut on her wrist, trying to take the edge off the sting. "I wouldn't say it's something I'm passionate about."

Gail rolled her eyes. "I read online you can use it to close wounds."

"Do it." Tess showed the palms of her hands, both covered in red-brown stains. Blood that wasn't hers, seeping into her skin. The longer it was there, the more it felt like it might never go away.

A constant reminder of what had she'd been through.

Of what she'd done.

Tess's chest tightened. "I don't know how much longer I can go without a bath. Let's just get it over with."

Luke handed her a glass of water. "Super glue sounds like a terrible idea."

Tess shrugged, opening her mouth so Gail could drop a painkiller onto her tongue. She rinsed it down and finished the water in one go. How long had it been since she'd had anything to drink? At the hospital?

Gail took the empty glass from her hand and disappeared into the kitchen. She came back with a refill, a small white tube, and a roll of cling wrap under one arm. "Hold still."

Tess took the water, closed her eyes and waited, trying not to squirm as Gail glued the gash on her forehead closed. It didn't hurt as much as she feared. Definitely less than the alcohol had. She relaxed a bit when Gail moved on to bandage the cut on her wrist.

Tess rotated her hand up and down to inspect the result. "Not bad."

"You don't raise three sons without learning how to tie a bandage." Gail adjusted the clip holding the gauze in place, wrapped the bandage in cling wrap, and sat back again. "That'll keep it dry until you've had a chance to get cleaned up, then we'll take care of the rest." She got to her feet, one hand pressed to the small of her back. "All the rain we've been having's hell on my joints." She grimaced. "Luke, help Tess to the bathroom. I'll go find her something to wear when she's done."

Luke put out a hand, then drew it back, uncertainty in his eyes.

"It's okay." She reached out for him. "Really."

He helped her to the bathroom, his body a warm comfort against hers, despite Tater's best efforts to trip them along the way. Her feet sunk into a thick white bath rug as she stepped into the small room. Square white tiles extended from the floor half-way up the walls. The space clean and spare.

Gail crowded in behind them, reaching over the dog to put a folded towel and a pair of cotton pajamas on the counter. "There should be everything you need in there." Gail nodded toward the shower, her hand still pressed to her back. "Do you need help?"

Tess shook her head. "No, I think I'm okay. Go take some Advil."

Gail took a step toward the door, then stopped, her forehead wrinkled as she turned back. "I think I should—"

"It's okay." The last thing they needed was for Gail's back to go out. She'd seen her friend go through that enough times to recognize the signs. "Luke's here, if I need help."

Gail gave a low hum, one eyebrow raised. She looked from Tess to Luke, then back again, lips pursed. "You call if you need me. I'll go see if I can find something for you to eat." She was gone before Tess could tell her she wasn't hungry. There were too many feelings inside her, not enough room for anything else.

Luke leaned into the stall and started the tap, holding his hand under the faucet until steam rose from the water. He switched on the shower and turned for the door. "I'll be right outside if you need me."

She spoke without thought. "Stay."

He turned, his voice quiet. "I don't think that's a good idea."

Tess stripped off the jacket, kicking the foul thing away from her when it hit the floor. She stood in her underwear, nothing else covering her nakedness now but blood.

He looked away. "Are you sure you're comfortable? Having me here, like this?" He swallowed. "After what happened." He rubbed the back of his neck and stared at the mirror over the sink, which was already too fogged to reflect anything.

"Luke, look at me." She waited until he did. "I don't want to be alone."

He rubbed the back of his neck again, then shooed Tater out and closed the door. "I'm just going to help you clean off."

"I know. I trust you." And she found that she did, completely. Not just because he'd come for her or because she'd so misjudged him when she'd run away, leaving him alone in her bed. But because some small part of her, some piece of her heart, had felt connected to him — called to him — even before they'd met.

He searched her face and nodded, as if something was decided. Then he undressed to his boxer briefs and draped his clothes on the counter. His body was just as gorgeous as she remembered.

He still didn't look at her, but he held her hand as she stepped into the shower. "Watch your step."

She kept her back to the showerhead, careful to shield her burns from the spray. The water drummed warm between her shoulder blades, and she tilted her head back, letting the flow dance over her scalp and run through her hair. It felt wonderful, but with her eyes closed, the world shifted, her equilibrium off. Everything slid sideways.

She smacked a hand against the shower wall to catch her balance. Waiting until the world stilled to open her eyes.

Luke stepped into the shower, his eyes worried. "Careful." He didn't touch her, but he stood close enough to brace her, if she needed him.

Tess pulled a bar of soap from a small built-in shelf and held it, looking down at a body she hardly recognized, not sure how to begin. She had so many cuts, scrapes, the burns. Would the soap sting? Did it matter? Maybe the wounds needed to be cleaned? She turned the bar over in her hand, a red smear where her fingers had been.

And even once she'd washed off the blood, would she ever really be clean?

What she'd done wouldn't wash off. No matter how hard she scrubbed. No matter how evil she told herself that man was. She'd killed him. She'd watched the life fade from his eyes.

She turned the soap over again but still couldn't figure out how to get started.

Luke lifted it from her hand and worked the bar between his until they were covered in suds, and the shower smelled of lavender. He ran his soapy hands down her arms and legs, across her back. Every movement as careful as it was gentle. And, after a moment, she relaxed, trusting him not to hit her injuries. She closed her eyes, lost in his touch. Then his fingers were in her hair, as he massaged in shampoo. Washing out the dirt, the blood, everything that remained of the man at the warehouse. Under the spray of water, Tess leaned into him, hiding her face against his chest.

He spoke, soft against her ear. "Until this virus is under control, we stay together. From now on, okay?"

She nodded. It wasn't even a question in her mind. She looked up at him, and he cupped her face in his hands, leaning down to kiss her forehead. Her breath came out in a sigh as she tucked herself back against him. Safe and warm. The water pouring over their bodies ran red, then rosy, and then finally clear and warm, swirling down the drain at their bare feet.

CHAPTER 39

Tess rolled over, waking to the clatter and sizzle of a late breakfast being made in the other room. Light streamed in through the bedroom windows, the sky a brilliant, cloudless blue between the curtains. Gail had left her side of the bed neat, the sheet and duvet pulled back into place, a ruffled linen pillow on top. Tess burrowed down into the covers, every part of her body a steady, persistent ache. She willed herself back to sleep.

But her mind refused to cooperate.

Nothing about the past few days made sense. Everything she'd been through was because of a stupid document she couldn't decipher? It didn't feel possible that was true.

And yet it was. Worse, she couldn't shake the feeling she was missing some connection. Some forgotten thing that might help her understand what had happened. And why.

Why her?

Her mind swirled with it all — the outbreak, her abduction, the document. Like broken pieces of an incomplete puzzle. As she sifted through the details, one thing stood out.

The man's voice from somewhere in the dark beyond the lanterns' glow.

"... wiped the hard drive ..."

"... the container that broke open ..."

"... nothing left to connect to you."

At the time, his words meant nothing to her. She'd been too focused on the pain and survival to recognize them for what they were. Half a phone conversation. Whatever he was doing, he wasn't in it alone. Which meant someone else could come looking for that document.

A chill crawled over her skin. They could come looking for her.

She pulled the duvet closer. Then threw it off.

Let them try.

This time, she would be ready. She still had the pistol Pop had given her when she moved away from home tucked into a shoebox in the top of her closet. She hadn't touched it since she shoved it there, behind tennis rackets and old photo albums. She'd never been comfortable around guns. But she knew how to use it, and she would, if it came to that.

Except how would she get to it?

From what Luke had said, it wouldn't be easy to get back into her neighborhood. Not with the roadblocks and her not having any ID to prove she lived there. Never mind that the place was full of desperate people infected with the virus. What good would a gun do her if she caught Marburg trying to get it?

Fuck.

Tess rolled out of bed, ignoring the aches of her body, and did her best to make her side of the bed match Gail's. When she finished, it was lumpy and lop-sided but as good as it was going to get. She followed her nose toward the kitchen.

Luke met her coming down the hall, a mug in each hand. "Oh, good. You're up." He handed her a cup of ink black coffee. His gaze flicked from her bandaged head to the gauze wrapping her wrists. "How are you doing?"

Tess took a sip and smiled at him over the cup's edge. The fact that he'd remembered her coffee order made her unreasonably happy, and the scalding brew was exactly what she needed. "I'm okay." She wasn't, but it wouldn't do any good for him to worry more about her than he already was.

"Breakfast is ready." Gail came out of the kitchen with a platter of biscuits and a plate full of patty sausage. She slid both on the dining table and went back into the kitchen.

"It wouldn't be Gail's house without enough food to feed an army." Tess said under her breath, even as the smells coming from the table made her stomach grumble. She might not have been hungry last night, but today, she was starving.

Gail emerged again with a butter dish and a stack of plates, a jar of strawberry jam balanced on top. "I heard that." She pursed her lips as she arranged breakfast on the table, gathered a pile of silverware from one of the scalloped placemats, and handed them both a fork and knife. "Sit down. You need to eat."

"Yes, ma'am." Tess spread butter on a biscuit then topped it with jam. As they ate, she fell back into the same cycle of thoughts that had woken her — the outbreak, the abduction, the document. She finished her second biscuit and leaned back in the chair, hands clasped over her well-filled belly. "I've been thinking."

"Uh oh." Gail poured the last of the coffee into her cup.

Tess ignored her friend. "I know this is going to sound crazy, but the man who abducted me—" She stopped, trying to prepare herself to talk about something she'd just as soon never even think of again. She took a deep breath.

Luke did the same and held it.

The gesture made something warm grow in her chest. If there was a bright spot in all the terribleness around them, it was the bond formed between them. She had no idea how she could care for him so much in such a short time. Trust him the way she did. But the connection was undeniable.

She gave him a small smile before she went on. "The questions the man asked. They were about the document I found for the Ashbys. The one that had the number I called and got you. After your plane crashed."

"What?" Gail put her cup down on the placemat.

Tess looked off toward the living room, her eyes settling on the neat stack of sheets and blankets cleaned up from Luke's makeshift bed on the couch. Before she could think too much about it, she let it all pour out. She started with the stairwell. Then told them everything else. Even the details that hurt to say out loud. She made herself keep going. Saying it made it real, but it also made it over. It had happened, and she had survived.

The sound of Tater crunching his way through a bowl of dog food in the kitchen grew loud in the silence that followed. She looked around the table, but neither Gail nor Luke met her gaze. Gail stared off toward the kitchen. Luke had his eyes pressed firmly closed.

Did they blame her for what had happened? For what she'd done?

Killing someone that way. Leaving him to burn.

She was a murderer.

The word took root in her gut, sending tendrils throughout her body, each one growing bigger, until it seemed like the truth of what she'd done might not fit anymore. Like she might burst into a thousand minuscule pieces and float away. And maybe that's what she deserved. Because she didn't feel remorse for what she'd done. Not really. She was glad that man was dead.

She'd plunged a knife into his body. And, in that moment, felt nothing.

What kind of person did that make her?

Not just a murderer. A monster.

No better than the man she'd killed.

The tendrils wrapped around her heart and squeezed.

Gail cleared her throat, her voice still strained when she spoke. "So, you think Luke's passenger who died was connected to the man who took you?"

The man whose blood had coated her hands only hours ago.

Tess blinked a few times, trying to shake the image from her mind. "Right. He called Smith 'Dr. Haley,' and he said the only way

I'd have had the doctor's phone number was off of the document I found. That's why they came looking for me. And I… this is going to sound crazy." But what did she have to lose at this point?

Tess sucked in another breath. "It's more than that. I think the document and the outbreak are connected."

Luke's brow creased, and Gail cocked her head to one side. She opened her mouth, then closed it. As if what Tess had said were so insane she couldn't conjure a response.

Tess raised her hands. "Just hear me out." She turned to Luke. "Haley uses a false name and boards your plane with a bag he won't let you stow. But when the EMTs get there after the crash, the bag, the phone I called you on, and anything that might identify Haley is gone. At first, I thought maybe he left his ID at home, maybe the bag had been thrown free of the plane in the crash. Lost in the woods." Her voice grew stronger, her certainty building as she spoke the theory out loud. "But you talked to me on Haley's phone after the crash, Luke." She paused, waiting until he nodded confirmation. "Which means someone had to have taken it. They were there cleaning up evidence before the paramedics arrived."

"Who's they? And evidence of what?" Gail raised a pencil-thin eyebrow.

"I don't know exactly. But it must be something pretty bad for them to send a psychopath after me, just because they think I might still have that document." She paused. "They tried to kill me to get it back. It has to be important."

Luke nodded, but his expression was tight.

Tess plowed ahead, her heart beating faster as she felt the rightness of what she was saying. "And I left out the part, of course, where the psycho talked about containers breaking open in a crash and then the nurse who treats Luke at the hospital becomes patient zero for the fucking apocalypse." She threw up her hands. "It can't all be a coincidence."

She looked from one of them to the other, then back again, waiting for them to respond. To say anything, even if it was to tell her she was nuts.

Neither of them spoke.

Tess fiddled with the bandage on her wrist. There had to be some better way to explain. To make them see that—

"You're right." Gail turned to Luke. "She's right. It can't be a coincidence, can it?"

Tess sat back in her chair, lighter somehow. As if Gail's belief somehow halved the burden of carrying what Tess thought must be the truth.

"Maybe not. But I didn't get sick. So how would that work? Unless you think I'm a carrier?" A muscle in Luke's jaw twitched.

Gail shook her head. "If you were, we'd both be dead by now."

Worry played across his face before his shoulders relaxed. "I guess. But, if not, how could it spread from me to the nurse?"

"What if something Haley had in that bag 'broke open.'" Tess put air quotes around the words she'd overheard at the warehouse before she continued. "Something in it got on you, and then, when the nurse treated you, it transferred to her?" She shrugged. "Maybe you got lucky, maybe you're immune. I don't know, but it's connected."

Tess had thought she was making progress, but both of them looked wary again.

Gail turned the coffee cup in her hand. "What did it look like? The document, I mean."

"It was huge. Like a chart with these series of letters and numbers. And it was color-coded. Red and blue. Sort of like— " She paused, her eyes going wide as the realization hit. "Like an equation, or a formula."

Holy shit.

A formula.

Gail waved her hands around, as if she was searching for the right words. "Like for an antidote or something?"

Luke cocked his head. "I don't think that's exactly how it works. This is a virus. Not a poison. But maybe it could have something to do with the disease itself?"

Gail pushed away her plate. "Let's say it does. Who do we tell? And what would we say? If we had the document in hand, maybe. But all we have is speculation and Tess's memory." Gail turned to her. "Do you think, if we found someone who'd listen, you could pull it up again?"

Confusion clouded Luke's face. "Pull what up?"

"Tess has a photographic memory. Or sort of." Gail shrugged.

"No shit? Like a memory palace kind of thing?" He looked to Tess, eyes wide.

"Not exactly." Gail launched into an explanation of her condition. Something Tess would have hated under normal circumstances. The fact that it was unavoidable now didn't make it much better. She'd spent most of her adult life trying to pretend the memories didn't exist. She twisted a strand of her hair, waiting for Gail to finish.

Waiting for Luke to pull away from her.

Like Jay had.

"That's amazing." Luke leaned forward to take her hand.

She searched his eyes for doubt or suspicion but found neither. He didn't even seem freaked out. She gave him a slow smile and sat up straighter in her chair.

"How does it work? Do you really think you could access the memory? Explain the document to someone who could help us figure it out?" He raised his eyebrows.

Tess nodded. "I think so. And if there's any chance it could lead to a cure, it's got to be worth a try."

But even as she half-listened to Gail gush about her "gift," the reality of using it to explain the document hit her. The paper had been massive and packed with information. The time she would need to be in the memory to unravel it, even to accurately repeat it all to someone — there was no telling what it would do to her.

How long had she been in the memory of her father before she got sick? Half an hour? Maybe a little more?

There was no way to know for sure.

She'd been hiding in her dad's study, still wearing the itchy black dress Mom had bought her for his funeral. Trying to avoid the aunts and cousins buzzing around their house, making coffee, arranging whatever hot dishes had been dropped by. All she wanted to do was be where her dad had been before he died, breathing in the smell of dusty books and Old Spice. His smell. She'd been spinning herself in slow circles in his worn leather desk chair, when one of her episodes came on. The memory taking her back to a lazy summer day. Sitting side by side with him on the kitchen counter, eating boxed macaroni and cheese straight from the pot. Grass clippings still stuck to her toes from where she'd been running through the sprinkler while he tended Mom's roses.

It was all she had left of him. And she couldn't let go. Not even when the headache set in.

Not even when the real world slipped away without her.

Instead of letting the episode take its course, she'd fought it, forced it to stay. Long past the point when the headache became excruciating, the nausea overwhelming. She wouldn't let go of her dad.

When she'd finally opened her eyes, she'd been in the hospital. Gran asleep in a chair beside the bed with a book of daily devotionals open in her lap. And her mother nowhere to be found. Tess had been in the hospital for two weeks after the aneurysm.

And she hadn't seen her mother since.

A hollow ache beat time behind her ribs.

She tried to refocus on Gail and Luke's conversation instead, to pay attention as they debated what to do next. She knew she needed to tell them what they were planning could be dangerous for her. For all she knew, it could kill her. But she couldn't make herself say it out loud — she'd spent too many years trying to pretend there was nothing wrong with her.

Tess glanced up at the television playing on mute in the adjoining room. It showed a map with the projected spread of infection, red clusters blooming out across the United States.

If she could help, she didn't have a choice. Too many people had already died. It was time her memories did something positive. No matter the cost.

Luke's voice broke into her thoughts. "Definitely not the police."

"Wait, what?" Tess's face warmed.

Luke sat back in his chair. "I was just saying that we shouldn't go to the police."

"Right." Her breakfast turned in her stomach.

He glanced over at her. "What?"

Tess took in several, slow breaths. Knowing what he wasn't saying out loud. They couldn't go to the police because of what she'd done. Because of what she was.

A murderer.

No one knew what had happened in that warehouse but her. Who was to say the police would believe her? She'd basically gutted the man then burned all the evidence. She didn't practice criminal law, but she knew murder came with a mandatory life sentence in Georgia. As much as twenty years, even if they called it manslaughter. Maybe Luke was right. Could she really risk it? The back of her throat ached. "You think, once I tell them what happened, they'll arrest me. For what happened at the warehouse."

"No one thinks that." Gail covered one of Tess's hands with her own. "What you did was self-defense. No question."

Tess blinked away a burning behind her eyes and looked at Luke.

"If you hadn't killed him, I would have." His gaze, hard at first, softened as he focused on her. The look held no hint of judgment, and it reached her in a way words couldn't. Seeing herself through his eyes, she wasn't a murderer or even a victim. But a survivor.

She'd been through something awful, something she'd have to deal with for the rest of her life, but it wasn't her fault. She'd done the only thing she could. She gave him a small nod, and Luke continued. "I just meant I don't think the police are going to help. I tried that already. If they didn't take a missing person seriously, I can't imagine they're going to listen when we come in with a possible theory about a document we don't have or understand, that we think might be related to the outbreak."

"The FBI then? Or the CDC?" She looked from Gail to Luke. "If anyone would know what to do with it, the CDC would."

"Let's try all three." Gail cleared the table, porcelain clinking together as she stacked their plates. "It can't hurt." She disappeared into the kitchen.

Tess pulled Gail's phone from the wall charger. "Let's start with the FBI."

She tried their main number first but got no answer. On his phone, Luke tried the FBI's Atlanta field office, with the same result. They went through every number they could find: the Marburg hotline, the Atlanta Police Department, the CDC — no one answered. Or, if they did, it was an automated system directing her to call another number no one answered. They kept dialing until they both ran out of options.

Tess dropped the phone to her lap. "I think we're going on a road trip."

CHAPTER 40

Mara sat with her head in her hands, listening to the CDC's Marburg team call drone on in the background. Except that the transmission rate in the Minneapolis cluster seemed to be on the decline, news was predictably grim. One hundred and twelve confirmed infected in Los Angeles, eighty-six dead. Sixteen confirmed infected in Minneapolis, four dead.

Atlanta continued to be an entirely different story. Since containment had failed, some estimates had the infection rate as high as fifteen percent. What would that even be? If Atlanta's population inside the perimeter was 4.5 million… Mara tried to do the math in her head. Six hundred and seventy-five thousand people infected? Could that even be possible? And how many had died? No one offered an estimate for that.

Emmy's just one of the unnumbered dead.

She closed her eyes, weathering a now familiar burst of pain. Then forced herself to refocus. She had to keep going, one foot in front of the other. God knew how many more lives depended on it.

Jerry's voice came over the line. "Listen, before we all drop off, I wanted to give everyone a quick reminder that our data sets need to be shared with the folks at Maeler who are working on vaccine development. President's orders. I know you're aware—"

A knock came from Mara's door, and she jumped, punching the phone's mute button before she answered. "I'm on a call." Her voice came out sharper than she intended.

Mara reached to take the phone off mute. Another knock.

She rolled her eyes. "Come in."

After a brief pause, her door swung open. The nurse she'd sent to find Mr. Romero's family stood in the corridor, a grimace on her face. "So sorry to bother you. There's an urgent call for you from the CDC." Mara glanced at the phone, where, as far as she knew, everyone on the Marburg Hemphill team had already been patched in.

Apparently not.

The double-beep of people disconnecting from the conference call sounded one after another. She'd missed whatever Jerry'd said in concluding the call. But it couldn't be helped.

"I guess you'd better put it through."

The nurse disappeared into the hallway, and Mara picked up as soon as the phone rang.

"Dr. Nunez, this is Joey Morelli, from security... "

"Hi, Joey. I know who you are." She'd seen the man every morning since she first started with the CDC. Bone thin, except for a basketball-shaped belly that stuck out over his belt. She'd never made it past him without getting a cheerful "good morning" or "y'all have a good day, now."

"Yes, ma'am. I've got two folks here trying to talk their way inside the building. The National Guard guys are ready to haul them off to the dome, but I thought I should check with you first."

"I don't mean to be rude, Joey. But why ask me?" Building security was more than a little outside her field.

"They say they know you, ma'am. Claim to have something you might want. Something related to Marburg Hemphill."

She shook her head. "I can't imagine what that would be."

"Like I said, I wasn't even sure I should bother you." His voice lowered. "But the woman's all beaten up, and they seem credible. Man's name is Luke Broussard, and the woman with him is Teresa Oliver."

Mara sat bolt upright in her chair. A stack of patient files cascaded over the side of her desk and onto the floor. She ignored them. "One second."

Teresa Oliver.

Some part of her wasn't surprised the woman had turned back up. Mara had been so sure there was something odd about her case. Had struggled with the decision to release her from the hospital before she understood what it was. Mara clicked through folders on her computer, flying from file to file to confirm what she thought she remembered. "Holy shit." Like Oliver, Broussard'd had direct exposure to Sarah Baqri and hadn't contracted the virus. Now they were together. She tapped her fingers on the desk.

Why? And what would bring them looking for her?

Whatever it was, she needed to figure it out, now.

And maybe more than that — she'd run out of other ideas. She had done everything she could think to do. Ordered every conceivable test, read and assessed all the data she could find. None of it made a damn bit of difference when it came to improving her patients' chances of survival. At this point, she wasn't going to ignore anything that might help.

No matter how crazy it might seem.

"Put them on the phone."

▪ ▪ ▪

Luke waited outside one of a dozen orange plastic barricades surrounding the CDC's campus. Soldiers in masks stood guard every few yards around the perimeter. The closest stared in their direction, his face tight as he adjusted his grip on the assault rifle held across his chest. He looked young, barely twenty, and twitchy. Like he couldn't decide whether to throw up or shoot the first thing that moved.

Luke remembered that feeling from his first mission. His stomach knotted with too much coffee and waiting. Knowing the action could kick off at any minute. Terrified it would. And just as desperate to prove he could handle whatever happened when it did.

He'd probably never been more dangerous in his life. Luke glanced at the soldier again, only to find him still looking their way.

Not comforting.

Luke leaned toward Tess, keeping his voice low. "Still think this is our best plan?"

"I think it's our only plan. And anyway, this is a better reception than I expected." She shrugged, pinching the top of her mask against the bridge of her nose.

It certainly hadn't been what he had expected. He'd thought there'd be a crowd of people surrounding the place, either looking for help or protesting the government's handling of the outbreak. But they'd only found soldiers.

And the same had been true on the drive over. Empty roads, abandoned cars, hardly anyone in the streets. And no police presence at all. At first, he'd assumed people must be sheltering at home, keeping a safe distance from each other.

But what if that wasn't it? What if they were all sick?

Or dead.

Luke swallowed hard. Other than the wind in the leaves of the trees lining the front sidewalk and the occasional garbled chatter over the soldiers' radios, the street sat silent as a tomb. Beside him, Tess had her arms wrapped around her middle. She rocked back and forth heel to toe, her face tense.

Luke forced a smile. "I guess they did ask us to go home twice, before they asked at gunpoint."

"Well, if that isn't Southern hospitality at its finest?" She barked out a rough laugh, and a second soldier scowled in their direction. But she'd stopped rocking, and her arms had loosened.

He smiled down at her.

Tess waited until the solider looked away before she spoke again. "At least you thought to ask for that doctor. Dropping her name seemed to turn things around."

"Let's hope." Because there was another explanation for the lack of a crowd. Anyone who had shown up to protest, who'd refused to leave when asked, could've been detained.

They could all be locked inside the Dome.

He choked on the thought. At any other time, in any other circumstance, he would've dismissed the idea as impossible. Some conspiracy theory pulled from a dystopian movie. But now? When a fence had been erected seemingly overnight to lock them all in together. Was it really that far-fetched people who resisted would be held in the Dome against their will? Really any different at all?

And if this didn't go as planned. If the doctor didn't remember them, or if she thought they were a bunch of crackpots not worth her time…

He and Tess could be next.

A pot-bellied security guard stepped out of the glass doors at the main entrance and waved to one of the soldiers. "Sergeant? Would you escort our visitors inside?"

Luke let out a slow breath and took Tess's hand as the man led them into what turned out to be an impressive gray stone lobby. The guard circled around to the far side of a reception desk and held out a phone and a pump bottle of sanitizer.

The man motioned toward the desk. "I have Dr. Nunez on the line." He held the phone out to Tess with one hand, a pump bottle of sanitizer in the other.

Tess cleaned her hands and took the receiver. "Dr. Nunez? Sorry to bother you, I know you're busy. But I have information about a document I think might be related to the outbreak." In less than ten minutes, Tess had laid out all the relevant events, starting with her discovery of the document and ending with the conclusions she'd drawn after her near death at the hands of the man who was searching for it.

Luke should've let her do the talking when they'd gotten to the CDC. Listening to her now, he could see why she was a good lawyer. She was sharp, efficient with her words, and painstakingly logical. If he hadn't been entirely convinced they had done the right thing in coming before, he was now.

After a long pause, Tess continued. "Sure, of course. It started on one side with 'L0,' then branched off from there..." She ran through her description of the document again. When she finished, Tess nodded along with whatever Dr. Nunez was saying. "And how will we get there? ... Okay, I see. And how will we—" Her brow furrowed as she listened, the room silent except for her occasional "uh-huh" or "okay." By the time she was done, he'd imagined a dozen outcomes. Most began with them in police custody.

She hung up. "Ever been in a tank before?"

CHAPTER 41

The scene outside Tess's window went from strip malls to pine trees as they turned into an area she thought might be Brookhaven. She picked at a stitch on her sleeve, then shoved her hands under her legs. Gail was already mad Tess had made her stay home, shredding the shirt she'd borrowed wouldn't make things better.

It wasn't that she hadn't wanted Gail to come. It would have been a comfort to have her friend there. But there was no reason for her to risk exposure again.

And Gail would've noticed something was up if she had come with them.

Tess blew out a long breath, trying to clear the bramble of fear stuck in her windpipe. The closer she got to accessing the memory of the document, the riskier it seemed. She could have another aneurysm. She could go into a coma. And, this time, not wake up.

The bramble shifted from her throat to her chest, embedding itself into her sternum. She forced out another breath, but thorns of "what if" still snagged as it left her body.

She could die.

Another deep breath. And another.

But if she could have helped all the people who were sick or dying, and she didn't try… she'd never forgive herself.

She had no choice but to do it. And worrying about what might happen when she accessed the memory wasn't going to help. She might be fine, maybe walk away with another headache. How many times had she been through that before?

More than she could count.

Maybe this would be no different.

"You do know this is not a tank, right?" Luke said from the back seat.

She twisted around and gave him a grin, glad for the distraction. "So maybe when I heard 'military transport,' I got a little excited."

A flicker of amusement crossed their driver's face, and she read the patch on his chest. "Thanks for the ride, Cooper." With his jarhead haircut, brawny shoulders, and a smashed nose that screamed "I like bar fights," Cooper looked the part of a military man.

"I'll take this over Dome duty any day of the week." He pulled the Humvee to a lumbering stop in front of an eight-foot security fence. "Here we go."

Tess craned forward for a better view of what was beyond the razor-wire. A nondescript single-story concrete building squatted in the center of the property. Its facade bore no signs or decoration beyond a series of narrow windows that slashed the building at irregular intervals. Only the half-dozen guards who paced the property in black fatigues gave any indication of what might lay inside.

Smart.

There would be no way to keep people out if they announced the place as a vaccine development center.

Cooper rolled down his window. "Afternoon."

"ID." The guard nodded a gruff hello then peered around the inside of the truck, his mud brown eyes grim and assessing. "I'll need one for everybody."

Another guard, this one with several days' stubble on his chin, leaned out of a shack to the left of the gate, yelling something unintelligible to the man with his hand through their window. The first guard shook his head. "One second." He clomped back to the shack, head bobbing up and down as he talked to the other man.

This was not going to be good.

Tess turned, watching Luke dig out his wallet. "I don't have my ID."

He froze, one hip in the air. "What do you mean?"

"I mean," she paused, cringing, "it's still in my purse at home."

"Not sure what we can do about that." Cooper moved his head in a slow back and forth. "Wait here." He climbed down from the truck, letting the heavy door clunk closed behind him as he headed for the shack. Both guards rested a hand on their holstered weapons as he approached. Tess couldn't hear what they were saying, but the scruffy guard looked up toward the truck and shook his head.

Oh crap.

The guard leaned into the shack and emerged with a phone pressed to his ear.

She turned around in her seat to face Luke, wincing as the seatbelt slid across one of the burns on her chest. "We can just go get it, right? I mean, we're in a—" She stopped herself, holding a hand up before he could correct her. "We're in a Humvee. Is there anywhere we can't go?"

Luke stared out the window, watching the men talk. "Let's just see what they say."

Cooper waited, arms-crossed, kicking pebbles off the side of the pavement until the guard got off the phone. After a brief conversation, he trotted back to the truck and yanked open the door. "They say she can go in, but we can't."

"What?" Luke sat forward in his seat. "That doesn't make any sense."

"Clearance." Cooper shrugged. "She's got it. We don't."

Tess nodded. "Because I'm the only one with the memory." Which meant she was the one who might be able to help. And she had to try, no matter the risks. No one else could.

Cooper raised an eyebrow, but he didn't ask for an explanation.

Luke also sat silent as his gaze swept over the armed guards surrounding the building. But she still heard his words in her ear, the two of them under the spray of water in Gail's shower — "We stay together. From now on, okay?"

She'd agreed with him, and she'd meant it, but, "the longer it takes for them to find out what they need to know and finish the vaccine, the more people will get exposed. The more people might die. And anyway…" She gestured toward the guards. "Security's crazy tight here. I'll be fine."

I hope.

After a long pause, Luke nodded. "Okay. I'll be here. Right outside. We'll wait until you're done so we can bring you back. Right?" He directed the question to their driver.

Cooper dipped his head. "We'll be here. My orders are to escort the two of you here to the facility and back again. Job's only half done."

"It's settled then." Tess reached between the seats and pulled Luke forward by his shirt front. She brushed a quick kiss across his lips, holding his gaze as she pulled away. Then leaned back in to kiss him properly, committing every bit of him to memory. His taste, his smell, the feel of his lips against hers. Tess ignored Cooper's chuckle, pressing her lips one more time to Luke's before she let go. "See you soon." She didn't wait for him to respond before she jumped down from the Humvee and started toward the gate.

▪ ▪ ▪

A masked man met Tess at the door. "Ms. Oliver?" He was older than she expected, maybe seventy, with a full head of silver white hair. He wore a lab coat over a light pink polo that offset his tan.

Something about him made her think of golf and cotillions. "You must be Mr. Sullivan."

"You can call me Sully." The skin around his eyes crinkled, and she could hear the smile in his voice. He swept a hand behind him.

"Please, come in. I'd shake your hand, but that's discouraged these days."

She stepped into a small, worn reception area, empty except for an unmanned desk. A bland nautical print hung on the back wall. Through a glass door to her right, fork-lifts beeped as they moved between pallets, each holding a perfect cube of smaller boxes marked with the Maeler logo. She stopped, eyes going wide. "Is that the vaccine?"

Maybe they wouldn't need her help after all. She wouldn't have to access the memory, wouldn't have to risk what might happen.

"Oh my, no." Sully answered. "I wish it was. Our people have been working around the clock, doing everything in their power to get it finished. When this whole thing started, we were already several years into the process of developing a vaccine for previous Marburg strains, and that gave us a real advantage — thank God — but we've had some staffing issues and, we're just not quite there yet. What you see out there is just the logistics team shipping out the remainder of what this facility usually produces. Vitamins, supplements, and what not."

Her heart sank as she stared out into the warehouse. She hadn't even considered the possibility of a reprieve as she'd walked in, but now she felt the loss of it in her bones.

"I understand that's what brought you out to see me." He opened an unmarked door on the other side of the lobby and, standing back a safe distance, gestured for her to go ahead of him. "Dr. Nunez tells me you think you may have information that could help?"

"That's right." She set her shoulders and walked through. "Or, at least, I hope so."

"I've got an office set up this way where we can talk." He led her down a series of short hallways, past several closed doors marked "Restricted Area."

"I know the facility doesn't look like much, but she's state of the art where it matters." He pushed open a door to reveal a small office, with a desk and two chairs. One of the long, thin windows she'd seen from outside ran down the far wall. Beyond it, lay the front lawn of the facility and the gate where she'd come in. The Humvee was roughly where she'd left it, now parked on the side of the road. The knot of anxiety in her chest eased with the thought of Luke still so close, just outside the gates.

"Please, have a seat. Can I get you something to—" A phone rang, and he patted both his sides, before pulling a cell phone from an inside coat pocket. Tess sat on the edge of the chair in front of his desk, trying to look composed. Coming across twitchy wasn't going to help her credibility.

"Joseph. Is everything okay?" He took the chair on the opposite side of the desk, and the worry lines in his face relaxed. "Ah, of course. My fault. When she gets done with PT, tell her I'm sorry I missed our call. It's been a busy morning." He glanced up at Tess, and smile lines creased around his eyes again. "Time got away from me."

Sully finished his call and slipped the phone back into his pocket. "Sorry about that. My wife worries if she doesn't hear from me." He shrugged out of the lab coat and hung it on the seat back. "She wasn't too happy to have me working inside the perimeter."

"I'm surprised they set up the facility here. I would've thought they'd want you safely out of harm's way on the other side of the barricade."

"Well, Lynn certainly does." He chuckled, a deep rumble that started in his chest. "But, no, you're right. When we agreed to convert this facility to vaccine production, I don't think anyone had even considered we might get to the point of needing a cordon. But here we are. And once the perimeter was erected, the decision was made not to lose the time it would take to relocate. The right decision, I would say, given where things are now." He shook his head slowly, as if to acknowledge the surreal situation in which they found themselves. "Why don't we get started with you telling me what brings you here? I'm afraid what Dr. Nunez shared with me was… confusing."

She shifted in her seat. "I can see why it might be." Tess braced herself, then told the story again. This time, she started with finding the document, explaining the basic way her memories worked, and then gave him the whole picture of the past few days. She described the questioning at the warehouse the best she could remember it, noting the man's fixation on the document. But she left out the details of her torture and what had become of her tormentor, saying only that she had escaped. She needed to stay focused on what had to be done — which meant she couldn't let herself get bogged down in all the feelings that came with the other details. She ended with their trip to the CDC. "So, that's it. I wasn't sure if it would help, but it certainly seemed like it might be important. I didn't feel like I could just keep it to myself." Tess leaned back and let out a breath. All she could do now was hope he believed her.

"Fascinating." He blushed, looking away. "I'm sorry, that's not what I mean to say. That must have sounded terribly callous."

She smiled at the old man, who was now the one shifting around in his chair. "Don't worry about it. I know it's an odd situation."

"I hope I don't offend you, if I haven't already. When I say that I still have my doubts about this whole thing." He clasped his hands on the desk. "It isn't that I doubt you. Just that it seems… a little fantastical."

Tess's face went hot. Before she could respond, he continued. "With that being said and, given what we're facing out there, I do think Dr. Nunez was right to have you come see me. We'd be remiss not to see if we can get to the bottom of whatever this document is. And I would be most interested to hear what you remember of it." He pulled a small black device from a desk drawer and held it up for her to see. "Okay if I record you?"

She nodded, and he pressed a button on the recorder before sliding it on to the desk.

Tess closed her eyes, took a deep breath, and willed the memory into focus.

But it was different, pulling a memory up. She'd spent so much of her life fighting them. To invite it in was surreal, knowing what she was asking for. She braced herself, waiting for the flood of unwelcome stimulus, followed by a booming headache.

Nothing happened.

She cleared her throat, squeezing her eyes tighter shut. But she could still feel the man watching her, waiting. It didn't help. Her skin went clammy, sweat beading on her forehead.

She could do this. She had to.

Tess tried again, purposefully pulling the memory forward from her subconscious, willing it into view, letting it surround her. The process both gradual and immediate. Her senses increasingly muting out the present to let in the sensations of the past. One reality displaced by another, no less real despite having been lost to time. The chill of the air-conditioned bank vault, the glare of the overhead florescent light, the sickly, fruity-floral smell — the document lying on the table before her.

CHAPTER 42

"Nothing like a little deja vu." Mara muttered into her respirator as the elevator doors rattled open to Grady Hospital's basement floor. She'd begun this thing in a morgue, and here she was again. No closer to finding a way to stop the outbreak than when she'd started. And she was getting desperate.

Desperate enough to send some random woman to Maeler.

What would Jerry think of that?

"Ma'am?" A figure in full protective gear identical to her own approached from the hall. "Thanks for coming on such short notice." He fidgeted, as if unsure where to put his hands. "I'll walk you in." Without meeting her eyes, he led her down a short hallway and through a set of double doors. They both moved slowly. Their suits made for safety, not dexterity. He stopped to let her pass. "This way."

Even through the respirator, the room smelled of bleach and, more faintly, copper. Empty examination tables sat in the middle of the space, and body bags lined the room, two rows deep. Three in some places. In each row, bags had been stacked three or four high, one on top of the other.

Which one is Emmy?

Mara winced, the thought sent a sharp sting to the center of her chest. Her friend lay zipped up in one of the unmarked bags. There but not there, and—

"This is why I called you." The young man stepped into the room behind her, his voice timid.

"What am I looking at? How does something like this happen?" She walked the perimeter, counting bags.

Twenty-two, twenty-three, twenty-four…

He stood, hands-clasped, just inside the door. "The guy that picks up the bodies to take them out for cremation, he stopped coming."

"Stopped coming? Did you call to find out why? And why am I only hearing about this now?" she asked rapid-fire, pacing around the abbreviated perimeter of the room. She lost count of the bodies at forty-one.

"Don't know why they stopped coming, ma'am. The collection folks haven't returned my calls or my supervisor's. I didn't want to get them in trouble. Terry, the one who collects the bodies, he's a nice guy. Got a family, three kids. But—" He gestured toward the bodies piled around the edges of the room. "Things are getting bad down here, and I was hoping you'd have better luck getting them to come back."

Mara stopped. One of the bags nearest the corner had a dark, brown-red spot seeping out from underneath its furthest end. She lowered her head, her lips pressed into a grimace. "Was absorbent material not placed under the bodies? And why aren't they double-bagged? Weren't you given the print-out explaining how to handle the remains of a Marburg patient? This is basic, standard procedure."

Behind his plastic face shield, the young man's cheeks reddened. "We're nearly out of bags. I sent word upstairs yesterday." He shrugged, but his expression was pained. His voice came out tight. "We thought one was better than nothing. If we don't single-bag them, and the bodies keep coming like this, we'll be out altogether by tomorrow morning."

Mara forced herself to take several deep breaths. "I understand. You were right to ration the body bags." She met his eyes. Whatever was going on here, it wasn't his fault. "I'll go back upstairs and make sure you get what you need. And I'll find out what the hell happened to our cremation pick-up."

His mouth crimped in an upside-down smile. "Thanks, ma'am. And sorry again."

She nodded and tried to look reassuring. But she didn't trust herself to answer. Frustration crackled under her skin as she slammed her way out of the morgue doors.

Hijo de puta.

Whoever had side-lined body pick-up was going to get an earful. And the ones responsible for the failure to resupply the morgue with body bags were going to be jealous of what those cremation fuckers got. It wasn't like they were dealing with normal human remains that could be released to the family. Each of those bodies posed a real, imminent threat to anyone who came in contact with it. Mara stormed off the elevator and into the decontamination area, ripping off the protective suit.

She made herself slow as she went twice through the hand-washing process. Who should she reach out to first? Jerry? The health department? Maybe their contact at Maeler? What would it take to get refrigerated trucks to the hospital?

Mara flew through the outer door of the isolation wing and ran directly into the unwelcome scowl of Colonel Fitzgerald. He wore civilian clothes, but his drill sergeant expression was in full uniform.

"Dr. Nunez." He looked her up and down, no doubt noticing the utter disarray of her hair and clothes. "There's something urgent we need to discuss. I've been waiting in your office for the better part of an hour."

"Have you?" She smoothed her hair into place.

And here she'd thought things couldn't get worse.

"Sorry to hear that." She said, even though she wasn't. She had less than zero interest in dealing with whatever his bullshit power-grab du jour might be. Mara strode past him and into her office. "As you can imagine, things here have been busy." She stopped, crossing her arms over her chest as she turned to confront him. "Were you aware our requests to restock body bags have gone unanswered for days? Right now, there are bodies waiting to be picked up lying in stacks in the basement, one on top of the other, like trash. I'm sure you know the hazards of leaving dozens of infected corpses lying around."

Fitzgerald stood, frozen in the doorway. "What?"

She briefed him on the disaster-in-the-making she'd been called to downstairs. He listened, his skin paling as he nodded. When she'd finished, she watched his expression but saw none of the ego or entitlement she'd sensed from him before.

"Give me five minutes." He stepped out of her office, phone already pressed to his ear.

Mara collapsed into her chair. The day was too much, even by the standard of days that had set the bar for "too much" at a nearly impossible level. She let her head fall back, and her eyes closed. How in God's name had they gotten to this point?

"Can I come in?" Fitzgerald asked from the doorway.

She straightened, waving him to the only other chair in her make-shift office.

"First, let me start by apologizing for the way I behaved when we first met." He sat down, hands on his knees.

She leaned back in her chair, arms crossed over her chest. She trusted Fitzgerald's apology about as far as she could throw him.

He went on. "As you know, Marburg, like other Level 4 hot agents, is found in only a few laboratories world-wide. For reasons more obvious now than ever, those laboratories are highly regulated and open only to a limited group of doctors and scientists. When this outbreak occurred, and particularly when it became evident it may have been an act of bioterrorism, USAMRIID had to consider the possibility the virus originated from one of those sources. Which meant, when investigating what happened, we had to silo each possible source." He looked down his nose at her. "Including the CDC."

Including the CDC.

She straightened. What the hell was he implying? Blood rushed to her cheeks, the heat crawling down the neck of her scrubs.

He gave a short bob of his head. "I understand your feelings. But I ask you — and, please, be truthful with yourself — would you have handled it differently if you'd been me?"

She stared at him a long moment. If this was an act of bioterrorism, it made sense to assume that one of the handful of people with access to the Marburg virus could be responsible. And any proper investigation would've meant looking into all of them. No matter who they were.

"No." She finally answered, releasing the grip she had on her forearms and forcing her hands into her lap.

He nodded. "I've dealt with your supply chain issues. You'll have more body bags by nightfall. And I've sent men out to determine what became of the body removal service." He lowered his voice. "If I had my guess, though, they'll be among your patients soon."

Mara flinched. "Thank you." How had she not considered that possibility?

Fitzgerald nodded, leaning back in his chair. "I'm glad I could help." He cleared his throat in a getting-down-to-business sort of way. "I came to see you because Jerry shared your disparate transmission theory with me."

Of course.

He's here to mansplain why that's not possible.

Mara braced herself for the inevitable.

"We noted the same trends but couldn't explain them." Fitzgerald shook his head. She sat up straighter, as he continued. "But then, we turned something up." He paused, shifting in his chair. "In addition to the siloing of the organizations I mentioned, I tasked a small, trusted group within USAMRIID with a separate off-the-books investigation of every individual we could identify who had access to the Marburg virus."

Mara stiffened. Was he accusing her?

His mouth twitched up on one side. "You were among the first cleared."

She relaxed into her chair. "Okay."

"Which is why I'm here." He pulled a phone from his pocket. "I spoke with Jerry, and we both think there's something you should hear." Fitzgerald pushed the cell onto her desk. "This is highly classified. The contents were obtained by means that may be less than legal and they cannot, under any circumstances, be disclosed to anyone outside this room." He waited for her to nod then clicked through to an audio file, sitting back in his chair as a hiss of static came from his phone.

"You know I value your counsel and your support," a familiar voice said, but she couldn't place it. After a pause, the clink of a teacup placed on its saucer, and the man continued. "However, there are limits to what I can do."

"When have limits ever applied to you?" A second man chuckled, in a good-old-boy way. "No, I know you can't act unilaterally, Mr. President."

Mara sat forward, her eyes going wide. She looked to Fitzgerald for confirmation. "Is that?"

He nodded, and tilted his head toward the phone, where the audio file continued to play.

"You know you can call me Nate."

"Thank you, Nate. You may not be able to take some actions without Congressional consent, but you aren't entirely without the means to make real change. And when we put you— " The second man stopped and started again. "When we helped you take office, it was with the understanding you were of the same mind as the people who financed that run."

A long pause stretched out before the President responded. "I do not need to be reminded how I got here."

"My apologies. I mean no disrespect. But take it from an old friend, you will need those same supporters when you run for reelection. And, if they feel you haven't delivered on your promises, it may not go as smoothly as we'd like."

The President's voice was quiet when he spoke again. "What exactly are you asking me do?"

"For starters, stop letting them in. We are a hair's breadth from winding up just like Europe. Hundreds of micro-states governed by Sharia law, where it isn't safe for any Christian man or woman to go. You know what those people are like. The U.K. is on the cusp of becoming an Islamic colony, and, if it keeps going like this, we're next."

A short hiss of static then, "There's only so much I can do by executive order."

"Maybe under normal circumstances, that would be true. But we're at war. Islam is the most anti-Semitic, genocidal ideology in the world. They are the only religion who seeks to impose their religious laws upon people who don't belong to their faith. If you can even call it that."

The President spoke. "You know I don't disagree with you on the dangers of radical Islam, but you still haven't answered my question. What else can I do about it? I've limited the entry of Muslim immigrants to the country to the greatest extent the courts will allow. I've given federal law enforcement a mandate in the strongest terms possible to eliminate any threat of jihad on American soil. What else would you have me do, Sully?"

Mara jerked her head up. "Sully, as in—?"

Fitzgerald nodded again. "He's talking to Warren Sullivan."

Holy shit.

They both stared down at the phone. Another teacup rattled, and the recorded voice of Warren Sullivan shook with anger. "I would have you take real action. We have done nothing meaningful since 9/11 to stop it from happening again. The time for discussion is over. The time for legislation is over. We've lost the war on free speech. Our countrymen have had the wool pulled over their eyes by the left, and they genuinely believe in the myth of a moderate

Islam. You and I both know that's bullshit. There is no such thing as moderate Islam. It is an incurable disease of the Arab mind, and we need to stamp it out at the source."

Fitzgerald stopped the recording.

Mara's mind raced to catch up. Maeler had been working on a Marburg vaccine for years. They'd have had access to the virus. "You think he—?" She pressed a hand to her temple. Could that research have led to what they were seeing now? If she thought about it that way, it gave a whole new meaning to the document in Tess Oliver's memory. "You think Warren Sullivan may have been involved in this. In causing the outbreak?"

"Possibly. But it's not an accusation I could make without something more than this." He swept his hand toward the phone. "The recording is more than a year old. And there are obviously other considerations, given where the conversation took place."

Mara bristled. "You mean with whom it took place." She shook her head. "But it doesn't make any sense. Sullivan is here, inside the cordon, working on a vaccine. I just sent a patient to him."

"You what?" Fitzgerald crinkled his brow. "Why would you send a patient to Maeler?"

Mara took a deep breath. Where to start? How was she going to explain a series of events she barely followed, to Fitzgerald, of all people? Mara rolled her shoulders back and gave it her best shot — the plane crash that immediately preceded the spread of infection, Teresa Oliver's torture and interrogation, and the document she claimed to remember.

When Mara finished, he sat, quiet, his eyebrows pulled low in thought. "I know we're at the point of exploring every option. But that just doesn't strike me as credible."

Her cheeks warmed. "I had my doubts, too. But then Ms. Oliver described the document. She said one of the lines started with 'L0' and branched out from there into lots of other entries, mainly Ls at first, then other letters. Some numbers, too. What does that sound like to you?"

He leaned back, lips pursed, and shrugged.

"I sent her to Maeler to get an independent assessment, but I think the patterns of letters and numbers she described may be haplogroups. And the other entries track mutations."

His brow furrowed, but he didn't speak.

She pressed on. "In human genetics, we most commonly look to Y-chromosome haplogroups — those passed down from father to son — and mitochondrial DNA, which is passed down from mothers to their children, regardless of sex. Because neither recombines, Y-DNA and mitochondrial DNA change only by chance mutation in each generation. And—"

His already thin lips grew thinner. "I know the basics of DNA, Dr. Nunez."

"I'm getting to it." All she needed was the latitude to finish. "As populations migrated out of Africa, genetic mutations appeared in groups that went north, for example, that would not appear in the DNA of groups that took a different migratory path, say east into Asia. And, of course, those eastward-bound groups and sub-groups would have naturally occurring genetic mutations that would not appear in the group that went north into Europe."

She looked at him, expectant. His face didn't change.

Mara blew out a breath. "I think the document in Teresa Oliver's memory may be a map of DNA mutations. One that's color-coded to identify the groups selected for immunity. So, if you have a 'desirable' variant," she made air-quotes, "one that, for whatever reason, is viewed as a favored population, you could render them safe. And wipe the rest of humanity off the face of the Earth."

He took a long time to respond. "If that were possible — and that's a big 'if' — it could explain what we're seeing in the patient population right now." Fitzgerald tugged at one of his ears, concentration on his face.

"Right. I know it's a big 'if.' But if someone was motivated by hatred for a certain religious group — say Islam — it wouldn't take much to figure out which haplogroups were predominately Muslim."

Fitzgerald's eyebrows went up.

"And there's something else. I asked Jerry to have someone look into the rest of Teresa Oliver's story. See what they could confirm. The body of the passenger on Luke Broussard's plane was identified as Dr. Edmund Haley, as she said."

Fitzgerald nodded. "Okay. That's something. But just because she's telling the truth about that doesn't mean—"

"Haley was a virologist, top of his class at Vanderbilt, published a number of cutting-edge research papers on genetics and immunology before he lost his medical license because of something to do with opioids. Then he just disappeared. No trace of him at all, except for some reference to a real estate scam here in Atlanta." She paused for emphasis. "Until his body was found in the wreckage of a private plane, apparently booked under a false name, along with a man who could be our actual patient zero."

"Dear God." Fitzgerald looked away then quickly back to her. "If you're right… whoever's doing this could kill millions."

She nodded. "Just like Sullivan wanted."

CHAPTER 43

A dull ache throbbed in Tess's temples, but it was nothing like the brutal aftermath that usually followed one of her episodes. Her breath came easy, and her heart kept a comfortable rhythm in her chest. Maybe something about the way she'd accessed the memory had changed her body's response?

They normally took her over, her body invaded by something foreign and incompatible. A time and place she didn't belong in anymore. But today, she'd gone in with a purpose, directing her consciousness, controlling how immersed she became. She listened to her body's cues. Paid attention when they told her to drill in or pull back. Worked with the memory, instead of against it. She'd stayed in control.

Tess rolled her eyes back and forth under her lids, then blinked them open, her focus coming back to the small office. To the man looking at her expectantly across the desk.

"Amazing. Just amazing." Above his mask, Sully's eyes shone with a fevered light. A shade too bright, his assessment almost predatory.

Something curled uneasy in her gut.

Tess blinked again. And as her vision cleared, his face returned to normal. Everything about him spoke to the same grandfatherly man she'd met before the memory started. She searched his face, looking for insincerity or disbelief. But he held her gaze, his eyes a clear, guileless blue.

"I've never seen anything like that before. I've read about eidetic memory, studied it in medical school. But your case is... extraordinary." He pressed a hand to his chest, fingers splayed. "Truly." He leaned toward her, his mouth turning down. "But I have no idea what that document might be."

Tess winced, lowering her head as her ribs grew tight.

She had been so sure it would help. Had been willing to risk everything on the chance that it might. And for what?

He held up a hand. "Please, don't be discouraged. If you don't mind waiting here just a moment, I'll bring my notes and the recording to the lab. If anyone can decipher the document in your memory, it'll be them." He rose from the desk, the tape recorder in one hand, a document filled with his handwritten notes in the other. Most of what it said, she couldn't make out, but the words "Carolina Variant" stood out across the top.

Tess furrowed her brow. What the hell did that mean?

He moved toward the door. "Sure I can't bring you anything? Coffee? Tea?"

She shook her head and did her best to return his smile as he left. Hers disappeared as soon as the door closed. She crossed her arms on the desk and lowered her head, the headache still a faint thrum. First Dr. Nunez, and now the man in charge of vaccine development; neither of them had any idea why the document might be important to somebody dangerous or what it was. Maybe she had imagined connections that weren't there. Maybe everything she'd gone through had been for nothing.

Not that she should be surprised. Even if the memories hadn't made her sick, it wasn't like they had ever been anything more than a liability. Her stomach roiled with everything they'd cost her — Jay, her career, her mother, even her friendships. The law school friends who stopped speaking to her after she busted the curve, whispering behind her back about how she'd used her "photographic memory" to cheat. Even though that wasn't at all how it worked. Or the girls who stopped talking to her in high school after she'd had an episode in AP English.

Fuck them.

All of them.

She sat up straight in her chair. None of it was true, not really. Her mother had been in and out of her life long before the memories made Tess sick. Jay left because he was an insecure asshole who couldn't handle her getting the partnership position he assumed would be his. And she'd left her career in Chicago because she hated it. Also fuck those law school bitches. She had Gail, and now it seemed she had Luke, too. A warmth spread through her. Gran had been right. Her memories could be a gift, even if this one did turn out to mean nothing.

A knock sounded from the door, and Sully stepped back inside. "Ms. Oliver?"

She glimpsed an armed guard in the hall as the door swung closed behind him. He wore the same black fatigues as the guards she'd seen earlier but carried a much larger weapon across his chest. The kind that began with an AK or AR and always seemed to end in mass casualties.

She frowned. The hall had been empty when she'd arrived. Why would he be there now? She chewed her top lip. But then, there seemed to be guards everywhere around the facility. And with what they were working on, she could hardly blame them for keeping security tight.

"Sorry to leave you waiting." Sully came around to her side of the desk and leaned against it with his hands clasped together in his lap. "I wanted to make sure you knew how much we appreciate your help." He dipped his head. "I left everything with the lab. I don't know what they'll make of it, but I know it took a lot of courage for you to come see me, given what's happening out there." He opened his hands to reveal a syringe.

She leaned back in her seat, another curl of uneasiness in her stomach. Why would he need that?

He gave a small smile and went on. "I don't know if this will be of any use at all. We haven't had the opportunity to test it properly against Marburg. But the aid workers were all given the Ebola vaccine. As a sister filovirus, there is at least some chance it may help avoid infection." He placed the needle on the desk beside him. "I want to be clear. There are no guarantees, and we haven't been authorized to administer it to the public." He shook his head, then shrugged. "I guess I get it, we don't want to give people a false sense of security. But I sure felt better after I got mine. And given what you've been through… it was the least I could do."

"I don't know what to say." She held his gaze, uncomfortable with the idea of getting a vaccine she knew nothing about. And, maybe even more than that, a vaccine so many other people needed. She swallowed, her throat thick. Why should she get it when they didn't?

It wasn't like she'd done anything to deserve it.

"You don't have to say anything." Sully ripped open an alcohol prep pad and gestured toward her arm. "May I?"

For all her reservations, could she really say no?

Tess pushed up the sleeve of her borrowed tunic.

He sucked in a breath. Her gaze followed his, and she frowned. The raw red mark circling her wrist looked even worse today. If he hadn't already guessed the truth of what'd happened when she'd been held captive, he knew now. She pushed the sleeve the rest of the way up, looking away from the needle in his hand. "It's okay. Go ahead."

After a second's pause, he used the prep pad to rub a small, cold circle on her upper arm. "Okay, here we go."

Tess nodded and snuck a peek through one half-open eye. As he leaned toward her, the expression on his face changed, the fevered shine back in his eyes.

A flash of instinct, of warning, had her pulling back. "Wait, I— "

His hand clamped down on her arm, his grip stronger than she'd have thought the old man capable. "Almost done now."

She struggled to pull free, but he wouldn't let go. Her mind went blank, her body flooded with adrenaline. The feeling of being restrained was still too fresh — her hands bound to the chair, the glowing iron coming closer. She couldn't think. The hot breath of cinnamon on her skin. She couldn't get loose. Tess slammed her free hand into the side of his head, her palm connecting with his ear.

He gasped, and his hold went slack.

She yanked free, backing away as he clutched the side of his head with one hand, the syringe still hanging from the other.

His face hardened. "I was hoping it wouldn't come to this."

He reached behind his back, and pulled a gun from his waistband. A Glock. The same kind she and Pop had used for target practice.

Her breath froze in her throat, reality slowing to the space between heartbeats. Sully pointed the weapon at her head. He shifted back and forth on his feet, the gun swaying. Like a snake waiting to strike.

This couldn't be happening. She backed away as far as she could, only stopping when she bumped into one of the chairs behind her. "I don't understand what's going on."

He gestured for her to sit. "I know you don't."

Tess looked to the Glock, the closed door, then at the window. More men with weapons waited outside in the hall. The window didn't look like it would open. And, even if she could disarm him or distract him long enough to break the glass, the opening would be too narrow for her to fit through. She looked back at him, and he nodded toward the chair again. No doubt waiting for her to draw the same conclusion he already had.

She had no way out.

CHAPTER 44

Tess's vision narrowed on the small black hole at the end of the gun barrel. What would it feel like when that bullet found its target? Would she even know it'd happened? Her gaze flicked to Sully's finger on the trigger. The tiniest of movements, a flinch, and she'd be dead. She swallowed hard.

She couldn't let that happen.

Sully held the gun one-handed, his fingers white-knuckled and too low on the grip.

The exact opposite of how Pop had taught her.

"Don't make this harder than it has to be." He gestured toward the chair again with the gun. This time, more aggressively. He swung it far enough to the right that, if he fired, he might not—

She threw herself at him. His eyes went wide as she grabbed the gun, shoving it toward the floor.

He barked a curse as he lurched forward.

The Glock clunked to the carpet between them.

Within reach, if she could just—

They both went for it, moving in the span of a breath.

She shoved against him. His elbow caught her chin, a sharp jab that made her eyes water as they fought for position. She blinked the burn of tears away as she scrambled, her hands scratching against the carpet.

The gun.

Tess snatched it up, the weapon cold and heavy in her hand.

She turned it on Sully and exhaled, willing herself steady. She checked to make sure the safety was off and held the gun firm, one hand wrapped over the other, her pointer finger resting along the barrel. Pop's voice in her head.

"Never point a weapon at someone unless you intend to fire it."

And no matter how good you were…

"Give yourself the biggest target you can."

She lowered the gun from Sullivan's head to the center of his chest.

He held both hands up. "Okay, now. Let's just relax. Everything's fine." He shifted toward the door.

"Stop." She kept her voice quiet but moved her finger to the trigger.

He froze, his throat bobbing.

She stepped toward him. At this distance, no matter how long it'd been since she'd been to the firing range, she wouldn't miss. "We're going to call the police. And when they get here, you're going to explain to them whatever the hell is going on."

He glanced toward the door, as if considering what she'd said. "You don't understand what you're asking." He shifted closer to where his guard waited.

Maybe not, but she was sure as hell going to find out. She chambered a round.

Sully stopped moving, indecision playing over his face, before his expression crumpled. "I'm sorry it came to this. Truly." His gaze flicked to the bandage on her head, then at the door again. He closed his eyes, and when he met her gaze, his eyes had lost their fire. "You know, you remind me of my daughter." He sank to the floor, the lines of his face gone slack.

She let out a breath but didn't take the gun off him.

He scooped the syringe from the floor and plunged it into his arm.

She jerked forward then stopped, her grip tight on the gun.

What the hell?

Sully slumped back against the wall behind him with a loud thud.

She glanced at the door. Blood pounded in her ears. Would the guards help her? Kill her?

No one came in.

"What did you do?" She stared down at the syringe as she took another step toward him and stopped. He could be faking, trying to lure her closer so he could regain the upper hand. Or was he dying from whatever it was he'd injected into his arm? If that was true, could she just stand there and watch?

She frowned, and her stomach tightened, but she didn't lower the gun. He'd meant that syringe for her.

"Only what I had to." Sully pulled off his mask and let it drop to his lap. He fell silent for a long minute before he spoke again. "And it was worth every penny, worth every sacrifice. Even this one." He nodded down toward himself. "With me gone, the project can go on. There'll be no way anyone can stop it."

"What are you talking about?" Tess shifted on her feet. Right now, she had control of the situation. But that would change as soon as she wasn't the only one with a gun. She needed to figure out what to do next, and she needed to do it fast.

This time, when she bit her lip, she tasted blood.

"Carolina was a beautiful girl." His face softened. "You have the same color hair." He looked away, his words slurred. "She was our only child, over-indulged maybe, but such a good-natured girl. Too innocent to see Hasan for the charlatan he was."

She frowned. He wasn't making sense. Whatever drug he'd injected must already be taking effect, drawing him to thoughts of the past when she needed him conscious and coherent. Needed him to explain what was happening so she'd know how to get herself out of it.

Sully's eyes grew dull, and he mumbled his words. "First he took her away from our faith. Then from me."

"What are you talking about?" She didn't have time for this.

He kept going, as if he hadn't heard her. "Carolina was arguing with Hasan when her car went off the road." His voice broke, his eyes gone misty with unshed tears. "She was pregnant. She wanted her mother and I to be involved. To give that child a chance to know its heritage. I'd hoped maybe even a chance to one day be saved." Sully shook his head. "That man, his 'religion.'" Sully spat out the word. "He might as well have killed her himself. Knowing she and my grandchild died outside of God's grace, that they'd be barred from heaven as non-believers. That I'll never see her again, never meet her baby, even there." Sully shook his head, a single teardrop snaking down his cheek. "I couldn't let it keep happening. Let his kind do the same thing to other good, Christian families. I had to do something."

Tess's frown deepened. Whatever part of his past Sully had fallen back into in his delirium, it wasn't going to help her out of this mess.

He wiped at his face. "Then when I met Haley, realized what his research could mean... what he could do with the right funding. You can't deny the hand of God in that. The Lord gave me the very tools I needed in the moment I needed them. You have to see that." He wheezed, a wet rasping sound. "I need you to know that I regret the human cost, regret what Martin did to you."

Her skin went cold. "You're saying... you can't mean that..." It didn't make any sense, but then some part of her knew it did. That Warren Sullivan, as the head of a large, powerful pharmaceutical company, would've been in a position almost unlike anyone else. He'd had access to the virus, the means to manipulate it. And then there was Haley, on Luke's plane, the containers. Her breath froze in her throat. "You mean the virus, this outbreak, you created it?"

He coughed, his head weaving side to side. "We perfected it. And this virus will change everything, will separate the innocent from those who would destroy us. Those people have to be stopped." He met her gaze, seeming to find a moment of lucidity.

Righteous fire burned in his eyes. "It's God's plan. And it's Carolina's legacy. She won't have died for nothing. She can't have."

She let his words sink in.

Those people.

Whatever it was that Warren Sullivan had done. It hadn't just been out of love for his daughter.

But hate for someone else.

She swallowed. "You mean Muslims?"

He narrowed his eyes, his pupils no bigger than pinpricks. "They aren't like you and me. They're soulless. Godless people."

She recoiled away from him, anger catching fire in her chest. "None of the innocent people out there dying did anything to you or your daughter." How many had died? How many would? All because of his bigotry. "You're no better than a suicide bomber in a crowded market."

He waved her off, not even bothering to look affected by the disgust in her voice. "If I had any doubt about the rightness of what I've done, it disappeared when Haley's plane went down." Sully paused, his breathing heavy. "I wouldn't have had the stomach to release the virus here. But our heavenly father knew America needed to be cleansed." Sully coughed again, his face turning a blueish-gray.

He wheezed and went silent, his eyes open and staring at nothing.

Tess pressed back against the wall, watching Sully's chest. No matter what he'd done, she willed his lungs to fill with air. Willed him to breathe. But he lay on the floor, perfectly still, his hands loose at his sides. She put the gun on the desk and inched closer, crouching down to check his pulse. She waited, listening. But there was nothing.

She closed her eyes. She'd watched two people die in two days. Been responsible for those deaths in one way or another. Tears leaked out before she could stop them.

Tess swept an arm across each eye, wiping the wet on her sleeves. She had to get her shit together, needed to focus on how she was going to—

A knock sounded at the door. A muffled voice. "Mr. Sullivan?" The door swung open.

The guard she'd seen earlier stood in the threshold, the assault rifle still slung across his chest. His gaze took in the room — her crouched over Sully's crumpled body, the syringe on the floor, the gun on the desk. His face tightened, and he nudged his chin in her direction, telling her to move away from Sully.

She got up, her knees protesting she stood and moved backward until she'd pressed herself against the wall. Now on the opposite side of the room from where she'd left the gun.

The guard stepped into the room, gripping his weapon tighter as he crouched down at Sully's side. He looked up at her with dull eyes, his voice flat. "What happened?"

"I… he…" No version of what had just happened sounded plausible. Tess struggled to find the words to explain.

The guard touched the side of Sully's neck, gave a tiny shake of his head, and picked up the older man's arm, holding it by the wrist.

Tess held her breath while she waited, praying he'd find a pulse where she hadn't.

A crackle came from the walkie-talkie on the guard's belt, then, "Tony, we have a situation."

The guard held the walkie to his mouth, his eyes on her. "Handle it."

"I would, sir." More static. "But there's no protocol for this."

The guard rose to his feet, his face hard. He held her gaze as he collected the gun from where she'd left it on the desk, never shifting his own weapon away from her.

Fuck.

"Stay here." He backed out of the room, his walkie-talkie still blaring garbled voices. "All hands… report to—"

The door closed, but Tess didn't move. She waited, listening. A murmur of voices, then distant shouting. Too faint for her to make out what they were saying. Something hard formed in her throat.

She needed to get out. To get help.

But how? She looked back to the desktop where the gun had been. A few loose stacks of paper, a cup of pens. Not even a phone. No way to call for help.

Why hadn't she held on to the stupid gun?

Tess looked out the window to the Humvee where Luke waited. With the sun high in the sky, he wouldn't be able to see anything more than a reflection in them. Could she break the glass and call for help?

No.

That would bring the guards back for sure.

Think.

She leaned against Sully's chair, her hand resting on the collar of the lab coat he'd left there. The coat.

Sully had a cell phone.

She pawed at the pockets, squeezing the fabric until she hit something hard.

"Bingo." She pulled out the phone and punched the home button.

A number pad appeared on the screen.

Fuck, fuck, fucking fuck.

Of course it needed a passcode. She pressed her eyes shut tight, a wave of exhaustion pressing down on her. What now?

A rumble came from outside the window.

Tess looked up as a line of eighteen-wheelers rolled into view, driving away from the facility. The trucks came to a halt at the front gate with a squeal of brakes and a hiss. As the gate rolled open, they chugged back to life, and drove out past the Humvee.

The boxes.

She sucked in a breath. There's no way the pallets she'd seen when Sully led her into the facility were full of Maeler's normal inventory. She'd known that sounded wrong when he said it but couldn't put her finger on why. Now it was obvious. With all of their resources pulled paper thin, time and effort wouldn't be spent to distribute non-essential medications. Especially inside the cordon, where even basic services had stopped.

Those trucks weren't carrying vitamins.

CHAPTER 45

The driver sang along with Willie Nelson, loud and off-key. Luke shook his head. At least Cooper had good taste in music, even if he couldn't hold a tune.

Cooper's two-way radio garbled on, cutting him off mid-verse. A staticky transmission, a few words Luke couldn't make out broken by long bursts of white noise. Cooper clicked off the ancient CD player he had propped on the dash and leaned forward, listening. The walkie burst to life again, but whatever that transmission might have been was no more intelligible than the first.

As Cooper fiddled with the controls, something moved on the other side of the fence.

Finally.

Luke hadn't been able to breathe properly since Tess went inside. He sat up straight, shielding his eyes from the bright afternoon sun as he searched for whatever had caught his attention. The whole facility had been perfectly still since she'd disappeared behind its mirrored glass door. As if the building had swallowed its prey and was taking a satisfied nap.

An eighteen wheeler rounded the side of the facility.

He sagged back. Whatever he'd seen, it hadn't been her. And the longer she was inside, the more his gut told him something about this situation was off. The stronger his sense became that he'd missed something, made the wrong choice without even knowing he'd had one. The air inside the truck felt heavy, weighed down with tension and waiting. Somehow made worse by the insistent scratch of interference clawing out from the radio.

The facility's gate squealed open, and the semi-trucks pulled through, barely fitting past the fat chassis of their Humvee. Cooper smacked a hand against the top of the radio. The static changed pitch, but Luke still couldn't make out any words.

"You hear that?" Cooper cocked his head to one side. Over the rumble of the trucks came the faint sound of sirens, getting louder. The trucks jerked to a stop, the last of them idling a few feet from their rig's rear bumper.

The two guards who'd checked their IDs hurried off toward the source of the noise.

"Something's going on." Luke reached for the door.

"You stay here. I'll check it out." Cooper jumped out of the truck.

A waft of the semi's exhaust floated in, catching in Luke's throat. "Wouldn't it be better if—" The door closed before he could cough out the rest.

Guess not.

Shouting came from behind him, then a sharp rat-tat-tat-tat-tat.

Gunshots.

Luke hunched down in his seat.

What the hell?

Those weren't just gunshots, that was an automatic weapon. His senses sharpened, everything on high alert. He searched the inside of the truck for a gun but found nothing. "Damn it." Luke watched Cooper out the side window until the man disappeared from view. Another series of gunshots rang out, closer. Too close for him to just sit there and do nothing, especially if he couldn't see what was coming.

He craned around but couldn't see out the back of the truck. He eased the door open and peered outside.

Cooper crouched at the rear of the closest semi-truck, weapon drawn. His gaze met Luke's, and he held out a hand, patting the air in front of him. Signaling Luke to stay put. Cooper turned to round the side of the truck, pausing by the edge.

A crack of gunfire.

Cooper's head jerked, a red mist marking the doors of the truck behind him. The soldier slumped, going limp as he fell behind the Humvee.

Holy shit.

Luke whipped around to peer through the windshield. The shot had come from the facility. He couldn't tell which of them had fired, but guards in black fatigues moved toward the front gate. All held assault rifles across their chests as they ran down the long drive toward him. Luke froze, the image of Cooper crumpling to the ground replaying in his mind.

Jesus.

Please don't let him be dead.

Luke pushed open the door on the opposite side of the truck, where he might still be hidden from view. If he was lucky. He checked outside before he jumped down. Then crouched low and circled the back of the truck. The driver's door to the semi stood open. The driver had gone, and the truck's engine was now off, but the diesel stench of exhaust still hung in the air. Luke ran to where Cooper lay unmoving on the pavement.

The soldier had a gaping hole in this jaw, and one of his teeth lay on the ground by Luke's foot. Luke stopped, seeing nothing but that single, bloodied tooth. Almost the same shape and size as the gravel scattering the blacktop. He refocused on Cooper.

The man's chest rose and fell.

Thank God.

He checked the road beyond their truck. The facility guards were still coming.

He and Cooper weren't going to make it far. Not with the soldier in that condition. Their best bet was to find cover and hope the guards didn't spend too long looking for where the man they'd shot had crawled off to die. With shaking hands, he retrieved

Cooper's gun, clicked on the safety, and tucked it into his waistband. Then grabbed the soldier under the arms. He just needed his luck to hold. He'd get Cooper to safety, then go find Tess. "Hang on, buddy."

Cooper moaned as Luke dragged him to the side of the road, struggling against almost two hundred pounds of dead weight. Every tug sent a screaming protest through Luke's ribs and only seemed to move them a foot at a time. One, two, a yard, three.

He pulled harder, panting from the effort. And the pain. "Just a little further." It took all Luke had to get Cooper far enough into the trees and brush to hopefully hide them from view. Luke collapsed to the dirt. Breathing heavy from the effort, he pulled Cooper tight to his side as he watched for the men in black fatigues to appear. He pulled his cell from his pocket. No bars. He tried 911 anyway, knowing, even if the call went through, it would probably go unanswered.

A busy signal bleeped loud in Luke's ear as a man in black came into view on the road below. Huge, built like a college lineman, his hair shorn close to the scalp but still a bright orange-red. Luke scrambled to disconnect the call. He hunched behind a gnarl of kudzu, peering around the thick mass of vines. Praying the noise hadn't given them away.

Another guard followed the first, his movements purposeful. He went to the spot where Cooper had fallen, and looked left to right, scanning the forest on either side of the road. "Thought you said you'd hit one?" He turned to the man beside him. A lanky, pale guard whose face was all nose and chin.

"Thought I did." The lanky man's gaze fell on the thicket where Luke hid.

Cooper stirred.

Every muscle in Luke's body tensed. If Cooper called out, it would give away their position. And there was no way Luke could carry the man fast or far enough to get to safety before the guards caught up.

He dropped a hand to Cooper's shoulder, willing him to be quiet.

The lanky guard looked to the blood stain on the truck, a satisfied look on his face as he jerked his chin in that direction. "Gotta be here somewhere."

Luke held his breath. If they searched the area, he and Cooper were fucked.

The ginger-haired man mumbled something shaped like a curse, then turned at the thud of feet. At least a dozen more hard-faced guards in black followed. The man crossed his arms, barking out orders. "Secure the cargo first, then let's canvass these woods. We've got two in the wind, one injured."

Most of the men jogged forward out of sight. Another climbed up into the closest semi-truck. Luke couldn't see if any others remained behind the Humvee. Its bulk blocked his view. But the semi's engine rumbled back to life, and the noise gave Luke as much cover as he was likely to get.

"I'll be back as soon as I can." He whispered to Cooper, even though it didn't seem possible the man would make it. Part of him wanted to stay. To make sure Cooper didn't die alone with his body sprawled in a mound of snarled vines and weeds. Or worse, be found by the guards before Luke could get back.

But he didn't have a choice. Not with Tess still inside. Still in danger.

Luke slipped through the trees, careful to keep his body low and his footfalls soft. Adrenaline pounded in his ears. If he was careful, he could slip past any remaining guards, make it through the gate. But if anyone inside the facility was watching the front entrance, they'd have an unobstructed shot at him. The approach to the facility offered no cover. Nowhere to hide.

He pulled Cooper's gun from his waistband and tried to make peace with whatever came next.

. . .

Tess pressed her palms to the window glass, the surface hot from baking in the afternoon sun. She'd been standing there since the gunshots rang out, watching in terror as the guards encircled the truck where she'd left Luke. She let out a shaky breath.

Even now, after the guards had disappeared down the road, leaving the Humvee's doors gaping open, she peered into the truck's dark interior, looking for his silhouette. But, of course, she couldn't see a thing. And the rational part of her knew he couldn't be there. If he had been, if the guards had found him…

She shook off the thought. What mattered now was figuring out where he and their driver had gone. She scanned the area, the Humvee, the semi-truck, the guard shack. Back again, and again.

Please let them be okay.

The bushes to the left of the fence rustled, and Luke appeared, racing toward the fence. She let out a yelp of relief.

He stopped at the open gate, looking up to the building. Could he see her?

She smacked a hand against the window, her heart racing. "Luke, here. I'm here!"

He looked away, scanning the building.

She hit the glass harder.

He didn't look back. Just ran toward the front entrance. Toward the guards that must still be somewhere in the building.

No.

He'd be killed. He'd never make it. Tess raced to the office door. A guard probably waited on the other side, but, even so, she threw it open.

The hallway stood empty.

Her heart thudded loud in her ears, and the hair rose on the back of her neck.

But she didn't stop.

Tess slipped from the office, careful not to let the door slam closed behind her.

She crept down the corridor, careful of every footstep as she traced her steps back through the facility. She slowed at each corner, barely breathing. But nothing waited for her on the other side. The building had gone eerily quiet. She rounded the final corner, stepping through the door into the lobby where she'd first met Warren Sullivan.

The figure of a man appeared outside the glass of the front doors. Tall, broad-shouldered. A gun hung from his hand. Fear threatened to close her throat. She desperately wanted it to be him but—

The man turned, just enough to put his face in profile.

Luke.

She flew outside, wrapping her arms around him. "Thank God you're okay."

He squeezed her to him, once, tight enough her elbows jabbed into her sides. Then pulled back, his voice rough. "We need to get the hell out of here."

"I know." She glanced over Luke's shoulder.

A group of men in dull green fatigues advanced toward them from the front gate with guns drawn, as if she'd summoned them with her thoughts. Her fingers dug into Luke's biceps. "Oh my God."

"What is it?" He turned to follow her gaze and went rigid.

She held on to him, her mind racing. They could make a run for it. Maybe go through the facility? Try to find a way out the back? Except she had no idea where another exit might be or who could be between them and it. The fence surrounding the property was too high to climb and, even if it wasn't, the razor-wire around the top glinted in the sun. Its edges sharp and ragged. So far as she could tell, it encircled the property completely. The only exit sat behind the soldiers closing in on them.

Luke looked back at her, his face tight as he gave a small shake of his head. Even with the gun, they didn't stand a chance. They were outnumbered, outgunned, and outmaneuvered. He dropped the weapon and raised his hands in surrender, even as he shifted to put her further behind him.

What else could they do?

Nothing.

Tess steeled herself. It was over.

Or it would be soon.

As the men grew closer, they separated into smaller groups of two or three. Several split off around the back of the building. The remainder ran past her and Luke without a word, disappearing into the open facility door. They wore U.S. Army logos on their shoulders, and several gave her a short nod as they passed.

What the hell?

An older man, not in uniform, followed the soldiers up the hill. He had gray hair and eyebrows like two black slashes across his forehead. "Ms. Oliver?" He turned toward Luke. "And I assume that makes you Mr. Broussard?"

▪ ▪ ▪

Three soldiers — medics, Tess guessed — ran alongside Cooper's stretcher, pushing it toward the open bay of a military helicopter perched on the front lawn of the facility. Even at a safe distance, the *thunk-thunk-thunk* of the rotor made a deafening racket. Despite the noise and commotion around him, Cooper lay perfectly still.

The soldier was almost unrecognizable, his face a pale bloody mess. He looked nothing like the young man who'd driven them there only a few hours before. She sent up a quick prayer as the helicopter rose straight up from the ground, drifted forward, and away. It disappeared into the glare of the late afternoon sun.

"He's in good hands."

She jumped, looking over to find the man who'd introduced himself as Colonel Fitzgerald standing beside her. With the noise of the helicopter, she hadn't noticed he was there until he spoke.

"Apologies. I didn't mean to startle you." The old soldier stood, spine straight, shoulders back, his eyes hidden behind a pair of aviator sunglasses. Under other circumstances, she might've found him intimidating. But in the aftermath of what they'd through, she couldn't muster the energy to care.

"No, it's fine. I'm just a little on edge." She looked past him, to where Luke stood talking with some of the soldiers who'd arrived with Fitzgerald.

He met her gaze, clapped one of the soldiers on the arm, and came to join her. "Everything okay?"

"I think so." She took his hand and squeezed it. Not much about the situation was, but at least they were together. And no one was shooting at them.

Fitzgerald stared off in the direction the helicopter had gone, then refocused on her. "I know you've been through a lot, but I need you to tell me what happened here today."

Tess opened her mouth, then closed it, not sure what to say or what was safe to say.

"With all due respect, sir." Luke pulled her closer. "Shouldn't we be asking you that?"

Fitzgerald gave a quick nod. "I'll tell you what I can, although much of it remains classified. Right now, my priority is making sure we understand the scope of what we're dealing with. If there are other facilities, other trucks…"

A lump formed in her throat. She hadn't considered there might be more, that what had happened here might be happening other places, too. She'd been too preoccupied with what had happened in the facility. And what might happen next. The line of black SUVs that had pulled in after Fitzgerald's arrival. The grim group of men and women in suits who had climbed out of them and disappeared inside. None had come back out. And, whoever they were — she assumed the F.B.I. — must have found Warren Sullivan's body by now.

Tess chewed on her lip, reopening the cut and leaving a tang of blood in her mouth. "Sullivan didn't say anything about others."

Fitzgerald nodded. "What did he say?"

She had no way to know if she could trust the soldier. God knew her instincts had been all wrong about Sully. But with everything at stake, she couldn't see any other choice. "He didn't make sense… at least not at first." She took a deep breath. "It might help if I start at the beginning." She sat on one of the SUV's back bumpers and gestured for them to join her. "This might take a while."

Luke sat beside her, but Fitzgerald stayed standing. "Go ahead."

She did her best to explain how they'd wound up at the facility, what happened inside, what she suspected might be in the trucks Fitzgerald's men had stopped from leaving, and, with a souring of her stomach, what happened with Sully. What she'd done. Her mouth went dry, and in the pause as she forced down a thick swallow, Luke chimed in. As he described what they'd seen and heard from the gate, she drifted off. The image of Sullivan's vacant eyes burned in her mind.

Fitzgerald looked at her with pursed lips, his face shrewd. "Once we finish talking today, no one else needs to know your part in what happened here." He pulled off his sunglasses. His eyes were closely set and full of a certainty she'd guess came from decades of having orders followed. "I guarantee it."

She held his gaze. That seemed like a hard promise to keep, even for someone of his rank. But, after a moment, she nodded. It was the best pardon she could hope for under the circumstances.

Fitzgerald searched her face. "You look like you've got something else on your mind."

She shook her head, trying to calm the swirl of emotions clogging her throat. The terror of the day had wrung her out, leaving her little more than an exhausted shell of herself. And, at the same time, she'd never felt more alive. Never been more grateful to take another breath, and so glad Fitzgerald had come when he did… But "if Maeler doesn't have a vaccine, then what? Everyone dies?" Her voice cracked, and tears stung behind her eyes. "It feels like this was our last hope."

Fitzgerald tucked his sunglasses into a shirt pocket, the hint of a smile tugging at the corners of his mouth. "That's not exactly true."

CHAPTER 46

September 23, 2018

Mara sat on the edge of the hospital helipad, her legs dangling over the side. She leaned forward, peering down. A short drop from the landing area to the rooftop below, then another sixteen stories plunged from there. Up this high, even the light afternoon breeze had enough force to toss her hair around. It flipped around her face, into her eyes, one strand sticking at the edge of her mouth. She was too tired to coax it back into place, too tired to worry about what might happen if she fell. Too tired to grieve all the death around her.

And yet the grief wouldn't let go.

A plume of smoke and ash rose in the distance, drifting across the Atlanta skyline. A heavy gray stain bleeding out over the city.

Goodbye, my friend.

Mara had given everything she had to saving Emmy, to saving the others infected with this Godforsaken disease, and she'd failed. Her everything hadn't been enough.

The stairwell door slammed behind her.

Mara braced herself and turned, expecting to find one of her team come to tell her they'd lost yet another patient.

"The nurses told me I might find you up here." Col. Fitzgerald strode over the giant painted cross marking the helipad's landing zone. "May I?" He gestured to the edge of the pavement a few feet away from her.

Mara nodded and pulled her mask back into place. "So much for my secret hide-out." She'd been trying for levity, but even to her ear, it fell flat. "I thought you'd be back to Fort Detrick by now."

"I'm on my way. Just thought I'd make a quick stop here first." He followed her gaze out to the ashy cloud snaking north above them. "Is that—?"

She nodded. "The new cremation site."

They watched the smoke darken the horizon. There were no words for a loss of life on this scale. Nothing anyone could say that might capture the true horror of it all. Fitzgerald cleared his throat, breaking the silence. "Did you get the materials I sent over after we spoke last night? Sullivan's notes and the audio file?"

She dipped her head. "I half-thought we were all going crazy, to believe some woman had a map of DNA mutations saved in her memory… now that we know what Sullivan was up to, it seems almost mundane."

"We won't have Sullivan's tox report back for another week, at least. But the M.E.'s best guess is he died of a massive overdose of morphine." Fitzgerald crossed his arms across his chest. "We've recorded the death as a 'suicide in lieu of capture,' but publicly he'll be reported as another victim of the virus, of course."

"Of course." Mara pursed her lips. Disclosing what had actually happened would raise too many questions the government either couldn't or wouldn't answer. And she had no doubt Maeler's lawyers were all over it. "Did the tests come back yet for the cargo in the trucks?"

"Supplements, vitamins. All contaminated with the virus." Fitzgerald's eyes hardened. "Even the prenatals."

"Holy shit." The reality of what Sullivan had planned settled over her like an oily film that made it hard to see, hard to breathe. The scale of it. The complete disregard for human life. She forced air out of her lungs.

Prenatals.

Who could do something like that? To innocent people they didn't even know. To babies? She leaned back. A piece of loose gravel dug into her palm, but she didn't move to brush it free.

"I know. And there was enough in those trucks that, if it'd been distributed to the public, there's no way we could have stopped the spread."

She choked out a laugh past a growing tightness in her throat. "I'm not sure we're gonna be able to stop it as it is."

A police siren wailed in the distance, and he went quiet again. "That's actually what brought me here. I can't imagine what it's been like, fighting every day for lives you know you can't save."

She flinched, but he wasn't wrong. That's what they'd all been doing. Fitzgerald, too.

"I didn't want to say anything until I was sure." He adjusted his mask, finding her gaze before he continued. "It's vital this doesn't leak before it's confirmed. Unlike Sullivan's facility, the location of USAMRIID's lab is a matter of public record. And we need to focus on the task at hand, not crowd control."

She raised an eyebrow and nodded. "Well, now you have my attention. What are you trying to say?"

"USAMRIID has a vaccine effective against the Hemphill strain of the virus."

Her heart seized, and for the first time since Mara walked out of Emmy's morgue a week before, the warm glow of hope lit within her. "Say more."

Fitzgerald continued. "We'll need further testing, of course. And it'll take time to manufacture sufficient doses… I'd thought, at first, we might prioritize vaccination of the groups not assigned immunity in Sullivan's notes. But it's not like most people walk around with a complete genealogical chart on hand." He waved his hand in dismissal. "Even with that, we should be able to produce enough vaccine to make a real difference here within weeks."

Mara nodded along, but still couldn't quite believe what he was saying could be true. "How is that even possible?"

"It wouldn't have been without Richard Quinones."

She stared out over the rooftops of the buildings surrounding the hospital, trying to place the name. "Who?"

"He's Maeler's head of vaccine R&D. Or he was." Fitzgerald's eyes crinkled with what she assumed was a smile hidden behind his mask. "Now he's more of a government contractor."

Mara shook her head. "I don't understand."

"Maeler nearly had a Marburg vaccine complete before this whole thing started. Quinones ran the project for them for years, until he was promoted to some other role. And he's been working on Marburg Hemphill around the clock again since the start of the outbreak when he quit his job at Maeler."

She clenched her jaw, the flicker of hope in her belly going out. "How could you know he'd be willing to come on board with USAMRIID? That he wouldn't just run back to Sullivan or, worse, play mole for him."

"We didn't bring him on board." Fitzgerald chuckled.

She raised an eyebrow. "What do you mean?"

"He came to the F.B.I. a month ago as a whistle-blower. He didn't know what Sullivan had planned. Just that Maeler was spending far more money on paper than he could account for, all while Quinones's cancer research suffered for lack of funding. When he couldn't get Sullivan to address the issue, he suspected embezzlement and went to the Feds. Which is how we found him. No love lost between him and Sullivan."

"Hijo de puta."

"My thoughts exactly."

"Even with his help, how'd you get the vaccine pushed through so fast?" They could take years to get to market.

"If we'd been required to go through FDA review or make any of the normal license applications, you'd be right. But President Coates cleared the way for us to go straight— "

"Coates." His name left a nasty taste in her mouth.

Fitzgerald nodded, no doubt noticing the disgust on her face. "I know. It gives me heartburn, too. But for now, this is the best we can do."

"It can't be. These people developed a 'smart bug' they programmed to kill using ethnicity as a proxy for religion." She twisted to face him, hands on her hips. Heat spreading over her cheeks. "It won't be the 'best we can do' until each and every one of them goes down for it."

"I don't disagree. But we can't say yet if Coates was involved. We know he pandered to Sullivan somewhere along the way. That's it." He raised his brows at her. "Anyway, these things take time. Everyone we know to have been involved is either missing or dead, except for a few of the mercenaries from Sullivan's facility. And none of them seem to know what happened behind closed doors. Just that they were well paid to keep them shut."

Mara got to her feet, pacing the edge of the helipad. "I get it, but it's still not enough."

Fitzgerald stood, legs braced, arms crossed, every inch the military man he was. "Mara, stop."

She forced her body to still, despite the anger pulsing through her.

"The FBI has been through everything from the facility, Sullivan's office, and his home. They've done the same with Haley, although his situation was more complicated. Dozens of shell companies, each with their own accounts and holdings. Low-end properties all over the city. Part of some real estate scam he ran on the side and they— "

"I don't give a shit if it's difficult. People died. They're still dying. Here. Every day." Another pang went through her, memories of all the patients she hadn't saved amplifying her anger.

He held up a hand. "Listen. What I'm trying to say is that's where the FBI got lucky. According to my contact, they have a woman in custody. A nurse listed on the utilities for one of Haley's properties. They're negotiating an immunity deal with her now.

But she claims to have proof Haley experimented on people he duped into participating in a drug trial for Sullivan's virus. All the names she's given so far check out. Every one of them disappeared in the weeks leading up to the outbreak. Whatever she gives us could lead to the others, however many they are."

Mara went silent again, her anger draining away. Replaced by something heavier, a sadness she had no idea how to deal with. She stared back at the plume of smoke, hoping to buy enough time to get her emotions under control.

The wind picked up, a gust pushing her hair back from her face. It smelled of smoke and carried the faint sound of voices. She closed her eyes, tilting her head to listen. It was soft at first, almost a whisper. Then grew. The voices rose up in song, lyrics she knew. "Amazing Grace." She peered down to the city below. A crowd, at least a hundred people, maybe more, walked down empty streets toward the rising smoke of the cremation fires. Behind their masks, people of every color sang together of hope and love and faith and everything Sullivan couldn't destroy.

The tears she'd been fighting stood in Mara's eyes as she turned to Fitzgerald. "Go get me that vaccine."

He answered with a nod. "You have my word."

She turned back toward the hospital doors, to the people who needed her. The people she wouldn't let down.

CHAPTER 47

October 22, 2018

The pine trees surrounding Gran's house swayed in a stiff breeze that set her wind chimes clanging. Tess let the blinds in the kitchen window clack back in place. "Looks like a storm's coming."

"Mmm-hmm." Gran peered into her oven, where a taco casserole bubbled around the edges. "Little more rain'll be good for us." She closed the door and pulled on a pair of oven mitts. "Hardly saw a drop all those weeks you were in quarantine. I'm just glad it held off until y'all finally got here."

Rain or no rain, it felt damn good to be home. And even better that they were all together.

"Tess," Luke called out from the living room. "Come see this."

"Sorry, Gran. Be right back." She dropped a kiss on her grandmother's head and followed the sound of the TV to the living room.

Pop lay sprawled in his usual spot on the recliner. Luke had taken the couch. Both held Miller Lite tall boys in their hands. Luke glanced up, his face softening as he saw her. He tilted his head toward the image on the screen. "Look."

Fitzgerald stood next to a much smaller goateed man in a lab coat. The President shook their hands, then pinned medals to their chests. Text scrolled along the bottom of the screen. "Colonel Elias Fitzgerald and former Maeler scientist Richard Quinones awarded Presidential Medal of Freedom for development of Marburg vaccine, saving millions of lives." The three men stood side by side for photos, although Fitzgerald's expression was too grim to pass for a smile. The camera panned the gathered crowd. Cooper sat in the first row, his head wrapped in a bandage. She'd heard that he'd come through surgery, but hadn't expected to see him again. Luke gave her a smile as she settled onto the arm of the sofa beside him.

The screen split to a young brunette behind an anchor desk. "The President's announcement is particularly timely today, as it marks the third day in a row in which no new cases of Marburg Hemphill have been reported. Plans for the Minneapolis and Los Angeles memorials are underway. And, while certain areas of Atlanta remain under quarantine, the vast majority of the city's inhabitants have begun the process of returning to normal life." The image changed to an aerial shot of workers removing the fencing from the I-285 perimeter circling Atlanta.

Tess took Luke's hand. Half of her hadn't thought they'd ever get here. "I don't know how they pulled it off."

"Never under-estimate what the U.S. military can do with the right man in charge." Pop climbed out of his recliner as a clatter of dishes came from the kitchen. Tess watched him go. With Coates as their commander-in-chief, she wasn't sure that rang true.

Thank God for Fitzgerald.

It might take time, and it wouldn't be easy, but she had no doubt he'd make sure the people responsible for what had happened would be held accountable.

Pop called back over his shoulder. "I'm gonna go check on supper."

As soon as he was out of the room, Luke pulled Tess onto his lap. "Hi." He tilted her face toward his and ran his thumb over her lower lip. His eyes were dark and full of promise, the way they always were when the two of them were alone.

"Hi." She leaned in for a kiss. It deepened into another, and another. No matter how close he was, she wanted him closer.

"Y'all come eat now." Gran called from the kitchen.

"To be continued," Tess said against his mouth.

. . .

Tess pushed her heel against the porch floor's wide wooden planks, the swing protesting with a metallic twang. She let go, setting them on a lazy arc back and forth as rain drummed loud on the tin roof above their heads. She breathed in the clean smell of wet earth and leaned her head against Luke's shoulder. "Pop likes you."

"He does?" Luke relaxed back into the swing. "How can you tell?"

"Oh, I can tell." She grinned, remembering the look on Pop's face when she'd first brought Jay home. "You'd know if he didn't."

Tater lifted his head from the folded wool blanket where he and Pop's dog, Badger, had been sleeping since they arrived. He let out a short bark as the screen door banged open.

Pop ambled out with a folding chair under each arm. "Hush up now." The dogs each gave another woof, stretching in what looked like self-congratulation before they curled back up together.

Pop opened up the chairs, adjusting them opposite the swing before he gave Badger's ears a rub. "Thought we'd eat our dessert out here. House gets hot when the oven's on."

"Can I help with anything?" Luke stopped the swing.

"No, no. You two look cozy. Just stay there. Gran and I'll be right back. She's just dishing up some cobbler." Pop disappeared inside.

Tess raised one eyebrow in a "told you so" look.

"Feeling's mutual." He pulled her closer, and she snuggled in next to him.

Tess pushed her bare foot against the porch floor to start the swing moving again. "Gail got to South Carolina okay. I got a text from her as we were finishing up the dishes."

"Good, that's good. I bet her boys are glad to see her."

She hummed a response, absently tracing one of the scars peeking out above the neckline of her shirt. With everything they'd been through, the pain so many others were still going through, it didn't seem right for her heart to be so full of joy. But it was.

"What are you thinking?" Luke pressed a kiss to the top her head.

She took a minute to answer, needing the time to gather the loose threads of her thoughts into something that made sense. "It's hard to believe we're here. That it's over." She cringed. "I mean, I know it's not really over. Not for the people who lost someone. All the people whose lives will never be the same."

"I know what you mean."

"It's just that we are so lucky." She breathed in his scent, sandalwood and fresh laundry. It didn't seem possible that after everything, they were actually here. Together and safe. The world on its way back to something like normal. And letting herself acknowledge it made it all feel so tenuous. Like, even now, it could still slip away. "I can't stop thinking about what could have happened. About what Sullivan tried to do. To me. To everyone else. How close we came to losing each other."

Luke entwined his fingers with hers, resting their joined hands on the top of his leg. His jean-clad thigh warm against the back of her hand. "There's no telling how many people are alive because of you."

She puffed out a breath. "All I did was get abducted."

"That's not all you did. If it weren't for you finding the document Haley had stashed in that bank, fighting your way out of captivity. Twice. And being smart enough to get that information into the right hands. The world would be completely different now. To hear Mara tell it, without you, they would have been too late to stop it."

Tess shrugged, her cheeks growing warm. She pushed the porch swing again. "I heard from her today."

"Really? Is she still inside the cordon?"

Tess nodded. "She's in for the long haul." The containment area had progressively grown smaller, as the pockets of infection were isolated and the vaccine given time to work. Only a few small areas, including the hospital, remained. And, of course, Mara refused to leave until the job was done.

"She should have been up there on TV getting a medal with the other two."

There was no question that was true. Tess grew quiet, looking up at him before she continued, needing to see the reaction on his face when she did. "She asked me to come back."

He stopped the swing, looking down at her. Tension creased his eyes. "Back into the cordon?"

She shook her head, waiting until Luke relaxed before she continued. "They want to offer me a job with the Department of Health and Human Services' general counsel's office once the quarantine's lifted." She stared off into the yard, remembering what Mara had said. Half of the CDC's lawyers hadn't made it. The DHHS's Atlanta office was desperately in need of help. And she'd known the answer was yes before she'd hung up the phone.

She couldn't think of anything she'd rather use her law degree for.

Her work helping the Ashbys had been the only time she remembered her law practice feeling worthwhile. She hadn't understood that at the time. She'd been too preoccupied with finding something — anything — that would save her little firm from going under. But she'd found something else in fighting for the Ashbys. A satisfaction that came only from doing what was right. From helping people who needed it.

And if she could do that every day going forward. Use her law degree to help, to give back. Find a way to finally make sure the Ashbys were made whole. Especially if she could rebuild some of the things Warren Sullivan had broken…

She was in.

"Is that what you want?" Luke finally spoke. "To go back to Atlanta? Things will probably be tough there for a few years yet. So many people gone. So much unrest now after how the city government just fell apart. I mean, God, after what they did to those people in the Dome." He shook his head. "It'll be years before anything feels normal again."

She nodded. He wasn't wrong, but "it feels like I need to." She swallowed. "To try to do something to help." Although she hated the thought that accepting the job might separate the two of them. The wind shifted, a cold mist of rain blowing in on the back of her neck. What if he wanted to go back to Louisiana to be with his family? His mother and sisters had been calling every day since they'd been rescued from the facility. She wouldn't blame him for wanting to go home, where it was safe. Or, if not home, then at least somewhere new where he could have a fresh start. Where he didn't have to wake up every day and face all the death and loss Atlanta had suffered.

That it continued to suffer.

She tucked a loose curl behind her ear, trying to look alright with whatever he said.

Even if it broke her heart.

"Okay." He said, his voice even.

"Okay?" She sat forward so fast a throw pillow fell from the swing, bouncing onto the porch floor. Tater shot her a look, but she ignored him. A smile spread over Tess's face as she stared up at Luke. The only sound the slowing patter of rain and the happy yips of Pop's rescue dogs playing in the distance. "That's it?"

"That's it." He smiled back. "I need to get back in the air. And Parker says his dad's working on getting a new plane for us. Once that happens, we should be able to pick up pretty much where we left off." He squeezed her hand, running his thumb over her ring finger. "With some improvements, of course."

"Improvements?" She raised an eyebrow, her smile becoming a grin as her heart expanded in her chest. "Like what?"

He ran his thumb back over her finger, leaned in, and kissed her.

THE END

A NOTE TO THE READER

While much of the science behind The Carolina Variant is real, particularly as relates to historical events, several aspects are not.

The virus at the center of this story — Marburg Hemphill — is, thankfully, fictional. Marburg itself is a rare but very real and very deadly hemorrhagic fever, with a case fatality rate as high as 90%. The Hemphill strain I created for purposes of the book differs in a number of significant ways, almost always for the purpose of better torturing my poor, unsuspecting characters.

DNA based immunity of the type imagined in The Carolina Variant is not yet possible. A disease can be crafted so as to render a certain individual immune, but this is not yet viable as applied to entire groups of people. With that said, selective immunity has been explored by multiple governments, including our own here in the United States. For a deeper read on biological warfare, I'd recommend *Germs, Biological Weapons and America's Secret War* by Judith Miller, Stephen Engelberg, and William Broad.

Finally, while Tess's memory condition is loosely based on an eidetic memory, my version is entirely fictional.

ACKNOWLEDGEMENTS

Thank you to my boys for making me the luckiest mom on Earth. You are my greatest distraction and my greatest joy.

Thank you to Black Rose Writing for believing in my work enough to put it out in the world, not just once but twice.

Thank you to Heather Lazare for all her edits and support.

To C.S. Lakin for teaching me how to be a better writer.

To David Wright for letting me come see your plane and spending an entire day with me explaining how everything worked (and what might happen if it didn't). The chapter that came from your help is still my favorite of any I've ever written.

To my parents for forever being my biggest supporters. Mom, I still remember when you bruised your hands clapping for me at a high school recital. And Dad, this book is dedicated to you for a lot of reasons, but mainly because of all the time you spent talking through details with me, showing me FAA reports, etc. There's no one I'd rather crash a plane with.

To my writer friends, who are the absolute best community a girl could ask for.

And, finally, to my readers. You can not know what it means to me to see my books in your hands. It is a literal dream come true.

ABOUT THE AUTHOR

Brooke L. French is a recovering lawyer turned author. Her debut thriller, *Inhuman Acts*, came out in 2022, and her second novel, *The Carolina Variant,* in June of 2023. Brooke lives between Atlanta and Carmel, California with her husband and sons.

NOTE FROM THE AUTHOR

Word-of-mouth is crucial for any author to succeed. If you enjoyed *The Carolina Variant,* please leave a review online—anywhere you are able. Even if it's just a sentence or two. It would make all the difference and would be very much appreciated.

Thanks!
Brooke L. French

CPSIA information can be obtained
at www.ICGtesting.com
Printed in the USA
JSHW020321030323
38336JS00001B/1

9 781685 132187